continued...

The Moon Witch

"I can hardly wait to find out how she will [entwine] all the threads she has created!...This series is just too good to miss."
—*The Romance Reader*

"An enjoyable romantic fantasy that grips the audience... Action-packed."
—*The Best Reviews*

"A unique and imaginative realm...Prepare to be swept away!"
—*Rendezvous*

"[W]ill enthrall...Lushly imaginative."
—*Publishers Weekly*

The Sun Witch

"Entertaining and imaginative, with a wonderful blend of worlds and technology and magic. The characters are different and engrossing, the villain is fascinating."
—*New York Times* bestselling author Linda Howard

"Charming...Winsome...The perfect choice when you want a lighthearted and fun, yet sensual, romance...with all the magic of a fairy tale."
—*Bookbug on the Web*

"Fabulous...The story is spectacular and this author is unforgettable."
—*Road to Romance*

"Let the fireworks begin! This whimsical, entrancing tale will satisfy the romance fan demanding something unusual and wonderful. With a skillful blend of the fanciful and the mundane, author Linda Jones weaves a marvelous tale of love and happy-ever-after, with a twist. Remarkable in imagination."
—*Word Weaving*

"Amazing adventures unfold...Marvelously captivating, sensuous, fast-paced."
—*Booklist* (starred review)

"Hot."
—*Affaire de Coeur*

Untouchable

Linda Winstead Jones

BERKLEY SENSATION, NEW YORK

THE BERKLEY PUBLISHING GROUP
Published by the Penguin Group
Penguin Group (USA) Inc.
375 Hudson Street, New York, New York 10014, USA

Penguin Group (Canada), 90 Eglinton Avenue East, Suite 700, Toronto, Ontario M4P 2Y3, Canada
(a division of Pearson Penguin Canada Inc.)
Penguin Books Ltd., 80 Strand, London WC2R 0RL, England
Penguin Group Ireland, 25 St. Stephen's Green, Dublin 2, Ireland (a division of Penguin Books Ltd.)
Penguin Group (Australia), 250 Camberwell Road, Camberwell, Victoria 3124, Australia
(a division of Pearson Australia Group Pty. Ltd.)
Penguin Books India Pvt. Ltd., 11 Community Centre, Panchsheel Park, New Delhi—110 017, India
Penguin Group (NZ), 67 Apollo Drive, Rosedale, North Shore 0632, New Zealand (a division of
Pearson New Zealand Ltd.)
Penguin Books (South Africa) (Pty.) Ltd., 24 Sturdee Avenue, Rosebank, Johannesburg 2196, South
Africa

Penguin Books Ltd., Registered Offices: 80 Strand, London WC2R 0RL, England

This is a work of fiction. Names, characters, places, and incidents either are the product of the author's imagination or are used fictitiously, and any resemblance to actual persons, living or dead, business establishments, events, or locales is entirely coincidental. The publisher does not have any control over and does not assume any responsibility for author or third-party websites or their content.

UNTOUCHABLE

A Berkley Sensation Book / published by arrangement with the author

PRINTING HISTORY
Berkley Sensation mass-market edition / August 2008

Copyright © 2008 by Linda Winstead Jones.
Excerpt from *22 Nights* copyright © 2008 by Linda Winstead Jones.
Cover art by Danny O'Leary.
Cover design by Lesley Worrell.
Hand lettering by Iskra Johnson.
Interior text design by Kristin del Rosario.

ISBN: 978-0-425-22296-6

BERKLEY® SENSATION
Berkley Sensation Books are published by The Berkley Publishing Group,
a division of Penguin Group (USA) Inc.,
375 Hudson Street, New York, New York 10014.
BERKLEY SENSATION and the "B" design are trademarks of Penguin Group (USA) Inc.

PRINTED IN THE UNITED STATES OF AMERICA

10 9 8 7 6 5 4 3 2 1

This book is dedicated to Andrea Laurence,
walking buddy, sounding board, and "Child."

Prologue

**The Columbyanan Palace in the Sixth Year
of the Reign of Emperor Nechtyn Jahn Calcus
Sadwyn Beckyt
First Night of the Spring Festival**

ALIX watched silently as his brother, the emperor, toyed with the ministers and priests who had gathered around him. They did not see the muted sparkle of humor in Jahn's eyes, but Alix saw. He had watched his entire life as his brother—elder by a few important minutes—charmed and joked and glided his way to success. Whether that success was with women or gambling or ruling a country recovering from war, it came easily to Jahn.

Alix had spent many years trying to outshine his brother in some way, not that he would ever allow anyone to see his efforts. He had been a more disciplined soldier than the elder twin, but in their time of battle Jahn had fought with great heart and determination which more than made up for his lack of discipline. Alix could not equal, much less surpass, his brother's natural ease and charm, so he excelled in other ways. He was steady, whereas Jahn was unpredictable. He was even-tempered, whereas Jahn was occasionally emotional and reckless. He was a rock in contrast to Jahn's storm.

Minister of Foreign Affairs Calvyno turned his head

slightly and looked at Alix with more than a hint of accusation in his tired eyes. Alix knew there were many in the palace who wished he were emperor instead of his unpredictable brother. There were even those who expected bad blood between the brothers, who were quite certain that Alix would one day make a play for the throne. The outwardly unshakable Calvyno was likely among those who not only expected but looked forward to political excitement.

Alix took great satisfaction in denying them what they expected.

Beyond the open window in this large and elegantly furnished meeting room, revelers laughed and sang and danced as they enjoyed the first night of the Festival of Eramyn which ushered in the spring and said farewell to a cold winter. A large bonfire was visible, and now and then Alix's gaze drifted in that direction. Flames against the black night sky were more tolerable than the sight of Jahn arguing with those of power who surrounded him, those who insisted that it was time the emperor took a bride.

The twins had not always been Jahn and Alix Beckyt, emperor and prince. Until six years ago they had been known as Devlyn and Trystan Arndell, poor sons of a lost fisherman and a seamstress who worked hard to keep food on the table. They had been sentinels who'd gladly joined the fight against the demon-possessed Ciro. Those simple days might've been from another lifetime, they seemed so long ago. Alix very seldom thought of himself as Trystan Arndell anymore, and no one would mistake Emperor Jahn for a fisherman's son.

The majority of the common people of Columbyana had no idea their current emperor had come from such humble beginnings. They knew only that Emperor Sebestyen's twin sons miraculously had been found alive. However, many of those in power knew the whole sordid story, as did a large number of those who worked in the palace.

The sight of the bonfire did not distract Alix quite enough. He heard each minister and priest, one after another, wholeheartedly suggest a different woman to fill the position of empress. Each female was presented as more beautiful, more sweet-tempered, more *suitable* than the last.

After a short while the moment came when the emperor tired of playing with those around him. "Fine," Jahn said, a tenor of certainty and resignation in his voice. "I suppose I must marry." There was a collective sigh of relief from those surrounding him, but then the emperor added, "I will not, however, allow anyone else to choose my wife for me."

There was a flurry of argument as the men who had gathered around their emperor protested. They knew too well that Jahn's taste in women leaned to the unacceptable. An empress must be of an impeccable bloodline. She must not laugh too loudly or lose her temper or make bawdy jokes, and she certainly could not bare too much of her precious skin in public. An empress must be refined and elegant, a woman worthy of a country's loyalty and affection.

Jahn raised a hand, and the others were immediately silenced. The elder twin had taken quite well to his position, and he instinctively knew how to wield the power which was his by blood. "Those women who have been so glowingly suggested will be brought to the palace, where I will meet them all and make my choice."

"But, my lord," the Minister of Finance Tomos protested. He was pale and fleshy, looking very much like a man who spent his days bent over stacks of papers as numbers filled his head. "No woman of high rank will subject herself to such scrutiny and humiliation. These potential brides are not horses to be inspected and judged and . . . and discarded."

Jahn would not be swayed. "Any woman who wishes to be empress will agree to my terms."

A tall, thin priest, Father Braen, bowed with a modicum of respect. "I suspect Tomos is correct, my lord. No suitable female will wish to be examined and found lacking, only to be sent home in disgrace."

"Then perhaps I should marry them all," Jahn responded. "It's been a long while since the Emperor of Columbyana possessed a proper harem."

"You cannot suggest...," Braen snapped.

"I can suggest anything I wish," Jahn said coldly, in the voice he used to silence opposition. It was a voice Alix had not heard until his brother had been made emperor. "I can change the laws and take a dozen brides, if I so choose. I can ignore your suggestions and remain unwed. I can impregnate any number of immoral and willing women and allow you all to fight over who the heir might be. Anything is possible. *Anything.* Never forget that."

The smooth and seemingly unshakable Minister Calvyno bowed crisply. "My lord is correct, of course. I find his suggestion of bringing all the potential brides here for his inspection to be most"—he swallowed hard, unable to carry off his statement as smoothly as he'd intended—"reasonable," he finished in an uncertain voice.

"Excellent." Jahn stood. "I heard six names mentioned here tonight. Six of my most respected men will collect these women and bring them to me. Some reside quite a distance from the palace, so I suggest the bridal candidates be presented to me on the first night of the Summer Festival, in three months' time. Six of the fastest couriers should be dispatched immediately so the ladies will be prepared to be collected."

The men around the emperor nodded in approval—whether they actually approved of the plan or not. No one but Alix noticed the dulling of the light in Jahn's eyes. No one but Alix knew how deeply vexed the emperor was to be forced to take a wife.

"I will see to it, my lord," General Hydd said with his usual solemnity. "The couriers will leave at first light."

Jahn dismissed the crowd with a wave of his hand, and the men who had surrounded the emperor left quickly, almost as if they were glad to escape. Usually the emperor's meetings with his closest advisors were more genial, but the subject of an empress and a much-needed heir was a prickly one.

When Alix made as if to follow the others, Jahn stopped him with a raised hand and waved him to his side, just as the last of the ministers left the room and the heavy door closed with an ominous, dull thud.

"I should like to send you to Tryfyn to collect the Princess Edlyn," Jahn said. No one else would see the tiredness and even the surrender in his eyes, but Alix saw. He knew his brother well.

"It may be difficult to convince the King of Tryfyn to send his daughter to you for inspection," Alix said.

"Having a prince designated as her escort should ease his reluctance." Jahn shrugged his shoulders; wide, tired shoulders encased in imperial crimson. "If Princess Edlyn does not come, then it was not meant to be, and my choice will be all that much easier. She is of the highest rank of all those proposed, so I suppose she has a bit of an advantage, if she should decide to participate in the contest." He suddenly looked more Devlyn than emperor, his eyes hinting at the boy Alix had once known. "A contest for my bride. What do you think my closest advisors would think if I made it a real contest? I could bed them all and choose the one who pleases me most. I could strip them bare and search for imperfections. I can only imagine what Father Braen would think of that type of competition."

Alix knew that his brother was joking about testing the women in such a way. Jahn had taken too naturally to his position of power to throw it all away on such a whim. He realized that every word, every decision, was weighed and measured. Still, Alix breathed deeply before asking, "Are you sure about this plan of yours? Is it truly wise?"

For the first time in a long while, Alix saw a true smile from his brother. "I doubt anyone ever expected wisdom from Devlyn Arndell."

"True, but they demand it from Emperor Jahn." Alix bowed crisply. "I will, of course, do as you ask."

After almost six years in the palace, the twins had heard many tales of their conception and birth. The stories were told in whispers and tinged with magic, and it was impossible to know what was true and what was myth. No matter how it was told, the story was unsavory and sad. One they did not wish to dwell upon or examine too closely. Still, they could not ignore what they heard. They did not know all, would never know all, but one aspect of the tale was unchanging.

One twin had been conceived in darkness, the other in light. One twin was destined to wrestle with darkness, and the other was born of goodness and light.

Those who knew them surely believed that Emperor Jahn, a man who gambled and occasionally drank to excess and often enjoyed the company of inappropriate women, was the twin who struggled with a darkness of the soul, and Alix, who was noble and steady and well mannered, was the twin born to light.

Only Alix knew that they were wrong.

Chapter One

Four Weeks Later

THE court of King Bhaltair, ruler of Tryfyn and father of five princesses and one young son, was lavish and properly regal. The food was superb, the servants were ever-present, and Alix had been well entertained since his arrival four days earlier.

The castle which housed the royal court sprawled across a large plot of very green land lush with spring growth. A mere three stories high, the castle was very much unlike the narrower and much taller palace in Arthes. Some aspects were the same, of course. The castle was spotlessly clean, thanks to constant tending by an untold number of maids and manservants who were always underfoot. Stone walls gleamed and soft rugs lined oft-walked pathways. To welcome spring, the windows were unshuttered, allowing sunlight and fresh air to fill the confines of the castle on balmy days. The dining hall, ballroom, and private suite where Alix passed much of his time were lavishly furnished and adorned with potted plants and flowers in painted vases. Even the housemaids wore flowers in their hair. There were moments when Alix thought life in the castle too bright, too perfect, as if they were putting on a show for his benefit.

Each night, after a plentiful supper, there was music and dancing, or a well-acted play, or a sweet-voiced minstrel to sing tales of Tryfyn victory and beauty. There was even a lilting song to Princess Edlyn. The song praised her beauty, which was true enough, but did not mention her sour disposition or her spoiled demands.

The official color of the court of King Bhaltair was a dark and dreary green, much unlike the bright crimson which dominated in the palace of Arthes. Most days every member of the royal family dressed in that drab shade, but the women always adorned themselves with much gold to brighten the dreary green. They wore gold circlets in their hair, and jangling gold girdles to bring light and life to their costumes.

As a representative of Columbyana, Alix dressed each day in imperial crimson. Both trousers and vest were made of a fine fabric in that shade. Thank goodness the shirt he wore beneath the vest was plain white. His traveling clothes were plainer and more serviceable, though the trousers and vest were adorned with imperial embroideries, and he was anxious to get back to them. He did not care for standing out in a crowd; he did not like being the one bright spot of bloodred against a sea of dull green.

He was anxious to be on his way for many reasons, his wardrobe being the least of his concerns. With the entourage Edlyn's father insisted on providing for the journey, they'd be lucky to make it back to Arthes in six weeks. Having spent some time in Princess Edlyn's company, he suspected his sanity would be tested along the way.

As Alix had assumed from the beginning, Edlyn was not pleased to be offered for the emperor's inspection. Still, she was the only one of the five princesses that remained unwed, and if she often behaved as she had since his arrival, he could understand why she had not yet married—and why her father was so anxious to see her off.

Queen Coira was very well pleased. Any mother might

feel a pang of regret at seeing her youngest daughter ride away for potential marriage to a stranger—emperor or not—but the queen was Bhaltair's second wife, an exquisite woman not much older than Edlyn herself. She was all but smug about sending her stepdaughter away.

On this, Alix's final night in the Tryfyn royal castle, the dinner was sumptuous, the service was impeccable, and the queen could not contain her joyous smile. Princess Edlyn's mouth remained tightly pursed most of the time, and she seemed to fight back tears of outrage and disappointment. Alix studied her from his place at the table, not far from where she sat. Edlyn was beautiful, he would allow that much. Her hair was a nice pale yellow, and her skin was fair. Her eyes were a pale blue and hinted at a bit of intelligence—but not too much. That was just as well, as women who were too smart could be burdensome. Her mouth was nicely shaped, but since he never saw it curve into a smile or heard it speak a kind word, he wasn't impressed.

Traveling with her was going to be a nightmare.

Alix noticed that as the meal neared an end, the queen nudged the king more than once. Queen Coira nodded in Alix's direction, and then poked her husband in the ribs as she whispered a command. Finally, the king sighed and lifted his hand to signal the servant who waited at his side. The thin attendant obviously knew what was required, as he simply bowed and then exited the room with a quick and purposeful step.

"I do hope your brother will be pleased with our Edlyn," the king said with a forced smile. "She is a treasure."

Alix simply nodded, unsure of a response that would be both proper and honest.

"We are honored that the emperor will consider Edlyn to be his bride. To thank him for his generosity of spirit, we have a gift for him. A very special gift."

Alix could only hope the gift was small and easy to transport. One never knew what others would consider a proper gift for an emperor who had everything any man might ever desire. In the palace in Arthes, there were entire rooms devoted to the storage of jewels and pottery and woodcarvings which had been deemed by someone, somewhere, to be a proper gift for the emperor.

Every head in the room turned toward the dining hall entrance, and Alix did the same. He did not know what this night's entertainment might be, but he hoped it would be short in duration. As talented as the performers had been to this point, he really wanted nothing more than a good night's sleep before the long journey to Arthes began. This would be his last night in a proper bed for quite some time.

The two men who led the way, stepping into the dining hall with purpose, were dressed differently than the Tryfynians Alix had come to know in his days in the castle. The squat, muscled men wore bright, multicolored vests over smooth, naked chests. Their trousers were equally bright and ended just below their knees, above massive muscled calves and wide bare feet. Their skin was bronze, as if they spent all their days in the sun, and they were both bald and clean-shaven. Each wore a broad, curved sword at his waist.

His eyes did not remain on the men long, as his gaze was drawn to the woman who walked directly behind them.

Alix blinked as the woman stepped into the light cast by the many candles and lamps which filled the hall. She was blue. As she moved closer, he could tell that the blue was a powder of some sort, a flawlessly applied cosmetic. Every speck of exposed skin was covered—her face, neck, arms. Even her full lips were blue, but they were an even darker shade—almost black, it seemed. The rise of her bosom and the leg that peeked out of her skimpy skirt as she walked were a smooth sapphire blue, as was the curve of hip revealed beneath the low-slung band of the loosely fitted skirt. The woman was as tall as her escorts—perhaps taller than one—but instead of wearing colorful dress as they did, her outfit was entirely gold. The fabric shimmered and glittered as she walked into the room with a powerful and sensual grace that made Alix's mouth go dry.

Long, black hair flowed down her back, and amid the silky strands he caught the sparkle of ornate earrings that hung to her shapely shoulders. She wore many bracelets of gold and gems that caught the light, anklets that flashed gold with each step that sent the panels of her skirt dancing, and a low-slung girdle that looked to be made of many, many small golden coins. She jangled softly with each step, and the rattle of her adornments held a musical note that was unlike the clatter of the other women.

No one breathed, it seemed, as this blue woman took command of the room merely by entering. She moved with such grace, and her attire was so sensual, that Alix assumed this evening's entertainment would be an exotic dance of some sort. Moments earlier he had wanted only sleep, but to see this woman dance . . . surely it would be a most memorable diversion.

Sleep suddenly seemed unnecessary.

The blue woman had almost reached the main table, where Alix sat with the royal family, when he noticed that her wrists not only were adorned with many bracelets but were also bound with sturdy golden chains.

The guards before her parted and allowed the woman to come close to the table—close to the king, to be precise. Her eyes briefly met Alix's, and he saw no fear there, no hint of submission. Bound or not, she was proud and unbending.

The queen's mouth was thinned and hard, and once again she poked at her husband.

"Have you heard of the newly discovered Island of Claennis?" the king asked.

"I have heard very little," Alix admitted, "but yes, I did hear of its discovery." In the past few years brave travelers who ventured beyond the known world had returned with colorful tales, spices and fruits, and strange people. The world grew larger every day.

"I recently enjoyed a visit with the ambassador from the island country of Claennis, and he presented me with this gift. Sanura is one of a treasured tribe of that island, a tribe called the Agnese. Their women are possessed of great powers."

Good God in heaven, the gift the king had spoken of was a woman, and judging by the chains, she was a *slave*. Jahn would not be pleased. Women pleased him mightily, especially those who were beautiful and barely dressed, but he was staunchly opposed to owning another human being. "I can't possibly . . . ," Alix began.

"Take her," the queen said sharply. "If you do not, Sanura will be dead by morning, even if I have to see to it myself."

It was a bold statement, considering that the large dining hall was filled with many distant relations, close friends, and political allies.

The king blushed, and Alix understood. This Sanura had been given to the king as a gift, and his wife would not allow him to keep her. What wife, no matter how pretty and favored, would rest easy with a woman like Sanura living under the same roof?

Alix opened his mouth to refuse the gift, and then he remembered the queen's sharp words. Judging by the fire in her eyes, the promise of death for Sanura was not an idle threat.

And yet, the blue woman did not seem to be afraid.

"These men"—Alix indicated the two sword-bearing bald guards with a wave of his hand—"who are they?" They were not dressed like soldiers of Tryfyn.

"These are Sanura's keepers," the king explained. "I must admit, I am not entirely certain of all the rules concerning the Agnese, but I do know this. If any man other than he who owns Sanura touches her in any way, if any man is caught with blue marking his skin, these keepers will carry out an immediate execution."

So, he was to travel not only with a demanding princess and her soldiers and maids, but with this "gift" and her entourage as well. They would be lucky to make it to Arthes by the first night of the Summer Festival.

Alix considered refusing this gift, in spite of the price she'd have to pay. What did it matter to him if the woman was executed? She was not his concern, and in the end she would be much more trouble than she'd be worth. Once they reached Arthes, Jahn would surely give Sanura her freedom, anyway. The queen's threat was likely an idle one. Murder was an extreme reaction to her obvious jealousy. Surely there were others who would be happy to accept such a gift. A recipient from Tryfyn would be best.

As he was about to refuse the gift, Sanura's eyes met his. In spite of her cool and almost haughty demeanor, he saw the subtle touch of fear lurking there. He saw the almost hidden pleading in her eyes. Such deep and expressive eyes they were, a blue of such a remarkable hue that they were not dulled against her blue skin. Yes, she was brave and she was proud, but she was not fearless.

He could always free her along the way, since he was certain that's what Jahn would do when—if—he received this gift. "I'm sure my brother will be very pleased," Alix said in his most diplomatic voice.

Princess Edlyn pushed her chair back and jumped to her feet. "This is entirely unacceptable. It's bad enough that I'm forced to travel to another country to be scrutinized to see if I'm good enough for the blasted Emperor of Columbyana or not. Now I have to endure the journey with *her*? I refuse," she said tersely. "I absolutely, positively, *refuse*."

The king and queen did not react strongly to the outburst, but Edlyn's father did respond with quiet authority. "If you refuse to travel to Arthes with Prince Alixandyr, then I must insist that you accept the only other suitor who has persisted all these years. Tyren Mils is still willing to…"

"Tyren Mils is a pig!" Edlyn shouted. "And he's older than *you*!"

"The choice is yours," the king responded calmly. "Arthes and Emperor Jahn, or Tyren Mils."

Edlyn sat down hard, displaying not even an attempt at grace. "Arthes it is, but that perverted blue creature had best keep her distance from me."

Sanura, who had not spoken a word to this point, stepped toward Edlyn. The room was so silent it seemed that no one breathed. Every eye was on the blue woman, every ear strained to hear her words. Alix awaited an attack, but Sanura spoke to the princess in a calm, lightly accented voice. "I see who you are, sad little girl," she said with a hint of tenderness. "You are afraid, afraid to the pit of your soul, and that fear makes you strike out at those who only care for you. We are not enemies, you and I. We are much the same, given to men without the favor of a voice. We are given to others without considerations of love or personal inclination. You are crying inside, but you should not do so. This is who we are, little girl, and it is useless to fight against what is."

Edlyn stared at her dinner plate, and even from his position at the table Alix could see that her cheeks turned bright red. "Do not look at me, you... you witch. We are not the same, not at all! Turn away! I do not want you seeing that which is not yours to see."

"All is mine to see," Sanura said in a lowered, soothing voice, and then she did as the princess demanded and turned away. Her head twisted slightly and again she caught Alix's eyes with her own. "All," she whispered.

WHEN Sanura was returned to her room, Paki removed her chains. He did not like to see her restrained this way, she knew, but the resentful queen had insisted that whenever Sanura was not in her quarters, she would be restrained. Seeing Sanura in chains gave the queen a sense of satisfaction, a sense of ease. Even though her skin was slightly chafed, Sanura did not hold a grudge against the queen. The pitiful woman was insecure. Jealous. Lacking.

If it were entirely up to the queen, these quarters would likely be in the dungeon of this fine castle, or else Sanura would be forced to share a stable with the horses. The king was smarter than his sad wife, and understood that he was obligated to care for the gift he'd been given, even if he did not wish to—or was not allowed to—touch her.

When Paki and Kontar, her guards and countrymen, left her alone, Sanura sat before the small mirror in her room. She opened the ornate box at the center of the table, then took a fine brush and dipped it into the powder there. When she touched the powder to her skin, it turned almost liquid, it became the paint which covered her. She repaired the makeup on her wrists, where the shackles had very lightly marred their smoothness. The dense powder was not easy to remove, but the constant rubbing of the shackles had marked her. She had been assigned two maids who could see to such ministrations, but the servants disliked her as much as the jealous queen, so it was easier—and more pleasant—to see to such simple matters herself.

As she tended to the imperfection, Sanura's thoughts dwelled upon what tomorrow would bring. She was ready to leave this place where her gifts were not appreciated, where she was forced to spend most of her days in this lonely room without sunlight or companionship. She did not know what her new position would bring, but it would surely be different from this lonely existence, and so there was hope that her circumstances would improve.

The one who was to escort her to another, the one they called Prince Alixandyr, was intrigued by the blue, as were many men who were unaccustomed to the ways of the Agnese, but he was not repulsed by her the way many men of this country were. So many she had met were either frightened of her gift or repulsed by the color of her skin. She did not care what any man who was so squeamish and narrow-minded thought of her, so her feelings were never hurt by their rejection. A man who was afraid to have another look into his soul obviously had something to hide.

Prince Alixandyr was unlike the others in more ways than one. Not only was he not frightened by her differences, he also had a black and empty space inside him that

she could not read. He did not always think of himself as
Alixandyr or Alix, but sometimes thought of himself by
another name, a name she could not quite catch. It was odd,
even alarming. Though he was not an imposter, he was
also not entirely as he presented himself. She could see
that he was a soldier and a politician, dedicated to his
country and his brother and not entirely happy with his
life—yet neither was he unhappy. He did what needed to
be done without complaint, and he possessed a nobility
which would not allow one such as the queen to do murder
in the name of jealousy.

Sanura had learned that very few people in this world
were honest about who they really were. Most hid behind
faces that were forced, and they pretended to be what they
were expected to be or what they wanted to be. For that
reason she never attempted to disguise who she was. She
never pretended, or hid behind false words and faces.

The females of the Agnese were not seers or sages. They
did not see what the future might bring, nor did they see
into the past. What they saw was who a person—especially
a man—was at the pit of his soul. Fears, desires, strengths,
and weaknesses, with a bit of concentration an Agnese female could see them all. When Sanura had looked into the
prince from Columbyana, she had glimpsed strength and
nobility and ordinary male desires, but there had also been
a blackness that hid from her, a darkness that slept.

If she joined with him, she would see past the blackness. If they had sexual relations, she would know Prince
Alix to his soul, because there were no secrets when she
and another were linked. Mere men desired the Agnese
because in an instant, every desire they possessed could be
realized and met. There was no physical sensation to compare with sex with an Agnese female. Silly men, they did
not know how deeply they were joined in that moment,
how much of themselves they gave to the woman they saw
only as a possession, an object of pleasure.

They did not know that with every joining, the woman

who pleasured them became stronger, that she took as much as she gave.

Prince Alixandyr would be a good lover, she suspected. He was handsome and healthy and well built. He had the look of a man who was more warrior than prince, more soldier than politician, more civilized than not. He was strong and considerate and—sleeping blackness aside— there was a kindness in his green eyes. What a shame that she was intended for his brother, the emperor. If the black-haired, green-eyed prince dared to touch her, if he caressed her skin and stained himself with her blue, Paki and Kontar would not hesitate to kill him.

LADY Verity of the Northern Province, only daughter— only child—of a wealthy merchant who owned nearly all of the town of Mirham and much of the land beyond the city, was filled with excitement. At last, *at last*, she was going to escape her sometimes dreary and always predictable life!

She did not bother to hide her joy from the two women who were in her bedchamber, as she tried to decide which of her many gowns to take with her. She certainly did not wish to drag them all, but there were a few things she would not leave behind. She looked excellent in blue and in rose. The green and yellow she could leave behind. Once she was empress, everything could be replaced, but until then she would need her favorite and most flattering things. She'd be leaving home in two days, and she was not at all ready! Well, mentally she was ready, but she still had so much to do.

Her mother tried not to cry but did not entirely succeed. Verity had told her mum many times that she would visit Arthes often, once she was mother to the empress. Those words didn't help much. Verity tried very hard not to let her mum see her own infrequent tears. Of course she was look-ing forward to being empress, but she would miss her parents. Still, she was nineteen years old, and it was time for her to begin the life she'd been promised.

Her mum's witch, the sweet if occasionally creepy Mavise, remained calm while the other two females in the room alternately sniffled and agonized over what to pack. Mavise had always known, of course, that this day would come. For the past nineteen years she had said that Verity was destined to be the wife of a great man who had come from humble beginnings. Verity had always wondered how that would be possible, since there were *very* few great men in the Northern Province and, thanks to her father's wealth, she knew none who had come from humble beginnings.

But when the request had come from the palace in Arthes, and her father had told her the story of the emperor's lost and decidedly humble years, she had known the truth. She was going to be empress.

"Do not waste your time packing too many things you will not need," Mavise said calmly. "Too many unnecessary possessions will only slow your journey."

"What do I need, then?" Verity asked.

"Only two things are of importance." Mavise smiled as she reached into the deep pocket of her plain dress and withdrew the objects in question. "First, this talisman I fashioned for you." She offered a wrapped amber stone at the end of a long silver chain.

Verity sighed as she took it. "Mavise, you know I prefer gold to silver. It's more flattering with my golden hair."

The witch continued to smile. "The silver has more magic, girl, as I have told you many times before. Wear it beneath your clothes. It will bring you much luck."

Verity was going to ask why she needed luck when marrying the emperor was her destiny, but she didn't get a chance before Mavise handed over the second object she held, a small cloth bag closed with a leather thong and thick with some hidden substance. The old woman laid the bag in Verity's hand and then covered it with her own. "Be very careful with this, girl."

"What is it?"

"A powerful love potion."

Verity's spine straightened and her chin came up. "I do not need magic to make a man love me." She was very pretty and young and magnificently charming, and could be sweet and well mannered when it suited her.

"Take it," Mavise said. "Your life will be much happier if your husband is madly in love with you and will do whatever you ask of him without question. One pinch of this, and he will be yours forever. One pinch, and your every desire will become his every desire. He will give you all that you wish, all that you yearn for. A few grains, and he will adore you for all of his days."

Verity took the bag. She did not think she'd need such a potion, but just in case . . .

She kissed her mother and hugged Mavise, knowing that she would see them often in the next two days but also knowing she would soon be leaving them behind. It was a little sad. Sad and exciting and scary and wonderful.

After the other women left her alone for the evening, Verity donned her nightgown and brushed her hair as she thought of the days ahead. The trip to Arthes would be arduous, she imagined, but it was also necessary. She pulled the lucky talisman over her head. Even though the plain adornment was made of stone and silver, she realized she could not have too much good luck in the weeks to come.

As she was ready to douse the candles, she heard laughter. She walked to the window to look down from her second-story bedchamber at the men who had gathered below to drink and laugh and share stories. Sentinels! The torches which surrounded her home on this mild spring night were bright enough to illuminate them all. There were only three of them, but they were a rugged and uncivilized lot.

One of the sentinels looked up, even though she had not made a sound. Their eyes met, and he smiled at her. She had noticed this one before. Laris, as she had heard him called, did not seem as uncivilized as the others.

"Are we disturbing you, m'lady?" he asked in a voice just loud enough to reach her.

The other two sentinels continued their discussion and laughter, not at all concerned about whether they were disturbing her. Only this one seemed to care. "A bit," she said. "Tomorrow will be a busy day, and I need my sleep." She was such a grouch if she did not get proper rest, and there was so much to do before she departed home for her new life as empress.

"That will not do at all, m'lady." Laris gave a curt and very manly bow, and then he led the others away from her window. He looked back once and smiled, before the light of the torches no longer reached far enough to illuminate him.

Verity dismissed the handsome sentinel from her mind, doused the candles, and crawled into bed. Yes, she needed sleep, but could she? Could she rest at all when her mind was spinning so? Yes, she could, she thought with determination. She would dream of being empress, and of having an emperor husband who adored her beyond all reason. She would dream of being the wife of a great man, of having everything any woman might possibly ask for.

Yes, *everything*.

Chapter Two

THE traveling party was much larger—and much slower—than Alix would've liked. Still, he remained his usual stoic and calm self as he led Princess Edlyn, the beautiful blue Sanura, their collective guards and servants, and his own sentinels toward Arthes. As the days passed, he remained uncomplaining and courteous to all those around him, even though inside he was near boiling. Jahn would be in an absolute rage by now if he were subjected to the women and their demands.

The princess did not care for riding on horseback, so she was pulled along in a boxy conveyance that moved at a snail's pace. She insisted upon stopping frequently to stretch her limbs and complain about the bumpiness of the ride. Edlyn commanded that Sanura remain as far away from her as possible, so if the princess's slow conveyance was at the rear of the party, as it usually was, the blue slave was forced to ride at the front. As Alix led the procession, and as he did not care to be anywhere near the complaining princess, he was forced to travel with Sanura practically at his side.

She did not ride astride, but made the journey very gracefully perched in a massive sidesaddle. With her back unbendingly straight and her long legs more revealed than not, she was truly a sight to behold. Alix was accustomed to her blueness after more than a week of seeing her on a daily basis. It suited her, as did the black hair which was usually pulled atop her head in a pigtail that spilled out into a thick, straight fall which bounced with the horse's gait.

As they'd begun their journey he had insisted that Sanura not be chained. It was impractical to travel with a bound prisoner. If she decided to make off with her two surly guards, then all the better for everyone involved.

Sanura was unlike the princess in every way. Not only did she not complain about the conditions of travel, she did not often speak at all. She never spoke to Alix. In fact, if she was aware of his existence, she did not show it in any way. Edlyn passed most of her days hidden in her dreary coach and spent every night in her private tent. Sanura seemed to love living under the open skies. She all but basked in the sun, and though she had a private tent of her own, she retired there only to sleep. In her waking hours, night and day, she moved among the others, silent and sensual and oddly peaceful.

Whenever he heard the rattle of her girdle and bracelets and long earrings, Alix was reminded of music. The swish of the golden fabric which draped her body was just as harmonious. Other women so adorned clattered when they moved; they rustled and clanked. Sanura sang, and her song reached inside Alix and made his gut dance. When her movements made that song, he could not think of anything else—at least for a moment or two, until he forced his attention elsewhere.

And still, in his mind she was as contrary and bothersome as the princess. He was constantly aware of her, and though she was not demanding, her guards and the two Tryfynian maids who traveled with her insisted on stopping more often than he liked.

Sanura had to be aware of the curious eyes which were constantly upon her, but she never seemed nervous or ill at ease. She had to know that the men who watched her had, at the very least, passing lascivious thoughts. Her keepers did not even glance at her in an inappropriate way, but in their party there were four Columbyanan sentinels and six Tryfynian guards, all of them young, healthy, and distracted by the half-naked, curvaceous woman in their midst.

Her body was more revealed than not in the foreign costume she wore, and the unnatural color of her skin drew the eye to every curve, every angle. Sanura was forbidden, and for some men that made her all the more attractive. Not Alix. He had always staunchly avoided that which was truly forbidden. He followed the rules, always. He did not reach for those things which were not meant to be his, whether it was a woman or the ruling of a country.

But even he looked.

Alix had never lacked for female companionship. Even before he had discovered his true heritage and found himself in a position of power—as next in line for the throne of Columbyana and as an influential advisor to the emperor—women had been drawn to him. Unlike his brother, he was discriminating, and he preferred short-term monogamous relationships to bouncing from one woman to the next with abandon. Those relationships never lasted very long. As soon as any woman got too close, as soon as she looked at him with curious eyes that asked too clearly, "What are you hiding?," he found a reason to walk away. It was best that way. It was the only way.

Now past thirty years of age, Alix had considered marriage a time or two. The same priests and ministers who had been demanding that Jahn marry had also been hounding Alix—though less strenuously and less often. Still, he knew the time was coming when he would be forced to take that step. His position demanded it. When the time came, he would be obliged to choose a woman who would be a distant wife. He would be forced to choose a woman he did not like too well, a bride who would not look too closely or ask questions he could not answer, and yet he did not wish to be shackled with a wife he did not like at all.

The demands on a soldier were simpler, and there were times when he wished he could return to that time in his life.

While the sentinels saw to the horses and the Tryfynian soldiers and servants began to erect the tents the females insisted upon each night, Alix walked away from them all, moving toward a shallow stream they had just crossed. He needed a moment of silence, a chance to breathe deeply and still the stirring at his core. He would not allow that stirring to rule him. He would not give in to the animal inside him.

He would not become his father.

Alix squatted beside the stream and splashed water on his face. The chill was refreshing and stimulating, and served to bring him into the reality of now. There was no need to ponder what might happen in months and years to come. First he needed to get through this trial and deliver Princess Edlyn to Jahn. Somehow he thought his brother would not choose the Tryfynian princess, even though she was more highly placed than the others who were being fetched for the same purpose. She was too harsh, too petty. A shiver of warning ran up Alix's spine. What if his brother insisted that Edlyn become *his* bride, in the name of keeping peace with the neighboring country? What if Jahn chose a more agreeable bride, and forced his brother to wed the demanding, petulant Edlyn?

Inside, a part of him rebelled against the very idea, but he understood himself well enough to know that if that sacrifice was asked of him; he would agree without argument. Whether he was called Alixandyr Beckyt or Trystan Arndell, he always did his duty without complaint. That was who he was, who he insisted upon being.

"You confuse me."

Alix turned his head toward the woman who surprised him with her lightly accented voice. Annoyed at being disturbed, but also intrigued, he said, "You do not know me. How can you possibly be confused?"

Sanura—blue-skinned, bright-eyed, and scantily clad— sat down beside him, not too close but more than close enough to make Alix's mouth go dry. "Seeing into people is my gift," she said, her blue eyes alight with that curiosity which always sent him running. His eyes were drawn to her full lips.

"So I have been told," he responded in a calm voice.

"While it is true that some people are more complicated than others, at their core most are simple. Kind, greedy, cruel, needful...there is always a strong foundation deep within that we are forced to call upon or disguise or embrace."

His heart skipped a beat. It was not possible that this woman could see anything of the struggle he lived with every day. She could not know.

"But you," she continued, easing her body closer to his, "you are not so simple. You are at war within, in a way I have never seen before. I did not understand until last night, when I saw you wandering through the camp at midnight."

Alix breathed easier. The woman was a charlatan. "I was sound asleep at midnight."

"A part of you, the part you have chosen to embrace, slept," she said. "The other part, the dark side you seek to hide, was not."

"Impossible," he muttered.

"Apparently not," she answered just as softly.

He decided to change the subject. "Where are your guards?"

"I told those who have my keeping that I needed a moment alone to see to private matters." She nodded her head and that long, black pigtail swayed. Jewels sang, and he heard the music at his very core. "I thank you, Prince Alixandyr, for ordering that I not be treated as a prisoner during the journey. It has made my days most pleasant."

"We have no prisoners here."

"What of my life at our destination? Will your brother accommodate me as King Bhaltair did? Will he lock me away and keep me in chains in a small room where the sun never shines?"

"No," Alix responded quickly. "My brother does not believe in slavery of any kind. I'm quite sure he will free you." Sooner or later. Jahn was sure to be intrigued by Sanura; what man would not be? Would he be intrigued enough to keep her around when he was surrounded by potential brides? Was Jahn brave enough to sleep with a woman who could see into the pit of his soul?

"I am not meant to be free," Sanura said without rancor. "The emperor may give me to another, but he may not release me. It is not the way." She took a deep breath that did interesting things to her bosom.

"Surely you desire freedom."

"The women of the Agnese were not created to have desires of their own. We hear the desires of others, and when it is acceptable, when those desires emanate from those who possess us, we fulfill them."

"Everyone has desires of their own," Alix insisted.

Sanura smiled, her wide mouth twisting into a seductive grin. "I came to speak of your lot in life, not my own. Your darker side intrigues me. I have never seen anything like it."

His inner battle was a subject he would rather not explore, but Alix found himself drawn into this conversation he could never have with any other. Only Sanura saw. "If I have, as you say, a dark side, then why do you speak to me of it? Aren't you afraid?"

"No," she whispered.

"Why not?"

"I'm not sure. You are different," she said, as if she did not entirely understand. "I see the struggle inside you, but I cannot be afraid." She looked at him intensely for a moment, and then she glanced away as if embarrassed. "Perhaps I am unafraid because you saved me. The queen we left behind would've gladly taken my life."

"Surely not..."

"Yes. She dreamed of the ways in which she might end my life. In the moment when you were undecided about escorting me to your brother, she thought of how the deed might be done. She relished the thought of seeing me dead, so you see, you did save me." Her fingers clenched and unclenched.

"You are not obligated to me in any way," Alix said, calling upon his most distant tone of voice. How would a woman like Sanura repay such a debt? He could only imagine...and he should not imagine . . .

"I have another reason for speaking to you privately," she said, putting a hint of false bravery into her slightly accented voice as she deftly changed the subject. "One among us is planning aggression. I see no specific plans, no hatred of a person among us, but I sense that the violent thoughts grow stronger each day. There will be death before our journey is done, I fear."

"I was told you do not see the future."

"That is true, but I do see what is in men's hearts and souls. With that knowledge, certain behavior can be predicted. Your sentinel, the one with the fair hair and brown eyes, he hides feelings of hostility."

"Vyrn is a warrior," Alix responded. "Hostility is his livelihood."

Sanura nodded. "I do not believe that is true, but it is possible that the violence he conceals may sleep within him for the rest of his life, the same way that which you hide may sleep. That is a comforting thought, I suppose. I have done my duty in telling you what I saw. The rest is up to you, Prince Alixandyr." Again, she looked him in the eye. Yes, this was a woman who looked too deeply and saw too much.

"I will release you and your guards now," he said, anxious to be rid of this woman who looked into him so. "You are free to leave us at any time."

"I told you, I am not meant to be free."

Her acceptance of her lot in life angered Alix. She

seemed to think it was an honor to be owned by another, whereas she should be outraged. "Perhaps where you come from that is true, but you are in Columbyana now, and we have no slaves here. Jahn outlawed the possession of another person his first year on the throne."

"I answer to my own laws."

"I cannot believe that you don't wish for freedom," he said, his voice sharp with frustration.

Her face remained calm, her eyes serene, her breath slow and even. "I would not know what to do with freedom. To be free and alone is not who I am. I was born, raised, and trained to be possessed."

"Everyone wants to be free."

Sanura smiled. "No man or woman is truly free, Prince Alixandyr. We are all owned by something or someone, are we not? You yourself are possessed by responsibilities, by your brother, by your country. Is that so very different from my own circumstance?"

"Yes."

Again she looked at him with eyes which saw too much. Her smile faded. "You are also possessed by that which you hide so well. It rules your life as surely as the laws of the Agnese rule mine. May I speak once more about your own soul and heart?"

Alix's instinct was to say no, but he hesitated. No one else knew of the struggle within him, no one but this odd, blue, beautiful woman, and he did want to know exactly how much she saw. "If you wish," he said.

She lifted a hand that skimmed his face—not quite touching, but so close, so very close. "I like your eyebrows."

"My eyebrows," he repeated.

"Yes. They slash slightly upward in a very manly fashion. With your narrowed and piercing eyes, which sometimes seem to see miles ahead of the others, and the slashing eyebrows, you can appear quite demonic. I imagine the Angel of Death himself has such eyes. And yet, I also see that you are kind and brave and much like an angel of another sort entirely."

Her observations made his stomach clench. "I thought you wanted to speak about my heart and soul, not my eyebrows."

"I am simply taking my time, my prince. Does it bother you that I study you so?"

"No." What a lie that was. She had his heart beating too hard and too fast, simply with a glance, simply because she was too near.

"You have buried a part of yourself for so long, and you think you have won this very personal battle," she said. "You think that darkness is buried. But of late it does not always rest as you wish it to, Prince Alixandyr. Of late it awakens while you sleep and it rules. It lives. If you wish to be done with the darkness once and for all, you must first allow it to live, to breathe, to be your own. Only then can it be truly controlled." She moved closer, rising to her knees and leaning over him so that her body almost touched his. He could feel the heat rolling off her body, and he wanted to reach out and grab her so badly that he had to clench his hands into tight fists to keep from grabbing her. Even this close, the blue of her skin was flawless and smooth. He wanted to rake his fingers across the forbidden flesh, he wanted to taste the blue. He wanted to pull her body against his.

"I am not supposed to have desires of my own," she whispered, as if she were afraid someone might hear, "but on occasion I do. Right now I wish you were the one who possessed me, who owned me body and soul, who took pleasure within me," she said, so casually it was as if she were asking for a sip of water or a slice of bread. "If we were joined, I could see more of you, I could know the darkness you battle in a more complete way." She licked her lips and tilted her head, and her hair swung forward and brushed against him. "I would also know all that you most desire."

In spite of the earlier, less pleasurable subject of their conversation, Alix was hard. Perhaps it would be worth death to lie with such a woman. Perhaps it would be a fair trade—her body against his for the blade of her keepers' swords. His breath did not come easily, and he could feel his heart pounding in his chest. His mouth was dry, his hands trembled, and in his mind he could see the two of them together, their bodies bare and joined and screaming. He felt, almost as if it were real. He saw her blue body and his ordinary flesh meeting and joining, felt the heat and the pleasure she promised.

She was a sorceress, that was the only explanation.

"The darkness is a part of you, Prince Alixandyr," Sanura whispered. "It cannot, will not, remain buried forever. Claim the shadows and control them, or they will win the battle for your soul and the man you have become will be no more. The man you have become will be buried, struggling to rise to the surface as the darkness now struggles."

"I won't allow it," he insisted hoarsely, as Sanura moved impossibly closer. She was all but straddling him, and though her skin did not touch his, the loose golden skirt she wore brushed against him.

"Perhaps if your brother does not wish to keep me for himself, he will give me to you, as the king gave me to him." She licked her lips. "In the world I left behind, men do not so easily toss away a treasure such as a woman of the Agnese. All my life I have been told that I am precious and special, that all men will want me for their own. It is disconcerting to be unwanted. Untouched. If I were your gift, would you give me away?"

"No," he whispered. "I could not."

She smiled a slightly crooked, almost sad smile. "That is good."

He knew the blue before him was a powder, but it was so perfectly applied that it looked as if her skin were actually that sapphire shade. Was the cosmetic applied to the swell of her breasts, which he could not see beneath the low-cut gold blouse she wore? Were the nipples blue, or did they blush a soft pink against the unnatural color, the way her tongue blushed between the parted dark lips? Were the most private parts of her body covered in that powder? He wished very much to know, to see, even to touch.

Sanura pulled away, slowly but decisively. "I can see no more," she said as she resumed her seat a safe distance away. A moment later she rose to her feet, moving more quickly than usual, and turned from him. Without another word she walked away, leaving Alix to the solitude he so needed.

SANURA walked away from the prince without a glance back. No one would know, by looking at her face, that the man by the stream left her confused and unsure, and somehow heartbroken.

Her heart never came into consideration. She was of the Agnese, a gift to be owned, a treasure whose concerns were never for herself but were only for the man to whom she belonged. At the moment she did not even know the man to whom she belonged. Was the emperor kind or brutish? Would he care for her and be glad he had received her, or would he dismiss her with barely a thought? Would he be thankful for her, or would he toss her away? This part of the world was strange. Men did not always behave as they should, and at times like these she wished only to go home.

Home, where she was wanted. Home, where the sun always shone and men and women bowed to her when she passed. Home.

She had never before questioned the way of her life. She'd never wondered why she could not be like other women and choose her own lovers. Prince Alixandyr made her wonder. His complicated nature intrigued her, but she would notice him as a fine specimen of a man even if he were like all others. He had the body of a soldier, fit and strong and kissed by the sun. His visage was not pretty; it was not even and soft enough to be called pretty. Instead, his face was masculine and handsome, with calculating eyes, a blade of a nose, and a mouth that was wide and hard and interesting. The line of his jaw was as bladelike as his nose, and she had been so tempted to touch him there—even knowing that such a touch would mark him for death. His black hair was almost as long as her own. Instead of being straight it waved wildly, even though he had most of it restrained behind his head with a silver clip. She had very much wanted to run her fingers through the wild and curling strands.

Sanura tossed her head and tried to shake off her interest in the prince just as she shook off the foolish notion that what she wanted mattered in any way. She would do well to stay away from one who battled with darkness, no matter how he intrigued her.

As she crossed the camp to the tent Paki and Kontar had erected for her, she decided to maintain a distance from Prince Alixandyr for the remainder of their journey. Princess Edlyn was a difficult companion, but perhaps it would be better to deal with the disdain of a simple woman than to be washed in the complexities of a man who made her wonder about things she should not.

She had been too long alone, that was the reason for her confusion. If Zeryn were still alive, if his blasted brother had not given her to the King of Tryfyn as a gesture of goodwill, then she would not be faced with such a dilemma. After her period of training, Zeryn had purchased her. She'd been pleased, as he was kind and handsome and a good provider. They'd had four years together, and she'd expected that she'd spend her entire life as his, treasured and pampered and devoted to him who possessed her. Life had other plans for her, it seemed, as Zeryn had died much too soon and his brother had decided she'd make a nice diplomatic gift for a leader of the new world which had so recently been discovered.

The women of the Agnese were not meant to live alone. They were not meant to forever sleep alone, to pass the nights in solitude in a too-quiet room or a too-small tent.

They were not meant to hunger for that which was, by right, theirs. Warmth, pleasure, companionship, they were all meant to be hers. Instead, she passed each day and night with no one but her keepers and two surly maids for company. No one treasured her. No one wanted her.

Her eyes were drawn to the sentinel who hid such hostility beneath a constant smile and easy banter. Even from a distance, she saw who he truly was. She felt it, was assaulted by it. She wanted to believe that Prince Alixandyr was right and the man was merely a soldier whose life was touched with violence, but in the pit of her soul she knew better.

Vyrn caught her looking at him, and in a shy manner that was unlike her, Sanura turned away when their eyes met. Deep down, she shuddered. She'd do well to steer clear of that one. She did not sense that his hatred was aimed toward her, but she could not be certain. Her gift was not one of absolutes, but was based on emotion and spirit and possibilities.

The prince was not far behind her, and Sanura wondered if anyone in the camp wondered that they had come from the same direction, not so long apart. They would know that he had not touched her. The blue was easily transferred from skin to skin, even though it was not at all easy to wash away. If he had touched her, everyone who saw him would know.

And as far as they were concerned, there was no reason for the prince to have anything to do with her if he could not touch her.

Sanura watched as the sentinel who concerned her walked to his prince and said a few words. She wondered if the prince would betray her confidence and tell his soldier what she suspected. What she knew. Their conversation was short, and the sentinel did not seem alarmed. Sanura soon breathed easier.

Beyond Prince Alixandyr, one crimson and one dull green flag, each dutifully planted upon their arrival at this campground, whipped in the wind. The prince's long hair was caught in the breeze, too, as was the traveling cape which fell to his thighs. He would not tell, she knew it.

No, the part of him she knew would not tell. She had no idea what the darker side of his soul would do.

"Your evening meal will soon be ready." The cool voice came from behind her, and Sanura slowly turned to face one of her young and reluctant Tryfynian maids. Tari was plain of face and too thin, but she did have very nice red hair which was usually caught in a too-tight bun. She didn't like her duties any more than the other maid, a prettier brown-haired girl called Phyls.

Whenever she was close to them, she felt their disdain, their dislike, and even their disgust.

"I will take the meal in my tent tonight," Sanura said, being careful not to give away her sadness as she looked toward the stream she had left behind. "The wind is picking up."

Tari curtseyed sharply and then turned away.

At home, young girls vied for the position of maid to a woman of the Agnese. It was an honor to serve one so blessed, not a bitter trial. At home, at home, at home. Sanura bit back the bitter realization that she would never see home again. She was destined to live in a world where no one wanted her.

As Tari walked away, Sanura glanced back at the prince. He wanted her, in an entirely male way. There were others who felt a basic urge to touch her, but they were also afraid and uncertain. Prince Alixandyr was neither.

Her heart sank. It didn't matter that he wanted her. He was too noble to take a woman meant for his brother and emperor, too upright to break the rules—whether they were his rules or another's. The part of him she could see and understand would never take a gift which was meant to be his brother's.

The dark side of him, the shadowy part of himself that he denied and fought, was too protected, too mysterious for her to be sure what might happen if it were in control.

She had a sudden and unpleasant feeling that she might find out before they reached their destination.

AFTER their traveling party stopped for the evening and Verity had taken the time to give her mare, Buttercup, the care and attention she deserved after a long day's ride, she caught Laris's eye and nodded. A few moments later she casually made her way around the bend so the campsite was no longer in her view—and she could no longer be seen from there. Their group was small and no one paid her much mind, which was just as well.

Verity found a rocky hollow and leaned against the wall of stone, taking a moment to straighten her mussed hair and smooth her wrinkled blue traveling skirt. Before she had time to do more than briefly admire the quickly setting sun, Laris joined her. She found herself smiling at him more widely than she'd planned. He did not smile often and did not smile now, but instead simply looked at her with pained eyes and thinned lips.

"Are you well?" he asked, concern evident in his deep, smooth voice.

"My backside is sore," she said honestly. "Though I am accustomed to riding, I have never spent so many hours in the saddle." There were too many hills and narrow paths in this part of the world to accommodate a proper coach, not that she would've hidden in one all day even if it were possible.

"I'm so sorry," Laris said with heartfelt emotion. "Is there anything I can do to help?" He blushed, as he did on occasion. Perhaps he wondered if she'd ask him to massage the abused area, and that's why he blushed.

Verity felt an unexpected heat in her own cheeks. "There's nothing to be done, of course. I should not have complained."

"I only want your comfort and happiness, Lady Verity. I will do all that I can for you." The way he looked at her, as the light faded, cut to her heart in an unexpected way.

She'd had to test the love potion on someone, and Laris had been the logical choice. The handsome sentinel, one of the three who had accompanied the fat, grumpy diplomat who'd fetched her, was one year older than she was and relatively new to his position. He was a handsome young man, with hair fair like hers and remarkable brown eyes. To be honest, he was the only acceptable candidate in their party. If she was going to have a devoted and adoring man constantly at her side, then he might as well be young and easy to look at.

Verity looked up at Laris, catching his lovely dark brown eyes and holding them with her own. "I am ready for summer. As soon as the sun sets, I grow cold." She hugged herself, and very soon Laris was there, wrapping his strong, warm arms around her. She let him. She even rested her head on his chest and listened to the beat of his heart.

All her life Verity had been told that she would be the wife of a great man, so traveling to the capital city to become empress did not scare her. It did occur to her, however, that Mavise had never told her she'd be happy in her new position. Not once. That didn't mean she couldn't or wouldn't be happy as well as powerful. Mavise should've been more thorough.

Verity should've thought to ask before leaving home, but she'd only recently begun to consider the matter.

When she was in a position of power, she would make herself happy. She would *insist* upon happiness. With the help of the love potion, she could be assured that the emperor would adore her, but would she adore him? Would she feel a real, true love for the man she'd call husband?

The future was uncertain, but Laris made her feel steadier and less afraid—even though she was *not* afraid. Not at all.

His heart thumped steadily in her ear, and she took comfort from the sound. "Sometimes I get cold at night, too," she said hesitantly.

The heartbeat she listened to grew a bit faster. "Do you?"

"Yes." And sometimes she could not sleep. Some nights her thoughts spun and spun and spun, and all she wanted was something—or someone—to hold on to. "Perhaps when it is your watch you could..."

"I could not," he said hotly, before she had a chance to finish the invitation.

What good was a love potion if she could not compel the afflicted man to do as she wished? "Please," she whispered, "just visit me for a while. We cannot...well, you know what we cannot do. It wouldn't be proper at all." Very nice, judging by the way he held her, but not at all proper. "I don't want you to think that I desire anything more than a friend's comfort, but it's a comfort I would very much like to have. Please, Laris. Please."

He sighed. "If you truly wish it."

"I do."

"I'll visit you tonight if I can."

With her face against his chest, she smiled. Yes, the love potion Mavise had provided was quite effective and *very* handy.

Chapter Three

HE argued with himself on occasion, but Alix couldn't bring himself to entirely dismiss Sanura's warning about violence within Vyrn. If she saw his own struggle, a struggle he successfully hid even from those who knew him best, then how could he dismiss what she claimed to see in others? As the days passed and the traveling party moved toward Arthes at an achingly slow pace, he kept a close eye on the young sentinel, trying to see for himself what Sanura claimed was there. All he saw was a smiling, flirtatious, seemingly reckless sentinel who made small talk with the Tryfynian maids whenever the opportunity arose and happily took on whatever chore he was assigned.

Maybe the blue seductress was wrong. Worse, maybe she was lying. Maybe, for some reason which was thus far hidden, she wanted to create a division between him and his men. Divide and conquer, was that her way?

Alix took a deep breath to calm himself when he saw Princess Edlyn stalking toward him, two humorless and dedicated Tryfynian soldiers at her heels. The skirt of her green traveling gown snapped behind her, and her mouth was set in a hard, straight line. For all her physical beauty, she was as drab and unappealing as the color she wore. For a moment he imagined himself married to this sour woman, enduring her demands and petulance day after day, keeping his temper in check in the name of diplomacy and peace. He tried to imagine her lying beneath him, lost in the throes of passion, but he could not. From what he could see, this woman had no passion within her, no warmth, no love. She was as hard as any sentinel, in her own way.

His eyes were drawn over the princess's shoulder to watch a still and serene Sanura. She waited silently as her guards set up her small tent. Behind her the sun was setting, coloring the sky pink and orange and violet. A gentle breeze caught her skirt and made it dance, and even though he was too far away, he was certain he heard that music her jewels made when she moved. He could very well imagine her beneath him. She would cry out in pleasure, she would laugh in bed and in his arms, she would scream, and she would likely make him scream as well.

And she would see all of him. She would know every secret, see every lie. Marriage to a cold princess would be better.

"Would you do me the courtesy of *looking* at me?" Edlyn snapped as she came to a halt before him.

Alix dragged his eyes from Sanura and pinned his gaze on the princess. Again he imagined himself married to her, shackled in the name of diplomacy, once again a prisoner in the name of doing what was right, and he felt a rush of anger as he caught and held her eyes with his own.

The princess blinked hard and took one step back. "I...I'm sorry." She glanced to the side and down. "Obviously I've caught you at a bad time."

"Not at all," Alix responded. "What can I do to make your journey more comfortable?" His voice was sharper than he'd intended, but perhaps that was for the best.

Edlyn frowned and wrinkled her nose, then she cautiously stepped forward once more. "It is that heinous blue creature my father insisted upon sending along who causes my distress. Having her along for the journey is a punishment," she muttered. "My own father hates me."

Did the spoiled princess want Alix to do what her stepmother had not? Did she wish to be rid of Sanura before they reached Arthes, and if that was the case, did she expect he'd do the dirty work for her?

"Perhaps you should take your complaints to Sanura herself," he suggested, knowing that she would not. Haughty and arrogant as Edlyn was, she was more than a little afraid of Sanura.

"I'd rather not," Edlyn muttered, confirming Alix's suspicions. Her chin came up. "In the early days of our journey she rode near the front of the procession, but lately she's taken to riding alongside my carriage. It's unbearable, I tell you, to look out my small window as the carriage bumps and rattles along and see *her*. She's taunting me. She's...she's...she's harassing me!"

"By riding too near to your conveyance," Alix said without sympathy.

"Yes," Edlyn whispered.

Edlyn surely knew that as a woman she paled beside Sanura. In character, in appearance, in sensuality, there was no comparison—at least, none which favored Edlyn in any way. Next to Sanura, Edlyn—pretty as she was— disappeared. What woman would not? Did the princess look at the gift her father had sent and realize that no man, emperor or not, would remember she existed after he'd had a look at a woman of the Agnese, after he saw Sanura's blue curves and heard the music of her steps?

"I will speak with her," Alix said, bowing curtly and with more than a touch of disdain.

Again Edlyn frowned. It seemed to be a normal expression for her. "I thought your eyes were a rather ordinary shade of pale green," she said as she studied them with a squint.

"They are," he replied.

"Oh." Edlyn backed up, and so did her soldiers. "It must

be a trick of the light." With that she turned and walked away, her steps a bit quicker than they had been on her approach.

It was easy, very natural in fact, for Alix's gaze to return to Sanura. She did not move, and even if she did, he would likely not hear the music from this distance. And yet somewhere inside he did hear. Even though his body remained motionless, even though no one could see his reaction, he danced to the tune Sanura sang. The dance was internal, private, and as hidden as the shadows he fought.

Perhaps it would be a kind of torture, but he would ask Sanura to ride with him in the morning. He would insist that she once again place herself at the front of the party. He would do as the princess demanded and put as much distance as possible between the two women for the duration of the journey, no matter what the cost to his own comfort and sanity.

He might cross the camp and ask Sanura about the new traveling arrangements now, but he didn't feel quite himself.

IN the confines of her tent, long after darkness fell and the camp grew silent, Sanura caressed the square box which held her cosmetics, brushes, and oils for scent and cosmetic repair. At home, maids would fight for the honor of assisting her in the application of the sacred blue paint. Here she did the work herself, calling upon others only when she could not reach a patch of skin which needed repair.

Lamplight flickered over the intricately carved box, which was a work of art like no other she had ever seen. Delicate flowers with curling stems covered the wooden container, and in many places there were inlays of shimmering stone which caught the lamplight and felt warm beneath her fingers. At home, this box was considered a treasure, as she was. Here no one seemed to pay it much mind. They did not know the years of work which had gone into the creation of the box. They did not realize how the craftsman had so lovingly carved the wood and shaped the stones. Like her, it was dismissed as beautiful but odd.

As Sanura caressed the box, she wondered if the emperor who now possessed her would be anything like his brother. If so, then Arthes would become her new home. She would forget all she'd left behind; she'd forget her old home and make a new one. Perhaps the emperor would treasure her as she was meant to be treasured. Perhaps Columbyana would be different from Tryfyn. Less cold. Less lonely. Perhaps someone there would recognize her worth and the worth of her meager possessions.

Thinking of Arthes and the emperor naturally guided her mind to Prince Alixandyr. She had never longed for anything which was not hers. Not freedom. Not love. Certainly not a particular man to whom she did not belong. And yet she thought of Alix as she sat in her tent and pondered treasures of the past and things she could not have.

Sanura was surprised when the flap to her tent opened and the prince himself slipped inside, his manner and his movements surreptitious and furtive. He glanced at her and smiled—she had never seen him grin this way—and he laid one long finger over his mouth, cautioning her to be silent.

Her heart skipped a beat. His eyes were too dark, his smile too wicked.

The shadow walked again tonight. The darkness Prince Alixandyr fought lived while the man he had become slept inside that body.

He dropped to his knees beside her, his body long and muscled and strong, a man's body as certainly as hers was a woman's. "I could not stay away," he whispered.

"You should go," she answered, her voice even softer than his own. "If you are found here, you'll be killed."

"Only if there is blue on my skin, isn't that the way of the rule? Only if I touch you is my life forfeit." He leaned toward her, and she could see that his eyes were still green, but they had taken on a darkness which made them resemble the forest at night, or an angry sea. Lamplight flickered over one side of his face, which was so close she could see the small lines at the corners of his eyes, the creases by his mouth. His dark hair was more mussed than usual, loose and waving thickly to his shoulders and beyond. He was a hard warrior in many ways, outside and in, and yet he was also very much a man. A good man. A needful man.

"You want to touch me," she whispered.

"I do," he admitted with a smile. "So does he."

"Prince Alixandyr," she said softly.

"Yes, that cowardly, uptight, do-gooder Alix."

She wanted, so much, to reach out and touch him. "Like it or not, you are, in many ways, one and the same."

His eyes grew darker, and his mouth went hard. A long hank of hair fell across the illuminated side of his face, hiding so much. Too much. "We are not one. We are two very different men in one body, and I have been silent for far too long. I'm done with being silent, with being constantly imprisoned."

The prince's hand skimmed a fraction of an inch from her cheek. She closed her eyes, and still she could almost feel the touch of his hand. Even though it was forbidden, she wanted his warmth as much as he wanted to touch her. She held her breath as his hand moved so close, and beneath closed eyelids she felt her eyes roll up and quiver. A mistake on her part or his could mark him, so she was very careful to remain still, to soak in the closeness without losing control and reaching for what she wanted.

The part of him he had just denied—Alix, he said—remained within, sleeping but certainly not dead. Resting, not gone. The darkness and the light which had done constant battle from the time of his birth were a part of one soul, one man. He wasn't ready to hear that, however. In his eyes, in his heart, they were two.

In hers, they were one. One man who struggled. Which part of him would win? He thought the battle was over, but she knew it had just begun.

"You could make a man crazy." His hand floated over

her chest, almost touching, almost condemning. "You could get inside a man's head and overshadow everything else he holds dear. Duty. Family. Honor. Life itself. All gone, in the name of Sanura. Are you a witch who's cast a spell upon me? Upon him?" She felt and heard his sigh. "Upon both of us?"

"No." She breathed her answer. A shout would bring her guards to her, but she didn't want this encounter to end. Nothing could come of it, nothing could come of them... but she enjoyed having him so close. She enjoyed it much more than she should.

He buried one hand in her hair, catching the strands fast and holding on. She felt his fingers against her scalp, felt the warmth of his hand against her head. His cheek rested against her hair, but he touched her nowhere else and she could not touch him.

"If you claim you are not the man I know as Prince Alixandyr, what shall I call you?" she asked.

"You needn't call me anything at all," he whispered against her hair. "Simply snap your fingers and I am yours. Crook one finger in my direction, and I will come running. Even your hair smells good," he added. "Like flowers and sunshine and... woman. You smell like a woman, Sanura."

"I wish to call you something," she said. "Alixandyr or Prince, perhaps." Dearest or lover, even better.

He sighed, and she felt his warm breath in her hair. "Call me Trystan, if you insist upon giving me a name."

"Trystan."

"He was Trystan for many years before he became Alix." A thumb touched her nipple, not coming into contact with her forbidden bare flesh but warming and arousing through the thin fabric that covered her breasts. Sanura closed her eyes and held her breath as Alix—Trystan—made small circles with his thumb, circles which made her nipples grow hard and her body tremble. No one had ever caressed her this way, and she had been so long alone that her reaction was unexpectedly intense.

"Have I found a flaw in the laws that protect you, Sanura?" Trystan teased as his touch grew harder. "I can touch you very well." He removed his hand and a moment later his mouth was there, carefully and expertly suckling at her breast through the gold fabric. Her body shuddered. Her toes curled. His mouth lifted away and he blew a long, slow breath onto the damp fabric before saying, "If I'm very careful, I can pleasure you without getting a particle of that damned blue paint on my skin."

"You do not understand," Sanura said, her voice breathless and uneven. "The women of the Agnese do not take pleasure, they give it. The men who own us do not keep us for the offering of gratification, but for the taking. You can touch me thus without condemning yourself with the blue, but I cannot touch *you*." And she wanted to touch him, shadows or not. Alix or Trystan or Prince, she did not care.

He seemed amused. "So, no man has ever touched you like this?" Again he kissed her through the gold fabric. He caught a nipple between gentle teeth, and she gasped.

"No."

"What about this?" He reached between her legs and, with the fabric of her skirt against his hand, stroked her where she trembled for him. She could very easily clamp her thighs against him and spread the blue paint on his hand and his forearm, but instead she opened herself for his touch. His stroke continued, rhythmic and beyond arousing.

Since the first time she'd seen this man sitting at the king's supper table, she had often wondered what it would be like to have Prince Alixandyr for a lover. She liked him; she was drawn to him. He was kind and strong and everything a man should be. He was a protector, an honorable man, a noble and cautious and unbelievably stirring man. He stirred her body and her heart. He made her wish for a different kind of life.

But this was not Prince Alixandyr, not entirely. Not completely. This was not the man she had come to admire and to want. Her body stiffened as she made the distinction. Physically the two parts of him were the same, but if the darkness ruled his soul, as it did now, he would no longer be the man she had come to admire. Was she wrong in her understanding that they were one and the same? Or was he himself correct when he said they were two? She should know, she should be able to tell, but she could not. In many ways this man remained a mystery to her.

"What's wrong, love?" he asked.

Sanura looked him in the eye, studying the dark green and looking deeper, trying to see more. There was not much of the man she truly desired present, at the moment. "I want Alixandyr."

The man who touched her smiled crookedly. "No, you don't. Alix would never dare to touch you this way." His stroke continued. "It's not *proper*. It's not *right*." Every word dripped with sarcasm. "You are meant for his brother, after all, and Alix would never dare to covet what his brother possesses. Not a woman, not the throne, not even a mother's love."

"Is that why you want me?" Sanura asked. "Because I'm his? Because I have been given to the emperor?"

"Yes," he whispered, and she felt the truth of his easy confession.

He might as well have thrown a bucket of cold water over her. What had been wonderful and promising was now unclean. Her body grew cold, and she attempted to move away from his touch without staining him with the blue. Alix was not guilty. It wasn't easy to dismiss Trystan entirely, to shake off her womanly reaction to his attentions, to his touch.

She did not like the man before her, but the body he claimed was that of a man she liked very much.

"You should go," she said.

"Too bad." He moved away from her, taking his hand from her body and sitting back, but showing no indication of leaving. "I wanted to watch you scream, love. I wanted to hear you gasp and moan. I wanted to feel you lurch against my hand."

"I want Alixandyr," she whispered. "Go away and send him to me. Now." She wanted the warm green eyes, not the black/green that stared through her. She wanted the man of honor, not the thief who coveted what his brother possessed. "Go away, and send him to me."

She asked for Alixandyr even though she knew Trystan would touch her, take her, while the man she craved would not.

His smile did not fade. "No. You can't have him. I have learned to take control, and I won't relinquish that control easily."

"You're not as strong as he is," Sanura said softly. "He'll be back."

"I imagine so, but not now, and not permanently." He grinned. "I'm coming into my own, and I like it very much. Alix won't survive this journey, my blue seductress. If I think he's winning the battle, if I believe that I will never have possession of this body, I will take you, willing or not. I will cover myself in the blue that stains your skin, and then I will present myself naked and deliriously happy to your sword-toting guards." He moved closer. Too close, and yet still he did not touch her skin. "If I don't win the fight for this body before we reach Arthes, you will be the death of your precious Alixandyr."

ALIX woke feeling as if he had not slept at all, but there was no time to lie about simply because he'd passed a restless night. His first order of business was to ask Sanura to ride beside him as she had in the early days of their journey. Being near her was a kind of torture, but keeping peace between the two women he was escorting to Jahn was of the utmost importance.

Even though Sanura had been avoiding him since their conversation by the stream, he was surprised when she turned about, saw him, and visibly flinched. She was not a shy woman, and he had never seen her cower or recoil from anything. He had certainly never given her reason to fear him. He crossed the camp to speak to her, and she remained wary. Openly suspicious. He could almost swear that she was about to run from him—or at least she wanted to run.

Sanura did not flee as he approached, but she had told him more than once that what she desired did not matter.

"It would be best if you rode with me today," he said in an authoritative tone of voice. They would take this one day at a time, in a sensible manner.

She stared into his eyes, studying them more fiercely than was necessary, and then she relaxed. He could actually see the tension leave her body, he saw her limbs and her mouth relax until she was once again the sensuous and confident woman he had come to know.

"Why do you wish it?" she asked.

Alix attempted to inject a touch of cheerfulness into his voice, even though he did not feel at all cheerful. "Do you enjoy listening to the princess complain with each step the horses take?"

At this, she smiled. "No more than anyone else who travels at the rear of the column, I imagine. Is my comfort of such importance to you?"

He would not lie to her. "No."

A light of understanding came into her eyes. "Ah, this is Edlyn's doing, isn't it? She wants me as far away from her as possible."

"Yes."

Sanura cocked her head and studied him for a moment. He didn't like the calculating intelligence in her eyes, or the sense that she saw more than she should, as she always did. She was just a woman, no different from any other who was not his to take. And yet, he did not react to her as if she were any other woman.

"A more perverse woman would refuse your offer and spend the remaining days making conversation with our troublesome princess, simply to make the journey more difficult for you."

"Are you perverse?" Why could he suddenly smell her hair, as if it were directly beneath his nose? Why did he have to clench his hands into fists to keep from shaking? Such a woman could surely bring stronger men to their knees, but he had never thought himself vulnerable to such nonsense.

"On occasion," she admitted. "But not today. I will ride with you if it will make the journey easier for you...and for everyone else, of course."

Alix bowed to Sanura in appreciation, and then he allowed his eyes to roam over her body. Her outfit was still gold and scanty, but the shimmer was of a different and darker shade. "You changed your traveling outfit."

Her smile disappeared. "The top was stained."

"Traveling is often the end of a suit of clothes. You will ruin two instead of one if you are worried about something so insignificant as a stain."

She did not care for his observation, and he wondered if she blushed beneath the blue. It was impossible to tell. "Surely the emperor will replace any clothing that is damaged in my journey to him. Is your brother a miserly man? Will he expect me to adorn myself in a common fabric which is not the best?"

At the mention of his brother, Alix's jaw clenched. There were moments when he forgot that Sanura was Jahn's, a gift, an offering from the henpecked King of Tryfyn. "You will find the emperor to be most generous, especially where his women are concerned."

Sanura nodded. "I'm glad to hear it."

Women always liked Jahn. Sanura would be no different. It was a waste of time to wonder what might've been if he were emperor, if he had been born a few minutes before his brother.

One thing was certain. When Sanura saw what Jahn was at the pit of his soul, there would be no surprises, no battles, no shadows. No confusion. Jahn was exactly as he presented himself to the world: irreverent, fun-loving, and inherently good.

She was better off that Jahn had been born first.

WHEN the party stopped at midday to rest the horses and grab a bite to eat and a sip of water, Vyrn grinned at Tari and winked broadly. His mind was not entirely on the willing and suggestible maid, but was more focused on those at the head of the column.

Last night Prince Alixandyr had visited Sanura's tent. Vyrn had seen it with his own eyes. The prince and leader of this expedition slipped past the sleeping guards and into the forbidden tent. He had remained in the woman's tent quite a while. Long enough, at least. And this morning the blue whore rode at his side, as she had in the early days. The implications were most unsavory—and yet they offered a new and neater opportunity than the one Vyrn planned.

He had originally thought to make it look as if Princess Edlyn's suitor from Tryfyn, one Tyren Mils, was the guilty party, but he had not yet been able to come up with a proper and foolproof plan. He still had lots of time to see the deed done, but with each step they took toward Arthes that time decreased.

Vyrn very casually made his way to Tari. He gave her his most charming grin and a small, private wave of his hand. The homely girl smiled as he approached, happy to be chosen on this day. He'd taken pains to give attention to all the female servants, as he had not begun this journey knowing whom he might need. Now he knew. He needed Tari.

"You look lovely today," he said, staring into her eyes with sincerity and a touch of passion he knew she would see.

Tari blushed and glanced away. "Thank you. I know I don't..."

He grabbed her chin and forced her to look into his eyes. "Don't do that," he said sharply. "Don't pretend you don't see your own unique beauty."

Her skin was soft and smooth against his fingers. It was one of her few truly good features, and he could not say he did not enjoy the feel of it against his stronger, rougher hand. Youth was kind to Tari in that way, but the sharpness of her features would make her a truly ugly old woman. Not that he would ever see her in that state.

She blinked and met his stare. Of course she wanted to believe that she was beautiful, she wanted to believe that some man saw beyond the thin face and the slightly crooked nose. "Do you find me beautiful?" she asked, the uncertainty of her question tinged with hope.

"I do," he said with a forced smile. "In fact, I wish I could kiss you here and now, in front of all these people."

Again she blushed. Had she ever been kissed? Perhaps not. That was a pity, since girls who were unacquainted with passion made terrible lovers.

"Tonight," he said with yet another wink. "Tonight perhaps we can steal a moment alone. What do you say, beautiful?"

Tari nodded subtly and briefly, and Vyrn walked away from her with a satisfied smile.

Bedding one ugly girl in exchange for the perfect plan of action was a small price to pay. If he did not find Tari pleasing as a sexual partner, he would close his eyes and think of the former Empress Rikka and all she offered in exchange for his loyalty.

Chapter Four

THREE days passed, and Sanura saw no further signs of Prince Alixandyr's darker side. Trystan, as she had come to think of him in order to distinguish between the two very different parts of one man, had likely expended a lot of energy in rising to control on that night when he'd touched her, and was compelled to rest. At least for now. He'd seemed determined to take his place in the world, to send Alix into the depths where the shadows had been trapped for so long. Perhaps he had overestimated his strength. She could hope that was true.

The prince did deign to speak to her on occasion, but there was a formality in his air, a distance, a wall he created between them. She did not feel that she could tell him what had happened that night. He would not believe her, in any case. No, he did not think himself in danger of losing the inner battle he fought.

At the present time, he fought more than one battle. Though Alix did not remember that Trystan had touched her, he was sexually attracted to her and at times was certain he knew what she felt like, how she tasted. That lost memory had created a new conflict as his senses fought with his usually disciplined mind. That much of him she could see well.

Their travels had been blessed with good weather until the afternoon when clouds obscured the sun and the wind pulled with great force against the two banners which marked their party as regal and of two countries. Columbyana crimson and Tryfyn green whipped side by side, furling and snapping in the wind.

When the first drops fell, the prince's eyes turned to Sanura. "Will the rain wash away your cosmetic?"

As he asked, a raindrop fell on her shoulder and meandered down her arm, leaving no mark. "No," she said. "It takes the oil of another's skin or a special ointment to remove the blue."

"Then we can continue."

Sanura nodded. Princess Edlyn was safe and dry in her coach, and the others were of no concern to Alixandyr, who wished only to move forward as quickly as possible.

The rain felt quite good on her skin. It was gentle and not too cold, and while the other women—the four maids who served the princess and the gift—covered their heads and cowered beneath the falling drops, Sanura continued forward as the sentinels and soldiers did—spine straight and head high. She was unafraid of rain. She was unafraid of what awaited her in Arthes. The women of the Agnese knew no fear. At the very least, they showed none.

More than once, as the journey continued through the soft spring rain, she turned her head and caught Alixandyr staring at her. More rightly, he stared at the way the raindrops slipped over the blue without washing it away. He stared at the way her wet clothing clung to her body. Sanura did not pretend to be shy or demure, she did not pretend that she was ashamed for any man to see the shape of her body, whether it was bare or encased in wet golden fabric.

After a while the prince removed his crimson cloak and, moving his horse close to hers, draped the cloak over her shoulders and around her body.

"I am not the only one intrigued, Sanura," he said in a lowered voice only she could hear.

"It does not matter," she said as she clung to the cloak, which smelled of him. "I am accustomed to men watching me and craving what they cannot have."

"I am not," he said tersely.

She should feel a surge of pride that he wanted her so, that he went so far as to protect her from the prying eyes of other men. No one had ever really protected her, not even Zeryn, who had on occasion claimed to cherish her above all his wives. Alixandyr protected her. He asked about her comfort and shielded her from the eyes of the other men.

But she knew too well that nothing could come of it. Nothing could come of them. Her heart skipped a beat. At least, nothing *good*.

AS had become their custom in the past few days, Tari and Vyrn met in the forest after everyone else was settled for the evening and the camp had become quiet.

The kissing had always been nice, but at first Tari had not liked the sex much. It had seemed rough and quick and had even been painful, but after a couple of secret liaisons in the woods that had changed. Now she looked forward to having Vyrn inside her, she looked forward to the unexpected pleasure and the way he held her after, while they still smelled of one another and their hearts no longer beat in steady rhythms. All during the day, she found herself thinking of the night before and planning for the night to come. She cast surreptitious glances at Vyrn, and though she never caught him doing the same, she was quite sure he did, when she wasn't looking.

One thought remained with her day and night. If she caught a child, he would have to marry her. Long before leaving the king's castle she had given up on all hopes of marriage, but Vyrn saw in her a beauty others did not see. Perhaps that meant he loved her already. Her mother had said no girl should give all of herself to a man without marriage, but her mother did not understand. Tari knew this was her one chance at happiness. Vyrn believed that he had captured her, but in truth she had been the one to do the catching. The thought warmed and pleased her.

Every night she held her breath and waited for the words she longed to hear: *I love you* or *Will you marry me* or even another *You're beautiful.* None of those words had come. Not yet. They would, she was certain of it.

The damp ground was her bed tonight, but she did not mind. Perhaps her bed was hard and cold, but she was not alone upon it. Someone who thought she was beautiful lay with her, spent and satisfied. As usual, Tari's mind wandered as she and Vyrn lay together. A baby would change everything. She would no longer be a plain and virginal servant, she'd be a wife. Vyrn's wife. And he would love her. He would love her very well.

His heart beat very fast, as it often did after sex. She felt it pounding against her own. For a while they lay upon the chilly ground in companionable silence, a part of the night as surely as the moon.

"You have turned from a timid maid to a fine and vigorous lover," he said, his mouth close to her ear when he decided to speak. As he finished the declaration, he licked her earlobe. They were not done for the night. Not yet. The sex was new and fascinating, and she could not get enough. Neither could he.

"Do I please you, then?" she asked.

Vyrn lifted his head and stared down at her. He gave her that grin that always set her heart to racing. "You do." His fingers raked through her hair, and an unusually dreamy expression crossed his face. "You touch me more than you know, Tari. If only I could afford to take a wife..."

Tari's entire body twitched. Even though he did not finish that important sentence, these were the words she longed to hear. "I am not very needful or expensive to keep," she said, perhaps too eager.

Vyrn laughed softly. "A lowly placed sentinel can barely keep himself, dearest."

"Dearest." No one had ever called her dearest. She liked it very much. "Is there no way?" she whispered. "Nothing we can do to make what we want possible?" She raked her foot along his strong leg and swayed up to meet his body more fully with her own. Dreams could come true. The seemingly impossible might become reality, and she would gladly do whatever was required to make it happen.

"Well, there is a way, but it is a bit unsavory and I'm afraid it might not please you."

"Anything which would keep us together would please me," she confessed. "Anything."

"Anything?" Vyrn raked his hands down her sides and then gripped her hips.

"Anything," she whispered.

"There is a way." He did not often look squarely at her, but at this moment he did. His eyes were not closed, as they sometimes were when they made love. He did not turn his head to the side, as if distracted. No, tonight he was looking at *her.*

Tari nodded. She had always known there would be some way for them to be together permanently.

"I will need your help," he added.

Again, Tari nodded. "You shall have it. Whatever you need. Whatever it takes for us to be together forever...I will do it." She had always heard that no woman should utter the words first, but they were on her tongue and in her heart, and they burst forth. "I love you, Vyrn. I love you."

He did not respond in kind, but he loved her in his own way, and before too many moments had passed she did not care that he did not speak the words aloud.

"M'LADY," Alix said with strained patience, "I cannot alter the terrain or the weather in the name of your comfort. Much as I would like to do so," he added without sincerity.

Princess Edlyn pursed her lips. As they neared Arthes, she became more and more demanding, more and more difficult. With luck and a change in the weather, they'd arrive in the capital city in two weeks, perhaps a day or two more. If the weather and his luck did not improve, they'd be lucky to reach Arthes by the deadline.

Alix was now certain that the emperor would not choose the princess as his bride—Jahn was no fool. It was very possible that Alix himself would be called upon to wed Edlyn in the name of diplomacy. No matter what the plan, no matter that Jahn insisted on choosing his own bride, one simply did not return a princess.

"Perhaps there is a more gentle route," she suggested. "The hills, the constant up and down, it all makes me very dizzy." She placed a hand on her head as if to demonstrate her ailment.

"A more roundabout route would make the trip weeks longer." They did not have weeks. They were traveling at a snail's pace as it was, primarily due to the princess's demands for comfort.

"I do not care..." she began.

Alix felt a rush of anger, and he interrupted harshly. "You spoiled little twit! If I hear one more word of complaint from you, I'm going to lash you over a donkey's back, gag you, and race the horses all the way to Arthes, where I will gladly dump you in my unfortunate brother's lap!"

She blinked several times and backed up slowly. "How dare you..."

"Good Lord, no wonder your father is forced to send you to another country to wed. No man who spends more than two minutes in your company would willingly agree to a lifetime of misery as your husband." Alix knew what he was saying was wrong. He knew the Tryfynian guards were moving closer, ready to defend their princess if necessary. He knew the words which spilled freely from his mouth were not entirely his own, and yet he could not stop. "If I could save poor Jahn from the horrors of making your acquaintance, I would do so."

Edlyn did not cry, that was not her way, but she did pale and move farther back, as if trying to escape him one tiny step at a time. Her mouth moved as if she had an argument ready to fly forth, but no words emerged.

"Your tent is ready," Alix said tersely. "I suggest you retreat there and stay until morning. If I hear one more word of complaint, one more whining demand, I'm not sure what I might do."

She turned swiftly and raced toward the tent in question, not running but walking so fast she might as well have been. Alix smiled. He should've given her a piece of his mind at the start. Perhaps then this trip would not have been so miserable.

No one came near him as the sun set and the camp was prepared for the night. Only one even looked at Alex, and that was the blue woman, the slave who was to be presented to Jahn. Sanura looked at him with sad eyes and more than a touch of resignation. Death sentence or no, he was sorely tempted to grab her and plant his face to her breasts, to strip that scanty outfit from her fine body and bury himself inside her.

He shook off the thoughts. She was Jahn's, not his, and no woman was worth literally dying for. Not even one such as Sanura.

Alix decided that he would sleep beneath the stars tonight. Only the women would have the luxury of tents until morning. He grabbed a small tin bowl of stew when it was ready, and sat near his bedroll to eat. His men and the Tryfynians avoided him. They were unaccustomed to his display of temper, he who was always imperturbable and calm. Apparently he had scared them all, not just the spoiled princess.

It was the sentinel Vyrn who approached him first, braver—or stupider—than the others. He smiled as he offered a mug of cider. "Drink, sir. I think Phyls oversalted the stew tonight."

Alix took the mug. "The stew is a bit saltier than usual." On some nights they ate only dried meat and hard biscuits, but since there was game aplenty in these hills and there were women about who could find wild vegetables and cook up a decent meal, on many evenings they indulged in a hot supper.

A touch of gray still hung in the sky, but soon it would be dark. There was no moon tonight, and though the starlight on such a night was lovely, it did nothing to illuminate the world below. The women had already retired to their tents—one angry and hurt, the other tempting and forbidden. It was just as well that they were both out of sight.

SANURA did not attempt to see into everyone around her all the time. It would be too draining, too disconcerting.

But now and then, what a person was—or had become— was so strong she could not help but sense it. Like Vyrn's tendency to violence, like Alix's dark struggle. Sometimes she could not help but see.

When Tari entered her tent bearing a cup of steaming tea, Sanura caught a glimpse of what she'd been sensing for several days. Love. Warmth. Devotion. She did not know which of the men in the traveling party had made Tari fall in love with him, but it had to be one of the soldiers or sentinels. The timid maid had never even spoken to the prince, that Sanura could tell, and Paki and Kontar kept to themselves, outsiders in this traveling party as much as Sanura herself was. But the maids and the soldiers mingled on a daily basis, and the change in Tari had come during the travels. It was unmistakable and very strong.

Sanura was happy for the young girl. She wondered if she should warn Tari that not all men were as they seemed, but she quickly decided against it. Perhaps the man in question was toying with Tari, but it was just as possible that he had fallen in love with her. Even if her heart ended up broken, at least she knew love now, at this moment.

"A cup of tea, m'lady," Tari said meekly. "The night is a bit chillier than it has been of late. I thought you might need the warmth."

Sanura gratefully took the tea and wrapped her fingers around the warm cup. "Thank you." Tari's love had changed her, at least for now. She was not as harsh as she'd been before. She did not seem to hate the woman she was forced to serve. "Would you sit with me?"

Tari hesitated and then lowered herself into a comfortable and relaxed position on the floor. "If you would like."

Sanura took a sip of the tea. It was overly sweet for her tastes, but she would not complain, not when the young woman before her had made such a friendly gesture. "I have never been in love," she said. "Not the way you are now."

Tari blinked hard and then took a deep breath. "Of course, you see the love in me, don't you?"

"I do. It's very enthusiastic and very strong, and it eclipses all else." In that moment, Sanura envied the plain servant.

"I did not expect to fall in love," Tari said. "It just happened." She narrowed her eyes. "How is it that someone like you has never been in love? You're beautiful, and all the men want and admire you."

"A man cared deeply for me once," Sanura confessed. "I liked him, I admired him very much, but I did not find what you are now experiencing." Unwavering devotion. Unquestioning fidelity. "The women of the Agnese do not love the way other women do." Love had not been part of her training, it had not even been mentioned in her years of education. She took another sip of the tea, which was quite good. Nothing came free, especially not magical abilities. Perhaps thanks to her gifts she was incapable of the kind of love Tari had discovered. Perhaps the lack of love had nothing to do with her powers, but was a personal character flaw. Did she have no heart? Why had she never loved

Zeryn this way? In their years together he had treasured her. He had treated her well. Until his untimely death he had been the perfect lover—the perfect possessor.

Could a woman love a man who possessed her so, even if he gave her everything he had to give?

Senseless, useless thoughts. She had grown too maudlin of late.

She would sleep deeply tonight. Her eyes were already heavy, and she stifled a yawn. The day had been a long one, and she looked forward to crawling beneath her blanket and escaping to the land of dreams for a while.

Before she knew what was happening, Tari had risen and was there, taking the half-empty cup, assisting Sanura into a prone position and placing the much desired blanket over her body.

"Sleep well," Tari said, and again the warmth of love bloomed within her.

"I'm so tired," Sanura said, and her eyes went to the cup Tari held carefully in one hand.

"It has been a long day."

"Yes, it has," Sanura admitted.

"You travel like a soldier, m'lady," Tari said with a smile. "But you are not a soldier. You need your rest."

It was true enough, and Sanura nodded. "Will you see the man you love tonight?" she asked.

"Oh, yes," Tari answered with joy.

The physical act of love combined with such emotion would be remarkable, Sanura imagined. The heat of passion combined with the warmth of heart would take any woman, trained in the arts or not, to a very special place.

"I wish I knew such love," Sanura admitted with a sigh. "Perhaps it is not possible for me."

Her body was not to be touched by any but the man who owned her, but what of her heart? Did she have a woman's heart at all, or was she doomed to live a loveless life?

Sanura drifted off to sleep washed in Tari's love, reaching for a love which was not and could never be her own. For a moment she imagined it could be hers. She imagined she was capable of choosing her own possessor and even loving him. Tari's love was so deep it had wiped away everything else she was, at least for now. Perhaps the intensity would fade in time, but for now it was blinding.

When Sanura thought again of love, she saw Prince Alixandyr's face.

Or was it Trystan's face? In slumber, she shuddered.

VERITY snuggled beneath a blanket of fur, protecting herself against the cold spring night. Her tent was sturdy and she had many blankets, yet still her blood was chilled. In Arthes, the nights would be warmer. She thought of that fact, hoping to bring warmth to her blood.

Even though she had begun to suffer the occasional doubt, she could not, *would not*, return to the city of Mirham and the cold home where she'd lived her entire nineteen years. There was nothing exciting in the province where she'd been born and lived all her life, and Verity longed for excitement. Although she was very well aware that others would also be vying for the position of empress, she was quite confident that she would be the one Emperor Jahn chose. After all, she *was* very beautiful. Her hair was soft and fair, and she had a nice womanly shape, and her face was flawless. Absolutely *flawless*. What man would not want her?

Besides, Mavise had been harping on Verity's destiny to be the wife of a great man for many years, and there were the love potion and the lucky talisman to call upon, if they were necessary. A few tricks, in case the emperor was blind or foolish, couldn't hurt.

She sighed and closed her eyes, pushing aside the new doubts which seemed to grow as they traveled nearer Arthes. She'd make a fine empress. Empress Verity. She'd have jewels and the finest of clothes and so many servants she wouldn't be able to remember all their names. And oh, there would be grand balls every week!

Verity was not surprised when the tent flap opened and

Laris slipped inside. She smiled, even though her mouth was hidden beneath the edge of her blanket and he could not see. Those pesky doubts faded away, at least for now.

"Are you awake?" he whispered.

"Yes." She did not move.

"I had to see if you were well."

It was a ritual of sorts, a requirement for what was to come. "I'm cold," she said simply.

A moment later he was there, slipping beneath the blanket and wrapping his arms around her. Verity sighed and melted into Laris's warm, hard body. Here was the warmth she'd craved. Here were comfort and ease and even happiness. If not for Laris, this journey would be unbearable.

As was usual, his hands began to creep, gently and not too terribly bold. Verity did not mind a little hand creeping; in fact it was quite pleasant. His touch made her tingle, it made her more than warm, no matter how cold the night. They were close, their bodies crushed together beneath the blanket, so she felt the evidence of his desire pressing against her. Still, she was not afraid. Laris was entirely hers. She had seen to that, had she not?

Soon his hands strayed a bit too far. She rather liked the sensations which filled her as Laris caressed her breasts, breasts which were encased in the warmest nightgown she owned. She almost gasped when he cupped one breast in his large hand and placed his mouth against the back of her neck. She shuddered to her bones, and so did he. Lovely as this was, she was not entirely cruel, and she imagined his manly restraint could be stretched only so far.

"You know I must be a virgin when I wed the emperor," she whispered. "He will expect it."

"I know," Laris said, the pain in his voice as evident as the erection which still pressed against her. "You have told me so many times."

She soothed him with a hand on his broad, warm chest. He could not know that this denial was as painful for her as it was for him. "But once the wedding night is over, we can be lovers." It was a thought which had only recently occurred to her, a thought spurred by the stolen moments when Laris was supposed to be guarding the camp. He refused to neglect his duties for more than a few precious moments, but they did have those moments.

"I don't want to share you," Laris insisted, and a hint of anger slipped into his voice. "I truly hope the emperor chooses one of the other women to be his empress," he said sharply, "and then I can have you for my own." He sighed. "But I know he will not. How could he choose another when he might have you?"

"There, there." She patted his chest and snuggled even closer. "My marriage will be one of political convenience." After all, the emperor was more than ten years her senior, practically an old man. If she decided not to use the love potion on the emperor, they could still get along quite well. She could have all the power and things she wanted, without the annoyance of an overly attentive and possessive husband. If that were the case, she'd likely want a young lover to keep things lively in the bedroom. Laris would do, she imagined. Yes, she imagined he'd do very well.

Chapter Five

WITH a start, Alix woke to a shrill, female scream. He'd slept so hard it took a moment for his head to clear. His initial reaction to the scream was one of concern, but given the current state of peace in the country and the disposition of his traveling companions, he quickly decided it was more likely that the princess had seen a snake or a frog in her path as she'd made her way into the forest for a private morning piss. He groaned as he rose to his feet, only to see a commotion around the princess's tent. Tryfynian soldiers scrambled, and two maids, those who served the princess, held on to one another and cried—and one of them screamed yet again. It had been that scream to which he'd awakened.

The cause of the commotion was likely not a small, harmless creature which could frighten fine ladies with its very existence.

Alix reached for the sword which should have been close at hand, and was alarmed to find that the weapon was gone, not where he always placed it when he slept. The dagger which was always nearby was also missing. His stomach sank, and then his dismay was replaced with alarm. The soldier in him was on alert, ready to react to the next scene in this morning's excitement and possible danger.

The elder of the Tryfynian guards came bursting from the princess's tent, his face red and his sword in one hand. He was obviously ready for a fight. "The princess is dead, murdered in her sleep." In the hand which did not hold his own ready weapon, he held a familiar dagger aloft. "Her throat was cut with this weapon. Who claims this? Who among us would do such a terrible thing?"

The weapon he held aloft was Alix's, but he had certainly *not* murdered the princess. He stepped toward the scene of the tragedy, ready to explain that the dagger was his but that it had been stolen while he slept. The events of the morning were those of treachery and conspiracy, and they would need to work together to get to the truth.

Alix usually did not sleep so deeply that someone could come close and take his weapons without waking him. He had been a soldier before he'd become a prince, after all, and he still slept like a soldier. Lightly. One ear and one eye always alert.

Until now.

The two maids went into the tent where their mistress lay dead. The sound of their sobbing was muted, but even muffled by the tent those sobs spoke too clearly of sorrow and horror.

Thank goodness, a part of Alix whispered. *The world is a better place with that one dead and gone.* He shook off the unkind thought. Edlyn had been difficult and sour, but she'd also been a woman—not much more than a girl, to be truthful. To wish her dead was heartless.

"The dagger is mine," Alix said as he approached the angry soldier. "I assure you I had nothing to do with the princess's death. Someone took the weapon as I lay sleeping and used it for murderous purposes, no doubt hoping to throw suspicion in my direction."

The soldier turned accusing eyes to Alix. "You had words with the princess last night, before she retired."

"I did." Words he barely remembered. The journey had been a trial, and was obviously taking its toll. "But if I wished to kill her, which I did not, I would not be so foolish as to leave my own dagger at the scene. Obviously someone took advantage of our disagreement last night and went to great pains to make it look as if I did the deed." But who? Yes, Edlyn had been disagreeable, but who in their traveling party would wish to do murder?

His eyes turned to Vyrn. Vyrn, who had brought him the cider before his unusually deep sleep. Vyrn, whom Sanura said had murder in his soul. She had warned him of the lurking violence, and he'd foolishly dismissed her concern.

One of the maids came bursting from the princess's tent. "Look!" she shouted, holding aloft a thin yellow blanket. "Only one among us wears this damnable blue on her person." The girl turned tear-filled, hate-filled eyes to Sanura, who until this moment had watched wordlessly and without emotion. "Why would you kill her?"

"I did not," Sanura said, her eyes on the long, bright spot of blue which was stark against the yellow blanket.

It was Tari, the skinny red-haired maid, who stepped boldly forward. "They must've done the horrible deed together," she said in a surprisingly loud voice. She wanted to make sure everyone heard her words. "I did not want to speak of their secrets, but the prince and the whore have been lovers for many weeks."

"We have not!" Alix insisted.

"I saw you go into her tent many times, sir," Tari said. She was too brave for a lass who rarely opened her mouth in the presence of others. She was unusually confrontational for a plain, mousy maid. But he was without a weapon at the moment and she was surrounded by protective soldiers, so what was to stop her from speaking her mind—whether she spoke the truth or not?

How strange that while the other maids sobbed and held on to one another, Tari was dry-eyed and calm.

"I'm afraid I saw the same," Vyrn said in a solemn tone

of voice. He pointed to Sanura with an accusing finger. "Just a few nights ago I saw the two of them meeting after the sun had set and the camp slept, but I thoughtlessly turned a blind eye because I felt loyalty to my prince. I had no idea my blind allegiance might lead to a tragedy like this."

Someone herded Sanura toward Alix, and the other members of the traveling party surrounded them accusingly. Alix heard the whispers, whispers not only from the Tryfynians but from his own sentinels as well. Two others besides Vyrn spoke of seeing Alix go into Sanura's tent, on one night, at least. They spoke about the fact that the two of them had taken to riding side by side.

Alix searched for a friendly face, but found none. The four sentinels who'd accompanied him on this journey were not those he'd fought with just a few years ago. They knew him only as a prince, a politician, the emperor's brother. Their respect was commanded, not earned. None of them would defend the murderer of a young girl, no matter how fractious she had been. Even Sanura's guards, who stood apart from the others, looked shocked at the events which were unfolding.

Sanura sidled up beside him. The music she always made with her movements remained, but on this morning her tune was touched with fear. Alix wanted to reach out and place his arm around her, but of course he could not. Not only did her blue make her untouchable, he did not need to add fuel to the fire which was presently blazing.

"How do we know this is not a trick?" The one sentinel who had apparently not seen him sneak into Sanura's tent asked his question in a calm voice. "How do we know the princess isn't sitting in her tent, laughing at this scene she created? The blood on the knife and the blanket might've come from an animal. She might've set all this up to have a bit of fun with us. You cannot say she is averse to making trouble of any sort." He nodded his head as if this explanation made more sense to him. Indeed it did, but Alix suspected this was no ghoulish prank, and nothing made any sense on this mad morning.

At the instruction of the eldest Tryfynian, a young soldier went into the tent where the murder had apparently taken place. He returned moments later with the princess in his arms. She was dressed in a white nightgown which was soaked in blood, as was much of her once fair hair. Her pale throat had been cut, and she was most definitely dead.

The sight of the dead princess only inflamed the crowd. The rumblings changed, they grew more insistent. There was talk of vengeance, of justice, of not waiting for a proper trial, which would surely be a travesty since one of the accused was the emperor's brother. The only question seemed to be about the method of execution: decapitation or hanging.

Sanura looked at him and whispered, "We must run."

Alix shook his head. "Evidence aside, there is no logic in these accusations, and as soon as a bit of time has passed, the others will see it. When these men cool off, they'll listen to reason." He knew them. They had traveled together for many weeks, they had followed his command and would soon rein in their overwrought emotions.

"No, they will not," she insisted. "Paki and Kontar will try to protect me, but they care nothing about you, and even if they did, they have no chance against all these soldiers. They, too, will die. We will all die!"

"You're panicking, Sanura," Alix said calmly. "My sentinels will not turn against me. They're just upset about the princess's death, as we all should be. I can and will reason with them."

Sanura stamped her slippered foot and turned to face him. There was fear in her blue eyes, a deep fear such as he had never seen in her. "I want Trystan, now," she insisted.

He flinched at the unexpected sound of the name he'd used most of his life. "How do you know..." he began.

"Come, Trystan, come forth and save us," she whispered. She leaned closer and added, "Get us out of here, and I will give you what you most want."

Alix did not have to wonder what she spoke of. He knew very well what any man would most want from Sanura. His eyes were drawn to the swell of her breasts even now. Something deep inside him twitched.

"When we are safe, I will wrap myself around you and give you pleasure you never knew was possible. We will be lovers, Trystan, lovers such as the world has never before known, and I will be yours and yours alone."

Why did she keep calling him Trystan? No one used that name anymore. His hands clenched into tight fists.

"Isn't that what you want? Do not lie to me, Trystan. I see what you want. I know who you are."

Alix heard the others claim that the murderous lovers were plotting something, and should be separated and restrained. He heard Sanura's words, her offers, and in response he felt suddenly dizzy. The skies turned an odd, dull gray. His knees wobbled.

And then he was gone.

SANURA knew the moment Alix left and Trystan emerged. His eyes went dark, and every muscle in his body tensed. He smiled.

"Please try not to kill anyone," she whispered.

"Why?" he asked, his voice as soft as her own.

"I will make it worth your while, I promise."

She knew what Trystan wanted most from her. Her body. Her complete surrender. He wanted to own her in the way his brother was meant to. His entire body stiffened at her promise. His eyes went impossibly darker, and she shuddered because for one long moment they were the eyes of a wild animal, not a man.

With her gift, Sanura felt the swelling, murderous intent of the crowd. Some were more intent on justice than others, but none could be called friend at the moment. Not one.

One among them laughed on the inside. It was Vyrn,

who was very pleased with himself. Tari felt some regret for her part in this tragedy, but her love was stronger than her regret. The love Tari had found was so strong that Sanura had seen nothing else last night. She had certainly not seen treachery, even though it was now obvious that the tea had been drugged and Tari had taken a bit of the blue powder from the sacred box in order to point the finger at her, as well as at Alix.

Alix thought these men would listen to reason, but he did not feel what she felt, did not see what she saw. They were surrounded by hatred, anger, a need for vengeance which would not be quenched by any logic. Now that the shadows were at the surface, she expected Prince Alixandyr—Trystan—to do something which would save them.

She did not expect him to grab her and rake his beard-roughened cheek boldly and firmly against hers, but that's what he did. She struggled against the assault, but it was already too late. He held her in a firm grip, hands on her arms to hold her in place as he scraped his cheek over hers. It had been so long since she'd been touched that she held her breath and quivered. No one was meant to live without the touch of another human being, no matter how unwise and uncaring that touch might be.

When Trystan pulled away his stubbled face was smeared with blue. So were his hands, hands which had touched her briefly and unwisely as he'd pressed their faces together. His grin and the touch condemned them.

"What have you done?" she whispered.

Paki and Kontar stepped forward, their every movement slow but determined. They drew the short, curved, very sharp swords they had carried from Claennis and lifted the blades in a threatening way. The soldiers and sentinels watched, stunned by their prince's actions and the immediate response of the foreigners who were usually so quiet and unobtrusive.

Trystan reacted immediately. Instead of moving away from the two guards, he surged toward them. Determined as they were, they were surprised at the swiftness of his movements, at the laughter. They were then shocked at the accuracy with which the prince disarmed them and took the weapons they wielded.

The forbidden touch had not been foolish after all. Her guards were not as practiced as the soldiers and sentinels among them. The *appearance* of Paki and Kontar, their size, and their evident willingness to do what was necessary were enough to keep men at a distance. They had never been called upon to use their skills, because no one who did not own her had ever dared to touch her. Their presence was more ceremonial than truly threatening. Over the years they had grown careless—and Trystan had seen that in them. He'd disarmed them easily, and now gripped their swords with confidence, one in each hand, as he faced the others.

"The lady and I will be leaving. You!"—he nodded to the nearest sentinel—"ready my horse."

"I…I don't know…" The young man looked to Vyrn. Trystan responded by placing the tip of the curved blade at the sentinel's throat. "You do not turn to him for direction, boy. I suggest you turn to me. I will have my dagger, too, and your own sword, if you please. Oddly enough, mine has gone missing."

Vyrn nodded, and the young sentinel ran to do as he was told.

Trystan faced them all like a madman, a sword in each hand, a wicked smile on his face. If any among them had had doubts that he was capable of murder, they were now gone. "The lady and I are going to leave this inhospitable party. I suggest you do not give chase."

They would, Sanura knew. The men here would leave the women behind and pursue the supposed murderers as soon as possible. At the moment, however, none wished to face the blades Trystan wielded. None wished to face the insanely grinning man who looked as if he were not only willing but eager for a fight.

None but one, apparently, as an incensed Tryfynian guard drew his sword and ran forward. Trystan was ready to do battle, but Sanura reminded him, "Do not kill him. Remember my promise."

Trystan seemed a bit disappointed, but he did listen to her. He defended himself with two Claennis swords, meeting the soldier's metal with expertly brandished blades. Trystan was faster than the soldier, he seemed to know how and when his opponent would strike. There was no contest. Trystan defended himself and then, with a skilled twist, sent the opposing weapon to the ground. He could've run the young soldier through with his blades, and likely would've, if not for Sanura's promise. Instead of killing his opponent he deliberately scratched the Tryfynian's arm before kicking the sword aside. "Anyone else?" he asked tersely as the sentinel came near with his saddled horse.

Trystan easily mounted the horse, but the sheaths built for his long, narrow swords would not accommodate the broader bladed and curved weapons he had taken from Paki and Kontar. After he had the sentinel's surrendered sword and his own dagger, a dagger still stained with the princess's blood, in his possession, he threw the Claennis swords. They flew end over end and then landed as he'd intended, their blades buried deep in the ground. That done, he offered his hand to Sanura. No one ever touched her, no one assisted her this way, but it was already too late. He was stained with blue, and her face burned with the memory of his rough morning beard. She took his hand, and he gripped hers tightly.

"Did you kill her, m'lord?" the young sentinel who had delivered the horse and surrendered his sword asked as Trystan lifted Sanura and deposited her in front of him. "Did you murder the princess?" It was evident in the young man's voice, and in his heart, that he did not want to believe that his prince was capable of cold-blooded murder, even though he himself had no affection for the dead woman.

"No, I did not," Trystan answered crisply. Again, he grinned. "But I thank whoever did. The Princess Edlyn was a royal pain in the ass, and I'm not sorry to see her dead." He spared a precious moment to bend forward and rake his nose against Sanura's neck, to further mark himself, and then he turned the horse about and they made their escape.

The others would come after them, Sanura knew, and she wondered how long it would be before they were caught. Vigilant and capable of anything, Trystan could protect her, but she suspected he could not remain in this state for very long—and no matter which part of him ruled, he would have to rest and sleep on occasion. Would Prince Alixandyr be as diligent when he emerged once more? He was likely to present them both to their accusers, certain that the truth and logic would be enough to save them, certain that justice would be served.

"It was Vyrn and Tari," she called as the wind whipped her hair and her skirt about wildly. "I'm certain they killed the princess and set the scene to place the blame on us."

"I don't care," Trystan responded. "I don't care who killed her or why. I care only for your promise, love. I killed no one, just as you asked. I could've killed them all, if not for the promise of that which I desire more than blood."

She shuddered. She'd done what she had to do in order to save her own life and his, and to protect innocent lives. She would not break her word. Still, she wished it had been Prince Alixandyr who'd saved them—Alixandyr, who could not believe that his men would turn against him; Alixandyr, who was sure the truth would be enough for the others, because the truth was enough for him.

"I do care!" she shouted. "We must prove that Vyrn and Tari are guilty in order to prove our innocence."

"We are hardly innocent, love." At that, Trystan laughed harshly. The discordant sound rang in her ear.

IT could not have gone more smoothly. Vyrn suppressed a smile as the other men around him gathered their weapons and readied their horses. Two Tryfynian soldiers, including the one who had been slightly wounded, would escort the princess's body and her weeping maids back to King Bhaltair. The rest, four sentinels and four soldiers, would pursue the murderous couple.

Vyrn had not expected the prince's reaction to be so bizarre, but he could not be sorry for the strange outburst and the flight from the accusers. Prince Alixandyr now looked very, very guilty. Even if they did find his sword, which was hidden so deep in the woods it would likely never surface, they would not believe him innocent.

His primary goal had been the death of the princess, but there was a bonus to be had if the prince did not survive this journey. Vyrn was quite fond of bonuses.

Before he could mount his own horse, Tari approached at a run. Foolish girl. They could not be seen together, not in any way that might taint their stories and point to their mutual participation in this scheme. They were the only two who had claimed to see the prince in the whore's tent on more than one night. That could not come under question!

She waited until she was very close to say, "You are coming back, aren't you?"

"Of course." It was a lie. When the time was right, preferably after the prince was dead, he'd break away from the others and make his way to the Lady Rikka, who would reward him well for his work.

Tari's eyes narrowed. She handed him a bit of bread wrapped in cloth, which supplied for those around them a purpose for her coming to him. At least she was smart enough not to ruin their cover now. "Good. If you didn't come back, if you just left me here..." Her eyes met his, and they were stronger than he'd imagined they could be. At this moment she did not look so naïve. "I might be forced to tell all that I know. About you, about the drugs we put in the tea and the cider, about stealing the blue powder. About everything."

Vyrn was a bit surprised. He had taken Tari for a fool who would wait forever for his return, before slinking off to drown her sorrows in wine or other men. Somehow she saw through him. Somehow she knew he was going to flee, just as the prince had fled.

He soothed her fears. "Before I run, I'll come for you," he whispered. "How can you doubt that? After all we've planned, after all we've done in order to build our life together, I would not, could not, go on without you. Say nothing, dearest. Remain calm and stick to the story."

She nodded, and in her eyes he saw the love which made her his willing slave. Good heavens, the woman would do anything he asked of her. Hadn't she proved that?

A Tryfynian soldier shouted, "Hurry, you laggards! They're getting away!"

Another responded, "Steady yourself. Where can they hide? How many blue women do you expect wander the countryside?"

A couple of the men laughed. They'd put aside the horror of the morning for the more welcome thrill of the chase. A Tryfynian soldier pointed out that they were two on a horse, which would slow them down considerably. Another agreed heartily that there was no place for the criminals, the murderers, to hide.

They had all seen the slave stand in the rain and not lose her blue coloring. It was very likely not even possible to scrub her bizarre cosmetic from her flesh. Yes, they'd find her, and the prince, too. The prince would die first, of course, and then the woman might die as well. She did have some magic, he had heard, and might know more than she should. Her death might not be necessary, but Vyrn would feel better if he did not have to worry about her when he started his new and wonderful life.

When those two were dead, there would be no one to dispute the claims that the emperor's brother and his forbidden lover had murdered Princess Edlyn. What a scandal would ensue! What chaos! Yes, there would likely be war, but there was always a price to pay for change. It wasn't as if he'd be forced to fight in the war. By the time the fighting started, he'd be living in his own palace somewhere, rich and happy and surrounded by beautiful women. He'd have his own servants, his own sentinels.

But first, there was a job to be completed. Vyrn mentally went through his priorities. He had to find the prince and kill him—or arrange for his death to occur in some way which would not fall back on him—and then do away with the woman. When that was done, there would be Tari to dispose of—a job which should be easy enough—and a generous reward to collect so he could start his new and wonderful life.

Yes, all was going as planned, and life for Vyrn was very, very good.

Chapter Six

"DID I kill her?"

Sanura heard the pain in Prince Alixandyr's voice as he asked the question that plagued him; she felt the torment roiling off of him as if it were a wave of the ocean she had left behind to come to this cursed land. "No."

"But if I was not entirely myself..."

"No," she said again, her voice more forceful than before. "It was Vyrn and Tari. They drugged us, murdered the princess, and set the scene to make it look as if we did the killing."

He shook his head. "Why?"

"I don't know."

Trystan had departed and Alixandyr had emerged sometime before they'd stopped to rest the horse. Though there had been no physical signs of the change that she could see, since his eyes were not in her range of view, Sanura had felt the shift within him and experienced a wave of relief. Alixandyr remained the stronger of the two, though she imagined Trystan would return—and probably sooner than she'd like.

In the early days she had been so sure that the two men within the one body were one and the same, but since neither of them accepted that, they continued to act separately. More and more she thought of them as separate beings. One of them frightened her; the other she liked very much. In essence, they truly were two men, not one.

Alixandyr looked down at the blue stain on his hands. He'd tried to wipe the paint away, brushing his palms briskly against his trousers. He'd attempted to wash his hands in the stream where the horse drank. Neither effort removed much of the stain. Sanura did not yet have the heart to tell him that his face was also marked. She should be horrified that he had touched her so when it was not his right, but she could still feel the scrape of his cheek against hers and she liked that memory of connection, even if it had been his darker side which dared to be so bold.

"Can this damnable blue paint not be scrubbed away?" he asked tersely, standing and wiping his wet hands against his trousers. "Until we settle on a plan of action, we'd best keep a low profile. In this part of the world, you are anything but low profile. I suppose I could wear gloves, but you are not so easily disguised."

"With time and enough vigorous washing, the blue can be removed," Sanura explained. "The process takes several days without the oils made specifically for that purpose."

"We don't have days," he snapped. "Where might we obtain this oil?"

"In my tent," she said softly. "A large vial of the oil is kept in a box along with the paint and brushes necessary for the application and repair of my blue. A few drops will be enough to see the job done."

He stopped scrubbing and looked her in the eye. She was relieved to see that his eyes were still a nice light shade of green. "So our choice is to remain blue or else to return to a camp where everyone wants to execute us for a murder we did not commit, so that we might fetch your box."

"Yes." She did not tell him she wanted that special box for other reasons: that it was special, that it reminded her of home and of being cared for and appreciated. She did not tell him that she wanted the container, which was a work of art, because it was all she had left of who she'd once been.

"I could wear gloves," he said again, "but you..."

She reached up and touched his face, her fingertips very lightly raking along the section of his cheek which was more brightly blue than his hands, and then across his nose. Why did touching this man's nose, such an ordinary and unimportant body part, feel so intimate? She allowed her fingers to linger for a moment. "Gloves will not cover this," she explained as her hand fell away.

"I don't remember," he said softly, not bothering to question her assertion. Did that easy acceptance mean he trusted her? She knew he was not a man who gave his trust easily or often.

"I know."

"This darkness, this part of myself I can't control, what else might I have done?" There was such frustration in his voice. "I could've murdered the princess..."

"You did not," she assured him again.

"I could've done anything." His eyes narrowed. "More than one sentinel said he saw me go into your tent on at least one occasion. I do not trust the Tryfynians, but I see no reason for my own sentinels to lie." He hesitated before asking, "Did I visit your tent?"

"Yes. Once."

Muscles in his jaw clenched as he fought to control his emotions. "Why didn't you tell me?"

"Because you did not wish to know," she answered honestly.

He nodded crisply, as if that answer was sufficient, at least for now, and then he handed her the dagger he had retrieved before they'd run from camp. The weapon was well made and well cared for, but not at all fancy. He had cleaned it well even before trying to remove the blue from his skin. Surely he was as aware as she that this weapon had caused the princess's death. The sharp blade had sliced through her skin. A shiver worked its way through Sanura's body. She could see into people, not things, and yet at this moment the weapon in her hand seemed wholly evil.

She had never before touched a weapon, and she did not care for this one, and yet her fingers gripped the handle easily. Surprisingly, it was lightweight and more well balanced than she'd thought it would be. It was deadly, and forever stained with Princess Edlyn's blood.

"If I turn again..." Alix began.

Realizing what he was about to ask of her, Sanura gasped. "I could not!"

His hands were already marked, so he did not hesitate to grab her arms and hold on tightly as he stared into her eyes. "I don't know what I'm capable of when I'm not myself."

"Anything," she whispered.

"I don't want to hurt you," he said, and she knew he was sincere, at this moment when Alix ruled and Trystan slept.

"You will not," she promised. She did not yet fully understand all that she saw, but she did know one thing without question. "When you change, when the darkness takes control, you are still present. You do not leave, you are not buried. The one who calls himself Trystan will not harm me because you, the one who calls himself Alix, will not allow it." She returned the dagger to him, and he reluctantly took it.

"I wish I could be as sure as you are," he said. "If I remain present at all times, why don't I remember? Why don't I recall visiting your tent when the other took me there?"

"Are you sure you don't remember?" she asked, looking inside him for answers. "Do you not know at the very core of yourself how I smell, how my skin meets yours, how I reacted when you touched me?"

A part of him did recall, though what he found within him was so primitive that what he felt could not be called recognition.

"When I snapped at Princess Edlyn, when I lost my temper," he said, "I was not entirely myself then, was I?"

"Not entirely."

"That I do remember," he said with a touch of sadness in his low voice.

"You are always there, and you can be in control. Perhaps you must fight for that control, but it is yours. You won't hurt me. You won't let the other hurt me."

"You would stake your life on that belief?" Alix asked with a harsh and humorless laugh.

"I just did."

WITH just the two of them on horseback, they were probably two and a half days' hard ride from Arthes. Perhaps three, since carrying two riders would be demanding for the horse, and they'd be forced to stop more often for the animal to rest. With the princess's entourage and conveyance they'd been weeks from the palace.

Anything might happen in that relatively short time. The darkness he battled might rise and take control once more. The soldiers and sentinels who were certainly in pursuit might find them, or at the very least force them to take a roundabout path to their destination, adding days to the journey.

Those who gave chase likely thought the accused murderers would race for the palace and imperial protection, and their search would take them in that direction. Just as well. Perhaps it would make sense for Alix to rush directly to his brother, but two things stopped him from heading there. First, Jahn would feel obligated to protect his brother at all costs, and that cost would certainly include war with Tryfyn. King Bhaltair would surely be willing to go to war over the murder of a daughter, even a difficult one.

Second, and most important, Alix was afraid of what the darkness might do to Jahn if the opportunity arose.

He had always been aware of the dark part of his soul. No one else knew of it, and no one knew that the times when it was roused were very often connected with his brother. It roiled when Jahn—or Devlyn, before their lives had changed so dramatically—got something Alix himself wanted. As children, when their mother had looked into Devlyn's face with such love and remarked on how his eyes were like their father's. As young men, when the girls all swooned over Devlyn and kept their distance from the other twin, as if even then they sensed his darkness. When Jahn had been made emperor, thanks to a few moments of life which preceded Alix's, it had stirred.

It had never before stirred as it had when he'd been asked to take Sanura to Jahn. He wanted her, but she was not his to take.

No, he could not immediately retreat to the palace. The first order of business would be to remove the stain from his skin and from Sanura's. That meant that instead of rushing toward Arthes, they turned back toward camp and those who thought them killers and lovers.

As night fell, they walked the horse through a dense portion of the forest. Alix led the horse, and Sanura walked beside him. Their steps were slow and cautious, as they could not see well in the deep shadows, and here and there limbs and low bushes impeded their path. The silence in which they traveled was companionable at some moments and strained at others. Alix did not have Sanura's gift for seeing into those around him, but somehow he did connect with her. When she was tense, he felt as if the air around him changed, as if it grew heavier and denser. When she relaxed, he felt as if a weight had been lifted from his shoulders and the air which filled his lungs grew sweeter.

He wished he did not want her. Wanting her had awakened the part of him he had always fought—always denied.

"We need to sleep, at least for a short while," Sanura whispered, as if those who searched were nearby and listening.

"There is no time for sleep."

"I can hardly put one foot in front of the other," she argued. "A few minutes. Please."

He could've continued on all night without stopping, but the woman and the horse could not. For their sakes, Alix grudgingly found a suitable place in which to rest. They had no bedding, but he removed his cloak and spread it out so Sanura wouldn't be forced to sleep directly on the hard, cold ground. They were both hungry, but they had found water and edible leaves during the day, so their needs were not critical.

Sanura reclined upon his cloak as if it were the finest mattress. She sighed and closed her eyes, and almost immediately drifted off to sleep.

After Alix had tended to the horse, he lay down beside Sanura. The night had turned cool, so he thought it a good idea to share the heat of their bodies in the name of comfort. She did not seem to need the heat—her skin was warmer than his, warmer than that of any woman he had ever held. Even though her ankles and her worn slippers, which had not been made for walking, were exposed, she seemed not to feel the chill. Still, he flipped the end of his cloak over them, trying to offer some comfort.

He knew he should keep a distance from the sleeping woman, but his skin was already stained with the blue, and it wasn't at all easy for the paint she wore to transfer to cloth. It was an argument he would use in their defense, if it ever came to that. The only way that stain could've been transferred to the princess's blanket was if someone had purposely placed it there.

He doubted he'd ever have the chance to make that argument. He could not go to Jahn for help, and those who thought him guilty of murder would likely not allow him a second opportunity to escape. They'd be more vigilant if he fell into their hands again.

So he placed his body close to Sanura's and absorbed her heat. He placed his arms around her and pulled her body against his. She fit quite well. Exhausted and anxious and on edge, his body still responded to hers in an immediate and primitive way. His erection strained against his trousers, and he was acutely aware that very little stood between him and what he so desperately desired. A slip of cloth, a minor adjustment of their bodies, and he could be inside her. She was so soft, so warm...so gentle. Such was true of many women, perhaps even most, but everything about Sanura seemed more pronounced. To touch her would be extraordinary, he imagined. He imagined too well.

She would require little in the way of seduction. There had always been an unmistakable attraction between them, a physical draw, and Alix was experienced enough to know the attraction was not one-sided. Unfortunately, she was not his to take.

He tucked her head beneath his chin and held her close, and the sleep he claimed not to need came upon him very quickly.

SANURA had never slept so deeply, so blissfully. The events of the previous day had exhausted her completely, that was the reason, she supposed. That and the fact that a man's strong arms held her.

She had never before slept this way. Even when she had belonged to a man, even when she had been possessed and treasured, she had not been held so. After sex her man would need to be cleaned of the blue markings. She usually saw to the chore herself, which could be pleasurable if done correctly. There had been rare nights when she'd shared her bed with Zeryn until dawn, but no one had ever held her so close.

"You're awake," Alixandyr whispered in her ear. As he spoke, one hand slipped beneath her skimpy blouse and cupped a breast as if he owned it, as if she were his to fondle when and where he pleased. Her eyes drifted closed. When he raked a thumb across the pebbled nipple, she felt a rush of dampness between her legs, and her body instinctively swayed back and into his.

She had been taught to respond to a man's touch, and she did. For a while, a lovely while, she forgot her sad circumstances. She very gladly forgot that she was no longer at home, and she allowed herself simply to feel, to respond. This was who she was, who she had been born to be.

The morning was more dark than light, but it was most definitely morning. The day slowly came to life as Alixandyr brought her body to life with his hands. In the distance birds and small creatures of the forest stirred. She heard their distant chirping, their muted song, even the rustle of leaves as they scurried about. A touch of gray lightened the once black sky, but the sun had not yet risen to bring its warmth. She did not need it. The man who held her gave her all the warmth she would ever need.

Alixandyr pressed his hard length into her backside, simply and undeniably telling her that he wanted her. She swayed into him, she met his caress with enthusiasm, not shyness.

She wanted him. He was not hers, she was not his, but she did want him in a way she had never before wanted a man. As a female of the Agnese, she was *required* to please the man who owned her. As a woman, she had never been given a choice in the matter. Nothing in her life was progressing as it should, and it hadn't since she'd left her island home. But this—this moment was right in so many ways. For the first time in a long while Sanura experienced happiness. Pure, unadulterated happiness.

Perhaps she was living this new life she'd been given in the wrong manner. Perhaps she needed to throw off all the old ways and embrace the new, the way Alixandyr now embraced her.

He had told her that his brother would not keep her, that he did not believe in owning another human being. What if the Emperor of Columbyana did release her? What would become of her then? Until now such thoughts had brought panic, but perhaps there was no reason for that reaction. If her new life included a choice, if she could pick her lover, she would choose the man who held her. She very gently rubbed her backside against his erection, and he gasped. She felt his tongue flicker against her neck, in a sensitive place where no tongue had ever before tasted her. She had told him once that she had no desires of her own, but that was not true. She did have desires; she had simply never before dared to acknowledge, much less welcome, them.

He slid one strong hand up her thigh and pushed her skirt to her waist, then that hand delved between her thighs and stroked, his fingers hard and insistent on her welcoming body. Her thighs parted to give him greater access, and he immediately pushed those fingers into her. She quivered and her back arched. The sensation was intense, and she felt herself spinning out of control—she who never lost control, she who was always the one to do the arousing. She caused men to become undone; they did not undo her. And yet that was how she felt. Undone.

He brought her to the edge and kept her there as the morning came alive. With his fingers caressing intimately and his tongue flicking here and there against her neck and her back, he commanded her. Just when she was about to climax, his stroke changed. He did that to her once, and then again. She remained on the cusp of bliss, of release, of paradise. He aroused her and kept her there until she could no longer think of anything but the demands of her body. Everything else was lost. She felt his desire for her, a desire as real as her own. That desire eclipsed everything else, and yet he did not rush toward his own pleasure. Instead, he focused entirely on her, on her body, on her needs.

He trembled. She felt that quiver throughout his entire body. It was as if he passed that tremble to her, through flesh, through spirit. She did not know how, but he did share his desire with her. She had never been held so close, and yet she could not get close enough. Every inch of her skin was on fire, and inside she ached.

"Now," she whispered.

Alixandyr did not make her ask again. He rolled her onto her back and he was there above her, freeing himself and gently spreading her thighs wider. His hair was loose and had fallen across his face. He looked wild in his desire. He looked as frantic and lost in need as she felt.

For a fleeting moment, Sanura wondered if the man above her was Alixandyr or Trystan. In body they were one and the same, she realized that, but they were also very different men in many ways. Trystan would likely not have bothered to arouse her so beautifully. Trystan would've jumped on her like an animal; he would not have waited for her whispered *"Now."*

And still she wished she could see his eyes. The dark of morning and his fall of hair and the way his eyes narrowed worked against her.

She was slick and trembling, more than ready for the thrust that filled her. Immediately her body responded to their physical bonding. A moan escaped from her parted lips, and the moan was followed by a scream as she quickly found the release she so desperately needed. No physical act had ever been so intense. No release so powerful that it brought tears to her eyes. Her body jerked and trembled, and the release continued. Her legs caught and held Alixandyr's hips, as she lifted her hips from the ground and reached for all he had to give.

He continued to move inside her, more gently now that her climax had faded. He was of an impressive size, and she enjoyed the stroking, the joining, the bond they had created.

Now it was her turn to pleasure Alixandyr, to show him what she could do. There were tricks and ointments and magical potions which could be called upon, but she needed none of them. Instead, she gave all that she was to the man who loved her. He was inside her in more ways than he knew, and he spoke to her without words. Where did he wish to be touched? Did he wish for her to move quickly or with torturous slowness? Did he wish her to be passive or aggressive? If he secretly longed to hear words of love, she would deliver them. If he wished her to take command, she would.

She gathered her wits and concentrated on the man who was inside her, moving in and out with such delicious leisure. What did he most desire? What could she offer him which would take him to new and more blissful heights than he had ever known before?

His rhythm did not change, but hers did as the truth hit her. She faltered a little, her heart stuttered. The man who was inside her possessed the most primitive of desires. He would've roughly taken what he wanted from her, as she had known he was capable of doing, but another part of him would not allow him to hurt her, not in any way, and he was well aware of that. In order for him to remain in control, he had, by necessity, been very careful not to hurt her.

"Trystan?" she whispered.

"Yes," he responded. "Did you know all along it was me?"

"Of course I did," she lied. "Did I not tell you that you would have what you wanted from me if you saved us?"

"You did."

"Do you think me a woman who makes false promises?"

"Everyone makes false promises."

"I do not," she replied.

"If that is true, you are a rare woman indeed."

Sanura wanted to push him off of her, out of her, but she did not. Not only would it be impossible for her to physically overpower him, but she realized that Alixandyr was inside her almost as much as Trystan. It was he who kept her safe, he who was still in control in some very basic ways, though he was not at the surface in this moment. She contracted her inner muscles and swayed against the thrusts, and the man above her responded by moving faster, by giving himself over to desire just as she had. Her hands skimmed his body and found an unusual but potent erogenous patch of skin on his hip. Her fingers pressed gently and then made small circles. Again he responded, and she felt the control he held so fiercely loosen.

She knew how to make a man hers; she knew how to make a man fall apart in her arms and in her bed, even if that bed was nothing more than a borrowed cloak on a patch of hard ground. The man above her would've found his own release moments ago if he was not working so hard to maintain control. It distracted him. It kept him off balance. She took advantage of that weakness, arousing him to the point where he had no control.

When Trystan was right where she wanted him, Sanura reached up and took a handful of black hair in her hands. She held on tight and pulled his face closer. "I want Alixandyr," she whispered huskily.

"No." The answer was a gruff whisper.

"Yes. I see so much of you now, Trystan, when you are within me and your precious control is on the brink of cracking into a thousand pieces. You are not so strong after all. You are still nothing but a shadow. Alixandyr is a man. Alixandyr is the one I desire. Give him to me."

"Alix is a shadow of a man who will not take what he wants. That's why I'm here. You brought me out, Sanura, you and your forbidden body."

Recognizing that to be true, she experienced a wave of guilt she quickly brushed aside. "Now that you have had me, will you be sent into the depths again? Will you once again sleep, unable to rise to domination? Once you have all that you want of me, will you disappear? Will giving over to me send you to oblivion?"

Apparently he had not thought of that, and while she knew little of Trystan, she understood that he wanted permanent control more than anything else he could imagine. His body jerked, and in the faint morning light Sanura saw the change in his eyes as he once again became the man she truly desired.

She sighed in relief, not only at the sight of those eyes but also at the new rush of sensations she drank in. Alixandyr was kinder than his counterpart, more complicated but also more noble. He was a man worthy of loving, and while he was surprised to awaken in such a position, it did not take him long to recover and continue. After a pause of sorts, he drove deep within her and resumed the rhythm that would carry him to completion. Heaven knows, she was close enough to finding yet another release, and now that she knew who touched her, she could relax and enjoy the sensations dancing in her body.

Alixandyr was hers in a way Trystan could never be. He cared for her. He wanted the release, the pleasure that all men wanted when they joined with a woman, but he wanted more, so much more. He wanted to hear her scream and feel her body jerk beneath his. He wanted to feel the flush of her skin and watch the transformation that would come over her when she found that release.

She needed no tricks, no special maneuvers. Not now, not in this place. She gave Alixandyr what he wanted; she climaxed once again, and this time he came with her. Their bodies sweated and shuddered in time, their hearts pounded a rhythm that drowned out the sounds of the morning. Once again, she screamed.

In the faint morning light, she placed a hand in her lover's hair. Yes, he remained Alixandyr, but for how long?

He should be happy, but was not. "Sanura," he whispered against her shoulder. "Did I hurt you?"

"No." She soothed him with a gentle hand in his hair. "You did not."

"What happened?"

"You seduced me."

He gave a harsh laugh as he lifted his head. She was so very happy to see those pale green eyes.

"I've never before seduced a woman and forgotten. It was the other, wasn't it?"

"Yes."

"So why did I...why didn't he stick around to the end?"

She smiled and ran her fingers down a blue cheek. He was now almost as blue as she. "Are you asking why he left before you got to the best part?"

"Yes."

"Because I asked for you."

Alixandyr moved off of her and she sat up, taking a moment to rearrange her clothes so that she was at least partially covered. Her costume had not been made for modesty, and their frantic encounter had not helped matters at all. She was beyond disheveled.

"Why?" he asked. "Why did you ask for me?"

"Do you really need to ask that question?" She studied her arms. Thanks to all the sweating and holding that had been going on, she was in desperate need of a touch-up.

He sighed. "I suppose not."

He straightened his clothes, taking a moment to bemoan the fact that his cock was blue. Holding back a laugh, she had to point out that wasn't entirely true. He had a mere smudge of blue on his penis, that was all. Though their words were inconsequential, she felt the real pain beneath the banter.

Alixandyr was distraught because he had taken something which was not his. He had lain with a woman who was promised to his brother. And she now knew why Trystan had awakened during this particular journey. It was his desire for her, a woman he could not have, which had called the less noble shadow to the surface.

It took Alixandyr a moment to compose himself. "No matter which of us initiated the encounter, it was wrong, and I apologize. It will not happen again."

"Pity."

He lifted one imperious eyebrow.

"Well, you can hardly claim that it was not extraordinary."

"I can't say for certain," he said. "I was there only for the end."

"That's the best part for a man, or so I have heard."

"You're teasing me."

She smiled. "Perhaps a little."

"This is no time for teasing. Princess Edlyn is dead, we're wanted for her murder, and I am quickly spinning out of control of my own body."

"And a very fine body it is, Prince Alixandyr, blue penis and all."

For a moment he was stunned, and then he suppressed a smile. "You should call me Alix. It's a common enough name in Columbyana, so if we run into anyone along the way, it will hardly cause suspicion." Inside he uncoiled, he relaxed, he let go of at least some of the agony he carried within.

"Is Sanura a common name in this country?"

He shook his head. "Not at all."

"Then what will you call me, if we find ourselves in the company of others?"

"Woman," he said simply. "I will call you woman, if I find it necessary to call you anything at all."

Sanura was indignant for a moment, and then she laughed. At this moment she could not remain angry, certainly not over something so insignificant. "You may call me anything you like."

"We must hurry," he said, abruptly ending their conversation. "We slept too long."

"It was more than sleep that delayed us, Alix." She tested the short name on her tongue, and liked it.

His mouth was set in a tight line, but she could see him too well...she could see him much more clearly than before. In fact, she could see him more clearly than she had ever seen anyone, joined or not.

Perhaps because after all these years she had finally found the man she was meant to belong to. It was a startling thought, not at all like her. There was no true forever for a woman of the Agnese. No choice, no love.

"We shall hurry, then," she said as she straightened her skirt and walked toward and then past Alix. "We need that oil more than ever."

He studied his stained arms as he strode beside her. "I don't suppose I want to see my face at this moment."

"Likely not," she said lightly.

He grumbled something she could not understand, and she turned to look at him. And she smiled. The tender and joyous feelings she experienced would probably not last, but while they remained, she would enjoy them.

"This will not happen again," he said, his voice much more determined than his heart.

"If you say so," she responded in a carefree voice.

"It was entirely improper."

"Yes. You'd best not let Paki and Kontar see you before we get our hands on the oil and make use of it."

Again he grumbled.

His grumbling did not ruin her joy. "By the way," she said as she walked slightly ahead of him, "I suppose you should know that your tongue is even bluer than your penis."

Chapter Seven

"I'VE lost their trail!" the Tryfynian soldier shouted, and Vyrn cursed aloud in the morning sunlight. The squat, incensed moron who was leading this search party of eight—four Tryfynians and four Columbyanan sentinels—had led them in circles. If Prince Alixandyr reached the palace and was protected, and perhaps even pardoned, by his brother, one part of the plan would've failed.

No, failure was the wrong word. Perhaps he wouldn't get his bonus, but Princess Edlyn was dead and that had been his primary assignment. Even if Prince Alixandyr escaped "justice" for a while, in the end the result would be the same. If the emperor and the prince led the country into war over the death of a woman, they would both fall, and the bitter woman who had once been married to their father would have what she wanted.

Still, the prince's immediate death would be both neater and faster. And the extra pay would be very nice. One could never have too much money.

"He will go to his brother for help, but not directly, I imagine," Vyrn said calmly. "The woman is too difficult to disguise, and he will not leave his whore by the side of the road. We should check the nearest farmhouses and villages, and ask if they have been seen."

"I suppose you think you should lead this pursuit," the Tryfynian soldier snapped.

Vyrn looked the man dead in the eye. "Yes, I do. I have allowed you to lead until this point because it was your princess who was murdered, but this is my country, and the people in these parts will talk to me much more readily than they will talk to you."

The man sighed, recognizing the wisdom of Vyrn's plans. "I am tired, and I do not know the countryside. You may lead for a while." His eyes hardened. "If I think for even one moment that you are purposely allowing your prince to escape, I will gut you."

"I possess no loyalty for a man who would murder a defenseless woman, prince or not."

The Tryfynian soldier, as well as the others surrounding them, nodded in agreement.

Gullible idiots, each and every one of them.

Vyrn changed the course of their chase, leading the party toward a small village they had passed through on the journey to Tryfyn, many weeks ago. The prince and his slut would need food, clothing, and soap. As he was at the front of the column and no one could see his face, he allowed himself a smile. Yes, they'd need lots and lots of soap. Someone, somewhere, would talk; someone would tell all they knew. He'd make sure of it.

It would be best if he could go alone, but that was not likely to happen. Still, he turned about—smile safely hidden away—and said, "I think we should split up into four groups of two. We can cover more ground that way."

A couple of the men were not certain about the plan, but others recognized the benefit of covering more territory in a shorter amount of time.

"Rolf, you come with me," Vyrn said, choosing the slowest of the Tryfynians to accompany him into the village.

It occurred to Vyrn as he watched the others pair up and ride off that if he could not find the prince, he could surely find a way to paint the man and his motives more clearly and more darkly. With enough evidence against him, there would be no hope for the prince. No hope at all.

AS Alix and Sanura traveled toward the site of the camp they'd run from just yesterday, they walked more than they rode. On occasion he led the horse while Sanura rode, as her inadequate shoes were so ruined they were almost gone. Such pretty and delicate slippers were not made for hours of walking across rugged terrain. Neither was the woman who wore them, though she did not complain. Much.

As Alix had suspected, those who were not in pursuit had broken camp and headed back toward Tryfyn, no doubt to deliver the princess's body to her father. Once that was done and the king was told that the prince he'd entrusted with his daughter had killed her in her sleep, there would be hell to pay.

He preferred to think of that hell, rather than dwelling on the hell in which he was currently living.

Wanting Sanura and realizing he could not have her had always been difficult. Having her, remembering the feel of her body and his together, being washed in the vivid memory of how he'd awakened this morning and then continuing to keep his distance was physically painful. If he'd had his way, if he were not the man he was, he would've stopped to relive that experience at least twice during this long day. Knowing they did not have a moment to spare, knowing those who were in pursuit might be closer than they realized... he would still gladly stop to relive the pleasure of being inside Sanura. From the beginning, this time, so that he could see her passion grow.

He worked at remaining alert and in command. All his life, he'd realized there was something different about him, something dark that others did not see. Fighting the dark impulses had become second nature to him, and yes, he had been foolish enough to think, on occasion, that he had won.

He had won nothing. That darkness would always be there.

Never had he expected that it was possible for the darkness to rise up and take complete control of his body and mind. Body, mind, and soul? Was everything of himself lost when the other was in command? It was worse than he had imagined it might be, so he fought for cool, calm control as he and Sanura traveled through the forest to retrieve her box of oils and paint and implements.

Though the company headed to Tryfyn had disbanded a day earlier, they would be moving slowly. It was impossible to travel quickly with that many women and the conveyance which would be necessary for the proper delivery of Princess Edlyn's body. Surely at least one of the Tryfynian soldiers had remained with that group as a guard; perhaps more. Alix wished he knew how many men remained with those headed back toward Tryfyn, so he'd know how many he might have to fight for Sanura's oils.

Alix had no doubt that he and Sanura could catch up—perhaps even by tomorrow morning, if they traveled for a while after dark. Once they had recovered the oil which was made for removing the damnable blue, he and Sanura could resume their flight from injustice.

He would love to have a few words with Tari, if the opportunity arose. Sanura was certain the maid had something to do with the princess's death. To avoid war, he would have to prove that he was not in any way involved in the murder.

Even though he had not killed the annoying girl, and according to Sanura the other had not killed her, he still felt responsible. Princess Edlyn had been in his charge. If he had heeded Sanura's warning that Vyrn planned violence, if he had been more diligent in seeing that the princess was well guarded, then she might still be alive. Instead, he had imagined the worst disaster that could befall them was for him to be forced to marry the disagreeable girl.

Sanura walked close behind him, rarely complaining about the long hours of travel, never asking him for favors or indulgences. She traveled very much like a soldier. A beautiful, blue, oddly happy, jingling soldier.

Before they reached the others, he'd have to do something about the noise she made when she walked. Sneaking up on even an untrained maid would be impossible as long as she jangled so. He had not insisted that she remove her decorative girdle and bracelets and anklets before now because he liked the music she made with each step. The sounds she made soothed him, even as they reminded him of what he could not have again.

She was Jahn's, and he himself was irreparably broken.

Still, they had a long way to go before it would be necessary for her adornments to be removed, and until then he would allow himself the joy and the pain of listening to the music she made with each step she took. There were moments when he was certain the words to her song were "Not yours, not yours, never yours," and still he took solace in the sounds.

It was the scent of something sweet and warm that broke the monotony of the day. Alix's mouth watered. They had found plenty of water along the way, as well as bitter spring berries and a few edible but equally bitter weeds which grew near streams of cold water. The food they foraged kept them from going hungry, but the aroma which interrupted Alix's thoughts was sweeter than any he had ever imagined. He stopped in midstride.

"That smells delicious," Sanura said, her voice filled with an entirely different kind of desire than the one he'd been mulling over before the aroma had stopped him. "The source can't be too far away."

Alix turned to look at her, and found her as he had all day—smiling, gently joyous, filled with contentment in this time when she should be anxious and afraid. "We have no time for such distractions."

"Surely it won't take long," she said, backing away from him. There was a devious sparkle in her eyes, one he had never seen before. She looked like an impish little girl set on something she should not have. Alix's eyes were drawn down. Her slippers were in shreds. A gold anklet sparkled there, tempting and beautiful against her blue skin and the torn slippers. He sighed. They didn't just need food, they needed inconspicuous clothing, blankets, a canteen, another horse, and sturdy shoes for Sanura. But first, they needed that oil. They were much too conspicuous in their current state of blueness.

"I never thought I'd stoop to being a thief." Alix tied the horse's reins to the low-lying limb of a tree near grass perfect for grazing, and he followed Sanura toward the scent that had captured their attention.

"I did not say I would steal the food which is creating that marvelous smell." Sanura removed one bracelet, slipping it from her slender wrist and over long, lovely fingers. "I will buy what we need with this."

No! Would the loss of a bracelet harm her tune? Would she sound the same when she moved if she gave away even one small instrument? "You are blue," he reminded her. "So am I."

Sanura grinned widely. "I know." This morning's episode had not disturbed her at all. She was able to embrace the joy of the experience and forget all the reasons why it should not have happened.

She had called his darker side to the surface once before, when he had refused to flee from the camp without attempting to reason with his men. Had she done so again this morning, in order to get what she desired? Who—what—did she desire? Him or the other? The noble man he had fought to become, or a darkness concerned only with its own needs?

Alix followed Sanura, one hand on the grip of the sword he had found himself carrying when the other had gone deep and Alix had come to the surface to find himself rushing away from execution. It was not his sword, but it was a proper sentinel's sword, and of a style with which he was familiar. He kept one hand on the grip, in case he and Sanura were headed toward more than food. She was drawn to the aroma of something freshly baked. He was drawn to her. In the early morning hours he had smudged her once flawless blueness, but she looked none the less beautiful. The curve of her hip, just above the low-slung skirt; the grace of her arms, bare and slender and long; the willowy movement of her legs, legs which had once been wrapped around him... all was perfection. He watched the sway of her hips, listened to the gentle song of her movements, and wished he were another man.

If he were another man, they could run and never look back. There were many sparsely populated areas of Columbyana where a man and a woman who did not wish to be found might live a very nice life. They could farm a bit, perhaps fish if they lived near the sea. He did know how to fish. They could build a small house, a home smaller but also warmer than the palace in Arthes which he now called home. They could make babies and laughter, and keep one another warm in the wintertime.

Foolish thoughts. Not only was such a life impossible for him, it was surely not what a woman like Sanura wanted for herself. She had had jewels and servants and the finest of clothes. A small, isolated farm and a fisherman husband were surely not what she desired from her life.

Not that such a choice would ever be his. He had responsibilities, and once he cleared up the confusion surrounding Princess Edlyn's death, he would once again devote himself to those responsibilities. He was a prince; he was his father's son.

Soon a small cottage was in sight. Puffs of white smoke drifted from the stone chimney. In a house this small, the cooking was probably done over the fireplace at the base of that chimney. He could picture it well, as he had grown up in a cottage no larger than this one.

Sanura looked over her shoulder and smiled at him, and his stomach dropped.

Take her. Wipe that disgusting grin off of her face.

He shook off the hateful words, words he knew were not his own. "I won't let you harm her," he whispered as Sanura's gaze returned to the cottage.

I know. That's why I haven't done so, yet.

That "yet" was frightening, but not altogether unexpected. "Go away." His words were so soft they could not rightly be called a whisper. "Damn you, go away."

I can't go away just yet, Alix. You need me.

"I do not."

Again, Sanura glanced at him. "Did you say something?"

"No," he said sharply.

You're the one who's going away, Alix, prince, do-gooder, noble ass that you are. I am what you truly are at the pit of your soul. I am your essence, your true self, and in time I will be where you are, and you will not even be able to whisper "no" as I give in to every impulse you've denied me for so long. I'm hungry, Alix, I'm so very hungry.

Was it his imagination, or did the voice grow stronger as it spoke? As they stepped into a clearing, his eyes fell to the sway of Sanura's hips. The thing inside him, the darkness he had fought all his life, wanted to make Sanura a slave to his own desires. Not a pampered possession as she had once been, but an abused and miserable thing.

He barely knew Sanura. They were lovers, they were partners on the run together, but he could not say that he knew her at all. And yet he realized without doubt that he'd take his own life before he'd allow her to be possessed by the other. He'd said more than once that he did not know what horrors he might do when the darkness within him ruled, but in truth he *did* know. He knew too well.

WITH every step Tari took, she grew more anxious. She was moving away from Vyrn, and though he had said he'd be back for her, the farther apart they were, the more uneasy she became. The thought of never seeing him again, of never touching him, of not having all that he promised—it was a nightmare. She'd had no hope of love and happiness before meeting Vyrn, but now that she had those things, she would not allow them to be snatched away.

Besides, if they reached King Bhaltair's court and one of his wizards or witches looked at her and saw the truth of what she'd done...Even Vyrn couldn't save her from the king's wrath.

When the others stopped for water and a quick bite of lunch, Tari slipped away. She wrapped some bread in a kerchief, hid it in her apron pocket, and then she stepped into the forest as if she needed to relieve herself. Once she was away from the others, she began to run. Back the way they'd come, back to Vyrn, she ran. After she'd run for several minutes, she made her way out of the forest and onto the road, where she could run more easily. She glanced back once, even though she knew no one would be following her. A missing maid was not important enough for them to give chase. She was merely a serving girl, and when she did not return from the forest, they would assume either that she'd run away or that a vicious woodland creature had eaten her. They would not even wonder about the fact that they'd heard no screams.

Here in the road there was nothing to impede her progress as she ran. The wind whipped across her face and mussed her hair, and she found herself smiling, even when her legs began to ache. When she'd left the castle, forced into serving the blue slave who was everything Tari was not, she'd been miserable and without hope. Now she was filled with hope. Hope and love.

Such a change did not come without a price. She would never forget the startled look on the princess's face when the poor girl had awakened to find the knife at her throat. Princess Edlyn had been surprised for only a moment before Tari had sliced her throat with the knife Vyrn had given her. In that moment, the princess had known she was about to die. Tari had not given her the opportunity to scream. A scream would've brought soldiers running, and that could not happen. All would be ruined if the truth were known.

Tari had wisely worn an apron for the killing, since Vyrn had warned her that there would be a lot of blood. That blood-stained apron was buried in the forest not far from the campsite where the killing had taken place, and not far from where Vyrn had hidden the prince's sword. No one would miss that common and insignificant garment, one of many from the castle laundry. She'd buried it so deep that no one would ever find it.

As she ran, she thought of Vyrn and all he promised. Love, marriage, children, love, love, love. She had come to enjoy the sex, but it was much more than that which bound her to Vyrn. Any man would likely fill that need for her, if she required it. It was the love itself that spurred her on. A handsome man loved her. He needed her. He wanted to marry her. A once hopeless future had vanished, and a new and brighter one had taken its place.

Tari had never thought herself to be a cruel person, but in order to have what she wanted, she would do anything. Anything at all.

SANURA was charmed by the small cottage and the woman who had done the baking which had called them in this direction. After a diet of weeds, berries, and water, the roasted meat and garden vegetables—along with the sweet bread they had smelled and a tankard of cider—made a most scrumptious meal. There was a small barn where the horse Alix had collected after their welcome had been assured could rest—with the woman's donkey for company—and there was hay and fresh water for the animal, as well.

The woman, who introduced herself simply as Donia, was a pretty, dark-haired woman who did not look to be more than thirty years of age. She seemed genuinely glad to see other people, and yet inside she hid something.

Donia had a secret, and it frightened her to know that others might discover what she hid. If Sanura looked deeper, she might discover this secret, but she did not attempt to do so. Behind the secret there was a simple, good woman who would do them no harm. Nothing else mattered. Besides, it would be rude to pry, to push for information about their hostess. She would see what she was meant to see, as always.

Donia was very much isolated in this cottage in the woods, and at a quick glance Sanura saw no evidence of a male resident. There was a doll sitting by the fireplace, but no child about. It would not be polite to ask questions, especially as she and Alix did not wish to answer questions themselves, but Sanura was most definitely curious. A woman as pretty as Donia could marry well. With her baking skills, she could support herself as a baker in a village, large or small. Why was she here, apparently alone? The secret she hid kept her here, no doubt. Yes, she was a prisoner to the secret; she protected it with her very life, and would continue to do so.

Donia had easily accepted Sanura's outrageous story of an unfortunate mishap with a vat of fabric dye, and she was very happy to take a gold bracelet in exchange for the food she so generously shared. It was obvious from the way she smiled at and wore the bracelet that she was unaccustomed to fine things but was certainly not averse to owning them.

They ate and drank and enjoyed not only the food and cider but the much-needed rest.

Donia was not afraid of Alix, but she was certainly wary of him. She kept her distance from him, though she was very much at ease with Sanura. Of course, Alix was a large and obviously powerful man, and might be seen as a physical threat to any single woman, even though he had done nothing to make Donia fear him.

After a fine meal and a short rest, Sanura could tell that Alix, who had been very quiet since they'd entered the cottage, was ready to resume their journey. He was tense, his neck and jaw and lips tight. No wonder Donia was wary! Alix needed a long, luxurious massage to relieve his tension, or perhaps an orgasm. Either would do. Given his current state of mind, neither was likely in the near future.

Of course, if Trystan decided to rise once again, that would change. Sanura wanted Alix, but she was afraid of Trystan. And yet in so many ways they were one and the same. If she were going to suddenly dismiss all that she'd been and all that she'd been taught in order to choose a man for herself, then why could she not have fallen for a simple, uncomplicated man? Why was it this one who seemed, so very much, to be hers?

They were saying good-bye when the door to the cabin swung open so swiftly that Alix reached for his sword. He relaxed when he saw the child standing there.

Sanura did not relax, and neither did Donia.

The child who had thrown open the door with such force was exquisitely beautiful, and looked to be five or six years old. Her hair was a pure white gold, and it fell to her waist in thick, straight strands. Her eyes were a brilliant blue that bordered on purple, and her face was without flaw. There was nothing to rival a child's unblemished, fat cheeks and soft mouth, no beauty could compare. The dress the child wore was white and plain, and even though she'd been outdoors, it was unstained.

On the outside this was the perfect child. Inside, she was not so beautiful.

This was Donia's child, and she was also Donia's secret. This little girl was the reason a young woman hid in the woods, isolated from all others as much as possible. The appearance of the child frightened her, even though there could be no reason for anyone to fear such an innocent little girl.

Perhaps not so innocent, perhaps not so flawless.

"I told you to wait..." Donia began.

"I grew tired of waiting." Though the tone of the voice was that of a child, there was an adult tenor that put even Alix on edge. The little girl came into the cottage and slammed the door behind her.

Sanura tried to look into the girl. There was something of Donia here, yes, but there was also something dark. This darkness was nothing like that which Alix fought. It was deeper, darker, *demonic.*

The little girl turned her eyes on Sanura. They were cold and fierce and not those of a child. "Do not use your witch's powers on me unless I give you permission to do so."

"I cannot help what I see," Sanura said honestly. "I did not mean to pry."

"Mali," Donia said. She wrung her hands. "Our guests were just leaving. Please, let them pass."

"Not just yet," Mali said.

Alix, who knew nothing of the child before them, raised one eyebrow. He was more amused than concerned, but he did not sense the dark power in the innocent-looking Mali. Who could look upon such a child and see anything of danger?

Sanura relaxed a little. She didn't attempt to see into Mali any more than she already had, but she knew that, like Alix, this child struggled. Like Alix, this little girl fought for her very soul. Even though Donia believed that all was lost for her and her daughter, that there would never be anything for them but fear and seclusion—she was wrong.

Without fear, Sanura dropped to her knees so she was eye to eye with Mali. "May I take your hand?"

"No!" Donia took a frightened step forward. To Alix it likely looked as if she were afraid for her daughter, but Sanura knew she was more afraid of what her daughter might do to their guests. There was great power in this child, some tapped, some as yet untapped.

Mali offered one small, delicate hand as if she were a queen. Sanura took it, and she was immediately washed in a power like no other she had ever known. Good and light from her mother, mixed with a demon's powers and greed, a violent gift from her father, made this child what she was. In a flash, she saw an unwanted glimpse of this child's creation. Sanura saw it all in an instant, even though to see into the past was not her gift. She saw all because the child wished her to see. Donia had been kidnapped by vicious soldiers and then delivered half-dead to their leader, a demon-possessed man who had raped her, beaten her, and even bitten her before leaving her for dead.

But Donia had not died, and Mali had been born of the night of terror.

"All is not lost," Sanura whispered.

"All has been lost for a long time," Donia answered just as softly.

The hand in Sanura's was a child's, soft and pliable and fragile.

"No," Sanura said, "there is as much of you in this child as there is of her father."

Donia flinched at the word "father."

"Teach her," Sanura said. Her eyes met Mali's, and there within the cold she saw light. She saw hope.

"How can I?"

Sanura lifted her head and looked at Alix, who was thoroughly confused. "This child possesses great powers and is in need of a teacher to help her harness them. A great tutor will be required."

Alix's eyes narrowed, his jaw clenched. He saw this diversion as a waste of time, a distraction. He was impatient to move on, not yet realizing what was truly before him. "I know of a wizard who lives near Arthes. Sian Chamblyn. He and his wife, Ariana, have trained witches and wizards in the past. I'm sure they would not mind working with another. This child is very young, however, and we have other matters to..."

"They will kill her," Donia whispered as she shook her head. "I did not ask for this, but Mali is mine and I will not let them kill her!"

A light of understanding came into Alix's eyes, and he smoothly drew his sword. "She is a demon's child."

Mali did not let go of Sanura's hand when she waved the other, as if she were shooing away a pesky fly. Alix's sword was magically plucked from his hand. The weapon went flying away from the people in the small room. End over end, the sword tumbled through the air before twisting one last time and ending with the tip embedded in the wooden floor.

"I could've killed you," Mali said calmly, "but I did not. Do you still wish to kill me?" She was unafraid in a situation which would terrify most adults.

Sanura lifted her own stilling hand. "Mali won't harm us," she assured her companion as he retrieved his sword. *She is like you*, she wanted to say, and yet she could not share Alix's secret.

So many secrets.

Sanura took Mali's hand in both of hers, and she smiled. "You have great powers, child. I am gifted, but I possess nothing near your gifts."

"Mother says I will bring disaster wherever I go," Mali said. "I was born to bring misfortune." She shrugged as if that prediction did not concern her, but it did.

"That is not true," Sanura said. "You are as much your mother's daughter as your father's, and with training and determination you can be a great force for good in this world." Again, she looked at Alix. "We must get her to this teacher you know."

While Alix did not make a move toward Mali, not for good or for ill, he was horrified by her suggestion. "I cannot, I *will not* subject Sian and Ariana's children to this...this monster." He lowered his voice as he said the final word, but that did not negate the hurtfulness of it.

Sanura glared at him. "Mali is no more a monster than you are." The words had more meaning for the two of them than for Mali and her mother, and Alix got the message loud and clear.

"Still..."

"Choose another teacher, then," she interrupted. "There must be someone who can help."

After a moment's hesitation, he nodded in reluctant agreement. "We must first finish the task at hand."

Mali laid her hand on Sanura's arm. "You wish to remove the blue," she said.

"Yes."

"Why? It's very pretty. I wish I was blue."

"No!" Donia shouted, but it was too late. Mali's skin began to turn. Shades of blue drifted across her skin, coloring her face, her hands, her arms.

"Your wishes come true," Sanura said with a smile.

"Sometimes," Mali said with a shrug. "If I wish it for myself and I wish hard enough. I suppose I should wish it away now, though it is very pretty. I look like the sky on a fine winter day." The next wish must've been silent, because the blue gradually faded until Mali's flesh was once again pale and creamy white.

Alix was now more intrigued than horrified. "That's very interesting. Can you wish the blue from our skin?"

Mali rolled her eyes in a very adult manner. "Of course not. Don't be ridiculous."

"It was just an idea," Alix muttered.

Mali gave her attention to Sanura. "There is a plant which grows nearby. It will remove the stain from your skin."

"And his?" Sanura asked.

"No," Mali said petulantly. "He wanted to kill me. He doesn't like me. I think he should remain blue."

"He's very sorry, now," Sanura said.

"I don't think he's sorry at all," Mali said with a pout. "He has not *said* that he's sorry, and he doesn't *look* sorry."

"Alix, apologize," Sanura ordered.

"I will not. She's a demon's offspring, and it is my duty…"

"Fine," Sanura said. "Remain blue." She stood and grasped Mali's hand in her own. The child looked at those clasped hands curiously, and Sanura realized that no one had ever walked hand in hand with this child before. Her own mother was as afraid as she was protective. Donia needed as much tutoring as Mali. Perhaps more.

They walked toward the door, and with a careless flick of her free hand, Mali opened it. Afternoon sunlight spilled across the floor.

Behind them, Alix groaned. "All right," he said, his boot heels clicking on the wooden floor of the small cottage. "I'm sorry. I could never kill a child. The drawing of my sword was simply a reaction to the disclosure of your true parentage. It was a shocking revelation."

They walked out of the cottage and toward the woods which lay in the opposite direction from which they'd come. "You would not have killed me in any case," Mali said calmly.

"Of course not," he said, very convincingly.

"I'm not at all easy to kill," she explained, and she glanced over her shoulder to look squarely at Alix. "If you don't believe me, ask Mother."

Chapter Eight

THE plant the little girl led them to appeared, at first glance, to be ordinary enough. It grew close to the ground and was mostly hidden beneath the larger leaves of other low-lying plants, but Mali knew exactly where to look. She dropped down and broke off a thick leaf, and when she did so, a thick, pale green substance oozed from the plant's broken edge.

Mali turned to Sanura first, gently placing the torn side of the thick leaf on one blue arm. Sanura jumped when the gooey substance met her skin, and Alix instinctively leaned forward, ready to lunge and separate the two females. The plant wasn't helping Sanura, it was *hurting* her.

Sanura laughed before he could do more than tilt his body in her direction. "It's much colder than I expected it would be."

Alix settled back, but not without noticing that Mali looked his way and smiled mischievously.

A mischievous half-demon child.

There were many rumors in Columbyana about the possibility that the Isen Demon's offspring had survived, even though the demon itself had lost the war and had been forever buried. Alix knew of one such child with certainty. Linara was being raised by Sophie Fyne Varden, who was a powerful witch in her own right. Last he'd heard, Linara was showing signs of developing her own gifts—or curses—but she was not at all mischievous or dangerous.

Mali's existence gave greater credence to the argument that many such children survived. He now knew of two half-demon children who lived among them. Were there more? More rightly the question should be, how many more? They would all be five or six years old, not much of a threat at first glance, but what would happen in ten or fifteen years, as they grew to adulthood? Some of them would perhaps be like Linara, and receive the proper training to help them choose the right path. But what of the others, the ones who had been hidden away from the world as Mali had been hidden?

Kill her, kill her now.

No. She's just a child.

A demon child. She sees me, did you know that? She sees us, and she knows that the two of you are very much alike.

We're nothing alike.

Alix pushed the dark thoughts down and turned his attention to the transformation taking place before him. Together Mali and Sanura worked the gel from the thick leaves over her exposed skin, and the blue disappeared. Beneath the blue paint Sanura's skin was golden and flawless, smooth and warm. He wanted to reach out and touch the natural-toned flesh which was revealed, to run his fingers against every inch as it was uncovered.

The necessary plants were small but abundant, and when they had taken a few leaves from one, they moved on to another, so as not to kill the plant. Mali had no problem finding the vegetation, no matter how well the thick leaves were hidden.

Alix wanted to help with the chore he watched so closely, but knew his assistance in this endeavor would not be welcomed, not by the demon child Mali and not by Sanura herself. He tried to tell himself that he wished only to assist in order to speed along the process, but that was a blatant lie. He wanted to be close to her again, to touch her in any way—innocent or not so innocent. As if he could run his hands over Sanura's body and not become aroused all over again. As if he could touch her and not have her.

Sanura sat on the ground, the blond child leaning over her. Mali ran a newly broken leaf over Sanura's long and slender blue throat. Sanura tipped her head back to allow the child better access. The substance from the leaf's core dissolved and then wiped away the blue paint, stripping away that which had protected Sanura from the touch of those men who were not allowed the honor.

He had touched her. No, no, the other part of himself had done the forbidden touching. If not, he never would've dared to start that which he had gladly finished just that morning, no matter how strongly he was drawn to her, no matter how much he craved her. He had trained himself to be better than his baser instincts, to ignore the calls within him which spoke of need and darkness. Nothing had ever been as difficult as ignoring the call to Sanura.

When all of Sanura's exposed skin was devoid of the blue, the two females turned to Alix. Two women, one fully grown and one a child, both of them powerful, both of them seeing too much. Mali broke off a new piece of the plant and threw it to him. More rightly, she threw it *at* him. Alix caught the surprisingly heavy leaf in one hand.

"It wouldn't be wise for me to get too close to you, splintered man," the girl said. "You'll have to manage without me."

"I won't hurt you."

"No," Mali said easily, "but *he* will, if he gets the chance."

Alix did not protest that there was no *he*, as he ran the leaf across his arm and watched the blue fade away. He had fought, denied, and suppressed that other all his life, and now two females he barely knew saw through him with surprising ease. Splintered man, the little girl called him. How could he argue with that?

The substance inside the thick leaf was indeed much colder than he had imagined it would be. Still, it would take more than a bit of chill to make him squeal as Sanura had. Alix was nothing if not controlled. The plant's inner substance removed the blue and then seeped into the skin, leaving very little residue behind. It was not magic, exactly, but came very close.

Sanura took another piece of the leaf and began to help. She removed the markings from places he could not see or reach properly; she removed small bits of blue he missed in his haste. The back of his neck, a place on his shoulder, beneath his ear, she gave them all her attention. She even ran a bit of leaf across his nose, making sure he'd removed all the blue there. He watched her closely as she tended to him.

He had expected that without the blue paint she would look ordinary, but she did not. She was beautiful, and he wanted her again. She was so close he could feel her body heat, he was assailed by her scent, and he was reminded of that afternoon by the stream, when she had come so close to him but had not touched. She was as enticing now; more so, since he knew what she felt like, how she laughed, how she gasped when she reached orgasm. He thought of that isolated farm, he thought of the life she would never settle for...the life he could never have. His hands itched to touch her, but he did not. Mali watched closely, and Sanura was still not his to take.

When all their exposed skin was cleaned of the blue, they broke off a few pieces of the plant with which to finish the job at a later time—when Mali was not watching. For now, the job they had done was sufficient. They could walk among others without drawing attention to themselves.

Well, almost. He looked Sanura up and down, taking in the skimpy and foreign outfit, the gold and jangling girdle at her hips, the bangles at her wrists, the anklet adorning a shapely ankle. There would be no more music, and he already mourned the loss.

"Mali," he said calmly, "Does your mother have a dress she'd like to sell?"

IT was much later than they'd intended when they left the cottage. Sanura fidgeted and pulled at the collar of the uncomfortable dress Donia had sold her. The fabric was heavy and it itched. She was covered from neck to foot. The boots were a nice change from the torn slippers, as they protected her feet from the hard and often rocky ground, but the rest of the outfit was horrendous.

And oddly enough, she felt naked. More covered than she had ever been, she felt horribly exposed.

The blue paint had protected her all of her adult life. It kept her apart. It screamed *don't touch* to all those who saw her. Now her skin was like everyone else's, and there was nothing to protect her. Nothing but Alix and Trystan.

"We will come back for Mali when we can, won't we?" Sanura asked, her eyes on Alix's back. She rather hated watching his back. It was his eyes which revealed so much, his eyes which told her what part of him was in control.

"We will fetch Mali and Donia when the time is right," Alix said.

"Of course," Sanura whispered, agreeing even though she knew Alix was wrong. Donia did love her daughter, but she would be very glad to see Mali in someone else's care. Permanently. The young woman longed for a husband and other children, she longed to have friends again, but did not dare to chase that dream while Mali was a part of her life. Mali would flourish away from her mother, she would do well away from a woman who was afraid of her. One would not think love and fear could live together in one heart, but they did.

Sanura and Alix walked in the direction of the closest village, which was half a day away, according to Donia. They would ride part of the way, but most of the time they would walk. The horse could not carry two riders endlessly, and as Alix often pointed out, they might find themselves in a circumstance where they'd need the horse to be well rested and ready to run.

Once again they would spend the night on the ground. If it was cool tonight, as it had been last night and probably would be again, they would keep one another warm. She did not think the night would end as last night had, however. Alix was stronger than Trystan at the moment, and though he wanted her, he was staunchly opposed to taking that which was not his to take.

Noble to a fault, the prince was.

Trystan was not at all noble. He took what he wanted without concern for others, without thinking. He was a slave to his impulses, just as Alix was a slave to his rules. For many years, the darker side had slept, but now that he had tasted freedom, he would not rest so easily, he would never sleep. Trystan would fight for control. So would Alix. Who would win? Who would be sent into the depths to live in darkness, and who would live?

It was unthinkable that Alix, a good man, might lose this battle, but Sanura could not say with any certainty that he would prevail.

They traveled for quite a while before Alix chose a proper camp for the night. A flat section of ground was protected from the wind on two sides by massive rock walls. A gentle creek bubbled nearby. No one could approach without being seen.

For a while after they'd stopped, Alix gave his attention to the horse. He brushed the animal and spoke to it in hushed tones, checked the hooves for damage and pebbles, and fed the animal a handful of the oats Donia had provided. Thanks to Donia, this part of the journey was much more pleasant than the first part had been. They had a blanket, a small sack of food, and a tin cup with which to catch and drink the water they found along the way.

Nice as those luxuries were, Sanura and Alix were still wanted for murdering the princess—and Alix continued to battle his own demons.

It was well dark before he joined her. He started a small

fire—for warmth, as their bread and fruit needed no cooking—and they ate in silence. They had pieces of the plant which would remove the blue, and should perhaps see to the task of removing what they had missed earlier, but that would mean undressing and tending to their most private body parts. Her breasts and buttocks, his penis and fine behind. Given the tension in their camp, perhaps that chore should wait.

Then again, perhaps it should not. Never before had she been concerned with what she wanted, what she desired.

Alix was bothered; she caught that much from him as she watched him eat. Of course he had a right to be worried, given all that had happened of late, but this felt like a new worry. She could not tell what that worry was until he looked at her and asked abruptly, "What if there is a baby?"

Sanura blinked, and she immediately dismissed all thoughts of seducing him on this night. He could not know that his question hurt, that he had found and irritated her deepest heartbreak. "There is not."

"How can you be certain?" he snapped. "Do you take a potion of some sort? Is a part of your magic the control of your childbearing abilities? Was it simply the wrong time for you to…"

"I cannot have children," she interrupted to end his questioning.

He seemed deflated but also relieved, and he was confused by the warring responses within him. "I did not know," he said softly.

"The women of the Agnese are created to give pleasure, and to be in a constant state of pregnancy would be inconvenient for those who possess us." A flare of anger rose within her, even as she kept her voice even and calm. "Most men who are gifted with one such as I do not wish to be bothered with bastards or the distended bellies of their lovers or the squalling of babes when they wish only for their own desires to be fulfilled. It is the males of the Agnese, my brothers and those like them, who assure that the bloodline continues. They marry outsiders who become mothers to the gifted ones, like me, and to sons who will ultimately insure our survival. The females born Agnese are all as I am, owned by others, gifted and barren."

Alix either saw or heard her pain. "I'm sorry."

She had never before complained about her childless state. What purpose would such complaints serve? Any sacrifices she had been called upon to make were offset by the gifts which were hers to share. She was a woman of the Agnese, and other women envied her. They wished to be like her—no, they wished to *be* her. Still, on this night when it seemed that in this new world all that she was, was not good enough, when she was trapped in a place where she did not belong, where she was despised and distrusted, what had been taken from her seemed more egregious than ever.

"When I was fifteen, just before my training began, I was taken to a special and isolated encampment and given a concoction which sent me into spasms of pain for five days and five nights." She could still remember the sharp anguish, the way she had gripped her abdomen and shouted for her mother. The pain had continued. Her mother had not come. "I cried. For two days I thought I was going to die. For the next three days I wished to die, for the pain was like a knife ripping through my insides, day and night. That's why the camp designed for this purpose was so far away from everyone and everything else, you see, so no one else would be bothered or frightened by the screams of girls in agony." Remembering, she could easily cry for what had been lost, but she did not. "In the end, all that died was my womb, as was intended. I do not bleed as other women bleed, I do not worry about catching any man's child, and you, Prince Alixandyr, do not have to worry that I might present you with an inconvenient bastard in nine months' time simply because the part of you which you cannot control took what you will not."

When she was done, she turned her head and looked into the night, hoping that Alix would not see the shine of tears in her eyes.

"I am so sorry," Alix said again. "What was done to you

is not right. If I had been there, if I had known, I would never have allowed such an atrocity to take place."

She heard the sincerity in his voice, she felt it, and somehow his outrage eased her heartache.

"I feel as if I should hold and comfort you," he said, "but I cannot. I cannot hold you and not have you, I cannot wrap my arms around you and go no further."

"Of course not," she whispered. She did not expect comfort. No one had ever offered such a luxury, and she did not want or need it now. Yet, she did remember what it had felt like to wake that morning with Alix's arms around her. She should cease her prattling and leave the man in peace. She had lived with her heartbreak for many years, always accepting that to remain childless was a small price to pay for being cherished and honored. "It's Mali who has stirred these feelings to the surface," she confessed, her tone changing as her anger faded. "She is unwanted, even by her own mother."

"Surely you understand. The child is half-demon, and her creation was likely not pleasant for Donia."

His defense of Donia made her angry. "And yet, Mali is still a child who has no choice about who she is, just as I have no choice." She looked squarely at Alix. "Just as *you* have no choice." She was glad to see that his eyes remained a pale green. Even in the firelight, she could tell which part of him was in control.

"What of you? Do you have children?"

He shook his head.

"Do you want them?"

"I've never given it much thought."

Sanura smiled wanly. "Do not lie to me, Prince Alixandyr. I see you too well, even now."

"I suppose I have thought about it," he confessed. "It is expected that I will marry and have children. It's my duty as prince."

"I did not ask if it was your duty," she clarified, even though he knew quite well what she'd asked. "Do you want children?"

"Yes," he whispered.

Of course he did. Almost all men wished to see themselves in their offspring. They wished to teach and play and train and watch their bloodline survive. That was not her purpose, and it never had been.

"You can hold me, you know. Now, tomorrow morning, whenever you wish. We can have sex again, as often as we please, and no one need ever know. There will be no child, and I expect nothing of you but pleasure given and pleasure taken in the days we are together." She looked him squarely in the eye, brave as she had always been. "What you deny yourself is the reason I was created. Sex. Pleasure. A moment of physical wonder in which we can forget the darkness of the world."

"You are Jahn's," he said simply.

"Not yet," she whispered.

Alix shook his head. "You are Jahn's," he said again. He studied her quizzically. "Will you call the other to you if I won't accede to your commands?"

"I make no commands; I merely offer suggestions."

"That does not answer my question."

"I don't want the other, I want you. You possess a kindness he does not. He scares me," she confessed. "I called him to me once before, when we escaped the camp where we were accused of murder, but I won't do so again."

"You did not call him to you early this morning?"

She shook her head. "He came on his own. I did not know it wasn't you until it was too late."

Alix nodded, and she was relieved to see that he believed her. "I think you are the only one who can call him. He has appeared a time or two on his own—when I've been sleeping and on that afternoon when I lost my temper with Edlyn—but if I work very hard, if I try, I believe I can keep him contained." His large hands flexed and he rolled wide, tired shoulders. "It won't be easy, I suspect. He wants you."

"So do you," Sanura said honestly.

"Yes, but I can and will control my impulses. That's the only way to keep him down. He's stronger than he's ever been, and I'm afraid the time will come when he is here and I am gone. What if he learns to keep me in the shadows, as I have learned to restrain him?"

Sanura knew she could have what she wanted from Alix. He would hold her, make love to her, offer her pleasure and connection and even the affection he denied. All she had to do was move closer and place her hands on him. If she made the first move, if she practiced all that she had been taught of seduction, he would not be able to resist her.

But she did not move. "Are you not stronger than he is?"

"I used to think so. Now I'm not so sure."

VERITY was annoyed. She wanted to retire to her tent and wait anxiously for the other travelers to sleep so Laris could join her, but her Aunt Louiza insisted that they all sit around the campfire and share stories, as the night was mild and no one felt the need to rush immediately to shelter.

Their traveling party was fairly small: Verity herself; Aunt Louiza, serving as the necessary chaperone; Gregor Wallis, the pompous deputy minister of something or another; Laris and the other two sentinels, Alroy and Cavan. She'd paid those two little mind on the journey. Until tonight she hadn't been sure which was which. Now she knew that Alroy was the older, quieter sentinel with the slightly crossed eyes and the horsey laugh; Cavan was younger and not quite so shockingly unattractive, though he did not hold a candle to Laris, who easily outshined them all.

Her father had wanted to send a maid along, but Verity had refused. No, she had *insisted* that a maid who was not accustomed to traveling on horseback would only slow their progress, and she was anxious to get to Arthes and have this whole empress episode taken care of so she could begin her new life. It would be best if she had a chance to settle in and learn her way around the palace before the wedding took place.

Her father always gave in when she insisted. The emperor would be the same way, she imagined.

Louiza laughed at something Wallis said, and then she began, "When Verity was a child, she was such a trial. Why, I remember one time…"

Verity shot up from her uncomfortable position by the fire. "No! You cannot tell amusing stories about me as a *child*." After all, one day these men would be her sentinels, her minions, if you would. She could not openly declare that she was confident she'd be chosen, but she *was* confident, and to have these men laughing at her childhood exploits was unacceptable.

Louiza's smile died. "I didn't mean to embarrass you, Verity. You were a funny little girl." Her father's younger sister was a sweet enough woman, widowed too young and too often at loose ends. It was no wonder she'd volunteered to chaperone on this trip.

Verity hated to be the one to spoil her aunt's fun. She resumed her seat. "Oh, all right. Go ahead and humiliate me."

She noted that Laris was paying extra attention as Louiza began her tale. Of course he was paying attention. The love potion made everything about her more special, more important. Louiza went on and on about one winter's holiday, and with a long sigh Verity realized which story her aunt was sharing.

The bucket tale.

"We stepped outside," Louiza said, her grin widening, "and there was Verity swinging a tin bucket toward her little friend's head. Her mother screamed, 'Don't hit Jana in the head with a bucket!' Verity turned about and looked at her mother with a very grown-up expression and said, 'Well, then, what can I hit her with?' "

Everyone laughed, even Laris.

"She had ripped the head off my favorite doll," Verity whispered beneath her breath. "One whack with a small bucket didn't seem like such a harsh punishment for the crime."

Across the fire, she caught Laris's eye. She could not afford to hold it for too long, she could not afford to let anyone else see that she took great comfort from that gaze and the smile he sent her way. It was a smile meant just for her, she knew, and in that moment she felt a burst of emotion wash through her. What was it? Affection? Desire?

Guilt?

THE night was warmer than it should've been, and Sanura was more comfortable. A blanket kept away the night's chill, and arms surrounded and cradled her.

A child's arms. Mali's arms.

In her short lifetime Mali had been held no more than Sanura had, though the reasons they were rarely touched were very different. Sanura wore the blue; Mali was rejected and untouched because of her mother's fear.

This was a dream and yet more than a dream, Sanura knew. Mali was experiencing the same vision and sensation at the same time. The child, too, longed to be held. She longed to be touched by someone who did not fear her.

The child whispered in Sanura's ear. "Mother thinks I don't remember, but I do. When I was an infant, she placed a pillow over my face, but I did not die. She fed me poison weeds, but I did not die. She tried to take a knife to my throat, but could not make herself finish the task. She did not wish to see my blood spill, even though she despises that blood. Even if she had, I would not have died."

"She loves you," Sanura said.

Mali sighed. "Sometimes."

They held one another, and it was very nice. In the way of dreams, one minute they were both blue and the next they were not. They were connected; they belonged to one another. Sanura felt so much love for this child, she thought her heart would burst.

Mali was the daughter she could never have, and in that same way Sanura was the mother who was capable of accepting and loving this child for who she was, not how she had come to be. She could not hold her tightly enough, for she knew the dream could not last. She knew the comfort was temporary.

"Come back for me," Mali whispered as she began to fade away.

"I will," Sanura promised.

"He doesn't like me."

"I do."

"Don't forget me," the child commanded.

"Never."

And then Mali was gone, their connection severed but not forgotten.

When Sanura woke before dawn, the dream was still clear and real to her. She could remember every word, and more important, she could remember holding Mali and soothing the child. She had long ago put away all maternal inclinations, knowing them to be senseless and a waste of her time and energy, but Mali brought them all to the surface.

Alix was already awake. No, Sanura realized as she looked at him, he had never slept. He was afraid the other would rise to control while he was sleeping, and so he did not allow himself that luxury. He had spent the night watching her, watching and wanting what he could not have.

What he truly wanted at the moment, what he wished for himself more than anything else in this world, was to prove himself innocent of murder and be rid of her so he would not be pained by his physical desire. Seeing the truth in him, seeing who he was and what he wanted, hurt her to the core. Here was a man she could choose, a man she could love no matter what inner battles he fought, and he wanted nothing from her beyond the sex they had already shared.

Physical pleasure was the reason for her creation, it was the gift she offered, and yet at this moment it was not enough. It was not close to enough. Not for him; not for her. A rush of emotion brought heat to her cheeks. If she was going to live in a land where she could have the luxury of choosing, she would insist upon more. She would insist upon love.

Chapter Nine

AS she got ready to mount her horse, Verity smiled at the pompous ass who was escorting her to Arthes. She was not a seasoned traveler, yet she seemed better suited to the harsh conditions than the diplomat Gregor Wallis. He rarely smiled, and she sometimes felt as though her own smiles annoyed him. All the more reason to flash her teeth at him and toss her hair. Sure enough, he grumbled.

"Isn't it a beautiful morning!" she called.

His answer was no more than a grunt.

She wanted to smile at Laris, but did not. In the past few days she had started to feel a bit ill when she looked at him. More rightly, she felt guilty when he looked at her with those moony brown eyes of his. She never felt guilty! Still, if he was ever caught in her tent, or creeping in or out of it, she'd have no choice but to make it clear that he had not been invited. He would likely be killed if that happened, and that would be a pity.

Verity patted Buttercup on the neck and then stepped into the stirrup and lifted herself up, unassisted, to take her seat firmly in the saddle.

Immediately, Buttercup bucked and tried to throw her off. Verity hung on tightly. As there was very little else in the way of entertainment in the Northern Province, she was an accomplished horsewoman. Thank goodness she didn't ride sidesaddle! Without a firm hold on the horse she would've been thrown to the ground. Her neck might've been broken. At the very least, she would've been badly bruised, and it would surely hurt to hit the ground so hard. Verity was not fond of pain, especially when it was her own.

She held on, as the horse took off at an uncontrollable run. With the air rushing in her ears she couldn't hear the shouts of the others, but surely they were concerned. Surely someone would save her! Holding on for dear life, she glanced back briefly. Already many horses were in pursuit, but it was Laris who was in the lead—Laris who bent low over the saddle and raced toward her.

Thank goodness for that love potion.

The horse beneath her was wildly uncontrollable. She'd ridden this mare for years, and Buttercup had never behaved in this way. Verity leaned down and tried to whisper to the animal, to calm her, but the mare was wild. Something was horribly wrong.

The mare was running for the hills, where there were steep drops and rocky cliffs and a rushing river and many, many other places an out-of-control horse should not go.

Again Verity glanced back. No one, not even Laris, was able to keep up.

She would have to rely on herself, she imagined. How annoying. She held on tightly with her arms and her thighs, and she leaned down until she felt as if she were a part of the horse—a part of the wild animal. Her heart pounded too fast, but there was no time to feel sorry for herself. That would come later.

Buttercup bypassed a turn that would've taken them both over a cliff and to their deaths, and Verity sighed in relief even as she was mercilessly jostled and tossed about. The animal stayed on a path which would take them through rough hills and to the river—but not at the crossing place where they were headed on this once-fine morning, where the ferry took horses and people safely across.

"No," Verity whispered as the mare raced headlong toward the banks of the rushing river. "Good heavens, *no!*"

Buttercup did not even slow before flying down the steep bank and plunging into the cold water. For a few moments Verity continued to hold on, and then the animal twisted in a new manner and finally managed to throw her—right into rushing, icy cold water. Verity's traveling gown immediately grew heavy, taking on the weight of the water and dragging her down.

For the first time, she was truly afraid. Not just afraid, but terrified. She'd thought Laris and her lucky talisman and the fact that she knew the mare well and the animal knew her and was accustomed to her voice and weight would protect her. Apparently that was not the case. Nothing and no one was going to save her. She was going to drown.

The current carried Verity along at a frighteningly rapid pace. Now and then she managed to raise her head for a gulp of precious air, but she realized that soon it wouldn't be enough. Soon she'd be dragged to the bottom of the river, where she'd get caught in the rocks, or else she'd just be too exhausted to move and she'd run out of air. What a horrible way to die. Her chest hurt, and she was so cold she felt as if she were encased in ice. She raced along out of control, so fast, so frightened. The world started to go black. Her plans to become empress and have fancy parties and take lovers and have many devoted servants seemed so silly, when all she wanted was to breathe.

Something touched her, and she panicked. Rushing along, cold as ice, not getting enough air, she was grabbed by an animal or a monster that lived deep in the river. She kicked, but had little strength with which to fight. The river beast held on tight, it had her in its grip and would not let go. The monster led Verity up to the surface, and once

again she took a gulp of air. That done, she struggled to
free herself from the grip which held her so firmly, even as
the current took them both. The creature called her name,
screamed her name, and she lifted her head to look at it.

Him, not it. Laris held her. It was Laris who struggled to
keep both her head and his own above water, as the current
steered them toward a nasty-looking outcropping of rocks.

ALIX became more cautious as they neared the village,
where they would be able to buy supplies. According to
Donia it was a small and isolated place, so it was likely that
the news of Princess Edlyn's murder had not reached the
inhabitants. Even if they'd heard everything, they'd expect
Sanura to be blue.

He packed his cloak, which was too fine for a common
traveler, in the saddlebag with what remained of the food
Donia had given them. He'd spent part of a sleepless night
removing imperial insignias from his vest and a pocket of
his trousers, and though the removal left a ragged mark, he
doubted anyone would notice.

The sentinel's sword he carried might alarm anyone
who looked too closely, as it was finely made and not at all
common, but he would not part with it, not even for the
short amount of time they'd be in the village.

"You should not speak," he instructed Sanura as they
approached the town. They left the woods and walked
upon the road, which looked to be well traveled but was
deserted at the moment.

"Why should I not speak?" she asked, openly incensed
by his request. "Are you afraid I will say something stupid?
Do you think I will give away your secrets?"

She had been in a foul mood all morning. "You have an
accent," he said simply. "If we are to pass for common
travelers, it would be best if we do not have to answer questions about where you are from."

"I worked very hard to learn your language, and my accent is not vile."

No, it was not. It was just enough to give her speech an arousing lilt, just enough to set her apart, just enough to make his gut dance in anticipation of what he could never again have. It was also just enough to raise questions. "I will tell any who ask that you are mute."

"Mute!" She ran until she was alongside him. "I will not be able to speak at all! Do you expect me to walk behind you, head down and mouth shut like a meek little wife? Will you call me *woman* so no one will hear you speak my name?"

"Yes," he answered without heat.

She snorted, but did not argue.

"We will not be in town long," he said. He had a plan, of sorts. Though he was not ready to run to Jahn, he did need help. Someone would need to get to Jahn with a message, and Sian Chamblyn was the perfect choice. The enchanter and his wife were regular visitors to the palace. They came and went quite often, so no one would question Sian's request for an audience with the emperor.

Sanura did not argue again, though she was no happier than before. Alix was not thrilled himself. Her bracelets and earrings and girdle had been left behind, but she still sang. She still made music. Now it was the swish of her plain skirt and the sound of her boots in the dirt and the rhythm of her breathing that made music.

Music only he could hear. She was in his blood, and he wouldn't be rid of her until he was *rid* of her. When he proved his innocence and presented Sanura to the emperor as the gift she was intended to be, it was likely she would be released. Still, Jahn was nothing if not unpredictable, and it was also likely that he would keep the scandalous gift simply to annoy the more staid ministers and priests who would certainly be shocked.

Besides, what man would not want her? Bride or no bride, Jahn might very well see the benefits of keeping Sanura. If that happened, there would be no way Alix could remain in the palace and watch the two of them together, knowing what they shared—realizing what he could never have for himself.

"I wish you would stop this," Sanura muttered.

"Stop what?" Alix asked. Was she already tired? Did she need to rest? He turned and looked down at her.

She waved a slender hand at him, in obvious frustration. "Your insides are so jumbled and uncertain, I can see nothing."

"Oh," he said, relieved as he resumed his walk toward town. If his indecision confused her, all the better. He didn't much like the idea of Sanura using her gift to study the very essence of his being.

"It's disconcerting," she explained. "Most men are very simple. Their desires are superficial, and they are easy to read and understand. You are not."

"There is no need for you to understand me at all," he argued.

"That is true, but if we are to journey together for a while longer, then it will be easier for me if I can understand your motives and your intentions."

"I won't hurt you," he assured her, not for the first time.

"I know that."

"Then what's the problem?"

She sighed. "You could never understand."

Alix took a few more steps before saying, "We'll reach the village soon. Perhaps you should practice pretending to be mute for a while."

"That is not at all funny," she said sharply, and then, with pursed lips, she settled into the silence he had requested.

Soon he saw a rustic building in the distance, the first structure of the village where Donia sold baked goods and bought the supplies she could not grow or make on her own. What he could see from this distance was roughly made and plain, but there were a number of buildings which likely supplied all the surrounding farms, as well as the occasional traveler. There they would stock up on supplies and...

His thoughts were interrupted when Sanura grabbed his arm and pulled him back in a display of surprising strength. "Wait," she whispered. "We can't go there."

He had learned not to dismiss her feelings. He'd done so once before, when she'd warned him about Vyrn, and that had led to disaster. They were still a good distance from the town, so whatever she was sensing must be very strong. "What's wrong?"

Her black hair was pulled back into a braid, much as his was, and he was still unaccustomed to the paleness of her skin. Her eyes were a brilliant blue, now that they did not have to compete with the blue paint that had covered her face until yesterday. He'd thought she'd be less tempting when she was presented like other women, without the paint, without the sensuous clothing, without the jangling gold. Somehow she was more tempting than before.

Her hand on his arm was warm, and she gripped him tightly.

"Fear," she whispered. "Fear and...violence, the same violence I sensed from Vyrn in the early days of the journey." Her eyes caught and held his. "I think he might be there. We must not go to the village. He is there, looking for us."

"And the fear?" Alix asked.

Sanura's face paled. "It is the fear of many. That is why it's so strong."

Alix placed his hand over hers. "If what you sense is truth, then I cannot turn away."

She blinked twice and her spine straightened, then she sighed. "I know."

VYRN leaned forward to place his face close to that of the innkeeper who was bound to a plain wooden chair from his own common room. The man was middle-aged and gone to fat and his hair was more gray than brown, and he was very, very stubborn. The two of them were alone in this room made for merriment, drink, and food. The Tryfynian soldier Rolf held many of the village's residents prisoner in the feed and metalwork shop two doors down from the inn. Vyrn had insisted on speaking to the innkeeper alone. No one else could know of his actions and his plans, especially not Rolf.

His plan to divide the searchers had been a brilliant one.

"Simply admit to the truth, and this will all be over very quickly." So far everyone he had spoken to had denied seeing any strangers of late. A blue woman and a prince would've stood out quite prominently in this backwater village, so he had to assume they were telling the truth. However, a witness or two who could claim to have seen the odd couple, and perhaps even overheard a confession, would lend credence to the story Vyrn had fabricated.

"They stayed here, surely," Vyrn said calmly as he grabbed a strand of the older man's thin hair and yanked the innkeeper's head to one side. "I imagine you heard them share whispers of confidence, I'm *sure* you overheard them bragging about the murder of a defenseless princess from Tryfyn."

The innkeeper knew what Vyrn was capable of. Upon their arrival, the villagers had been welcoming enough. They didn't see many travelers, and it was thought that a sentinel, an official representative of Columbyana, might bring news and gossip from the capital city. It wasn't long before Vyrn made his purpose known, and he'd shown them that he had no patience with those who could not deliver what he requested. Those who had given him trouble had been restrained. Those prisoners and the cowards who did not dare to act were all in Rolf's care.

One overly enthusiastic young man had made the foolish mistake of rushing Vyrn with a tiny dagger in one hand, and had taken a sword to the gut for his folly. The body still lay on the town's muddy, main street.

The innkeeper had seemed to be the perfect choice as a

corroborator. One could not expect a woman like Sanura and a prince to sleep on the ground. They would've sought out a bed, a roof, warm food, the bath they so desperately needed. It would be perfectly believable that an innkeeper might overhear their conversation.

And yet the stubborn old man insisted on telling the truth, even now.

So far Vyrn had limited his blows of persuasion to the midsection, where the marks he made would not be seen. A bruised and bloody witness would not be as believable as one who appeared to be unharmed. Still, if the old man refused to cooperate...

"Are you looking for me?"

His heart skipped a beat as he straightened and spun about. The prince himself stood just inside the rear door to the rustic inn. Prince Alixandyr held a sword steady in one hand, and he was not at all surprised or concerned.

Vyrn knew that if he shouted loud enough, Rolf would hear and would come running to his aid, but it would be so much better if he could simply kill the prince and be done with it. That had been the plan from the moment he'd seen Prince Alixandyr enter Sanura's tent, after all. Kill the princess, frame the prince for the deed, and then see him dead so he could collect that additional pay from his employer.

"Thank goodness I have found you, m'lord," Vyrn said with a smile. He stepped toward the prince. "After you fled, we discovered the true murderer. It was Tari, that plain, mousy maid." And that was true enough. How convenient that the woman he had chosen to use as his accomplice had been so eager to do her part. "She was jealous of the princess's privilege, I suppose."

He expected the prince to lower his sword in relief, but that did not happen.

The blasted innkeeper was no help. "Do not listen to him, m'lord! He means you harm."

"Yes, I know," the prince responded. "What I don't

know is why." He moved forward, poised as if ready to strike, coiled like a venomous snake. "Why, Vyrn?" he asked coldly.

Vyrn drew his sword. It would've been easier to make his move while the prince was unprepared, but he was certain his skills were a match, even in a fair fight. After all, of late the prince had spent more time as a politician than as a soldier. Perhaps once he had been a fearsome opponent, but those days were gone.

"Sentinels receive a miserly pay, m'lord," Vyrn said as he sidestepped, his eyes never leaving the prince's face. "I found another who is willing to pay much more handsomely."

"You became a traitor to your country for money?" The prince sounded incredulous, as if the concept were unthinkable.

"Yes, I suppose I did."

Vyrn lunged forward, hoping to take his opponent by surprise, but his maneuver was expected and easily evaded. Blades met, again and again, as they danced among and around the plain wooden furnishings and a bound old man who had proved most unhelpful. Vyrn soon found himself sweating, struggling to interpret and outwit the prince's tactics.

Apparently the prince had maintained his sword-fighting skills more diligently than Vyrn had realized. Soon Vyrn was tiring more quickly than his adversary, his moves became entirely defensive, and he was unable to make a single offensive strike. Sweat trickled down his face, and his arm trembled. He backed toward the front door of the inn. If he could escape and call for help, the prince would have no chance. He would be no match for Vyrn's sword when it was combined with the fury of a Tryfynian soldier who believed the prince guilty of murdering one of his own.

Vyrn stepped backward, his eyes remaining fixed on the prince's intense face. He had not bargained for this. He had not bargained for real combat. Fairness was highly overrated, and had never been one of Vyrn's sought-after attributes.

A few more steps, and he'd be able to make a run for it.

Without warning the wind was knocked from his lungs and he hit the floor hard, with a weight atop him. The old man, bound to a chair and badly beaten, had found a surge of energy and had lunged forward to knock Vyrn to the ground. The man and the chair to which he was attached scooted away quickly, and then the prince was there, kicking away Vyrn's sword and placing the tip of his own blade to Vyrn's throat.

He opened his mouth to scream for help, and in answer the prince pressed the blade more deeply into Vyrn's throat, drawing a little blood. "Shout, and you'll be dead an instant later."

He could not very well spend his hard-earned money if he was dead. "Don't kill me! I'll tell you everything I know. Please." The prince looked as if he could do murder. In a small voice Vyrn said, "I surrender."

For now.

"HOW many?" Alix asked crisply. Vyrn's former prisoner responded.

"One other."

Alix knew he could easily take care of two, but his mind sought another way. For all he knew, Vyrn was the only one involved in the scam. The others likely believed him guilty of murder, and he could not imagine killing a good man for believing what he'd been told—what he'd been shown.

"Sanura," he called in a slightly elevated voice, "it's safe to come in." She had been waiting outside the rear entrance, and was inside the room before he'd finished his sentence. "Free the prisoner," he instructed.

She did as he'd requested, taking Alix's dagger from his belt and then dropping to her knees to cut the bonds. The older man and his chair were on the floor, both lying to one side.

The freed captive needed to be assisted to his feet, and he gladly took Sanura's hand for that assistance. "The sentinel said you were blue," he said as he rubbed his reddened wrists. "I should've known he was mad."

Sanura did not respond to that comment, but remained silent and tense.

"Tie him up," Alix ordered, his eyes flitting briefly to Sanura and then to the remains of the bonds Vyrn had used on his prisoner.

He was distracted for only a moment, but it was enough. Vyrn burst into action. He rolled toward the door, grabbed for his sword, and screamed loudly for help.

Alix made sure that Sanura and the gray-haired man were behind him and safe. "I will kill you," he promised the traitorous sentinel.

The door burst open and the Tryfynian soldier Rolf entered the room, his sword ready, his eyes blazing with anger. "You murdering bastard," the big man said as he stepped forward.

"No!" the gray-haired man behind him shouted. "The prince is innocent. I heard the sentinel himself admit as much."

"The innkeeper is lying," Vyrn said through clenched teeth.

"He said it was someone named Tari," the innkeeper added.

"Don't listen to him," Vyrn snapped. "No doubt the prince has offered this poor man a nice reward for such lies. Who knows how much the old man has been paid for his assistance?"

The innkeeper's words had made the Tryfynian doubt what he believed to be true. Alix could see the uncertainty in his eyes, in the set of his mouth and, most important, in the way he held his weapon.

"We were made to look guilty by those who want death and war," Sanura said softly. There was strength and serenity in her voice. Who would not believe her when she spoke so? "Do you want war, Rolf, or do you want the truth?"

The soldier heard the truth in Sanura's voice, just as Alix did. Rolf's brows drew together, his sword fell. For a moment, one fleeting moment, Alix believed this could all be over very soon. If Rolf believed, then others would, too. He never should've run from camp and made himself look guilty ... but then, he had not actually been the one to run. That had been the other, the darker half of himself. His moment of relief did not last long, as Vyrn swung about and ran his blade through Rolf's midsection.

Rolf fell, realizing too late whom he could trust and whom he could not.

Vyrn backed toward the door. He did not like being outnumbered. He faced Alix's sword, the innkeeper's raised chair, and Sanura's knife. Alix made to follow, sure he could take the man on his own, but at that moment a thin, gray-haired woman rushed into view.

The traitorous sentinel grabbed her by the collar of her dress and held her body before his. "This is no longer a fair fight, m'lord."

"I did not know you were interested in fairness." Alix stopped his pursuit when Vyrn's stance changed and he held the edge of his sword to the woman's throat. One gentle motion, and she'd be dead.

"You should not have killed Rolf, m'lord," Vyrn said loudly, his words meant for the ears of those who streamed onto the boardwalk. "You should not have killed that poor boy who lies on the street." He smiled.

"Lies," Alix said. "And these people know it."

Vyrn made his way toward his horse. "These are *your* people, m'lord. They would likely say anything you ordered them to say. Do you really think the Tryfynians will believe their words of defense? Do you think the king who will soon bury his precious daughter will believe you to be innocent simply because your own people spin a protective tale?"

Vyrn made the woman he held hostage unhitch his waiting horse, and with the sword steady he put a foot into the stirrup and sat a well-worn saddle. The long blade of his sword remained threatening until he drew it away swiftly, then turned and spurred his horse down the street. The people watched him go. More than one held their breath as the man who had terrorized them escaped.

"Will you give chase, m'lord?" the innkeeper asked.

Alix longed to do just that, but with Sanura riding with him he'd have no chance of catching Vyrn, and he refused to leave her here unattended. If Vyrn turned back . . . if the other soldiers came here and found her . . . "No." He sheathed his sword and turned to face the innkeeper. "When I arrived, Vyrn was attempting to coerce you into admitting that you heard my confession. I can see for myself that he hit you several times. He might've killed you. Why did you not simply give him what he wanted?"

In spite of his pain, the old man smiled. "You don't remember me, do you, m'lord?"

"Have we met?" Alix searched his memory and came up with nothing.

"During the war with Ciro and his Own, you and a handful of other sentinels came to my rescue. More rightly, you came to my daughter's rescue. She was only nine years old at the time. You stood toe-to-toe with a monster and protected us."

The man's face was familiar, in a vague way. "I fought my share of monsters during the war, as did many others," Alix said, "but I was never in this village."

"No. I lived near my wife's family at that time. We moved here three years ago." The innkeeper gave Alix a belated and oddly graceful bow. "There are many who do not know that a soldier who fought Ciro and saved many became prince, but as I spent some time in Arthes, I know. I saw you in a holiday procession there shortly before I settled in this small town. Yours is a face I will never forget. I owe you a debt."

"Consider that debt paid," Alix said.

The old man grinned. "Not quite yet, m'lord."

* * *

PAKI did not care for the sentinels or the Tryfynian soldiers who believed the blessed Sanura was capable of murder. Still, following the heathens would likely be the easiest way to find the woman he protected. It certainly would make no sense for them to return to Tryfyn without her.

Sooner or later they would find Sanura and the man who had dared to touch her. She, they would protect with their lives.

The prince would die.

Paki and Kontar both felt shame for losing their weapons to the prince, for however brief a time, so they remained vigilant. They were confident that they would find Sanura, one way or another.

When the soldiers had paired up and gone in four separate directions, Paki and Kontar had chosen to follow the two they disliked the least. The Tryfynians and the Columbyanans were not well suited to one another. They did not trust one another—which was why each group of two was made up of a representative from each country. All those who searched had become frustrated at the fruitlessness of their efforts, and they snapped at one another over the smallest matters.

Paki and Kontar traveled at a short distance from the others. They did not care about the murder of the princess; they cared only for Sanura and the fact that the heathen prince had touched her, openly and defiantly.

More than once during this leg of the journey Paki had suffered a rush of fear. Would a man who would stoop to butchering a defenseless princess do the same to Sanura? Was her body somewhere in the woods along the road they'd traveled for the past two days?

He wondered if Kontar had considered that possibility. "Do you think he killed her?"

"Perhaps." Kontar's face remained calm, but his fingers flexed. "His eyes were less than sane when he took our weapons from us. Men with such eyes are capable of any atrocity, I would imagine."

Paki did not like being reminded of that dishonorable moment when they'd had their weapons taken away. "We have failed miserably in our task. What if we don't find her?"

"We must," Kontar said. "We must find her. Dead or alive, she is ours to protect."

Paki patted the distended saddlebag where Sanura's box of implements rested. When they found her, she would need repair of her blue. The heathen prince had smudged the paint when he'd dared to grab her.

The soldiers who led this small party changed direction and headed toward a farmhouse which sat in the distance. Gentle puffs of smoke rose from the chimney. It appeared to be a peaceful and simple home.

"If he is here and alone, don't kill him immediately."

"Why not?" Kontar asked, outrage in his voice.

"We must know where Sanura is, even if she no longer lives."

Reluctantly, Kontar nodded in agreement. "He will tell us all we wish to know, and then we will kill him."

"Slowly," Paki said.

"Of course."

"WE can't stay here very long," Alix said as he followed Sanura up the stairs of the inn where they'd spent most of the day. "Vyrn could come back with others, and if he does..."

"Vyrn won't return to this village," she assured him. "As I told you earlier, he does not like the numbers being stacked against him, and he does not want to take the chance that some of his comrades might believe you and the innkeeper, as Rolf did. There were many witnesses to the death of an innocent villager, and more than one witness to Rolf's death. Even if he can round up all the others on such short notice, he cannot and will not bring them here, to the site of his defeat." She reached the top of the stairs and turned toward the room the innkeeper had assigned them.

"You seem so sure," Alix said in a low voice.

"Do you remember that I told you most men are very easy to understand?"

"Yes."

"Vyrn is like most men, simple and even primitive in his thinking. He believes himself to be clever, but in fact he is little more than an animal in a man's skin." She shuddered. Vyrn was an animal who would kill without conscience anything and anyone who got in his way. He was the worst of men, worse even than the shadow Alix fought. Even though Trystan was primitive, Alix was always there to curb his appetites.

"Besides," she added, "you need to sleep, and I crave a night in a warm, soft bed. Just a single night before we take to the road again." She forced a haughty expression onto her face, and wondered how she might look without the blue which was so much a part of her. "I would also like a hot bath, scented oils, a dress which does not scratch, shoes which are not falling apart, my gold bracelets, and a bowl of freshly sliced *tangitos*."

"What are *tangitos*?"

"A red and lusciously sweet fruit, which grows only on the island of Claennis, and a craving which is as unlikely to be granted as the others." What she really wanted, the craving she refused to voice because she knew it would be denied, was Alix.

"We will leave before sunrise," he said.

Before entering the small room they would share for the night, Sanura attempted to look deeply into Alix once more. At the moment he was not so complicated, not so difficult to understand.

Perhaps more than one of her wishes would come true after all.

Chapter Ten

THE small inn where they found themselves for the night was situated in a village which saw few travelers or visitors, so he could've insisted upon a separate room for himself. He had not. Sanura was correct when she said he needed to sleep, and Alix knew he could not rest if she was out of his sight. She was positive Vyrn would not return to this village. He could not be so sure.

While the room they would share could not compare with the luxury and spaciousness of the palace Alix now called home, it was certainly acceptable. The chamber was small, but was large enough to accommodate the wide bed, a bedside table, a battered desk, and a chair. A tattered rug covered much of the wooden floor, and though the bedcovers and the curtain over the single window were threadbare, they were clean, as were the sheets which covered the thick, sagging mattress.

The past two nights had been spent with the ground as a bed, so perhaps he was being too kind, yet Alix did take some comfort in this clean, private room.

He had not been able to obtain all that Sanura desired,

but he had managed to arrange for a basin of warm water and clean towels, a better-fitting pair of walking boots purchased on credit from the innkeeper, a waterskin for their coming days of travel, and a warm supper which they had shared in the room. The innkeeper's blushing daughter had delivered the food. She was no longer the child he had supposedly saved, but was a pretty and shy young woman who lived a quiet, safe life. Alix tried to remember saving her but could not. He had fought so many monsters in that damned war.

A single candle burned, and by its light Sanura slowly removed the dress she'd bought from Donia. The sight was enough to make Alix forget old battles—and new ones. Perhaps she did not intend her disrobing to be seductive, but it was, painfully so. She could not make a move which was not arousing. The way her freshly brushed hair swayed, the way her arms moved so gracefully, the way she turned her head... they were all seductive. Her sensuousness was a part of her, just as the darkness was a part of him. They could never escape who they truly were. Never.

When she was completely naked, Sanura opened the sack which held the broken leaves that would clean the blue stain from her skin—and Alix's. She grabbed one and walked slowly toward the bed where he sat. His eyes were drawn to the blueness of her breasts and hips, to the line where her golden skin turned to blue. He could not forget being inside her, could not forget the sensation of her body swaying into his to meet his thrust. She did not demur, showed no hint of shyness, of modesty. She was entirely bare and comfortable with her nakedness, as if it were the most natural thing in the world to present herself to him thus.

"Will you?" she asked simply, offering him the broken leaf.

Alix hesitated. "Are you trying to seduce me?"

"Yes," she whispered. "Is it working?"

"Yes," he answered honestly.

She smiled, and her smile was as seductive as the sway of her breasts and the movement of her hips when she walked. Everything in him came alive, twitched and screamed for what he knew he could not—should not—have.

"I do not fool myself into believing that we can be mated forever," she said sensibly, "but that does not mean we cannot enjoy what we both want in this perilous time. As I watched you fight with Vyrn, I realized with great clarity that our lives are very uncertain. If I die tomorrow, I will be very glad that this night was one of joy. If I find myself at the end of a hangman's noose for a crime I did not commit, I might die with a smile on my face as I remember a finer moment."

"The fact that our lives are uncertain does not free us to take anything we wish."

"Not anything, perhaps, but we can have one another for a while." Sanura sat beside him on the bed, offering her body for his attentions. He did not rush, but gently ran the broken end of the plant over the swell of her breasts until they were as rosy as her cheeks, unstained and unmarked. There were many other places on her body which remained blue, and he gave them all his attention. Her thighs, her hips, the rounded cheeks of her ass, they all needed his ministrations.

Now and then he lifted the plant from her and replaced it with his hand, stroking her bared and clean flesh, absorbing her heat and reveling in the comfort of simply touching her.

"I know you worry about him who lurks within you," Sanura said as he stroked his fingers along her spine, "but you are so much stronger than he, Alix."

"Am I?"

"Yes," she whispered.

She did not speak again as he finished tending to her. Often she closed her eyes and seemed to savor every brush of the leaf, every warming sweep of his hand. As he saw to the task, he studied every inch of her body with leisure, in a way he had not before. He had never allowed himself the luxury of admiring her this way. He had always been too cautious, too aware. Too afraid.

Now and then he gave in to temptation and placed his mouth on her, tasting the warm flesh she offered so willingly, losing himself in her scent, her warmth, the flavor of her skin. How could there be anything evil or wrong in something which felt so good? How could a darkness he had suppressed all his life keep him from taking something which was only right? If he walked away from Sanura, did that darkness win another battle? Did it make him die inside a little more?

When the job was done and her skin was entirely free of the blue stain, Sanura began to undress Alix, her movements slow as she removed his vest, his shirt, his belt, and then his trousers. Like her, earlier he had removed only the paint which was visible when he was dressed, and beneath his clothes he was well marked as one who had touched that which was not his.

At the moment he did not care that Sanura wasn't his to take. He wanted her anyway. He certainly wished to believe what she said about taking joy while their lives were uncertain, and he wanted to believe that he was indeed much stronger than the shadows he had always fought. He'd lived his life restrained by caution, afraid to release what he knew slept within him. He was tired of being cautious, of not living fully and taking what that life offered.

There was joy in this, in touching, in pleasure, in the promise of so much more which danced just out of reach.

He waited for that dark part of him he denied to speak up, to urge him with a whisper to conquer or harm this woman who had changed his life, but the other remained silent. Maybe that part of him was sleeping. Maybe it was finally dead, killed by the myriad emotions Sanura brought to the surface.

Alix had always denied himself emotions, believing them to be a weakness which might awaken his demon. Perhaps that was wrong. Perhaps those emotions which marked him as entirely human meant the end of a darkness which was entirely unhuman.

Sanura removed the blue stain from his thighs, where those thighs had once rubbed against hers. She worked gently on a spot of blue on his side. Her fingers were warm, especially when they followed the touch of the cooling leaf. When all else had been cleaned, she rubbed a bit of the leaf's substance onto the palm of her hand and stroked his erection. Alix closed his eyes and savored the fluttering of her fingers, the strength of her palm, the stroke which almost sent him over the edge. The touch was cold and hot, and it was possessive in a way he had not expected.

"In all my life, I have never had a choice like this one," Sanura whispered as she stroked. "I was always told that I should feel honored and blessed to be a woman of the Agnese, that I should be pleased that men wanted to possess me. You tell me that it is somehow wrong, that I should wish to be free to make my own choices, to be my own woman. The idea of true freedom is frightening. What if I choose poorly? Who will take care of me if I make a mistake?" She leaned down and took a moment to kiss his throat, to run her hands slowly down his thighs and then back up again to grab his hard length and stroke it. "In my lifetime I have been sold and I have been given away, I have been treasured and pampered and taken care of. In Tryfyn I was feared and restrained and finally given away, as if my presence were a nuisance. In all that time, I have never chosen a man."

She straddled him with strong pale thighs and guided him to her, into her wet heat. "I choose you, Prince Alixandyr. Because my body wants yours, because my heart feels something I do not understand, because in my soul I am yours ... I choose you."

She should not choose him. He was broken. The sad thought rushed through Alix even as he reveled in the feel of her warm body around him.

"You are not broken," she whispered as she moved slowly, swaying into him and up, then plunging down to take him all again.

"You can read my mind?" he asked.

"No, I read your soul, Alix. When we are linked, I see your very soul, I see all that you are, all that you want. Together this way, linked and soaring, we are truly as one."

She saw him, she saw all of him, and she was not frightened by all that he was.

Sanura's words stopped and her speed increased. She rose and fell quickly, stroking him, taking him deep, accepting all of him, body and soul. She undulated over and against him until she found completion with an arch of her back and a strangled cry. As her inner muscles clenched and unclenched, Alix gave over to his own fulfillment, and in that moment everything else went away and there was nothing in the world but her body and his. Nothing.

Sanura collapsed atop him and settled her head on his shoulder. "I feel so much better," she whispered, and then she sighed and pressed her lips to his neck. "Do we really have to bother to prove our innocence? How do we prove that Vyrn and Tari did the horrible deed? What if no one believes us?" She rose and smiled down at him. "I think we should collect Mali and make our way to the coast, where we will steal a boat and sail to an island near Claennis. This island is small and verdant and warm, and no one would ever find us there."

It was a nice enough fantasy, and was very much like his own. "Would we live on *tangitos*?" he teased.

"*Tangitos* and fish and sex," she clarified.

With one hand, Alix shifted her face so her lips were upon his. He very gently moved his mouth against hers, allowing himself to get lost in the simple touch. When he started to draw away, she stopped him with her hands on his face.

"Don't stop," she whispered almost frantically. "My first kiss should not be so quick."

"FIRST kiss?" Alix whispered.

Sanura nodded as she pressed her mouth to his. Kissing

was very nice, and much more powerful than she had expected it to be. It sent chills down her spine, it sent a spark of fire through her blood.

Alix rolled her onto her back without breaking the kiss. He held her, kissed her, cared for her in a way no other man ever had.

It was nice not being blue, not being untouchable.

For tonight she had Alix alone, without the darkness of Trystan. Of course, Trystan knew that when they were joined, she could see into his soul, and he did not wish her to see him clearly. Why? Was there a weakness he hid? A vulnerability he wished to keep from her?

Alix's tongue slipped into her mouth and she forgot Trystan. "This is so very nice," she whispered, her breath mingling with his. "If we were to run away, we could kiss all the time."

He did not have to say aloud that running was not his way. She felt it. He wished for the same simple things she did, the same simple life, but he denied himself, as he had always done.

"I know what I must do," he said as he kissed his way down her throat.

"Yes, so do I," she responded breathlessly as she caught his hips between her thighs.

He laughed—*laughed*—with his lovely mouth between her breasts. "That, too, but that's not what I meant."

"What did you mean, then?" And how could he think of anything else when they were entangled so?

"I have been hesitant to go directly to my brother, because I don't entirely trust myself. More correctly, I don't trust the other, the darkness."

"You are afraid of what Trystan might do if he rises while in your brother's presence," she clarified.

"Exactly so," Alix said with a rush of sadness. "And yet, we cannot continue to run, we can't hide forever. Like it or not, I need Jahn's help. We will go to Jahn, through Sian Chamblyn if need be, and we will tell him everything."

"You said it yourself. No one will believe us without

proof. There will be war," she whispered. She feared what would happen when they were no longer alone, when they had to face and deal with others.

"Perhaps, but as things stand, there will be war in any case. I don't know how to prove our innocence, but perhaps Jahn will have some ideas. He's very clever that way."

The brilliant shine of her happiness dimmed. "So, we will go to Arthes and you will give me to your brother, as was intended."

For a moment Alix was silent, and then he said, "No. I will not."

He did not elaborate, and she did not ask him to. Instead, she snuggled against him and rested there, in a way she had never before been able to do. Her life was in shambles, yet she was not alone. Everything she knew of who she was, who she'd been meant to be, did not work in this new land. She did not want to think of that tonight, not when this man she had chosen held her so well. They settled onto their sides, still in one another's arms. Her soft chest against his hard one was a comfort. His hands, hands which touched her as if she were truly precious, caressed and held and explored.

Soon Alix was ready again, and so was she, so she was not surprised when he rolled her onto her back and filled her quickly and thoroughly. "I will never give you away, not to anyone, not for any reason. You're mine, Sanura." He was still, deep inside her and so very still. "You're mine," he said again, truly believing the words for the first time. "Jahn will understand, and if he doesn't, I will fight him for you. I will take you, if I must." He began to move, to arouse her, to make her truly his own. "In our lifetimes he has possessed many things I wished for myself. I have never thought of fighting him for anything, I've never even dreamed of taking that which might be mine but was not. Not until now."

"Yes," she said simply.

"I love you, Sanura."

She had heard those words before, uttered by Zeryn in

moments of passion, but she had never felt them the way she did now: pure and bright and so true it seemed nothing could ever dull the brightness. "Yes."

He stopped speaking, but then, they needed no words. They spoke with their bodies, moving with the rhythm of their heartbeats, whispering with the linking of their souls. Sanura was far from an untouched maiden knowing a man's touch for a first time, and yet in many ways this was a first for her. First choice, first surrender, first love.

"I love you, too," she whispered as she began to climax once again. "Alix, I love you."

Again they found blissful release, and then Alix kissed her again. Moments later he was asleep, and she cuddled against him to get her own rest. She was not glad that Princess Edlyn was dead, but she could not help but be happy that circumstances had led her from the path which had been set before her. "I am yours," she whispered to a sleeping Alix. "I am so very much yours."

She fell asleep snuggled against his side, and had dreams of *tangitos* and Alix.

VERITY shivered so hard her teeth clattered. Being wet and cold had been difficult enough when the sun was shining, but now that they walked in darkness, the chill cut her to the bone. Her hair was a matted, undignified mess. Her once-fine blue riding ensemble was filthy, wet, and torn in many places. Her shoes squished. But most of all, she was cold. She dearly hated to be cold!

Only one hand was warm. The hand Laris held in his own.

"How much farther?" she asked.

"I'm not sure," he said. His voice didn't crack and flutter as hers did, but he had to be every bit as cold. "If we follow the riverbank, eventually we'll come to the path your horse took."

Eventually. That was less than comforting.

He had asked her more than once what had happened to

spook her horse, and each time she'd told him she had no idea. At the moment she didn't care. Cold and miserable and lost, she was so blasted glad to be alive that she didn't care what had happened.

"I really should thank you again for jumping in after me. I'm not a good swimmer at all."

"You've thanked me enough," Laris said, his voice affectionate and gentle. He had a nice voice, which made her glad she'd chosen him to be the recipient of the love potion.

She was not only glad to be alive, she was very glad not to be alone in the forest. Critters scurried here and there, though none came too close, and at times her imagination ran away with her. All her life she had heard stories of vicious shape-shifters that lived in the forest, of monsters which owned the night in such dim places, of dark witches who practiced spells much more ominous than love spells and lucky talismans.

"My feet hurt," she said in a small voice. "Can we rest awhile?"

Laris stopped, turned to her, and without warning lifted her into his arms. She was so surprised, she squealed a little. "I didn't mean that you should carry me! I'm too heavy."

"You are not," he protested.

"My dress alone is heavy, wet as it is."

"Your clothing is more damp than wet at this point," he argued.

Verity pursed her lips. Was she going to be forced to purchase an obedience potion as well as a love potion? Laris's step slowed, but he held her snugly as he moved through the forest. The river rushed to their right. To their left, forest creatures scurried and chirped. Eventually she rested her head on Laris's fine and equally damp shoulder. To think she had once been willing to let him die for coming to her, when his presence in her tent had been at her initiation. No, if it had come to that, she would not have allowed anyone to hurt him, even though her reputation would've been ruined and no matter what Mavise said about her destiny, the emperor would not have chosen her. Emperor Jahn would likely not want to wed a woman who sought comfort in the arms of one of his sentinels, even if that comfort was of a nonsexual nature.

Well, mostly nonsexual.

Of course, she *could* make use of the love potion, if it came to that. It was obviously quite effective.

Before much time had passed, Verity found herself drifting off to sleep in Laris's arms. Jostled, held precariously, she slept. She even dreamed. She woke momentarily when Laris placed her on the ground in a small and shallow cave which protected them from the wind, but went right back to sleep as he settled himself beside her and took her in his arms. She woke again, just as momentarily, when he hooked his leg around hers in his sleep, as if she might escape if he didn't hold her fast. She dreamed of being caught in the river's swift current, but she did not panic as even in her dreams Laris was there.

When she woke again, Laris's hand was clamped over her mouth, and he crushed his body against hers. For the span of a heartbeat, she panicked. What was he doing? Why?

And then she heard the voices, speaking not far away. Surely hours had passed, but the night remained dark.

"She must be dead!" one man's voice insisted. "It is only logical."

"I need proof, not logic."

This voice Verity recognized. It was that ass, Wallis. She'd show him she was not dead! Laris would not allow her to move, much less speak. He held her tightly, much too tightly. Didn't he recognize the voices of those from their party? She tried to pat his arm in assurance, but she could barely move.

"The horse threw her into the river, just as I planned." This time Verity recognized the voice of the sentinel Cavan. She became still.

"A cliff would've been better," Wallis said, sounding

very disappointed. "Then we would've had a body to present for proof of her unfortunate demise." He cleared his throat. "The mare carries no signs of the agitating herb you gave it?"

Verity held her breath. Buttercup's strange actions had been planned! Wallis and Cavan wanted her dead! Her brows knit together. Why would anyone want her dead? She was pretty and sweet-tempered and only a little bit spoiled.

Instead of fighting Laris, she held on a bit tighter. In response he eased the hand that rested over her mouth.

"What of the other sentinel, Laris?" Wallis asked. "Was that his name?"

"The fool jumped into the river to save the girl," Cavan scoffed. "I knew he was sweet on the girl, but I had no idea he'd give his own life in an attempt to rescue her."

"What if he *did* save her? What if they're both alive?"

"Then they will blithely and ignorantly make their way back to us, and we will try again," Cavan said calmly. "If the girl lives, and I doubt that's possible, Laris will deliver her to us like the obedient sentinel that he is. Never fear, m'lord. If by some miracle she survived, she won't last much longer."

The two men were walking away from the cave now, heading toward the riverbank, where they no doubt hoped to find her battered and broken body. Verity felt a tear slip from her eye. They didn't even use her name. She was just *the girl*, a nuisance to be dealt with. How dare they?

When all had been silent for a while, and she was certain the men who had tried to kill her were gone, she whispered, "They want me dead!"

"So I heard," Laris whispered. His body remained atop hers, warm and hard and wonderfully protective.

"They gave Buttercup something which might very well have killed her!"

"It sounds as though the animal is well," Laris assured her.

"She had better be." It was bad enough that they'd attempted to kill her. If they harmed Buttercup... "What are we going to do?"

Laris stroked a strand of horribly mussed hair away from her face. "I will take you to Arthes myself, Lady Verity. You will be safe there. The emperor will protect you." He kissed her forehead. "He is a good man." The words were grudging, but seemed honest enough.

"I'm sure he is," she responded.

At the moment Verity didn't want or need the emperor to protect her. She had Laris.

THEY'D gotten an early start, leaving the inn well before first light. Now that Alix had a plan of sorts, he seemed to be in better spirits. There was less turmoil, less of that annoying indecision which made him difficult to read. Sanura smiled as they walked through the forest. She grinned as they rode together on horseback for a while. When they stopped for a break at midday, she kissed Alix for no reason. Not for seduction, not to reach more deeply inside him for the purposes of her gift, not for any reason but that she wanted to kiss him.

Sanura had this nonsensical feeling that all was right with the world, even though logically she knew very little was right. She and Alix might never be able to prove their innocence. The murder of the princess would very likely bring war. Given the opportunity, Vyrn would kill them both. Paki and Kontar would not hesitate to take Alix's head.

But he loved her. She knew it to be true, because she felt that love so very strongly. Alix had never loved before, not like this. He had never given so much of himself to any woman, yet he gave all of himself to her. And she loved him! Just a few days ago she had wondered if she was capable of love, and here she was awash in its brilliance. She was loved. She loved.

And she was happy, perhaps truly happy for the first time in her life.

It was late afternoon when they stopped to rest the horse and feed the animal another handful of oats. There was a stream nearby where they could refill their waterskin and wash their faces. This time of year in this part of the world, the nights were cool and the days were warm. The land was coming alive with spring. There were wildflowers and butterflies and fresh green buds on the trees, no matter what path they took.

Since leaving her home Sanura had often bemoaned the coldness and the ugliness of this new land, but today, thanks to Alix and the coming of spring, she saw the beauty in this strange place.

After washing her face and refilling the waterskin, she crept up behind Alix. He stood very still in a clearing where his horse grazed, his back stiff, shoulders back and spine rigid. Once again, he was in turmoil so that he was difficult for her to read. She lifted a hand to offer the small comfort of a hand on his back, but his voice stopped her.

"Don't touch me."

A chill danced down Sanura's spine. The change in his voice was subtle, but she heard it. She heard the nuance, the tension. The darkness. She knew, even before he turned to look down at her with those empty dark eyes, that Trystan was back.

"What are you doing here?" she asked, hiding her surprise by keeping her face and her voice calm.

"I told you I was going to reemerge. Didn't you believe me?" He gave her a chilling smile.

She had been able to summon Trystan and send him away. It was a power no one else possessed, and she wondered if she had that power because Alix had loved her from the beginning.

"Go away," she said confidently. "I want Alix."

Unconcerned, he leaned down and placed his nose close to hers. "You can't have him."

The confidence in his voice gave her a fright. Was Trystan so strong now? No. She had not been lying when she'd told Alix that he was the strong one, that he was in control. "You cannot stay," she said. *"Go."*

He reached around and grabbed her long braid, holding on tightly as he yanked her forward. "I'm not going anywhere."

She sensed a new strength in him, a new confidence, and it scared her. All her newfound happiness was washed away.

"I have you to thank for this, Sanura," Trystan said. "You're the one who weakened his defenses. You're the one who paved the way for me to emerge once and for all. He was right to fear giving in to you, but you insisted. And you got your way, didn't you? You seduced him, you made him want what he should not have." His smile was wicked. "When the one you call Alix broke all his own rules to have you, he knocked down the wall that had kept me under control for more than thirty years. I've been struggling all that time, I've been fighting to breathe and act and touch and control. My moments of victory were always brief and difficult, but that has changed. I'm free, and it was you who finally let me loose."

"No!" she whispered.

"And now, thanks to you, I'm going to have everything I want." He sounded so certain, as if he had not a single doubt.

"What is it that you want?" she whispered.

She had commented before that the slash of his eyebrows and the slant of his eyes could make Alix look demonic, malicious, and even soulless. He looked that way now, as he wrapped her long braid tightly around his wrist and tugged. "Everything that was once his will now be mine."

"You want all which was Alix's?"

"No, I want all which was Alix's as well as all that belongs to the other one."

"Your brother?"

"*His* brother, more rightly. I have no kin, no bonds of

blood, no soul. When *his* brother is dead by my hand, I'll be emperor."

She would shake her head, but he held her so tightly, so fast, she could not move her head. "Alix won't allow that to happen."

"Alix will soon be entirely gone."

Sanura almost cried in relief. *Soon*, Trystan said. At least for now, there was still a chance that Alix would once again take control. Perhaps she had not killed the man she loved by making him love her, by tempting him to take what they both wanted. If he didn't come back, it was her fault—hers and hers alone. She hit his hard chest with the palm of her hand. "Send Alix back *now*!"

The face she loved took on a smug and evil expression as the lips that had kissed her so well whispered once again, "No."

Chapter Eleven

THE one she called Trystan caught Sanura up in a grip she could not fight against. He held her tight, and he liked the feel of her body against his. He smiled. *His* body. What wonderful words those were.

There was more than a touch of fear in Sanura's eyes. She was afraid of him for so many reasons. She didn't know if he would kill her or fuck her. In truth, he wanted to do both, but for the moment he would do neither. If he joined with her, she would see too much of him, and until the other was entirely gone, that might not be wise. Her Alix was sleeping, pushed deep into the dark place where Trystan himself had lived the vast majority of his life. He didn't want Sanura to know that there was anything left of that man she loved, and he didn't want to take the chance that somehow the two of them would join.

For that same reason he would not kill her. If anything would awaken the sleeping one, it would be a threat to his woman.

He wanted Sanura to remain afraid, but he did not wish her to realize that he was more than a little afraid of her.

How much of him could she see? Not as much as if they were lovers, but still, she did see. He did his very best to think only of his strengths, to *feel* only his strengths, so that she would not see his weaknesses.

If he continued to keep the other down, soon the light would be gone. Alix did not have the strength to survive as Trystan had all these years. He would fade away, disappear—and then Trystan would be able to take all that he wanted without fear.

Standing there with that shocked and saddened expression on her face, Sanura eventually stopped asking for Alix. She eventually stopped ordering him to leave. Did she finally believe that the man she loved was gone for good? He hoped so. That would make the coming days much easier.

In order to keep the fear in her alive, he pulled up her skirt and exposed her trembling legs. She gasped, even though the clothing she had worn until so recently had exposed much more. Her body stiffened and she tried to pull away, but could not. He was much stronger than she was, and if he refused to allow her to escape, she would not escape. She was his as surely as Alix was his. They were equally helpless.

He was forced to release Sanura in order to grab the faded underskirt she'd bought from Donia. As soon as his grip loosened, she attempted to run, to pull the fabric from his hands and flee. Trystan held on tightly, and yanked hard to throw her to the ground. She landed hard, her skirt and her braid spilling around her. He stood over her and smiled, and she began to cry silent tears.

"You're not going anywhere," he said. He held her in place with the heel of his boot on her midsection, while he tore long strips of fabric from the underskirt.

"What are you doing?" she asked. Her voice trembled.

Trystan ignored her question as he admired the curve of her legs and the rise and fall of her bosom.

"Perhaps tonight you will show me what all the fuss is about," he said. It wouldn't do for her to know that he was afraid to have sex with her until he was certain that Alix was entirely gone. "I don't see how one woman could be

ny more pleasing than another. You all have the same ba-
c body parts, so any woman will do when the urge for
exual release arises."

"Tonight?" She sounded both relieved and confused.

Trystan dropped to his knees, straddling the terrified
voman. "I would take you now, but we need to make prog-
ess while the sun shines. The sooner we get to Arthes, the
ooner I can take what should be mine."

"Nothing should be yours," she whispered.

Trystan caught up her wrists with a length of the torn
nderskirt and tied them tightly together. "Alix doesn't like
o see you restrained, but I do," he explained. "In fact, it
ives me great pleasure to see you trussed up so neatly." He
ave the bonds a tug. "Too tight?"

She nodded.

"Good." When her wrists were well bound, he moved to
er ankles and tied them together just as tightly.

When that was done, he lay atop her, placing his face
lose to hers. He smelled her, felt the crush of her body
eneath his. What a shame that he had to wait to make her
ntirely his.

"I thought you were in a hurry to get to Arthes," she said.

"I am."

"Then get off of me."

Trystan smiled. She no longer asked for Alix because
he knew he was deeply buried and as bound as she herself
vas. So close, he could not help but remember how he had
educed her before, when she'd thought the other was in
ommand. He'd touched her, entered her, felt the squeeze
f her body as it took his. He told her one woman was like
ny other, but that was not entirely true. With blue or
golden skin, she was extraordinary. He ground his erection
against her. "If I wished to make quick work of you, I
vould take you now," he said, "but when I do take you
again, it will not be quick, and you will not be fooled for
even one moment that your precious Alix survives. He'll
e gone, thanks to you. Thanks to the walls you broke
lown for me, thanks to the way you forced him to break his

strict code of moral conduct. Thanks to the way you se
duced us."

"I did not seduce *you*," she argued.

"Yes, you did, and whether you'll admit it or not, yo
knew I was there, just beneath the surface. You've alway
liked me better than Alix." He grinned at her as he remem
bered what they had shared, how she had responded t
him. "He's boring and staid and ordinary. I'm exciting an
dangerous, and whether you admit to it or not, you like th
danger in me. A woman like you would never be satisfie
with the tedious prince." He leaned down and very slowl
raked the tip of his tongue against her throat. She shud
dered. She tasted so damn good. "You'd much rather hav
an emperor who takes that which is his, and you knew
was ready to have my time, to take my life." He rose slightl
and glared down at her. "Admit it, love, you knew fuckin
Alix would free me. You knew."

He rose, then took her bound hands and pulled her t
her feet. Not caring if she fell or not, he dragged her towar
the waiting horse. Even with Sanura bound and carrie
across his lap, they could be in Arthes in two days if h
rode hard enough.

"Wait, *wait*!" Sanura shouted. "Let me stand for a mo
ment and get my bearings."

"Why?" he barked.

"Because if you don't, I will likely throw up on you an
the horse. I hit the ground too hard. My head aches and m
stomach is roiling. Give me one moment to calm my in
sides and compose myself. Please."

He did not want to be retched upon, so he did as sh
asked and stood her on her feet. It wasn't as if she could ru
with her ankles bound as they were.

Standing, she found the nerve to look him in the eye
The fear remained, but so did a hint of defiance. He didn'
like the defiance, but he was sure it would not last long. A
few hours of riding tossed over the horse like a sack o
horse feed would shake the insolence right out of her.

She studied him for a moment, perhaps trying to se

to his heart. Trystan was not worried, as he was pretty
sure he didn't have one, not in the sense which would help
his witchy woman in any way.

When Sanura moved, she took him by surprise. Steady
on her feet, she swung her bound wrists and slapped the
horse on the rump. As she hit the animal, she screamed, letting forth a piercing cry which threatened to deafen him.
The animal reared back, and then it ran. Trystan gave chase
for a moment, following in the horse's path and calling for it
to return, but it was soon evident that the horse was gone.

He turned, expecting to find his prisoner attempting escape in spite of her bonds. She was not. Sanura stood where
he'd left her, her damned defiance more evident than ever.
"You whore," he said as he neared her. "You have cost me
days. Days!"

"I know," she said with serenity.

He raised his hand and curled his fingers into a fist, intent on bringing her to the ground with a blow. When she
was down, he'd knife her in the heart, he'd feel the blade
slip into her flesh, and he'd watch the life fade from her
eyes. Forget the sex, forget the sleeping Alix, he wanted to
kill her now.

His arm froze in midair, refusing to swing downward,
refusing to strike the woman before him. More than once
he tried to send his fist swinging, but his arm would not
move. Apparently Alix did not sleep as deeply as he'd
thought.

Trystan lowered his arm and pretended acceptance. "It
is of no consequence. The horse will return to me as soon
as the fright of your attack fades."

"I doubt that," she said confidently. "The animal under-
stands that you are not the man he knows. You are not the
horse's master, and though you may look and sound like
Alix, you are not him. I know it. The horse knows it. It will
not come back."

"I will simply steal another," he said, refusing to show
his anger. She could not know that the reason he did not
kill her for her actions was that Alix would not allow it.

Sanura glanced around, taking in the desolate for(
and the abandoned and rarely used path, pointing out wi
out a word that it might be quite some time before he fou
a horse to steal.

Trystan pulled the dagger from his belt and held it b
neath her nose. If she felt fear, she did not show it. If
intended to cut her, the other would know and would st
him, so he did not even think of drawing blood. He on
wanted to scare her, and he did.

Trystan dropped to his haunches and threw up Sanur
skirt. With a swift move, he cut the cloth that bound h
ankles. "We will walk instead of riding, thanks to you,"
said.

"I don't mind walking," she said.

He rose slowly and tucked his dagger back in its shea
"Don't think you won't pay for this," he whispered. "O
way or another, you will pay." He grinned at her. "But y
won't stop me."

HAVING her hands bound was inconvenient, but it was
as though she was unaccustomed to the circumstand
Queen Coira had insisted on chains whenever Sanura h
made an appearance in the Tryfyn court. She hadn't had
trek over uneven landscapes in the Tryfyn court, howev
She'd fallen three times this afternoon, and each tin
Trystan had only laughed at her as he'd tugged on the ro
he'd fashioned from what had remained of her underski
a rope with which he led her as if she were the horse h
lost.

She was not as stupid as he thought she was. His arr
gance blinded him. His joy at being free overshadow
much of what he should see. He'd wanted to hit her aft
she'd sent the horse running. He'd wanted very much to k
her for ruining his plans, and as he was so much a primal b
ing, he had been driven by his baser instincts to act. It had
been chance or luck which had saved her. Trystan had
harmed her in any way because Alix wouldn't allow it.

Alix wasn't gone.

She repeated those words like a mantra—*Alix isn't gone. Alix isn't gone.*—as she marched in Trystan's wake. It wasn't her selfishness which had killed him; it hadn't been her foolish decision to take what she wanted that had meant a defeat by the darkness he had successfully fought all his life. She would save him, somehow. She would bring Alix to the surface, and then she would leave him alone so that Trystan would never again be tempted—not by her.

All along he had known that the two of them together was wrong, that their surrender would lead to disaster. He'd told her many times that she was not his to take. Foolishly, she'd been certain that she could have all that she wanted, that she could embrace this new life and new land and choose the man who would possess her. She'd thought she could choose love. She'd been wrong. Horribly, disastrously, wrong.

Trystan's darkness made him more difficult to read than most others, but she did see his insecurity quite clearly. He might tell her that Alix was dead, but he did not believe it to be true. Trystan now fought to suppress Alix, just as Alix had fought the shadows for so many years.

Somehow she would save him. She would undo all that she had done in the name of desire and love. Love was never meant to be hers, and she'd been tempting fate to think she could take it, even for a short while.

Trystan would never love. He was incapable of doing anything more than taking what he wanted. Power, sex, food . . . sleep.

In the past, Trystan's possession, for lack of a better word, hadn't lasted for more than a few precious minutes. An hour, perhaps. He had never had to sleep, to rest, to let go of his tight rein of control. And yet, his body would eventually require sleep. When Trystan slept, would Alix have the chance to reemerge? While Trystan dreamed, would she be able to call Alix to her?

Sanura looked heavenward. She had always believed in the One God, but in Tryfyn there were those who prayed to many gods and goddesses. One for weather, one for abun-

dance of fish. One for health, one for the passing of th
moon. She could not begin to remember them all.

She did not know if the One God listened to her now (
if another god or goddess would hear her prayers. If ther
were many ancient powerful ones watching over her nov
surely there was a god of disaster or a goddess of doome
love. *Please. Please bring him back. I will leave him alon*
I promise, if you will only allow Alix to come back. Tear
filled her eyes. So soon after finding love, she had to giv
it away, she had to deny it.

They walked all afternoon without stopping to rest. Sa
nura was exhausted, but she did not complain or ask fc
even a moment to catch her breath. She knew Trystan wel
enough to know that such requests would only make hir
angry, they would only make him walk farther and faster

Trystan finally stopped when there was no more light t
illuminate their path. He didn't mind if she fell, but afte
he'd taken a couple of painful tumbles over unseen bump
and shallows in the path, he decided it was time to stop fo
the night.

In one way, Sanura wished they would continue onwarc
tripping and falling all the way to Arthes. Trystan had sai
he would take her when night fell. He had promised to hu
her. His body was the same as that of the man she loved
but she did not want him to touch her while Trystan rulec
Still, she braced herself for what was coming as he led he
to a small clearing just off the path. He carelessly hitche
the other end of the rope that encircled her waist aroun
the low-lying branch of a tree, and then set about collectin
wood and building a fire. He ignored her. There were n
threats, no jibes, no dark promises as he set about readyin
the campsite for the night.

Eventually he sat beside the fire and ate a handful o
spring berries he had gathered. Then he uncapped the wa
terskin, which hung from his belt. All afternoon they ha
pressed forward without stopping for food or water, anc
Sanura found herself horribly thirsty. She could go withou
food for a while, if necessary, but she needed water.

It didn't look as if Trystan intended to share. He stared into the fire as he ate and drank, not even acknowledging her existence. Perhaps it was best this way. She'd be parched, but would not have to endure threats or physical attack from her captor.

Relieving as that was, she could not help but wonder why. Trystan had always wanted her. That night in her tent and the morning she had believed it was Alix who seduced her, he had been very open about what he wanted. He had said he would take his time with her tonight, and yet now that they were camped for the night he ignored her.

His natural impulse was to take what he wanted. What stopped him from taking her now? She tried to see, tried to understand, and after a while she did.

He was afraid of what she would see. Not of Alix rising, not of losing control, but of her gift. What did he think she would learn? He was entirely open and honest about his plans and desires, so what did he hide?

Sanura held her breath for a moment. Only Trystan's primitive survival instinct would keep him from the sex he desired. He believed that if they were joined and she saw too much of him, she'd be able to discover his weakness and send him away.

He was afraid of her.

She swallowed hard before forcing herself to speak. "May I have a drink of water?"

Trystan lifted his head and looked at her. His hard face, illuminated by firelight, gave her a start. Those eyes, the slash of a mouth...he was a hard man who could hurt her, if he wished. "No," he answered simply.

"I can survive without food for a little while, but I must have water," she explained. She forced herself to look him in the eye. "I'll do anything for water, Trystan. Anything you want."

He cocked his head to one side and studied her quizzically.

"If you don't give me water, I won't be able to travel tomorrow. You'll be forced to leave me behind or carry me."

"Or kill you," he said without emotion.

If he'd wanted to kill her, she'd already be dead. "If y[ou] let me live, I will make it worth your trouble," she prom ised. "You know I can."

His eyes narrowed. "That sounds very much like a se[x] ual proposition."

"Perhaps it is."

"What about your precious Alix? I doubt he would a[p] prove."

"I loved Alix, but he's gone. You look like him. You w[ill] taste and feel like him. I might pretend that you are hi[m] for a while."

Trystan smiled. "You want my body?"

Again she swallowed hard, and gathered her courag[e.] "Yes."

He walked toward her, waterskin in hand. "Strange enough, knowing that you want me makes me want y[ou] less."

She was not surprised to hear those words. Trysta[n] would be aroused by fear, and to take what was not giv[en] would make him feel powerful. He craved power most [of] all, much more than he craved her.

He carelessly poured water into her mouth. Sanu[m] closed her eyes as she drank, as water spilled down th[e] front of her dress. She would do what had to be done [in] order to find out how to bring Alix back. She would [do] anything. Anything at all.

When Trystan pulled the waterskin away from her mout[h,] she gulped down one last drink and then opened her eye[s.] She looked straight at him, and she was not afraid. He was [a] man like any other, driven by darker desires and yet—st[ill] just a man. She licked her lips and lifted her bound hand[s.] "Free me, and I'll give you everything you want."

"It isn't necessary for you to be free for me to take wh[at] I want," he assured her.

She let her hands fall. "That's true enough. Is that wh[at] you desire, Trystan? I will scream for you, if you'd like. [I] will pretend to fight."

He smiled. "When I do take you, you won't be pretending."

Her wrists were tied together by lengths of soft, worn cloth, but they were not bound against her body. She lifted her hands and began to awkwardly unfasten the bodice of her plain dress. The fabric was wet and difficult to work with, but one by one she unfastened the buttons and spread the fabric wide. Trystan watched every sway of her fingers, he eyed every inch of skin as it was exposed.

"You kissed my breasts once, do you remember?" she said. "I was wearing the costume of my home, I was still blue, and you leaned in and touched me with your mouth. You drew the fabric and my nipple into your mouth. Do you remember?" she asked again, hoping to paint a picture in his mind which he could not shake.

"I remember well."

"I liked it," she whispered. "Even though I knew it was you and not Alix, I liked it very much. I almost experienced release simply because you touched me there in a way no other man ever had." Her breasts were bared to the cool night air, and her nipples hardened and peaked in response to the cold. "Touch me again," she commanded.

If Trystan would touch her just once, he'd be hers to command. He would not be able to stop, once they began. He did not have the control or even the desire to restrain himself when he had something he wanted in his grasp. Once they were joined, she'd be able to see what he hid from her: a way to bring Alix back.

His hand rose slowly, advancing toward her breasts. That hand stopped before it met flesh.

"You're very devious," he said as his hand fell. "Do you think I don't know what you're after? Do you think I don't know what you want, you witchy woman?" He stepped away from her. "Our time will come, but not tonight."

"Afraid?" she snapped as disappointment welled up inside her.

"Of you?" he laughed. "No."

"Then why won't you *touch* me? Why don't you take what you want?"

In the firelight, his eyes went hard. "Maybe I liked you better when you were blue," he said. "Maybe I liked you better when you were forbidden. Maybe I don't want you anymore."

She knew that wasn't true. He wanted her now, but in spite of his primitive instincts he denied himself. There was only one thing which would make him deny his urges. Survival.

Sanura refastened the buttons of her bodice. "You don't know what you're denying yourself," she said coolly.

"I do, actually," he said. "I have been inside you before, in case you don't remember."

"I remember," she said without emotion. "I also remember that Alix had to show up to finish the task you started. Why is that, Trystan?" she asked. "Are you damaged as a man? Are you unable to be a proper lover? Are you afraid that if you lie with me, Alix will once again have to rise up in order to do what you can't?"

Perhaps it was not wise to taunt a man as primitive as Trystan, but what choice did she have? If he didn't touch her, she might never discover how to save Alix.

After experiencing a flash of pure rage which Sanura felt even from this distance, Trystan laughed. "Maybe I won't kill you after all," he said. "You and I would make quite the clever couple. We're two of a kind, you know, two sides of the same dark coin."

"We are nothing alike!" she protested.

"You and I are very much alike, Sanura," Trystan said confidently. "We both know what we want and we'll do whatever is necessary to take it, to make it our own. You seduce with your body, I fight with my sword. I slay with a blade, you slay with a smile and a twist of your hips. You're cunning and devious just as I am, but in a sweet, feminine way which is not so obvious but is just as effective, perhaps more so. Yes, we are both willing to do whatever is necessary to have what we want." He grinned at her. "We're the perfect couple, Sanura. How would you like to be empress?"

TARI crept along the road toward the light of the campfire which was no longer so far in the distance. That had to be Vyrn's camp, it just had to be! She was tired and hungry and afraid, after two long days of searching for her soon-to-be husband.

When she heard the murmur of male voices, she smiled. Yes, this had to be the place.

She left the road long before the soldiers might see or hear her. Vyrn had been insistent that no one know of their alliance, so she would remain in the woods. She would shadow the soldiers until the time was right, and she would meet with Vyrn when he was separated from the others. He would be so glad to see her!

As she neared the camp, her steps were careful and very, very slow. She did not want to snap twigs and rattle downed and dried leaves, and call attention to her presence. She'd assumed the soldiers might have someone on watch, but as she drew closer and saw no signs of defense, she decided that was not the case. They did not expect resistance; the country was not at war and they were the hunters, not the hunted, so why bother guarding their camp?

Soon she was near enough to see that there were seven men gathered around the campfire. Where was the other? She did her best to see and identify each man. It was Rolf who was missing. Was he circling the campground, searching for intruders? Pissing in the forest? *Right behind her?* She hunkered down and made herself small. She closed her eyes to listen to their words, hungering for the sound of Vyrn's voice. The men talked about many things, important and unimportant. They were all determined to find the prince and the woman he had taken with him, and were frustrated that they'd had no luck thus far.

Eventually the talk turned somber.

"Rolf was a fine soldier," one of the Columbyanan sentinels said. His voice had that pleasant accent, but was not Vyrn's. "He will be missed."

There was a round of murmured agreement.

Apparently Rolf would not be in the forest searching for intruders. He was dead. Tari felt a rush of sadness. That was too bad, really. Rolf had always been an agreeable sort.

"The prince must be made to pay for murdering poor Rolf."

Tari smiled. That was the voice she had come here to find. The timbre of the voice sent a shiver of warmth through her. Since no one was in the woods on lookout, she lay on her belly and scooted into a better position. A glimpse of Vyrn's face would be nice. Just a glimpse. As she inched forward, the men continued to talk about Rolf. Apparently, after one was dead, his less desirable traits were forgotten and only the good remained.

"Rolf was a bit sweet on the maid Tari." The sound of her name caught Tari's attention. The speaker of the surprising words was Tenjin, who'd been friends with the deceased soldier and would surely know. Rolf had been sweet on her? She'd never guessed. Why, he had never spoken two words to her!

"Tari?" One Columbyanan sentinel said in disbelief. "Of all the maids, why her?"

Tari waited for Vyrn to come to her defense, to tell them all that she was beautiful and loyal and sometimes sweet, but instead he laughed. "Talk about an ugly woman! I'd have to put a bag over her head before I could screw her, and even then I'd have to be pretty damned desperate. Does she have any meat on her bones? There's likely nothing but a skeleton beneath her clothes."

Most of the men laughed. Another had something disparaging to say about her nose.

In the silent forest, a tear slipped down Tari's cheek. She knew she was no beauty, but to be called ugly, to be laughed at, hurt to the core. She knew Vyrn wanted to keep their relationship quiet for the time being, but that didn't mean he had to be cruel. That didn't mean he had to *laugh*.

It got worse as they began to talk about the women they did find attractive, the women they'd had pleasurable sexual relations with, the women they had loved. Her name was not mentioned.

All her dreams fell apart as Tari lay in the woods and listened to the soldiers' laughter and their boasts of exploits with loose women. Vyrn had more tales to tell than anyone else, more advice to offer the younger men. Things like *Make a woman believe whatever she wants to believe, and you'll get anything you want. Tell her whatever she wants to hear, but never be the first to say "love." If you're smart, you can make her think that anything you want is her idea.* They laughed at that one. His final bit of advice sent a chill down her spine and through her blood, then straight into her heart.

Screw 'em, tell 'em what they want to hear, and then disappear.

Before meeting Vyrn, she'd had given up all hopes of love and family, but he'd ignited those hopes. He'd made them seem real, but it had been a lie. It had been cruel to make her think she could have all she wanted, while the entire time he was planning to use her and then *disappear.*

Tari rested her chin on her hands. Soon her sorrow passed and a deep anger settled in. She'd murdered for Vyrn. She'd taken an innocent life because he swore it was the only way they could be together. He'd collect a fine reward for his work—for her work—and they would build a life together. Lies. All lies. But the blood remained on her hands.

After a while, after the soldiers slept and the fire died, the anger went away and was replaced with a coldness, an emptiness. If Vyrn wanted to disappear, she'd be glad to assist him.

Chapter Twelve

THEY walked for two days without seeing another human being. Trystan led her as if she were an animal. He fed her just enough to keep her alive, and he enjoyed talking about his plans—plans for her, plans for his brother.

Sanura knew without doubt that if Trystan killed Emperor Jahn as he planned, Alix would never reemerge. He would not be able to live with himself if his brother died at his hand. Even if he were able to muster the strength to fight and defeat Trystan, he would not. He would wither and die in whatever dark place he now existed. That horrible act would be the death of the man she loved, and complete victory for the darkness which now ruled his body.

But he was not gone yet.

It had surely been Alix's influence that kept Trystan from striking her on the day he'd emerged to take control. Would the same be true when he tried to murder his brother? Would Alix be strong enough to stop that atrocity as well?

Trystan seemed to forget about her for long stretches of time, even though he led her like an unwanted pet or an animal headed to the slaughter. Now and then he would look back at her and seem almost startled by her presence, and she finally decided that he had not slept at all last night. She had slept for a few short hours, exhausted as she was, and she'd assumed that he also slept. The body he now possessed would need sleep, and soon.

It was late in the afternoon when he stopped to relieve himself and to allow her the same privilege. He then tied one end of her tether to a low-lying limb and searched the immediate area for edible fruits and leaves. So far he had chosen wisely, and they had not gone hungry or gotten sick from eating the wrong sort of plant life. On her own she likely would've starved, or else unknowingly picked poisonous foliage. He disdained her, he insulted her, but he also kept her alive.

Even though she had decided it was safest for her to remain silent and on the edges of his thoughts, she had to look beyond her own safety if she wanted Alix back.

"You must sleep," she said, trying to force a tone of caring into her voice.

"Why?" he snapped, glancing up from his study of a clump of what looked to be tall, thick weeds.

"Because if Vyrn and the others catch up with us and you are in this state, they will cut you down before you realize they're upon us."

"I'm a better swordsman than Alix. No one will take me by surprise." He returned his attention to the task at hand, trying to dismiss her.

She could not allow him to dismiss her. "Without sleep, your mind will not function as it should. You will not see clearly." She lifted her chin haughtily. "I do not care for your life all that much, but if they kill you, I will surely be next. I'm not ready to die, Trystan."

He fought sleep, had almost fallen asleep on his feet as they walked, but he did not want her to know of his weakness.

"If I sleep, you'll escape," he argued.

"Where would I go?" she said too loudly. "I know no

one in this country or in Tryfyn who does not wish me dead. I would dearly love to make my way back to Claennis, but I do not have the resources to find my way there on my own. I despise you, Trystan, but you are the only person in this land who wishes to keep me alive."

"For now," he clarified.

"For now."

He stood, a handful of selected edible plants in his hands. Openly, he searched her face for signs that she lied, that she harbored nefarious plans, but as he did not have her gift, he would see only what she wished him to see. She remained passive and without the anger she felt for what he'd done to Alix. She showed him none of her fear.

"What of your guards?" he asked. "What of those two fat protectors who have vowed to kill any man who touches you?"

"I do not fool myself into believing that Paki and Kontar are any match for you, Trystan. You've proved that once. They will not confront you again." She hoped that was true. Unchecked, Trystan would quickly kill them both. Her protectors, her countrymen, were not her friends—she had no true friends—but they were good men who had left their homes behind to fulfill their duties. They should not die for it.

Sanura still believed that if she had sex with Trystan, she would be able to find his weaknesses, but last night he'd made it clear that he was not going to be swayed by an open seduction. She'd have to be much more subtle in order to make him put aside his fears to have her.

"And really," she said with a touch of disdain, "if you are going to pretend to be a prince, you must take more care with your appearance. Anyone who saw you now would never believe you're Prince Alixandyr."

"I am Prince Alixandyr," he insisted.

"You don't look like him."

Angry, he stood. "I *am* him!"

Sanura sighed and stood to face him without fear. "Perhaps, but Alix took greater care with his appearance than you have. I don't suppose we can do anything about the beard that's growing in until our circumstances change, and all you can do with your clothing is straighten it a bit. But really, your hair is a mess. The clip in back is hanging loose and half of your hair is in your face."

He roughly pushed the hair back and felt awkwardly for the clip. "Who cares about my hair?"

"Come closer and sit down," she ordered sharply, and surprisingly, he obeyed.

It was difficult to work with her hands tied, but she managed to remove the silver clip and move it to her mouth while she combed Trystan's hair with her fingers. She moved slowly, allowing her hands to linger on his scalp, to brush against his neck. Yes, the desire he always felt for her grew, and yet he did not realize that she was touching him this way with purpose.

She could do this only if she thought of Alix, if she assured herself that he was somehow present. As her fingers raked through his thick, wavy hair, she remembered the way it had fallen over her body as they'd made love and she'd looked into his emotion-filled green eyes. She could very easily cry for what was lost, but she did not allow herself even one tear.

His hair was never manageable, but by the time she was done, it looked much better. Less wild. Less untamed. Once the clip was in place, she ran her hands down the length of the curling strands, then settled them both on his shoulder.

"Much better," she said, making sure her breath made its way to his ear.

Beneath her hands, he shuddered. "Perhaps you're right," he said. "Tonight I will sleep. I can't afford to be less than alert, and it isn't as if…"

He did not finish his sentence, but Sanura knew what he meant to say. *It isn't as if Alix is strong enough to rise up while I sleep.*

As she stepped back, allowing her fingertips to rake over his shoulder, she prayed that he was wrong.

* * *

"WAIT here," Laris whispered.

"But why?" Verity held his hand tightly. She did not want to be left alone! After nearly three days of walking, they had finally arrived in a small village. She wanted a bath and a bed and clean clothes and a brush for her hair and *food*. Heaven above, she wanted food!

Laris placed his face close to hers and smiled. Heavens, she loved his smile! "You can't be seen, Lady Verity. If Wallis and Cavan ask questions about a beautiful and waterlogged lady, you will be remembered. One more sentinel passing through will mean nothing."

Of course he thought she was beautiful, even now when she was unkempt and her hair was matted and she was slightly sunburned. It was the love potion that made him think she was beautiful; it was the love potion that made him care for her so ardently.

She nodded her agreement, and he kissed her forehead before leaving her in this narrow, dank alley which ran between two of the town's four public buildings. If she hunkered down behind the woodpile, no one would see her from the main street.

When she was empress, she would never be dirty. Her feet would not hurt, and she'd have a hundred hats to keep the sun from her delicate face. She would have those who tried to kill her executed—though she did not want to watch as they died. She shuddered. That sight would be too much for her delicate constitution.

The words "when I am empress" no longer gave her joy, as they once had. It would be a wonderful life, she was sure of it, but where would Laris fit in? She could make him her private and most favorite sentinel, she supposed, and perhaps they would even become lovers—after the wedding, of course. In the past that plan had seemed most appropriate, but now she was sure that Laris deserved better. He deserved to be loved, to have a family and a home of his own. He deserved better than a sordid and secret affair with the woman he loved only because she'd used a witch's potion on him.

Just a few weeks ago, her life had seemed so wonderfully simple and clear. Mavise's prediction of her destiny to marry a great man who'd come from humble beginnings was so clear, so lovely, so *appealing*, and when the emperor's invitation had arrived and she'd learned of his own humble beginnings, it all made sense to her. Everything any woman could even imagine asking for would be hers. Empress! Who would not wish to be empress? And when she'd admired Laris, for so many reasons, it had seemed perfectly sensible to test the love potion and make sure she had a friend on the long journey to her new life.

She'd never planned for the chaos which had disrupted the journey, chaos which she felt inside and out.

Unwanted tears filled her eyes. She never should've used that blasted potion! It had seemed like a good idea at the time, but now...now she knew that the love she saw in his eyes wasn't real. He had saved her life, protected her from harm, cared for her, at times he'd literally carried her...all for a love which was not real.

What she felt for Laris wasn't love, she told herself as she wiped away her annoying tears. It was gratitude. It was relief. Her gratitude was so strong simply because without him she'd be dead. Without him, she would've drowned in the river, and even if she hadn't, she would've foolishly and blindly returned to the men who wished her dead, and they would have tried again. She did not fool herself into thinking the lucky talisman she wore would protect her from everything and everyone.

Verity was still crying when Laris returned with food, a rolled-up blanket, and a neatly folded dress. When he came closer, she saw that there was a hairbrush on top of the clothing. He hadn't had much money, she knew, and yet he had spent it on her. More tears fell.

Laris was alarmed when he saw her tears. He placed his purchases carefully on the ground, and sat beside her to wrap his arms around her and offer comfort. His large hand stroked her back, and he whispered into her ear. *Everything's going to be all right. You're safe, Lady Verity. I won't let anyone hurt you. I won't leave you alone again, I promise.* His assurances only made her cry harder, and she wrapped her arms around him to hold on tightly. He was warm and hard and strong, and maybe her love wasn't any more real than his, but at the moment it *was* love.

She was a wretched person for using the witch's potion on him. Wretched, wretched, wretched!

He took her face in his hands and looked her in the eye. His deep brown eyes were so warm, she felt as if she could fall into them. Her heart did a little dance.

"There's a creek just west of the village. Stop crying and I'll take you there. We can bathe and you can try on your new dress, and we'll eat."

Verity sniffled. "A picnic. That would be nice."

Laris laughed, and the sound was very nice. "Yes, Lady Verity, we will have a picnic."

She touched his face, ran her hand across the little bit of fair stubble which was growing there. "Call me Verity," she said, "just Verity."

"If you wish," he said softly.

"I do wish," she said. Of course, at the moment she wished for many things, and most of them would surely not come true.

Laris took her hand, gathered up his purchases in the crook of his other arm, and led her through the alley. At the rear of the buildings he stopped to glance in both directions, to make sure they would not be seen. When he felt it was safe, he held her hand more tightly and ran. Not as fast as he might've run alone, but as fast as she could manage. There was an expanse of clear green field where they were completely exposed, and then they burst into the shade of a green forest.

Once there, Laris slowed his step. They still held hands, and he pulled her closer to him. Verity was very glad to walk so close to him, to rest against his side on occasion, to take in his warmth.

They soon came to the creek, as he had promised. On the bank he released her hand and turned his attention to his purchases. The blanket he tossed to the ground, for now. The food he set aside. He handed her the dress and the brush.

"The dress belonged to the grocer's wife. She passed away last year. I know it isn't much, but..." He shrugged his shoulders. "I hope it fits well enough."

Verity looked down at her own ruined clothing and gave a little sigh of mourning. The riding gown was made of the finest material. It was blue, her favorite color. Unfortunately, fine material was not made to stand up to river water and mud, and her garment was now as stiff as wood in some places. It was no longer evident that this outfit had once been the shade of the sky on a clear morning in the Northern Province.

She took the dress Laris offered. It was green. Green was not her color *at all*. This particular shade made her skin appear yellow. She could tell at a glance that the dress was too large for her, and that the material would be scratchy against her skin. There was a stain on the bodice, as if the previous owner had spilled greasy food there and it had not quite come out. The dress had once belonged to a woman who was now dead.

She looked Laris in the eye. "I love it. Thank you."

He nodded almost shyly. "It isn't much, I know, but it's clean and simple and I expect it will be more comfortable than your ruined clothing."

Verity turned her back to Laris and began to unfasten the buttons that ran down the front of her riding outfit. A few buttons were missing, but there were so many the opening did not gap. Even if it had, she wore an undershirt beneath. Her movements were quick and efficient. She could not wait to get out of this horrid clothing!

As she pulled the top half of her outfit down and off, she glanced behind her to see if Laris watched. He did not. He had turned his back on her, not because he didn't want to watch but because he was a gentleman.

She stripped off all her clothing, ridding herself of the riding outfit and all her underclothes, and then she looked at the rushing water of the creek. From here it looked to be deep, for a creek, and the water rushed in a way that reminded her of the river which had almost taken her. She wished, very much, for a bath, but was afraid of even putting her feet into the water. Logically she knew the gentle current would not take her away, but there was more to life than logic.

"I'm afraid," she said simply.

Laris turned about quickly. He saw that she was still naked, blushed, and then turned about once again, presenting his fine back to her. "Why are you afraid?"

She explained. The water. The river. A bath.

"The creek is not at all deep."

"I know," she said.

"I'll be right here," he assured her.

Unfortunately, *right here* was not good enough. "Would you come in with me?"

He did not turn around, but she saw his shoulders tense. "Is that necessary?"

"Yes," she whispered.

Perhaps she should be embarrassed by her nakedness, but in her lifetime many personal maids and nurses had seen her without clothing, and she trusted Laris much more than she trusted any of them, even now when all she wore was a lucky talisman she was afraid to remove. She would never take it off! If she found herself in this dire situation with the luck of the talisman, where would she be without it? Dead, most likely. No, she was *not* taking it off.

Laris removed his vest and then his shirt, and he set his weapons aside. My, what a fine chest he had! He wasn't at all hairy, and she could see lots of fascinating bumps and bulges on his chest and his arms. His stomach was flat and ridged and not at all like her own soft belly. Interesting. He kicked off his boots and removed his belt, but began walking toward her without removing his trousers, though once he had a close look at the creek, he rolled his pants legs up to his knees.

"You're going in the water half-dressed?" she said as he took her hand.

"Yes." His voice was tight.

"That doesn't make any sense at all," she argued. She gripped his hand tightly as she stepped into the creek. "The water is cold!"

"Good," Laris muttered.

Goosebumps crawled up her arms and across her shoulders. Her nipples hardened. And still she kept moving deeper into the water. At the deepest point it barely came above her knees, and still the rushing water scared her. She hadn't told Laris, but for the past two nights when they slept, she dreamed that she was in the river and it was pulling her down to the deepest depths. In some dreams he arrived to save her. In others he did not.

She bathed quickly. That task required the freedom of both her hands, and she did her best to make sure she wasn't without support for any longer than was necessary. Her eyes flitted often to Laris, who was much nicer to look at than the stream at her feet or the green landscape which surrounded them. Even when he didn't hold her steady, he remained close. He was certainly close enough for her to notice that he was aroused.

All along she had told Laris that she had to be a virgin when she wed the emperor, but that when the wedding night was done, she could be his. Sometimes she'd even meant those words, usually as he held her late at night, but she had never before truly *felt* them. Not until now. She now felt that promise in her quivering belly, in the ache she had not paid much attention to until this moment, in the ardent desire to press her soft belly to his hard one to see how such a touch might feel. She wanted so much to reach out and touch the ridge in his trousers, to wrap her body around his and never let go.

She wished fervently that he was as naked as she.

Maybe the emperor would not choose her after all. She'd been so confident that he would, thanks to Mavise's prediction and her own self-confidence, but at the moment she thought that perhaps he would not. There was also the possibility that if she decided she did not want to be chosen, she could withdraw from the competition.

And then what? She knew Laris loved her; she had seen to that. But she couldn't be a sentinel's wife! Could she? What of the destiny she'd been promised? Could she, should she, turn her back on a promised future?

"You're clean enough," Laris said hoarsely. He took her hand and led her from the creek, not looking at her, not saying another word. He kept his back to her while she donned the dress he had bought for her, while he put on his shirt and vest and weapons, while he fastened his weapons to his belt. He didn't even look at her when she told him she was done and began to brush out her hair.

"You're mad at me," she said as she brushed out the tangled strands of her usually well-cared-for hair.

"I'm not mad," he said tersely.

No, he was miserably in need. So was she, truth be told. She could say a few words right now and they'd both be much happier. She could command—or ask—that he make love to her here and now, and he would accede. She could hint that perhaps she did not have to be a virgin when she wed the emperor—if she wed the emperor at all. She could just say his name in the right tone of voice, and he would be here.

A sadness welled up inside Verity. Would Laris want her so much if she had not given him the blasted potion? Would he have saved her, held her, cared for her, kissed her forehead? She wanted to know. She wanted him to love her without magic, the way she was beginning to love him. Anything else would be less than perfect, and she wanted perfection.

Perhaps in Arthes there would be a witch who could undo what she'd done.

* * *

TRYSTAN could barely keep his eyes open as the last light of day faded from the sky. Sleep, Sanura said, and perhaps she was right.

He fought the need for sleep because he remembered taking control for short bursts of time while the other slept. Would Alix be able to do the same? No. He had existed in darkness for years before he'd learned how to make an appearance while Alix slept. He was stronger than Alix, more determined.

He yanked on the tether by which he led Sanura as he moved into the forest which lined their path. In a way he wished Vyrn and the others would find him. He wanted a fight, he wanted to draw blood and expend some of the fury which was building up inside him. But he also knew that the woman was right when she said he needed rest before he took on the next fight.

What if she ran while he slept? He could, and would, make sure she was tightly bound, but that didn't mean she might not escape while he was senseless. She'd make her way to Arthes if she did escape, and warn Jahn that his brother was no longer entirely his brother, that the man who wore a prince's face wished him dead.

Would Jahn believe her, a strange, sensuous woman who dropped out of nowhere? Not necessarily. The thought soothed Trystan. He could kill Jahn while he was trying to convince him of the truth.

He'd been second best long enough. Born a few minutes too late, born to a battle which could not be shared—born in the shadow of his brother and destined to fight the shadow of his soul.

Trystan saw to Sanura once he had fed himself. He gave her some water, but not too much. He shoved a leaf wrapped around a small piece of wild fruit into her mouth, and before she swallowed, he followed with another, reminding her that if she had not scared off the horse, they might be eating bread and dried meat instead of foraged plant life. Her mouth touched his fingers, and he was reminded sharply that he still had not bedded her. He was also reminded that he did not dare.

Sleep was coming upon him; he felt it. He bound Sanura's wrists more tightly than before, and made sure that her ankles were lashed together as well. From about her waist he took the other end of the rope he'd fashioned from her underskirt and tied it to his own. If she moved about too much, she would wake him. There was little rope left after he attached it to his own waist, so they were forced to lie down close together. He expected she would stay as far away from him as possible, but instead she settled down close to his side. It was disconcerting.

He could feel her body heat, her closeness. Her hand settled on his side, soft and warm. The fingers barely moved, but they did move. She sighed, and he could feel her breath. Her body shifted and was suddenly closer to his, so close that he could feel the energy rolling off her flesh. She said not a word, and she did not blatantly touch, but she was there, so damned close he could feel her. She was still trying to seduce him; she was simply trying to be clever about it.

He could resist Sanura. She underestimated his patience. Thirty-one years of being restrained had forced that patience upon him.

Just as he was drifting off to sleep, she spoke. "Perhaps you are right," she whispered. "What you said about us being two sides of the same coin, I suppose that could be true."

"Of course it is." He was being pulled toward slumber, but she continued to speak.

"Besides, what woman would not want to be empress? I am so tired of walking, of being dirty, of wearing this horrid hand-me-down dress, of being forced to run and hide from men who think I'm a murderess." She sighed. "I want a bath and servants and clothes and jewels. I want to sleep in a soft bed and make proper love to a proper man. I want..."

"I don't care what you want," Trystan said testily. "Shut up, or I will kill you."

"No, you won't," she said confidently.

He rolled atop her, crushing her into the ground with the weight of his body, wishing he could see her face more clearly. In the dark of night beneath the heavy limbs of ancient trees, it was impossible to see more than the shape of her cheek and the very faint shine of her eyes. "Do you think what remains of Alix will save you? Do you think I'm incapable of wrapping my hands around your throat right now and squeezing the life out of you?"

"No," she whispered. "But I do believe you will keep me alive at least until you have what you want of me. If I can make you want me more, if I can make you need me, then perhaps you will allow me to live a while longer."

"You overestimate yourself," he said.

"I don't think so."

The fingertips of her bound hands raked against his stomach as they moved lower. Everything in him tightened. If she touched him, he would be lost. He would lose control and bury himself inside her, and then she would see. She would see Alix; she would see Trystan's weaknesses.

He could not lose control, but it would be lovely if she did. She thought she had command of this situation, of him, but she was wrong. He had command of everything—including her. He slid his body downward, moving his hard cock out of her reach.

"If you will not let me sleep, I suppose I should make the best of the night," he said as he pushed her skirt high.

"Yes," she whispered, and though he could not see her face, he heard the apprehension in her voice.

"This is why you were created, after all," he said as he slid his hand between her thighs. "You are and always have been a pleasure slave, an offering to men's needs and desires."

"Yes," she said again.

He lifted her legs and parted her knees, leaving her ankles bound as her wrists were. His fingers found her slick center. He stroked and she responded. "You said once that you were made to give pleasure, not to take."

"That is true."

"I can make you take," he whispered. "Not Alix, a man you claim to love, not Jahn, who supposedly possesses you, but me. A dark soul you despise, the death of the man you love...I can make you scream."

"You can," she whispered.

Sanura likely thought that he would take her on the ground, that he would jump upon her and penetrate her and allow her to see all that he was. She was wrong.

He slipped a finger inside her warmth. "Do you like that?" He could tell by her reaction that she did.

"Yes, but I want more."

"You'll get more," he promised her. "There is no need to rush."

He moved back up her body. A bit of moonlight broke through the limbs overhead and illuminated her face. It was flawless, no matter what the shade, and it was full of desire. Desire not for Alix, but for him. Perhaps her motives were not in his best interest, but she did want him.

"Unfasten your dress, as you did last night."

She did so, moving quickly and clumsily in her haste. When that was done, he grabbed her wrists and held them above her head so she could not touch him and take control of this game, then leaned down to take a nipple into his mouth. He suckled soft and then hard, deep and then shallow, while his free hand very lightly trailed against the soft folds of flesh he wanted so badly but would not take tonight. Soon her body took on a rhythm of its own, a rhythm that sang of the rush of blood and ancient need. Her hips rocked against his hand, her back swayed off the ground to bring her breasts closer to his mouth. Trystan trailed his mouth down to the tip of her opened bodice, then flicked his tongue between fabric and skin before allowing his mouth once again to find the swell of her breasts, her nipples, and her throat.

His touch was light and easy as he aroused her. She had begun this game thinking to seduce him, but he was the one seducing her. The thought made him laugh as his tongue found and tasted the hollow at the base of her throat.

"What's so funny?" she asked breathlessly.

"You," he said. "Me," he added. "Is anyone what they appear to be at first glance?"

"No," she said. "No one." Her body lurched and she gasped. "What are you waiting for?"

"Do you want me?"

"Yes."

He placed his face close to hers. "Are you imaging that I'm him? In your mind, do you see and feel Alix touching you? Don't lie," he added sharply. "I will know if you lie."

"Yes," she admitted. "I know that Alix is still within you, and I believe in my heart that it is he who touches me."

Trystan imagined that being so close to Sanura would awaken Alix, but he heard nothing, felt nothing that did not come from himself. Still, he could not be sure that the other was gone for good.

"Tell me that you want me."

"I want you," she said.

He slipped a finger inside her and felt her lurch and quiver. "No, say I want you, *Trystan*." If Alix heard that, if he *believed* it, perhaps what was left of him would slink away like the coward he was.

The woman beneath him hesitated and swallowed hard, and he felt her body stiffen.

"Say it," he commanded. "Tell me, tell *him*, that you want what I can give you. Tell your precious Alix that it doesn't matter which of us rules this body, it is only the body you care for."

"I care for much more," she said, but she continued to respond to his touch.

"Ah, that is too bad." He lifted his body from hers. He took his hand from between her legs, he released the arms he pinned to the ground.

"Wait!" She all but threw herself up and toward him, wrapping her restrained arms about his neck. "I'll do anything. I'll say anything, just . . . come back to me. Don't go."

He smiled as he slipped his head from her grasp. "Say 'I want you, Trystan.'"

"I want you, Trystan," she said obediently.

"Say 'I will die without you, Trystan.'"

"I will die without you, Trystan."

He placed his face close to hers. "Say 'I love you, Trystan.'"

She swallowed hard, then said in a weak voice, "It would be a lie."

"Have you never told a lie before?" he asked. "Have you never said what was expected in order to get what you desire?"

"Perhaps," she whispered.

"Then lie now. Lie to me."

He heard her breathing, he heard her clothing rustle as she squirmed. Finally she said, reluctantly, "I love you, Trystan."

"Very good." He kissed her throat and breasts again, but did not linger this time. He pushed her skirts higher and spread her thighs and circled his thumb against the nub at her entrance. She was so ready for him that she was about to scream. Yes, she was his. He had taken Alix's woman and claimed her for his own. It was another victory, as important as taking control, as momentous as taking command of the body they had once shared.

She thought he could not control himself, but he was so well acquainted with control it came quite naturally to deny himself. He was painfully hard, on the edge of his own release, but he did not dare penetrate Sanura as he wished. The time would come, when Alix was entirely gone and he was sure she would not see anything which might lead to his being banished into nothingness once again.

"Say it again," he ordered.

"I want you, Trystan," she said breathlessly.

"No, the other," he commanded hoarsely.

"I love you, Trystan."

At that moment she meant it, at least a little bit. He knew this because he heard the pain and the passion in her voice. She was not at all controlled, not as he was. Then again, she had never been forced to deny herself everything that she wanted.

He could pull away and leave Sanura wanting, but making her orgasm with his touch was another way of owning her—of possessing this treasure, this gift of kings. She jerked and trembled against his hand, she cried out, and though he longed to hear her call his name as she shuddered with release, she offered only a nameless cry.

He pulled away from her, rearranged her skirt, and arranged himself on his back beside her. Her hand or his would quickly take care of the pain he suffered, but he embraced pain. He embraced control.

For a moment he waited for Sanura's seductive voice to coax him to return to her, to finish what they had begun, but she remained silent. Perhaps she now knew that he was not as easy to manipulate as she'd thought he would be. The sleep he needed once again drifted upon him. Before giving in, he whispered once more, "Say it."

Sanura's response was immediate and not at all breathless. In fact, she sounded quite annoyed as she delivered a very convincing "No."

Trystan didn't push. He was too tired, and he was too hard. If he tried to argue with her, he would end up inside her, which was just what she wanted. An unpleasant thought stayed with him as the blackness of sleep came. He had longed for life and power and control for as long as he could remember, but he had never realized that he also longed for love.

The thought was startling, and proved to him that somewhere inside this body Alix still lived.

Chapter Thirteen

TARI wanted to rush the camp of soldiers and tell everyone what had really happened. To her, to Princess Edlyn. She could tell everything, and that would ruin Vyrn's plans.

But she quickly decided that strategy would not be wise. First of all, the soldiers might believe Vyrn's stories over hers. After all, it was clear that the men didn't like her very much. So instead of making her presence known and trying to ruin Vyrn's plans, she followed them for three days. During daylight hours they divided into groups of two or three and went in opposite directions to search for the prince and Sanura. They always set a meeting place a short way down the road, and they were always at that meeting place—unsuccessful in their search—by sunset.

Tari was always there, too, well hidden in the forest so she could watch and listen for a while before retiring to whatever lonely, dark hole she had chosen for her bed that night. Since she had the majority of the day to make herself comfortable, it was no trouble to find a hollow or a cave or a thicket where she might conceal herself. During the other hours of the day she collected herbs and mushrooms from the forest. The foliage here was a bit different from her homeland, but there were enough similarities for her to be certain about what she found. She avoided the few plants which were completely foreign to her, just in case. She ate very well, considering her circumstances.

She found fresh water aplenty, so she could bathe and drink, and she usually spent at least a small amount of time sitting in the sun and thinking about the days to come. Her initial anger turned into an unexpected serenity as she planned for the coming days. Perhaps tonight she would make her move. Yes, tonight would be fine.

SANURA almost wished the sentinels would find them, but her days and nights continued unchanged. She walked until she felt as if her legs would buckle beneath her, but they never did. Trystan led her, he fed and watered her just enough to keep her alive, and Alix seemed farther and farther away with each step they took.

Trystan had not touched her since that night when he'd made her lie and tell him that she loved him. She'd been desperate to get what she wanted—Trystan inside her so she could see all that she needed to see. But in the end he'd been stronger than her. He'd denied himself, he'd even laughed at her own need and easy response.

On some nights she dreamed of Mali, and in the way of their first sleep connection it was more real than not. Mali was distressed by Sanura's current situation; she was afraid there would be no one to come for her, to take her away from home, to hold and love her. In the dreams Sanura did hold the little girl, and she made promises she prayed she would be able to keep.

She took as much comfort in those dreams as she offered.

"We should reach Arthes by tomorrow afternoon," Trystan said in an almost jovial voice as he tugged on her rope. "I'm still a bit annoyed that you made me walk, and even more annoyed that we have not found a decent horse to steal, but I have been enjoying the anticipation of what's to come more than I'd thought I would. It's a pleasure I would not have enjoyed if not for you, so I suppose I should thank you properly." He turned and winked at her. "I do know how to thank you properly, don't I, Sanura?"

She did not respond, and he turned to the front again.

"There are so many different ways to kill someone," he continued, "and when that someone is one's own brother, well, the act should be symbolic and meaningful in some way, don't you think? I could run him through with his own imperial sword, or spear him with the emperor's ceremonial staff, or choke him with his own crimson imperial robe. I could smile and end his life quickly, or I could make his death last so he is sure to remember in the next life that it was his brother who ended his time in this world."

Sanura ignored Trystan's words. She had quickly learned that anything she said only spurred him on, only encouraged his ramblings.

He glanced back at her and grinned. "You condemn me with your silence, love. Don't be so harsh. Any man who finds himself emperor should surely expect political intrigue and assassination. It comes with the throne."

"Will it come with yours?" she snapped, in her anger unable to stop herself from responding, even though she knew it would only prolong the agony of this conversation.

His smile faded. "I suppose it will. I won't be as gullible as Jahn, however. No one will surprise me. No one will sneak upon me."

"No one will love you."

Trystan pretended not to care about such a trivial matter, but she felt the flare of anger within him. Only someone who wanted love would demand to hear the words, even if they knew the words to be false.

"You will," he said, and then he turned about and increased their pace. When he walked faster, she had no choice but to do the same. It was either that or be dragged. "You will love me."

Sanura had become accustomed to the constant trudge, the endless hours of walking. As she walked, she thought of Mali and of Alix and how she needed to find a way to save both of them. She thought of the love she'd found and how quickly it had been taken away. Sometimes Trystan rambled; sometimes he was silent for hours on end. She preferred the silence.

It was late in the afternoon when Trystan stopped abruptly. He came to a halt in the middle of the rough road they had been traveling all day. For a few moments he simply stood there, motionless and straight of spine.

"What's…" Sanura began, but Trystan quickly silenced her with a lifted hand and a glare before he dropped to the ground and placed his hand upon the path.

"Horses," he said. "Three of them, perhaps four."

"The sentinels who search for us?" she asked.

"I don't know." Trystan drew his sword and turned toward Sanura.

For a moment she thought he would kill her with that sword, rather than risk that she might tell all she knew about the prince and his other self. The sword swung and she closed her eyes, but she felt no pain. She opened her eyes to see that he had cut the tether which tied them together, waist to waist.

Of course, being tied to her would only hamper him if he had to fight.

He pointed the tip of his sword at her, seeming to aim for her nose. "Run, and I will find you."

Maybe—maybe not, Sanura thought as she edged toward the thick forest.

Trystan cocked his head to one side. "And if by some chance I can't find you, I'll make my way back to Donia's cottage and I will kill her and the demon child. They will never see it coming." He grinned. "They trust me."

Sanura's heart sank. He knew how much the child meant to her. Would he really go so far? *Yes.* Not only that, he could reveal Mali's heritage and be hailed a hero for killing the offspring of the Isen Demon. "I won't run."

He turned his head and grinned at her as she slunk just inside the shadows of the forest. "I never needed that rope at all, did I? Just the threat of harm to that demon child is enough to keep you under control."

Sanura did not answer. How could she love and hate the man behind the same face? How could she long to save him and to see him dead? As long as Trystan lived, Mali was in danger. As long as Alix lived, there was hope.

The horsemen were coming from the direction in which she and Trystan had been traveling, and they were coming fast. Since there was a curve in the road, they could not see the men who approached, but the noise of their advance grew louder and louder. It took Trystan only a moment to move a long fallen limb into the path. He stared at the limb for a moment, frowning, and then he looked to Sanura.

"Move to the middle of the path," he said.

"What?"

He grabbed her arm and all but threw her to the middle of the road, positioning her just behind the long limb. "Don't move. You know what will happen if you do."

Sanura faced the direction from which the riders would appear, bound hands at her waist, chin high as she tried to appear unafraid, even as her heart pounded. The horses' hoofbeats on the path grew louder with each heartbeat, with each breath she took. She imagined those horses' hooves knocking her down and running over her body, and she wondered if death from such an accident would be quick or painfully slow. Still, she did not doubt Trystan's threats, and she would not save herself and sacrifice Mali.

When it seemed that the riders were right around the corner, she closed her eyes.

THE spring weather in the Eastern Province was much nicer than the cold Verity had left behind, and as they moved farther south, the difference became more and more pronounced. There were flowers everywhere, and the warm sunshine felt nice on her skin.

Laris had led her from the creek where she'd bathed to a small and apparently rarely traveled path which wound toward Arthes. In the past three days they had seen two other travelers, and neither of them had been at all threatening. In fact, those two men had both studied Laris with suspicion, as the sentinel was armed and *far* superior physically to either of them.

She could almost hope they never reached the capital city, that she never faced Emperor Jahn at all. She and Laris could walk these roads forever.

In theory that was nice, but in reality her feet hurt and she was in dire need of another bath—a proper one, this time—and her legs ached horribly.

Laris glanced at her. "Would you like to ride awhile?" He always seemed to know when she reached the breaking point, when she felt as if her legs could take no more.

She nodded, and he squatted down slightly. Verity climbed onto his back, placing her arms about his neck and her legs around his waist. It was a totally improper position for her to assume, but over the past few days she'd grown accustomed to it.

Yes, she'd become accustomed to the feel of Laris's firm back and wide shoulders, to the smell of his skin and the sensation of his soft hair against her cheek. She'd become accustomed to the sound of his voice and the rhythm of his breath, and to the way he never complained about carrying her, not even when he grew tired and his shoulders began to sag.

Did he carry her because he loved her? Did he bear her weight because she'd tricked him with a witch's potion? How stupid that had been! She'd wanted to test the potion, just in case she one day needed to use it on her emperor husband, and she'd also wanted to make sure she had an ally for the long journey, but she had never considered that she might be ruining someone's life, that she might be creating a burden of another sort.

"Tell me about your family," she said, to take her mind off her own guilt.

"Again?" Laris laughed.

"Well, you have a lovely large family, and when you speak of your parents and brothers and sisters, it all sounds so very different from my own family tales."

Laris obliged and told her a story about his youngest brother, a boy who always seemed to be in some sort of trouble. This particular tale was about sneaking off to fish when chores were neglected, which seemed a common enough tale. It was the way Laris told the story that made it amusing, and Verity wished she had such tales to tell. Her privileged life seemed boring compared with Laris's family. During the telling of the fish story, he laughed and she laughed, and after a while she rested her head against his and held on tight. The miles went by too quickly. Every step took them closer to Arthes and her fate.

As empress, she would have all that any woman could desire. Money, clothes, servants, a fine home, power ... jewelry! She had almost forgotten about the fine jewels which would surely come with the position. Any woman would be impressed by the possibility of being constantly adorned with the finest of jewels. She sighed. Some of them would probably be horribly heavy and uncomfortable, a sparkling burden. She had never thought of jewels as a burden before!

Laris finished his story and grew quiet. His breathing was more labored than it had been before, so Verity told him she wished to walk.

"I don't mind carrying you a while longer," he said.

"I'm getting a cramp in my leg, and I need to walk to work it out." She lied rather than argue, because she knew carrying her was a burden—not a sparkling one—and she did not want Laris to suffer.

He would suffer when she married the emperor, unless she found a way to undo the potion's effects. She would suffer, too, but it would be of her own doing. Perhaps she should suffer.

Uh, no. How silly was that?

Laris put her down and waited a moment while she smoothed her skirt and her hair.

"At this rate we will probably be in Arthes in less than a week," he said.

Less than a week! Perhaps she should walk slower, or insist on more time to sleep at night.

"Unless, of course, you...change your mind."

Verity lifted her head and looked Laris in the eye. "Change my mind about what?"

He held her arms with his large, roughened hands. "They think you're dead, Verity. That is the message the emperor will receive when Wallis and Cavan reach Arthes. For all we know, they're already there and have already delivered the message that you drowned in the river. If you don't go to Arthes, if you don't present yourself as a candidate for empress, then..." He gulped once, and seemed unable to continue.

She held her breath. "Then what?" she said when she could breathe again.

"We could get married," he said quickly, as if he had to spit the words out to make them go. "You could live with my family until we can afford a place of our own. You could change your name and hide away and no one would ever know that Lady Verity of Mirham survived the journey."

"Not even my parents?" Verity asked in a small voice.

Laris's face fell and he lowered his eyes. "You're right. It was a stupid idea. I don't know what I was thinking." He turned and started walking again, his back to her so she could not see his face.

If he truly loved her, she might be tempted to say yes to his ridiculous proposal, even though it would mean sharing a small house with eight people for a while and doing without all the fine things to which she'd become accustomed. It also meant not being empress. If what he felt for her was true and not magically manufactured, she might change her name to Anya or Felyciny, or Leisa—well, not Felyciny, even though that was a common enough name. Anya or Leisa was more elegant and appropriate.

What on earth was she thinking? She was actually considering choosing a *false* name!

"I can't let my parents think I'm dead," she said as she hurried to catch up with him. "And I really should tell someone that Wallis tried to murder me. He should not be allowed to get away with such an atrocious act."

"You're right, of course," Laris said, even though he didn't sound as if he believed she was right at all.

"But…"

Laris turned and looked down at her. "But what?"

"But we really don't have to rush toward Arthes. I was told the emperor would make his choice on the first night of the Summer Festival, which is weeks away."

"What are you saying?"

"The next time my legs begin to hurt, perhaps we could just stop for a while." She glanced off the road to the gentle hills in the distance. "And perhaps we could veer from the path on occasion so I can see more of this lovely province. It's very different from home."

"What of informing your parents of your survival and informing the emperor that Wallis tried to kill you?"

"I doubt that Wallis will send word to my parents immediately, especially as there is no body to send home. And as to the other, well, justice will be served, but I don't know why it can't *wait*."

Laris smiled a little, and Verity reached out to take his hand in her own.

THE riders, three of them, came around the corner at a gallop, but reacted well when they saw Sanura standing in their path—just as Trystan had suspected they would. One rider veered to her left, the other to the right, and the man in the middle pulled on his horse's reins and reared back, barely missing her. The horse's hooves came very near her face. In that moment, Trystan's heart seemed to stop. He allowed his attention to stray from the riders and move entirely to Sanura. It was a luxury which could not last long.

As the rider in the middle of the road tried to bring his

horse under control, he fell off and hit the road hard, much
to the amusement of his companions.

The three men were armed, but did not wear the uni-
forms of sentinels. They were bearded and large and dirty,
and wore mismatched clothing, some pieces finely made
and others desperately in need of repair.

Mercenaries or highwaymen, then, searching for their
next victims.

Trystan remained hidden in the shadows of the forest,
taking a moment to size up his opponents. After a few sec-
onds he could tell which was the strongest and which was
the smartest, and which was so slow he could be saved for
last.

Sanura opened her eyes as one of the men, the smart
one, dismounted and walked toward her with an angry leer
on his face. "Woman, what on earth are you doing standing
in the middle of the road? Didn't you hear us coming?
Don't you have the sense the One God gave a toad? He
reared his hand back as if to strike her, and that was when
Trystan made his move. He tossed his dagger with preci-
sion. It flew through the air and landed, as intended, in the
man's raised hand.

The man who had thought to strike Sanura screamed
and clutched at his wounded hand as Trystan leaped from
the shadows.

His first opponent was the one who had fallen from his
horse—the strongest of the three, by Trystan's estimation.
The man wielded a short-bladed sword that had not been
properly cared for. He swung it with verve and strength but
very little skill.

The last rider to remain horsed—the slow one—
dismounted to see to his squealing, wounded companion.
That one was a follower, not a leader. He was a man who
did as he was told when he was told, and did not tax himself with making decisions.

Out of the corner of his eye Trystan saw the man who'd
thought about hitting Sanura yank the dagger from his
hand, grab her, and begin to shout.

The rider who fought Trystan made a mad stab with his blade, and Trystan skillfully finished him off with a single thrust.

Two to one was much better odds. Trystan turned to face the man who held Sanura, and he smiled. "Thieves or mercenaries?" he asked crisply.

The smart one held Trystan's bloody dagger to Sanura's throat. "What is it to you?"

"I wish to steal or purchase your fallen comrade's horse, as he no longer has need of it and I do, and I'm wondering if I'll have to kill all three of you in order to make that happen. Thieves I can bargain with. Mercenaries are likely to need killing."

"In that case, we're thieves."

"Good to know. If we're going to bargain, you can release the woman." Something deep inside him *did not* like seeing that blade at Sanura's throat. One smooth and relatively minor motion, and she'd be dead. He had threatened to kill her himself, and still might, but she would die by his hand—no other's.

"I don't think it would be wise to release her just yet," the man who held Sanura said. "You put a dagger through my hand, and it hurts! You also killed my cousin. By rights, I should kill your woman in return."

They called her *his*, and she was. Bound as she was, beautiful as she was, she was obviously a possession which could be bartered just as the horse was.

"My dagger could've gone through your heart or your throat, so you should not hold your wound against me. As to the other, he was your cousin, eh?"

"Not a favorite cousin, mind you," the knife-wielding thief said. "Lucky for you."

"How much for the horse?" Trystan asked. "Your cousin isn't going to need it anymore, and I do."

The thief looked at his fallen cousin, at the horse, and then at Sanura. "I'll trade you for the woman. She's pretty, and I haven't bedded a pretty woman in a long time. Is she agreeable?"

"Very," Trystan said in a flat voice.

"Does she have a name?"

"Call her whatever you'd like. It matters not." He did not want to tell the man that her name was Sanura. The name was for him alone, not for one such as this.

The wounded man looked at his hand and grimaced. It was still bleeding, but was far from fatal. "I'm not sure a woman is enough in trade for all that you have done."

Trystan smiled tightly. "This one is, I promise you. She begs for sex now and then, she likes it so well, and when she finds her pleasure, she screams loud enough to shake the walls around you, or the trees, if you have no walls. She will make you glad to be a man, and before you're finished with her, you will have forgotten all about your wounded hand and your cousin."

Sanura glared at him, hurt and angry and wishing him dead, no doubt.

"An unlikable cousin and a horse for such a woman seems like a fair enough trade," the thief said with a grin. "But if she is so wonderful, why would you let her go?" He was a suspicious man. As he was untrustworthy, he likely could not trust anyone else.

"I'm done with her," Trystan said simply. "She's been good fun on this journey, but I can't very well take her home with me."

The man who held Sanura nodded as if he understood. Perhaps he imagined that there was a wife waiting at home, a wife who would not be pleased to see one such as Sanura. "It's a deal, then."

Trystan sheathed his weapon in a show of surrender and agreement. "Done."

Sanura blinked hard, and her eyes went wide. Was she relieved or horrified that he would leave her here? He could not tell, and he wanted very badly to know what she was thinking right now.

He took a step toward Sanura and the man who held her. The knife did seem to slip a little from her throat. "It's not a bad trade for either of us," he said. "You've lost a cousin but gained a delightful woman, and I'll be able to ride the rest of the way home. I'm damned tired of walking."

He took another step, and the thief moved the dagger to a more ready position once again. "Stop where you are."

"I only wish to kiss the woman in farewell. She really has been quite pleasing. In many ways, I will miss her."

"You'll get no kiss. Take your horse and leave before I change my mind and kill you so I can have the horse and the woman."

Trystan held both hands up, and he smiled. "Fine. There's always another woman down the road to kiss." He stepped backward and locked eyes with Sanura. "Sorry, love. I need the horse more than I need you."

Trystan stepped over the man he had killed and hoisted himself into the saddle. When he was well seated in the unfamiliar saddle, he gave Sanura a casual wave of his hand, and then he turned toward Arthes. He spurred the horse onward and rounded the corner, moving out of sight and racing down the road.

SHE had never thought to be sorry to see Trystan ride away, but these men who now held her—they were worse. They had killed on many occasions, when killing had not been necessary, and the one who held her liked to hurt his women. He would make her pay for the wound Trystan had delivered, if he got the chance.

It looked as if he would get that chance. Trystan had traded her for a horse! He had left her with these nefarious men, knowing what they were and what they wanted, telling them that she would *beg* for sexual favor.

Alix would care, but Trystan did not.

The wounded man ordered her to remain still as he released her and studied his bleeding hand. He still held Trystan's dagger in his unmarked hand, but the other was all but worthless, and would be until it had healed. She took a step back toward the forest, but her smallest motion caught the man's attention and he threatened to hurt her if she moved again.

Hurt her, not kill her.

She had fallen so very low. No longer treasured, no longer revered, no longer protected. Maybe that dagger in the back would be better than what awaited her. Maybe death would be better than to be given to one such as this. Sanura wanted to scream at the horrible man that she would rather be dead than continue to live this way, but it was not true. She wanted to live.

She heard the approaching horse before she saw it. Trystan rode into view, his sword drawn and held high, his hair flying behind him. He was not smiling as he cut down the man who had already been wounded, and then the other—a man so stunned by Trystan's appearance he didn't have time to draw his own weapon more than halfway out of its sheath.

They were just a few feet away, and the commotion was so great, the screams so gut-wrenching, that Sanura dropped to the ground and covered her face with her arms. She did not want to see or hear as Trystan cut down the highwaymen. She did not want to see more blood, even though it flowed from unworthy men. She had seen enough blood to suit her since coming to this land.

"I want to go home," she whispered. "Gods above help me, I want to go home." As the screams fell silent, she added, "I want Alix."

As the horse's hooves moved closer, she dropped her arms from her face and looked up. Oddly calm, Trystan sat his horse and looked down at her. He offered her his hand. After a moment's hesitation, she stood and took it. Trystan lifted her easily and plopped her down in front of him, in a sideways position which was uncomfortable and unnatural but oddly steady. When she was seated securely, he slipped the blade of his sword between her wrists and cut the bonds which had restrained her for so many days.

Once he had returned that sword to its sheath, he turned

the horse away from the bodies and took off at a moderate speed. "Did you think I would really give you away?"

"Yes," she said honestly.

"I'm far from finished with you, Sanura," he admitted, and she could tell that the words were grudgingly said. Trystan did not wish to need anything or anyone.

For a moment she detected a light within him, just as she had once detected the darkness within Alix. Confused and agitated, that light struggled—as did the shadows. In that moment she knew the truth. Neither Alix or Trystan would ever win this battle. The struggle would continue for the rest of their days, dark and light vying for control.

No, the battle was not theirs, it was *his*.

She placed one palm against the side of a beard-roughened face, leaned in, and kissed the man who held her. For Alix, for the light, for not being able to allow those men to hurt her, she kissed him. The meeting of their mouths was brief, and took him by surprise.

"What was that for?" he asked, sounding more than a little annoyed.

"For saving me," she said simply.

He laughed harshly. "My intentions were not noble, so I hardly deserve your thanks."

She understood his intentions better than he did, and it was all becoming so clear to her. "You love me."

Again he laughed, but the sound seemed more forced this time. "I love no one," he said after the laughter died. "I took you back because you are mine. I own you as you were meant to be owned, I possess you as you were intended to be possessed. I would've just as ardently retrieved a horse or a sword, if I saw either of them in unworthy hands."

He spurred the horse to a gallop, and she held on tight. If she screamed, he would hear her, but she needed time to think. How best to save this man? How best to repair the damage she had done?

How best to love him?

Chapter Fourteen

TRYSTAN'S control was tight, if not complete, and Sanura knew she could not seduce him unless he wished to be seduced. He could not be tricked, and subtleties were wasted on him. She could not lie to get what she wanted, she could not pretend.

That left the truth, which was stark and painful, but also unexpectedly beautiful and full of hope.

Though he wished to race to Arthes, they did make camp for the night. Trystan was not taking any chances with the precious horse he'd killed to take, so there would be no pushing the animal, and no racing down dark paths where unseen obstacles might—and surely would—lurk.

This might be the last night they spent alone, the last night before they reached the palace and Trystan became the emperor who'd murdered his brother to take the throne. After that happened, would Alix retreat completely? Would he bury himself deep and stay there?

Trystan built a fire and cared for the horse. There had been hard bread and dried meat in the saddlebags of the horse he'd taken, and the meager meal seemed like a feast after too many days of foraging for their sustenance. They shared their meager rations in strained silence.

When Trystan took the bedroll which had also been a part of their bounty and laid it upon the ground for their bed, he did not threaten Mali or bind Sanura's hands and feet. He knew she would not run. He knew that she was his.

Before he could recline upon the rough blanket, she forced herself to stand before him and take his face in her hands. She did not tremble; she did not waver, even though the eyes which stared down at her were dark and unpredictable.

"I love you," she said simply.

Trystan sighed. "Good Lord, woman, are you trying to seduce me again?"

His sharp tone did not deter her. "No. I don't need to join with you in order to see who and what you are. I see all of you. I love all of you. Trystan and Alix, darkness and light, killer of thieves and noble prince—you are *one* and I love you no matter which part of your soul is stronger at this moment."

"You're confused," he said softly.

Sanura raked her fingers across his rough cheek. "No, for the first time since I met you, I am not at all confused. I don't understand how it happened, I don't know why you are two, but I do see. Your goodness is not without shadows, and your darkness is not without love. Threaten and glare all you want, I know you will not hurt me."

She went up on her toes and kissed him as she had that afternoon, softly and without demand. "There is no more need to hide from me, because I see all of you," she whispered against his mouth. "I will call you Alix or Trystan or whatever else you might wish. It does not matter. Perhaps I was given to your brother, but that was a lifetime ago and I am now yours. In ways I cannot begin to understand, I have always been yours."

He caught her up in his arms and lifted her off her feet and he kissed her hard. His tongue speared into her mouth and he parted her lips wide as he devoured her. She threaded her fingers in his hair and held on, kissing him back, giving as much as she took.

She felt it when the moment came that he gave over completely, when whatever within him fought his love for her lost the battle. He laid her on the blanket and kissed her again. Sanura could not remember ever being swept away quite like this. Trystan or Alix, she did love him. Trystan or Alix, he did love her.

For the first time, she made love without consciously using her gift. There was no search for more, no sought-after connection at the pit of her soul. Trystan undressed her, taking care not to tear her plain hand-me-down dress. He undressed himself with haste but not with frenzy. Bare body to bare body there was connection, but it was of a man and a woman, not of a gifted slave of the Agnese and he who possessed her.

Alix had made love to her; Trystan had made love to her. The instant he entered her, she knew this was different. This was both—no, that was wrong. This was Prince Alixandyr the whole man, good and bad, noble and wicked. She did not reach to grasp his desires or to know more of who he was or what he wanted from her, but the knowledge was there, flowing through her like the ocean before a storm, strong and sure and beautiful.

Fractured. The word teased her. *Broken.* Alix's word to describe himself and the darkness which he fought. *Endless*, to define the battle he fought every day.

And then it all went away and there was nothing but the way their bodies came together, the way the stroke and the press and the frenzy made her feel. They were skin and breath and sweat and heartbeat, they were need and love and possession, and then they were release. They were pleasure. They were screams and moans that sounded in the lonely black of the forest.

And neither of them was alone. They had both been so lonely, so isolated in their lives, but no more. Never again.

The body above hers stiffened and withdrew, but with

an easy arm she pulled him back to her. "Do not be afraid of me," she whispered. "I have not seen anything which I did not already know, and even if I had, I will not hurt you. I will not hurt any part of you."

"Don't care about me, Sanura. When I'm done with you, when I don't need you anymore, I will kill you."

"No, you won't," she said confidently. "A part of you might wish to kill me, a part of you might want to be free of all that I see, all that I know, but even that part loves me."

"You're very sure of yourself," he said.

"No, I'm very sure of *you*, Trystan or Alix or whatever you wish to call yourself. You do treasure me, even when my very presence maddens you. You do want me, even when you know such wanting is not wise. You do love me, just as I love you."

He looked her in the eye. The light of the fire was not enough for her to see the color of his eyes well, but she knew they remained dark, at least for now. "I have fought too long for what I want to allow a woman to ruin it all."

"I will ruin nothing," she said confidently.

"My plans have not changed. When we reach Arthes, I'm going to kill Jahn and take the throne."

She did not think so, but now was not the time to argue. "If you insist."

"I'm going to take all those things which the one you call Alix would not take."

"Will you take me?" she asked, lifting his hips to bring them closer once again.

"Yes."

Sanura pressed her lips against his neck and tasted his sweat. She flicked her tongue there and suckled his skin and wrapped her legs around his. "Good. Tonight nothing else matters."

THEY had found a narrow path which led them east of Arthes. No matter how many detours they took, no matter how often they stopped to rest or to admire the scenery, eventually they would come to the capital city. That knowledge weighed upon Verity every day and every night.

She could not sleep, even though Laris was close to her, offering her his magnificent warmth, and she'd walked more than she'd been carried today. She should've fallen into an exhausted sleep long ago, but her mind was spinning mercilessly.

It was so completely unfair that she could fall in love with a sentinel! Why could she not have fallen in love with a rich merchant or a prince or even the emperor himself? Why did she have to defy her own destiny to be the wife of a great man? No, she had to fall in love with a sentinel who had no money, no home of his own, no jewels to give her, no position of power, no land. All he had were strong hands which protected her, strong arms which had saved her life, sweet eyes which spoke of the magical love with which she had poisoned him, sweet lips which she was dying to taste.

She would be tempted to take him up on his offer of a new life, if not for the fact that his love for her wasn't real. Tears stung her eyes. She had done a few selfish things in her lifetime, that was true, but she'd never done anything as horrible as this!

Her sniffling woke him.

"What's wrong?" Laris asked, his voice sleepy.

"I'm a terrible person," Verity said in a small voice.

He pulled her close and laughed sleepily. "You are not," he said with confidence.

"I am," she insisted. "You just don't know…"

His hand settled in her hair. "You're spoiled and funny and beautiful and naïve and overly ambitious, but you are not a terrible person." He kissed the top of her head. "Go back to sleep. Morning will be here too soon."

If she didn't tell him now, she might never again find the nerve. While he held her, while it was too dark to see his face and the shocked reaction he would no doubt have… "I gave you a love potion!" she said quickly. "That's why you risked your life for me, that's why you hold my hand and why you sneaked into my tent all those nights before Wallis tried to kill me, it's why you're so nice to me. I tricked you! I gave you a witch's potion to make you love me."

His body stiffened, but he did not push her away. Not yet. "When did this happen?"

She hid her face against his chest, expecting him to push her away at any moment, now that he knew the truth about her. "The day we left home, I brought you a cup of cider. It was not just cider," she added with a sigh.

"Oh, that," Laris said, relaxing once again.

"Oh, that?" she said, sitting up to look down at his dim figure. She had basically poisoned him with a magical elixir meant to serve her own purposes, and he was so besotted he didn't even see the wrongness of her actions! "Oh, that? Is that all you have to say? I did a terrible thing to you, I tricked you and used you and you just say, Oh, *that*?"

He gently pulled her back down to him. "You're worrying about nothing, Verity. Maybe you gave me a love potion, but I didn't drink it."

"What?" Her heart skipped a beat. "But I saw you."

"You saw me put the cup to my lips. The cider stunk, thanks to the potion, I suppose, so I pretended to take a drink, and when you turned your back, I dumped it all onto the ground."

Verity rose up again. "Why didn't you just tell me it stunk and you wouldn't drink it?"

"I didn't want to hurt your feelings."

"Why not?"

Laris sighed and sat up. "Because I already loved you, that's why. Because you were, and still are, the most beautiful creature I had ever seen, and I didn't want to say or do anything to dim the brightness of your smile." He reached out and touched her face gently. "Why me? Why didn't you give the potion to one of the others?"

She could lie and tell him that he'd been closest, the most convenient, but she didn't want to lie to him, no matter how embarrassing it might be. "You were by far the most handsome of all the sentinels, and you have such a lovely smile, and on the second day after you arrived, I saw you speaking to the cook's son, who is not so very bright, and you were kind to him."

"You chose me," he said.

"I did." They lay back down in the dark, and once again Laris held her. Her heart felt so much lighter, she could not stop the smile that spread across her face. Whatever he felt for her, it was real, like her own feelings. He had not saved her because he was under the influence of magic, but because he cared. Because he truly loved her.

"I'm glad I chose you," she whispered.

Laris sighed sleepily. "So am I."

VYRN laid a hand over his stomach, which had not been quite right of late. Soon, in a matter of days at the very least, he would be forced to part from the other sentinels and soldiers and make his way to the house of the woman who had hired him. There he'd be paid for his efforts, and with any luck he could disappear before anyone thought to question what had happened the night Princess Edlyn died.

He didn't have a lot of time. Paki and Kontar, the blue whore's two surly guardians, just yesterday had separated themselves from the group to travel to Arthes and demand justice from the emperor himself. They were all frustrated at the lack of success, but those two had finally had enough of following the others and not finding their charge. Impatient fellows! Yes, it would be best if he collected his pay before too many questions were raised.

Vyrn walked into the forest to relieve himself, took care of the task, and then turned about. Tari stood there, her thin, drably gowned body positioned between him and camp. He blinked hard, wondering if she was a hallucination. His head was swimming and his legs were unsteady, so it was possible.

"Hello, Vyrn," she said in a lowered voice. "I got tired of waiting for you to collect me, so I decided to find you on my own. I hope you don't mind."

"We haven't yet caught the prince," he whispered. He stepped toward her, and when he was near, placed a hand on her shoulder, as much for support as to assure himself that she was real.

"I know."

Vyrn set aside his annoyance. Perhaps it wasn't a bad thing that she'd joined him. He'd eaten something bad or had picked up a disease from one of the villagers he'd questioned, and he could do with a woman to look after him. Besides, with her to help him through this bad patch, he could leave immediately and go collect his pay.

"I'm glad you've come," he whispered. "We can leave tonight."

She nodded, meek and agreeable as always.

"Wait here. I'll be back as soon as I can."

Vyrn returned to camp. No one else was sick, which made him think he'd caught a disease. They'd been eating the same food, after all. He'd caught something from one of the common folk he'd been interrogating of late. A farmer or a shopkeeper's wife had passed along this weakening illness. Maybe one of those annoying coughing children he'd had to deal with a few days ago had given him this sickness. Little monsters, he should've beaten them the way he'd beaten their uncooperative father. Dammit, someone had to have seen the prince, someone had to know where he was.

That no longer mattered. He was not going to find the prince and collect a bonus, but he still had a nice bit of pay to collect. Until he regained his strength, Tari would care for him. She'd be good for one last function before he disposed of her.

Without letting on to the others in camp that anything had changed, he volunteered to take the first watch, using the excuse that he did not feel like sleeping. When everyone else was asleep, which did not take very long, he grabbed his bedroll, saddled his horse, and entered the forest.

He found Tari where he'd left her standing.

"Did you bring your waterskin?" she asked as he led her away from the camp.

"Yes. Are you thirsty?"

She shook her head. "No, I just wanted to make sure you didn't forget anything that we might need along the way."

His stomach made an odd gurgling noise and yet another pain shot through him. Yes, it was a very good thing Tari had come along when she had. He had her right where he wanted her, and she'd do anything for him. Hadn't she already proven that point?

TRYSTAN held Sanura long after she slept, knowing that to hold her was a weakness he did not need or want.

Was she right when she said that he would never be rid of the other and the other would never be rid of him? Was she right to contend that he was only one? Was that why, in spite of his anger and his ambition, he wanted her to love him?

When the thief had threatened her, Trystan had felt anger and worry and a dark possessiveness, even though he had been the one to put her in the road, even though he had used her to stop the horsemen. Sanura was *his*. No other man would hurt her, no other man would touch her. He might've taken her and the horse and left the two thieves alive, but when the bandit had held a knife to Sanura, he'd gone too far. He'd been dead the moment he put that dagger to her throat.

This was a complication he could do without. All these years, his plans had been so simple. Take control, take the throne, *take* whatever he wanted to take! And yet here he was, enjoying the comfort of the even sound of Sanura's breathing, of the feel of her skin against his. He was hard again, he could not sleep, and yet he would not wake her to *take* what he wanted.

Trystan was not gone, he had not been pushed down into the shadows again, and yet he realized that he was no longer alone. Alix was with him—and perhaps had been for quite some time. Alix was influencing him, was affecting his mind. If Sanura was right and they were one, nothing would be as he'd planned—nothing would ever be the way it had once been, either.

He no longer knew what tomorrow would bring. He was not Prince Alixandyr, loyal and obedient servant to his brother the emperor, but neither was he a cold-blooded killer who cared for nothing but what he desired, what he deserved.

Perhaps that was why he held Sanura even now. In spite of his strength and his plans and the victories he had won of late, he was lost.

Sanura woke slowly. Her body squirmed against his, her breathing changed, her hands wandered. They had not bothered to dress last night, as the air was mild and they had one another to keep themselves warm, so her squirming was quite pleasurable. Her head tilted back, and in the first gray light of the day he saw her smile.

She *smiled*.

"Are you awake, love?" she asked, her voice husky with sleep.

"Yes."

"Good." She stroked him intimately, she kissed him, she raked her talented fingers across his body as she wished, and then she guided him into her. She sighed in contentment as he filled her. She moved against him in a slow and easy rhythm. They came alive as the morning did.

In this position he could only partially enter her, but for a while it was enough. There was no rush, there was no fury. There was sensation and possibility and love. There was desire and pleasure and the promise of more. She belonged to him, and he would never again be lost in darkness. He would never again be alone.

"I love you," Sanura said as her hips shifted so that she could take more of him into her. Just a bit more.

I love you. His words, his return of affection was silent

but no less heartfelt than her own, even though he realized that love was his undoing. All his plans were dust thanks to the love he had not wanted or expected. And yet, he did not care. Not at this moment when his world did not extend beyond this forest, his desire, and her body.

He rolled Sanura onto her back and thrust deep. She found release almost immediately, and so did he. She shuddered and screamed and gasped beneath him, and then she grabbed on to his hair and pulled him down for a long, passionate kiss.

"You should not love me," he said gruffly. "It's wrong."

"No, it is not wrong," she insisted. "Just because you did not plan to love me in return..."

"I did not say that I loved you," he insisted.

Sanura smiled. "No. You were so caught up in the physical, you forgot that I can see all of you, most particularly when we are joined. You do love me."

"You've bewitched me with your body, that is all. I cannot love. I am not capable."

"You can." She looked at his eyes, calculating and inquisitive. "You do."

Perhaps it was foolish to argue with a woman who had the power to see into a man's soul. He could profess to the heavens that he felt nothing for her but lust, but she would know it was not true.

"When we recover your box, I want you blue again," he said, anxious to turn the conversation from the subject of love.

"Why?"

"Don't you know?" he asked sharply. "You seem to be able to see everything else."

"Not everything," she said without rancor, "just most where you're concerned. Besides, now and then I like you to tell me things. I like to hear the gruff timbre of your voice."

"Fine. I want you blue so no other man will ever touch you. I want you blue because that was how I first saw you, how you first attacked my heart and soul. I want you to sing again, just for me."

Her brows drew together. "Sing? I have never sung. I have no gift for it."

Trystan sighed. "You sang for him with every step, with every sigh. I don't hear it the way your Alix did, and I want to. I want that very much. If you are painted blue once more and you wear the bangles, perhaps you will sing for me."

"I will sing for no one else," she said.

He remembered the feeling inside Alix when he'd heard Sanura's song. It had been pleasant and at the same time disturbing, perhaps because he already knew what that music meant.

"You will make a fine empress," he said as he forced himself to stand.

"Perhaps," she whispered.

He offered her a hand to assist her to her feet. "If we hurry, we can make it to Arthes by tonight, and you can be empress by morning."

She came to her feet with his help, and then her bare body fell against his. "I am in no rush to see Arthes or to be empress."

He knew what she was doing; he realized that she did not want him to kill Jahn and take the throne. He knew that she would do everything in her power to slow their journey and keep him from the end of his plans—and he did not care.

Chapter Fifteen

VERITY saw the farmhouse in the distance, and even though she was not anxious for their journey to end, she breathed a sigh of relief. The house was directly in their path, and Laris showed no sign of veering around it. She doubted he would stop there for very long, but shelter, food they did not pick or catch, a *chair*, all waited in that quaint cottage. Those simple things sounded so wonderful, she found her pace increasing. She almost skipped, but that would've been entirely inappropriate for a woman of her age.

The house itself was small compared with her home in the Northern Province, but it was far from tiny. It sprawled a bit, as if rooms had been added to the original structure. Smoke rose gently from the chimney, and the land surrounding the cottage was green and well kept. Farmland spread as far as she could see. Some of the crops had been recently planted, others were mature and green. She didn't know exactly what kinds of crops grew on the farm, but she could see that they were well tended and healthy.

A line of freshly washed clothes whipped in the breeze,

and Verity thought of what a joy it would be to wash the putrid green dress Laris had bought her. There had been a time when burning would've been her first thought, but since he had bought it for her, she would not destroy it, no matter what happened in the weeks to come. Besides, he had told her that her eyes were a more brilliant blue than ever before, in contrast to the drab green. When she was able to replace the clothing she had lost, perhaps there would be one or two green gowns in her new wardrobe.

She was practically joyous as they approached the farmhouse, and again she suppressed the urge to skip. The sun shone, the weather was mild, and Laris held her hand. Perhaps her good mood was colored by the fact that he loved her without the use of magic. She was not a terrible person after all.

Since running away from the potential assassins, she had not seen another living soul except Laris. He had seen only a shopkeeper, in that small town where he'd stopped for supplies. Verity was anxious about seeing the people who lived in this farmhouse. She was not afraid and she was not joyous, but she *was* anxious.

Would word of her death have reached such an isolated home? Probably not, but it was possible. They should come up with a good story and a couple of false names, just in case whoever lived here asked too many questions.

Before she could broach the subject, the door to the house opened and a young woman stepped out into the sunshine. Even from this distance Verity could tell that the woman was shapely and probably no older than she. The girl's dress was as plain as the one Laris had bought for her, but it was not green and it was of a better fit.

"We should have our story settled, if we're to see others," she said. "I suppose we will have to pretend to be married." Her heart did a flip and her stomach tightened. "That would explain why we're traveling together." And holding hands, too.

"We don't need a story," Laris said calmly.

"We do."

Verity said no more before the young woman who'd come out of the cottage saw them. And screamed.

The girl lifted the skirt of her plain dress high, and ran. She did not run like a lady, but flashed her bare legs and moved at an amazing speed. Verity stopped in her tracks. Was the woman mad? Had she been isolated on this farm for so long that the sight of strangers compelled her to run at the speed of a racehorse?

Laris dropped her hand and smiled at the madwoman, moving forward to greet her. The racing girl smiled widely, and she screamed again for no apparent reason. Then she screamed his name at the top of her apparently healthy lungs.

"Laris!"

His smile; her shout…this was a sweet reunion.

Verity's heart sank. Love-struck or not, Laris had a wife. A special friend, at the very least. No wonder he had never tried to make love to her as they slept entwined. He was already married, or promised. She placed her hands on her hips in outrage. He had asked her to marry him! How could he have suggested that she be his wife if he already had one? Of course, he had quickly admitted that his proposal was a stupid idea, so perhaps some baser impulse had momentarily carried him away, and then he'd had time to remember that he already had a woman and could not take her as a wife.

Verity no longer felt like skipping. Her heart was heavy, her stomach was one big knot.

If only the girl were ugly, she thought as the two met and threw their arms around one another. Instead, the girl was quite pretty, and had luxurious light brown hair and a pronounced womanly figure. Verity's knees wobbled. She wanted to fall into the dirt and sob, even though Laris was nothing to her but a sentinel who had saved her life and promised to protect her. He was just a man who loved her, even though he knew it was wrong.

He wasn't hers. He never had been.

Laris lifted the unladylike, screaming woman off her feet and spun her around. They both laughed. It was heart-warming and totally unacceptable. Verity stood her ground, crossing her arms over her chest and glaring at the happy couple.

"I didn't expect to see you for weeks!" the girl cried as Laris put her on her feet.

"This visit was unplanned," Laris explained.

The girl looked around him and smiled at Verity. "And you are not alone."

The smile was confusing. Verity knew that if she was married to Laris and he showed up with another woman, she'd be furious!

Laris took the girl's arm and led her toward Verity. She tried to keep her lower lip from trembling, but was unsuccessful. Laris looked confused, and then contrite. "Verity..."

So much for her false name.

"This is my sister Carina."

Sister. The word echoed through her heart clear as a bell. Sister! The knotted stomach eased. Her heart lightened. Verity put on her most brilliant smile and stepped forward. "It's so lovely to meet you. Really, so very lovely. Such a pleasure." Just because she was dressed like a beggar, that didn't mean she had to act like one. "Laris, you didn't tell me your sister Carina was so beautiful!" She reached around and pinched him soundly, to make him pay for causing her grief, no matter how short-lived that grief might've been. He didn't yelp, but he did jump a bit.

From what he'd said, there were three sisters and two brothers still living at home. He had mentioned all their names at least once, but she could not remember them all. He had never bothered with physical descriptions, and she had not asked since she'd thought she'd never meet them. She looked at the farmhouse and tried to imagine all those people living there. With their parents, that made seven in a house smaller than the kitchen of the home she'd left behind.

Of course, it was a *big* kitchen.

Laris placed an arm around her shoulder. "You don't

have to be in Arthes until the first night of the Summer Festival, so I thought we might stay here for a while, if that's all right with you."

"Yes," she said. "I think that's a lovely idea."

"It'll be much more crowded than what you're accustomed to," he warned her.

"I don't care."

"You'll have to share a bed." He blushed.

She blushed, too. "I don't care," she said again.

In fact, sharing a bed sounded very fine at the moment.

IN spite of his impatience to reach Arthes, Trystan led the horse at an easy pace. If they did not reach Arthes until tomorrow or the next day, what would be the harm? Jahn would still be there, and before it was all done, Jahn would still be dead.

There was more to this life he had craved for so long than the taking of power.

Sanura was perched in front of him, sideways so he could see her face when he desired to do so. He desired to do so often. There was something about the curve of her cheek and the softness of her lips and the gleam of her eyes that warmed him. He had not thought he wished to be warmed, and yet apparently he did.

"Tell me about your brother," Sanura said as they moved at a slow pace down the road to Arthes.

Instead of ordering her to cease prattling, as he should've, he asked, "What do you wish to know?

"You are twins. Do you look exactly alike?"

He gave a disgusted snort. "No. Jahn is fairer, and prettier in the face. You would find him handsome, I imagine. Most women do."

"I don't care for a man who's too pretty." Sanura twisted her head and looked up at him. "I prefer a man who looks like a man, as you do."

Was it his imagination, or did she stare too intently into his eyes? His insides tightened and quaked.

"Stop looking at me that way unless you wish to be taken here and now."

"You would stop so soon?"

"I did not say we would stop. I said *here* and *now*."

She laughed easily. "We cannot make love on horseback. Don't be ridiculous."

"I did not say we would make love." Such soft, easy words for such a momentous act.

"No, but that is what you meant," she said, relaxing against him as best she could. "And no matter what you call it, the deed cannot be accomplished on horseback, and should not be attempted unless you wish to die of a broken neck."

"But I would die happy."

She laughed. He smiled. *Happy.* In all the times he'd thought of taking control and taking what he wanted, happiness had never crossed his mind. It had not crossed Alix's mind often, either. He'd been too busy fighting to keep his most primal thoughts suppressed.

Was Sanura right when she insisted that they were one? That there was no Alix and Trystan, that there was no light and dark, there was only the man he had become. A single man. If she was right, then there was no other—and there never had been.

He'd planned to kill her once he'd had her, but he'd had her many times now, and he did not even wish to see her frown—much less see her dead. He would protect her with his life, if need be, and if anyone else dared to touch her, to hurt her, he would die to keep her safe.

She had ruined everything.

"Were you close growing up?" she asked.

"Jahn and I?"

"Yes, though when you were children, he was Devlyn and you were Trystan, isn't that right?"

"That's correct." He looked past Sanura's fall of hair, which was caught up on top of her head, silky as a raven's wing. "There were times when we were close, and times when we were not. He could be very funny, when he wished to be. He made our mother laugh when she was sad and nothing and no one else could ease her pain."

"Did he make you laugh?"

"Now and then." His gut clenched. "Don't think you will make me change my mind by urging me to remember better times. I know what I want and what is required to take it. I know what is mine, Sanura."

"I would never dare to try to make you change your mind," she said calmly. "I was simply curious, and trying to pass the time." He could see her face well enough to see the transformation that came over it. Her smile died. Her mouth went hard. He wanted to ask her what was wrong, but held his tongue.

Eventually, she told him what had made her frown. "I cannot be empress, you know."

"Of course you can." He would have no one else—he could trust no one else. "We will be married as soon as I'm declared emperor, and..."

"I can't give you an heir, and any woman you take as your wife must be able to bear your child. Is that not the reason for this silly contest to find an empress? Is it not required that the emperor produce sons?"

"I know a woman who has the gift of fertility. We will ask for her help..."

"I don't think even the strongest of magic can help me conceive and bear a child, and even if it were possible...is this woman a friend of yours and of Jahn's?"

"Yes."

"Do you really think she will help you after you assassinate him?"

"We will find a way," he said sharply.

"There is no way. Perhaps you will keep me as a concubine and marry a woman who will give you children while you keep me for pleasure. Was that not the way of old? I heard stories, while living in Tryfyn, of a Columbyanan emperor who kept a large and pampered harem."

Trystan sighed. "That emperor was my father."

"Then you can carry on the family tradition."

It did make sense. He would need an heir, and Sophie Fyne Varden would not only not assist him if she knew he'd murdered Jahn, she was likely to rain terror on the palace, if she got the chance. Still, he did not like the idea of taking another woman as wife. He also did not like the idea of keeping Sanura as no more than the sexual slave she'd been born to be. She deserved more. She would have more; he'd see to it.

SANURA knew she could not stop Trystan if he insisted upon killing his brother, so she did not even attempt to reason with him. Instead, she planted small doubts in his heart. It was easy, now that the part of him she'd called Alix was rising to the surface once again.

He would never again be the man she'd first met, she understood and accepted that, but he could be a new man, a happier man who did not do constant battle with himself. All beings had primitive desires and dark thoughts. What made a man or woman light or dark was what choices they made when those dark thoughts surfaced.

Trystan Arndell, who had become Prince Alixandyr Beckyt at the age of twenty-five, had been fractured at birth—or perhaps earlier, when he'd become life in his mother's womb. That fracture had existed all these years, until she'd drawn the darker half to the surface by making Alix take something which he knew was not his to take.

Because of her, he would never be the same, but she was not sorry. She could not be sorry that she loved him and he loved her. With luck, his long battle was over. She looked up and into his eyes once again, to see the streaks of light green that had begun to form amid the dark. Love did that. Love brought the light of his soul to the forefront even now.

"I should call you Alix," she said softly as they rode slowly—much more slowly than was necessary—down the path.

The body she leaned against jerked in surprise. "Why?"

"All those at the palace know you as Prince Alixandyr, do they not?"

"They do," he said grudgingly.

"If you show up with a woman who calls you by another name, questions might arise."

He shifted his body slightly, as if he had suddenly grown uncomfortable. "I suppose you're right."

"I've gotten so accustomed to calling you Trystan, I'll need to practice calling you Alix again until it feels right and natural."

"It does not matter what you call me," he said gruffly.

"In that case, I will start practicing now, Alix."

Again he was startled. She held on to him, burying her cheek against his warm chest. "I will call you Alix until you stop reacting so oddly. Those at the palace will wonder if you jump every time I say your name, Alix."

Her fingers raked against his side. She had not thought she would ever feel affection of any kind for the one who called himself Trystan, but now that she knew they were and always would be one, she loved that sad side of him, as well as the more noble Alix. If anything, Trystan needed her more.

No, Trystan needed *Alix* more, and she could be the one to draw Alix to the forefront once again.

"It'll be dark soon, Alix," she said. "Perhaps we should stop for the night.

"We can be in Arthes in a matter of hours," he argued.

"I doubt if the palace will move if we stop for food and sleep and other pleasant activities." She wanted to call him Alix as he made love to her. She wanted to say, "I love you, Alix," while he was inside her.

"You're right, of course," he said. "One more night will make no difference to my plans."

Sanura smiled and held on to Trystan—no, *Alix*—tighter than before. She wanted one more night to call to the light the man she loved, and she was going to have it.

* * *

TARI carried the tin cup of water to Vyrn's trembling, pale lips. The sun had just set, but they had stopped to set up camp hours ago.

Vyrn could barely put one foot in front of the other. His hands shook all the time, and after a few days of fighting his viciously rebellious bodily functions, he had nothing left to expel.

It was time.

Tari made him comfortable on his blanket, after being sure he swallowed a generous drink of the tainted water she'd been giving him for days. Even before she had revealed herself to him, she'd slipped the herbs into his waterskin. It had been very bold of her to sneak into camp and sully his water, but she had not cared what might happen to her if she got caught.

She had not cared then, and did not care now, because her life was over. It had been over since the moment she'd heard the soldiers and sentinels talking about her around the campfire, laughing at her appearance, openly abhorring the very thought of touching her. She did not care what the others thought, but Vyrn should've been better. He should think better of her. After all that she had done for him, he owed her that!

He looked as if he were drifting toward sleep, so she grabbed a hank of his hair and jerked his head very slightly off the ground. His eyes opened, but he was unable to focus on her. Dammit, she wanted him looking at *her*! She wanted him to know the truth.

"You have been so miserable these past few days," she said with sympathy.

He nodded.

"Do you know why you have been so miserable?"

"I'm sick," he said weakly.

"Yes, you are. You're sick because I fed you herbs and grasses which tear up your insides and sap your strength."

It took a moment for the truth to get through his muddled brain. "You...poisoned me?"

"Not precisely, no. What I gave you won't kill you, Vyrn."

He seemed relieved, but not for long. She held his own dagger to his throat. "What I gave you was meant to weaken you so I can cut your throat the way I cut Princess Edlyn's throat. For *you*!" she said sharply. "I killed a woman whose only crime was to be disagreeable, and I did it for you."

He tried to lift his hands, but could not. The last dose she'd given him had been doubly strong. "We're going to get married and be rich and happy," he argued, his words sloppy. "Why would you want to kill me?"

She grabbed one of his wrists with her free hand and carried it roughly to her stomach. "What do you feel here, Vyrn? A woman's body or a sack of bones? Do you want to poke me one more time? If you do, I'm sure I can find a bag to put over my head so you won't have to look at me."

It took a moment for Vyrn to recognize his own words, and when he did, he went even paler, which was a feat. She'd seen fresh winter snow less white than his face. "When I said that, I was only covering for us," he explained. "I couldn't let the others know that you and I were in this together. I couldn't tell them that I... loved you."

"Even now, when your life is in my hands, you choke on the words." She leaned down, placing her face close to his. "Say it again, and this time make me believe you."

"I love you, Tari. All this, everything I've done, has been for you. For us."

She wanted to believe him, she truly did. "I think I'm going to have your baby." Only in the past few days had she begun to suspect that she might be with child. If she had not overheard that awful conversation, she'd be deliriously happy.

"A baby." He managed to lift one trembling hand and touch her arm. "Isn't that nice? You don't want to murder your baby's pappy, do you?"

Tari was set to cut Vyrn's throat, but she hesitated. He did sound happy. Was it true that everything he'd said in camp had been intended to throw the others off their scent? Had he lied to the others that night? She did not fool herself to think that she was beautiful, that men lusted after her, but Vyrn had made her believe that he saw beyond the physical. Did he? Was it possible?

Vyrn moved more quickly than should be possible, grabbing her wrist, turning it sharply, and thrusting the knife into her side. His false face was shed, and he called her vile names as he twisted the blade. His strength was waning and all he could manage was that one thrust and a twist, but it was enough. Tari looked down at her side and the bloom of blood there, and knew he had killed her and their baby.

He fell back, exhausted by the effort of killing her. Sweat beaded on his face, and his eyes were more closed than open. She had to act fast while she still could. Life was slipping away; she felt it leaving her.

Without hesitation, Tari quickly swiped the blade across Vyrn's throat. She'd done the heinous deed before; she knew what to expect. She did not wear an apron this time, so the blood that spurted from the severed throat sprayed across her dress, mixing with her own and even marking her face with vile droplets. She didn't care.

"Why did you make me do this?" she asked as Vyrn's body jerked and then went still. "Why couldn't you love me?" Tears ran down her face, mixing with the blood there.

Killing him had taken the last of her strength, so Tari placed her head on Vyrn's stomach, resting there very comfortably even though they were both drenched in blood. "You made me do this terrible thing," she said. "It's your fault, all your fault." Her words had begun to slur, but she continued to speak to the dead man beneath her. "You should not have talked about me so horribly. You should not have lied to me."

When Vyrn had seduced her into killing the princess, he'd promised that they would be together forever. Tari was pretty sure this wasn't what he'd had in mind, but in the end he was entirely hers.

Chapter Sixteen

VERITY was very happy to make use of one of Carina's old nightgowns for the night. Who would've thought a plain, used nightdress that didn't fit all that well could be considered a luxury? A nightdress, a bath, hot food, a roof over her head when the rain came—it was all heavenly.

She lay in the center of the large bed she had been directed to, and waited anxiously for Laris to join her. Now and then she fiddled with the amber stone of the lucky talisman, which she refused to remove even for sleeping. She did not have any proof that the love potion—which had been left behind with her things when poor Buttercup had run amok—was effective, but she did believe that this talisman had assisted her. She was not dead, and she'd found Laris. All in all, she considered herself very lucky.

Though the farmhouse was far from large, there were a number of small private rooms, as well as a loft above the main room. Privacy was a good thing. After so many days of seeing no one but Laris, she missed their private moments; she hated sharing him, even with his own loving family. Soon he would be here, and she would not have to share him any longer, at least not for tonight.

Verity was no fool. She knew what Laris had been asking when he'd informed her that she would have to share a bed. For weeks the possibility of what might happen had danced between them, but now that they had a proper bed and she knew his love wasn't the result of trickery, everything had changed. Tonight Laris would do more than hold her in his arms, he would do more than protect her. Tonight he would make her his in every way. She was scared and excited at the same time, but still—what was about to happen was right and good, she knew it.

Once she was no longer a virgin, marrying the emperor would be out of the question. She didn't care. Destinies could be changed. She did have *some* control over her own life and destiny! There had been a time when she'd wanted to be empress more than anything else, when she was certain she'd been born to be empress! Now all she wanted was one handsome, sweet sentinel to come to this bed and show her what a man and woman in love might be.

The door to the small bedroom opened, and a figure slipped inside. Maybe she should've left a candle burning, but there was a hint of moonlight shining through the uncovered window, and that should be enough. Verity closed her eyes and gripped the stone she'd been caressing. She held her breath and waited for Laris to join her on the bed. The mattress dipped as weight fell upon it, and a very soft, very female voice, said, "Good night. I hope you don't snore."

Verity sat up abruptly and looked down at Carina's unmistakable head of hair, as Laris's sister turned her back and settled down with a sigh. Before she could think of a word to say, the door opened again and the youngest sister Fharis—easily identifiable thanks to her slim frame—walked in. She dropped to the other side of the bed and hunkered down quite comfortably.

"Are you going to marry Laris, do you think?" the girl whispered without preamble.

Before Verity could answer, Carina said sharply, "Hush, Fharis. That is not a proper question to ask. Go to sleep."

"I only wondered," the youngest sister whispered. "I always thought Laris would come home and marry Ellanie one day. So did Mama, so don't say it's not true."

Ellanie?

"Go to *sleep*," Carina said again. "Tomorrow morning will be here before we know it."

Verity lay back and tried to relax. The bed was large enough for two to be comfortable, but three? And who was Ellanie? The door opened again, and this time Verity was not surprised when the third sister, Robyn, slipped into the room. She shoved Carina to the middle of the mattress, where Verity was already lying quite miserably, muttered a tired good night, and laid her head upon a small pillow.

Verity snuggled into the mattress, disappointed and more than a little hurt. Was this what Laris had meant when he'd said she'd have to share a bed? Of course it was. Once again she'd misunderstood his intentions.

He loved her, she knew that. Did he not want her as a man wants a woman? Did he not believe that she wanted him? He probably thought she still wanted to be empress. A virgin empress, at that. She could not blame him, as she had never told him otherwise.

Somehow, she had thought she would not have to tell Laris how she felt. He should know, shouldn't he? He should look into her eyes and see what she wanted from him. Didn't love bring with it unspoken communication?

Apparently not.

Not that her actual communication had been without its problems of late. She had never told Laris that she did not wish to be empress. On many occasions she had told him that she would marry into that position. How was he to know otherwise? And still, she was annoyed that he did not.

Carina elbowed her, and Fharis kicked her ankle. The assault continued for a while before Verity became accus-

tomed to the other bodies in the bed, and the girls all settled down to sleep—quiet and still.

It was quite some time before Verity found the same
stillness and much-needed sleep.

"I suppose we will reach Arthes tomorrow," Sanura said as
she laid her head on Alix's bare chest.

"Long before dark," he said. For a man who had once
been so anxious to get to the palace, he did not sound happy
about the prospect.

She placed her hand low on his belly, pressing it there,
raking her fingers against his warm flesh. They were naked and entangled beneath a canopy of leaves. It was the
only bed she'd known of late, the only bed she wanted. For
now, lost in the forest, Alix was entirely hers.

"I will take good care of you," he said gruffly. "No matter what happens in the days to come, I will care for you
above all others."

A part of him, the part which had craved control for so
long, still wanted the throne and the power that came with
it, but another part of him, the man she loved, wanted
more. He wanted love and peace; he wanted the connection
they shared. Would it be the same when they were lying in
a large, soft bed as it was now when their bed was the hard
ground and their roof was the night sky? Would he still
love her?

Would he choose power over her?

"And I will care for you, Alix," she said softly. "When
you are well; when you are ill; when you are happy; when
you are sad; whether you are emperor or not ..."

"I will be emperor," he said.

Arguing with him when he was in this state would do
more harm than good, she knew, so she did not. Instead,
she brushed her thumb across a muscle. He had so many
fine muscles, and she was learning them all.

This afternoon she had noticed that his eyes had begun
to change. Not the instant and remarkable change from

light to dark that she had seen before, but a subtle blending. Streaks of light green now existed among the dark, as both parts of the man she loved merged. At the moment there was still more darkness, but every time she called him Alix, every time he questioned his intentions toward his brother, every time he realized that he loved her—the darkness became less pronounced.

Soon, if she was right, his eyes would be the light green she had first seen, light and beautiful green, perhaps marked with thin streaks that spoke of the darkness he could, and would, learn to control.

They slept awhile, and then they woke to make love without words. They simply came together as if being one were the most natural state for either of them. She called her lover Alix. She told him she loved him, many times. She found and gave pleasure in a way she had never known was possible, even though to give pleasure was her purpose.

No, to love was her purpose. She simply had not realized that until she'd come here and discovered Alix, this fractured man who needed her and her love more than she'd imagined was possible.

When they were joined, she could see deeply into his soul. Where there had once been light and dark in a constant battle, there was now a merging, a union—a truce of sorts. If she had more time before they reached Arthes, if she could have Alix to herself for just a few more days, she could be assured that the dark side would not win—she could be certain he would not kill his own brother.

But he could not be stalled any longer. If the one who had called himself Trystan was in control, he would kill his brother and take the throne, and Sanura would find herself the emperor's favorite concubine. If it was her Alix who won, then the emperor would live and Sanura might very well find herself a prince's wife.

Whatever the outcome, she was his. For better or for worse, bride or whore, in war or in blessed peace, she would be his.

It was for Alix's own sake that she wished the best of him would win. No man should have to live with the blood of his own family on his hands, no man should allow ambition to be more important than love. And she knew that if he did kill his brother, the best of him, the Alix she had first loved, would never recover.

Sanura would spend her life comforting him, if need be, but she would much prefer their life to be a celebration. She wanted to give this man who had known little true happiness the best of this life.

As the sun rose, she shattered and cried out as release cracked through her body. She called his name: *Alix*. She clutched his body to hers and felt the love he would not speak for fear of giving too much of himself to her. He climaxed and gave of himself, filling her with the seed which would not make a child, not ever, not for her.

"You will never again sleep on the ground," Alix whispered. "You will have the finest clothes, the most dedicated servants, the most brilliant jewels in existence. All will be yours."

"I want only you, Alix," she said honestly. In the new light of day she added, "Though a bath and warm food and a mug of cider would be very nice."

"You will have whatever you wish," he said, and in his own way that was *I love you*.

"If you really mean that," she said cautiously, "then reconsider your most immediate plans."

His body stiffened. "No. I must follow through. I must take what is mine."

She took his face in her hands and forced him to look at her. His beard was rough with neglect, his mouth was a firm and determined slash, and his eyes were, perhaps, a bit brighter than they had been last night. It was hard to tell in this light. "I am yours," she said confidently. "Nothing else matters."

"How can you be so blithely accepting? I bound you, threatened you, mistreated you, and placed you in the path of galloping horses. I degraded you with my words and with my actions, all to get what I wanted and needed. I would do so again, if necessary."

His words were harsh, but he had obviously forgotten that she could see inside him, that she knew his true intentions, his true self. "No, you would not," she whispered.

He did not argue with her, but neither did he agree.

PAKI and Kontar presented themselves at the Arthes palace and demanded to see the emperor immediately. They were not pleased by the response they received. First they were told it was impossible to have an audience with the emperor himself. They were dismissed by a lackey who was anxious to usher them out of the palace and send them on their way.

In fact, they received no respect at all until Paki told the attendant that the emperor's brother had murdered Princess Edlyn and stolen a gift which was not meant to be his.

The lackey paled and then disappeared, ordering Paki and Kontar to remain where they stood until he could fetch someone who could handle the particular situation. Eventually a nicely dressed older man who introduced himself as Minister of Foreign Affairs Calvyno greeted them with an unfriendly and tight smile, asking about the impossible rumors they were trying to spread.

Paki had studied the language of this land more than Kontar, thanks to a pleasant and pretty kitchen maid from Tryfyn, so he did the talking. "We do not speak nonsense. Prince Alixandyr murdered Princess Edlyn and touched that which was not his to touch. We are here to take the life he forfeited."

"You're here to execute the prince for killing the princess from Tryfyn," Calvyno stated.

"No," Paki said plainly. "We are here to take his life for daring to touch a woman of the Agnese, a gift from the King of Tryfyn to your emperor and a treasure which was not and is not his."

Calvyno licked his thin lips and wrung his hands. "I

cannot believe that Prince Alixandyr would commit any of the crimes of which he is accused. He is a fine, upstanding man, a noble and selfless..."

"We saw him with our own eyes," Paki said.

"You saw him kill the princess?" Thick eyebrows came together.

"No!" Kontar said, losing his patience. He drew his sword and threw it with a vengeance. It flew end over end past the minister's head and then pierced the wall solidly. "We saw him touch Sanura."

"Sanura, this gift of which you speak," the minister said as he glanced behind him to the quivering blade.

"Yes," Paki said, remaining calmer than Kontar. "I imagine there are those from Tryfyn who wish to make the prince pay for murder, but that is not our concern." He hoped that they were first to face the prince. Given the lack of good fortune the soldiers had in their search for the runaway pair, it was very possible the prince would arrive here without ever having faced a Tryfynian blade.

The Minister of Foreign Affairs, a man who obviously had a difficult job, was silent for a few moments. Minister Calvyno studied his visitors, taking in their costumes, which were as strange to him as the long red robes were to Paki, and glancing more than once at the sword which was stuck in the palace wall.

When the prince was dead and Sanura had been either recovered or avenged, he and Kontar would find their way back to Claennis, Paki decided. He missed the sea, and the laughing women, and the air of home.

But he could not return home until this job was done.

Finally, Calvyno spoke. "You will be the emperor's guests until Prince Alixandyr arrives and this mess can be properly sorted out."

"All will be *sorted out* when he is dead," Paki said.

"Every man deserves the opportunity to defend himself, don't you think?" Calvyno said with a touch of false joviality.

"No," Kontar said gruffly as he walked past the minister to retrieve his weapon.

Calvyno gave them a smile which was not true, and then he directed them to yet another room where they were to wait until their living quarters had been prepared. Paki did not wish for comfort, not while his job remained unfinished. He did not wish for a lavish palace life when Sanura's fate remained uncertain.

But Minister Calvyno promised them hot food and the company of women, if they wished it, and Paki decided a bit of comfort at this point in time was not unearned or unacceptable.

IF he traveled any slower, the horse would be walking backward.

The palace which had been Prince Alixandyr's home for the past six years loomed ahead, unavoidable. It sat at the western edge of a large, sprawling city, taller by far than any other edifice, imposing and elegant. The palace was the end of a long journey, the place he wanted and needed to be in order to accomplish what had to be done. And yet, he could not make himself race toward his destiny.

Sanura sat before him, as comfortable as she could be in such a position. His arms encircled her as easily and naturally as he held the reins. Her body resting against his was natural and comforting—yes, *comforting*, for a man who had never desired solace.

The palace waited, and it looked colder and more ominous than ever before. Jahn waited within, perhaps in his personal quarters, or in the office where he often met with those at his command. In his mind Alix could see the elder twin smile, then laugh, then take on an expression of determination. Yes, Jahn had always been determined. In many ways he had been a good emperor.

Alix stiffened his spine. When had he begun to doubt

his plan? When had he begun to have qualms about killing his brother?

When had he begun to think of himself as Alix again?

Inside her, he imagined. As she whispered his name, perhaps, or as she found pleasure in his arms. As she forgave him for all he had done to her.

As she told him that she loved him and he saw the truth in her eyes.

The man he had been a few days ago might've killed her for making him doubt, but he was no longer that man. He had not been that man since he'd turned away and left her in the possession of bandits who would've hurt her. He had not been that man since he'd turned back to save her.

"You will not kill him right away, will you?" Sanura asked, and he heard the uncertainty in her voice. She might say she would remain with him no matter what, but she did not like his plan for fratricide. "There's really no reason to rush."

"Nor is there a reason to stall," he said reasonably.

"We could have a bath together," she offered, "and I will shave your beard and wash your hair. You look quite the unkempt madman with your beard growing in so. If you insist upon being an assassin, you should at the very least look imperial when you carry out the act. No one would take you for an emperor at this moment, love."

It was likely the truth, given their difficult days of travel.

"Besides," she said, a sadness creeping into her voice, "what if you do not succeed? What if you're killed trying to take your brother's life? I should like to know one night in a proper bed with you, in case the worst occurs. One meal shared without the insects and the dirt." She looked up and back at him. "I should like for you to begin your new life, no matter what it might be, with the picture of me at my very best in your mind's eye. I want to give you strength, Alix my love, in the only way I know how."

"I will not fail," he assured her. "I will not be killed."

"You have not looked at yourself in a mirror lately," she said softly. "No diligent sentinel, no wary guard will allow you near the emperor with murder in your eyes and ragged, dirty clothing on your body. You are not the man I met in Tryfyn, love. The sentinels who guard the emperor will know you have changed. Your brother will surely know."

He had not thought that others might see the changes he felt, but it was likely true. Perhaps he was not ready to proceed; perhaps he did need preparation before he carried out his plan. "We can sneak into the palace and to my suite of rooms on Level Five. I know of secret passageways which will get us there without being seen, and there are many loyal servants who will remain silent about my presence if I ask it of them."

Sanura's body relaxed against his. In fact, it seemed she melted into him, warm and giving and *his*.

No one and nothing had ever been so completely his before.

VERITY ignored Laris all day, which was exactly what he deserved for tricking her as he had. She would snub him. She would not even look his way and smile. Of course, he made this all very easy, as he'd left the house before she got out of bed, and she had not seem him all day. How annoying! The best way she knew to punish him was to ignore him, and he didn't even know about it.

His mother was very sweet, and made the day go by faster than Verity had imagined it would. The older woman allowed her unexpected guest to help with the cooking and cleaning. It was all new to Verity, and she was more trouble than she was help, but she found it all very interesting. Well, the cooking was interesting. The cleaning was less than deadly dull only when she took out her anger in wild swipes of a cleaning rag or vigorous swipes of the broom.

All the girls had chores, as well. They mended, baked, cleaned, and worked in the vegetable garden just outside the rear door. They also laughed and teased and made plans while they worked. The boys were all engaged in farm chores, and as absent as Laris.

It was late in the day when the men returned from their work on the farm. Verity glanced at Laris only once, then she yanked her eyes away from him. Ignoring him was much more difficult when he was actually present! She listened to him talk—farm talk, which was as exciting as cleaning the fireplace—but she acted as if she didn't hear. All the while her blood ran hotter and faster, as the anger she could not contain grew.

Finally she dropped her cleaning rag, stalked toward the farmer-sentinel, and grabbed his arm. "I need to speak with you. Outside," she added sharply.

He came along obediently. His brothers and sisters all laughed, and one of the girls—probably Fharis—said, "Ooohhh, Laris is in *trouble*."

Verity didn't say a word until they were well away from the house and prying ears, though she did imagine more than one pair of eyes watched.

"Explain yourself," she said succinctly.

"How so?" He looked truly confused.

Verity leaned toward him. "You asked me if I minded sharing a bed and I said no, I did not mind at all. I thought that meant..." Her face flushed hot. "And then I end up in a bed with your three sisters, elbow to elbow." She looked into his eyes, those warm brown eyes she loved so much. "Do you not want me? Are you promised to another?" Ellanie, a woman she detested even though they'd never met. "Are your parents very strict about that sort of thing, because if they are, we can leave and go..."

Laris laid two silencing fingers over her lips. Those fingers were a little dirty, but she didn't mind. They were also warm and strong, and she liked the smell and feel of his skin. "You said you would be a virgin on your wedding night," he said in a lowered voice.

"Well, some things change..."

"Let me finish, Verity," he said, his voice taking on a

tronger, more determined tenor than she had ever heard
rom him.

She pursed her lips and nodded her head.

"You know I want you," he said. "We slept too close
ogether for too many nights for you not to know how pain-
ully that is so."

True enough.

"You know I love you. I've told you so on more than one
occasion, have I not?"

"Yes, you have," she admitted.

"In the early days of our journey, you mentioned more
han once that after you became empress, we would be
overs."

"I did say that." It had seemed like a good idea at the
ime—and still did, she supposed. Marrying the emperor
nd keeping Laris as a lover would logically offer the best
of both worlds. She'd have all the luxuries any woman
could ask for, and Laris in her bed. Such an arrangement
vould be perfection. So why did the thought give her no
happiness at all?

Laris shook his head. "That won't happen, Verity."

"But…"

He showed her with a lift of his eyebrows that he was
not finished. "I won't share you. I won't watch you marry
another man and then sneak into that man's bed and steal
hat which is not mine." Laris never lost his temper, so she
vas surprised to see the fire in his eyes. "You *will* be a
virgin on your wedding night, Verity. You deserve no less.
The question only you can answer is who your husband
vill be. Me or Emperor Jahn?"

Her heart sank and soared at the same time. She couldn't
marry a sentinel—could she? Could she trade the life of an
empress for a life like the one his parents led? A small and
warm home, lots of children, lots of laughter—lots of
work.

"I…" she began.

"Don't answer now," Laris said. "It's a big decision, and
not one which should be made lightly. I do feel obligated to

tell you, in case the thought has crossed your mind, that will not go home with you to the Northern Province and make being your husband my career, no matter how much money your father has. I am a sentinel, and I plan to make that service my career. It's a good, honest life, and though I will never be rich, I might someday rise through the ranks to a higher station, which would come with more pay and finer benefits. You won't have any of the things an empress might expect to have, but I will always love you."

That said, Laris wrapped his arms around her and pressed his mouth to hers, and he gave her a long, slow, heart-melting kiss that shook her to her toes. She saw stars, her heart pounded, her blood rushed. His lips were soft, not at all demanding or harsh, and she did not want him to ever let her go.

He did let her go, of course, though he held on to her for a moment while she found the strength of her legs and blinked back tears. Empress or sentinel's wife? A palace a home or a small cottage? Love or privilege?

Before she could give Laris her answer—which was not at all difficult to come to, in spite of its importance—he turned and walked away, spine straight and head high.

"Don't you want to hear my answer?" she called after him.

"Not yet," he answered, continuing to walk away. "Think it over for a spell."

"I don't..."

"Think, Verity," Laris said once more as he turned to look at her. She had never seen him look so determined, so stubborn. "This is likely the most important decision you'll ever make. Take your time. I won't be a whim." With that he turned once more and walked back to the house.

Eventually Verity followed him, muttering to herself about hardheaded, stubborn men who refused to listen.

Chapter Seventeen

ALIX released the horse a good distance from the palace, sending the stolen animal on its way. The horse turned and sauntered north, perhaps heading for home or drawn to a mare in heat.

Sanura stayed close as he led her toward the palace which loomed before them. In that place, Alix's future would be decided. Would he kill his brother, take the throne, and be forever dark? Or would he choose not to carry out that act, even though the shadows which had been loosed would never again be entirely contained?

He knew exactly where he was going and he moved with assurance, even though Sanura felt the trepidation within him. It was good that he was questioning his plans even as he crept toward the secret passageway he had told her about. She wanted him to question, to be less than sure about his plans.

He led her to a small door on the western end of the wall which surrounded the palace. It was guarded, of course, but as this was a time of peace, the sentinel there was less than vigilant. She and Alix waited until the young guard turned his back and walked toward another entrance, then they ran. Alix held her hand and all but pulled her along, but her feet flew and she was able to keep up with his pace.

They turned a corner, maneuvered around some bed linens which had been hung to dry in the sun, and then slipped through an open entrance into a small, bustling room. Four tubs of water were manned by women in long white robes. Two of them were young, two were much older. They all diligently scrubbed at stains. Two other women sat in plain wooden chairs and mended crimson clothing. Only one looked up to see who had entered.

"You're not supposed to come in this way," the young woman snapped.

Alix glared at her, and one of the women at a tub of water looked up. "Do you not know who this is, girl? This is Prince Alixandyr. He comes and goes as he pleases." The woman looked at Alix. "Forgive her, m'lord. She's new." The news was imparted with a rolling of her eyes.

"How was I to know he's a prince?" the new girl asked in an almost insolent tone of voice. "He doesn't look like much to me," she added in a lowered voice that carried more than she'd planned.

The older woman looked Alix up and down. "You do look a mite rough, m'lord."

Alix managed a small smile for the older woman. "I've had a trying journey and want only to rest for a while before I resume my duties. A few days of complete privacy away from prying eyes and questions are all that I need, and for that to happen, no one can know I'm home. Can I rely on your silence?" He glanced at the six women in the room. "I ask for discretion from all of you, if you please."

"How about discretion, a tub of hot water, and a warm meal?" the eldest laundress said. "I think I can even scrounge up some of your favorite sweet bread."

Without warning Alix grabbed the old woman, who squealed in surprise, and then he teasingly kissed her wrinkled cheek. "I would be forever grateful."

The woman straightened her spine as she was released.

"I've never known you to be so gregarious, m'lord." She followed the statement with a smile and a girlish blush. Only then did she pin her calculating eyes on Sanura. "Would you like discretion, water, and food for two, m'lord?"

"I would."

"You'll have it," she said in a conspiratorially low voice.

Sanura, who had been alone with Alix or Trystan for much of the past month, was assaulted by a wave of feelings from the women in the room. She was usually quite adept at controlling her gift, but she hadn't had much practice in recent weeks. There was admiration and curiosity and even a touch of fear in the room, as some of the women instinctively recognized the changes in their prince. There was loyalty here, too, so much so that she suspected Alix would get exactly what he had asked for from these women.

Except that one new girl, who was too curious for her own good.

Alix led Sanura through a narrow hallway and around a corner, then into another small room—where he quickly located and activated a hidden door which was made of the same stone that made up the walls. The door swung open on a dim space. Dim, but not dark. As they stepped into the hidden stairway and Alix closed the secret door, Sanura's eyes were drawn to the glowing stones which lit the space. There was a cluster of three stones on the floor near the doorway, and from what she could see from her vantage point, there was one stone placed at the far edge of every step. The entire stairway had an eerie, purple glow.

"Magic," she whispered.

"Yes. Jahn doesn't care for relying on magic, but in some cases it is the best solution to a problem."

"A problem like dark, hidden stairways," she said as he led her up.

He turned to smile down at her, and in the unnatural light he did look more evil than not. It was the slash of eyebrows and the wild hair, the humorless smile, the glint of darkness in his eyes. Her heart constricted, and she wondered if she could do what needed to be done.

All was not lost. She did see the Alix she had first loved there, in the eyes and in the face. More important, she felt that man radiating from the soul she could touch. He was not alone; he would never again be alone, but he was there and strong.

Could she make him shine once more?

ALL he had to do was follow the hidden stairway to Jahn's chambers and kill the emperor while he slept. It was possible he would run into a guard or two along the way and be called upon to kill or disable those who would protect their emperor, but if it was unavoidable...

No, Sanura was right. He would rest and make himself presentable, then tomorrow morning he'd ask for a moment alone with his brother—a request Jahn would not even question. When they were alone, he would drive a dagger through the elder twin's heart.

Alix sat in a deep tub of warm water, water carried to this room by a trio of young, strong servants who would do exactly as the laundress had instructed them. They'd carry water up endless stairs and keep their mouths shut about what and whom they'd seen this evening. They were loyal now, and they'd be loyal when he was emperor.

Sanura washed his hair, her movements sensuous and arousing, her hands and fingers gentle and loving on his scalp. He liked it. He liked it when she tipped his head back and rinsed the soap away, protecting his eyes with a hand so the soap would not sting. He liked it when she ran her fingers through the long strands, squeezing water out.

He especially liked it when she stepped into the large tub with him and settled down, facing him, to wash her own body.

She was entirely his, no matter that she'd been given to Jahn, no matter that they'd broken the laws of three lands to be together—she was entirely his, and he would not allow anyone else to have her, not ever again.

In all his imaginings, he had never imagined her.

"We could have a very nice life here," Sanura said as she soaped her body. He watched the motion of her hands against her skin, and his body responded.

"We *will* have a nice life here," he said.

"Even if you don't kill your brother..."

"You won't change my mind, Sanura," he interrupted.

She lowered her eyes and continued to wash. "You know I am yours no matter what you do, no matter if you are prince or emperor or fisherman."

His stomach flipped over and then knotted.

"I care for the state of your soul, Alix, and if you kill your own brother, it will never recover. Trust me, I know."

"If my soul is a sacrifice I have to make..."

"Don't say that." She looked up sharply and her blue eyes pierced him.

For a while, a very pleasant while, she did not speak. She washed her body and her hair, and she even allowed him to help, as she had helped him. He had touched her in many ways, but never quite like this, caring and gentle, tending to her without thoughts of the sex that would follow. Well, without too many thoughts.

Sanura's head was back, and he had just rinsed the last of the soap from her hair when she said, "I could kill him for you."

Her voice trembled as she made the offer, and a few unwanted tears filled her eyes.

"Why would you say such a thing?"

"He is not my brother. I do not even know the emperor, so..."

"The murder of a stranger is less harmful to the soul?"

"I don't know," she whispered. "It seems it would be so."

He leaned over and kissed her wet lips, and he tasted her passion and her love and her sacrifice. "No," he whispered against her mouth. "I have asked many sacrifices of you and I will ask for more, but I will not ask for this."

"You did not ask, Alix. It's my idea, and if it will save you from committing this atrocity, then I'll do it. Quickly and painlessly, if I can. The result will be the same as if you did the killing yourself. Once your brother is dead, you will have all that you wish to have."

I have all that I wish to have right here.

The thought came out of nowhere, and he shook it off.

He would have everything he'd planned, *and* Sanura. He would have the power *and* the woman.

His mouth on her wet flesh drove all thoughts of murder from her mind, and from his. Her body against his, wet and warm and searching, made him forget that he needed so much more. In the small tub they twisted their bodies, reaching for the connection they were driven to attain. Their mouths fused; their insides quaking, they came together.

Water splashed on the floor as they pitched and rocked. Sanura's fine breasts swayed close to his face, so that he could bend his head and taste as they moved in time. His tongue raked roughly across a hard nipple, and she whimpered in response. She held on to him, her fingers caught in his hair, her body wrapped around his.

She quaked and fluttered around him as she found release. She cleaved her body to his and cried out his name, and then she said those words he needed to hear: "I love you, Alix." His release came with hers, and though he did not speak the words as she did, he felt the agonizing and wonderful emotion she had brought to him so unexpectedly.

It was only when he was finished that he realized she was crying. She held him, they were still joined, and she cried.

"What's wrong?" He pulled her head to his shoulder and cupped her head with his hand, holding her there.

"I want so much to save you, and you won't let me."

Alix appreciated the honesty of her answer, even though he did not believe he needed to be saved.

SANURA could not sleep. She was well fed, clean, lying naked in the arms of the man she loved more than her own life—and still she could not sleep.

It was the middle of the night when she realized what she had to do. Alix might never forgive her, but what choice did she have? Tomorrow morning the dark side of Alix, the part she had set free, would kill his own brother. He would never recover. He would have all that he thought he wanted, but it would taste bitter and he would never again smile or laugh or love with his whole heart, because a part of his heart would be shriveled and dead.

He was sleeping deeply when she crept out of the bed. Earlier in the evening she had acquainted herself with Alix's suite of rooms and his belongings, and she'd noted the many robes and sashes which hung in a massive wardrobe, along with boots and weapons and towels and bed linens. She headed now for the wardrobe, where she retrieved four of the long crimson sashes.

If he woke too soon and realized what she was doing, he might kill her. She did not think he would do that, but if he reacted instinctively in his current state, it was possible. It was also a risk she was willing to take. She started with his right hand, wrapping one sash around the wrist and tying it tightly, then lashing the other end to the headboard of his massive wooden bed. Next she did the same to his left hand, and then she moved to the foot of the bed and his ankles.

She was tying the last knot when he woke, confused for a moment and then smiling. "I did not know you cared for such games, Sanura."

She crawled onto the bed with him and she kissed him gently. Thinking this part of some sexual pastime, he kissed her back without care or caution. She then left the bed and retrieved the sheet she had set aside. Her dress was ruined by long weeks of travel, and Alix's robes were all much too large. The bed linen would do, for now. She wrapped it around her body and draped the end over one shoulder, leaving the other shoulder bare.

"What are you doing?" Alix asked, his voice turning suspicious. He yanked at one of his bonds, trying to free his right hand.

"I am doing what you should not," she said.

His body stiffened, and he fought against the sashes as Sanura took another sash just like them and tied it around her midsection, crisscrossing the crimson strands to make the sheet she wore form to her body. It did not make for a fine gown, by any means, but at a glance it was acceptable.

"One scream, and sentinels will come running. They will stop you. They will kill you."

Unconcerned, she took the dagger she'd retrieved from his wardrobe and placed on a nearby table, hefting it in her hands and then hiding it in the folds of her makeshift dress. It was small enough to lie well in the folds. "One scream and the sentinels will come running and I will tell them everything, love," she said calmly. "Everything."

"They won't believe you," he said, ceasing his struggle.

"When they look into your eyes, they will," she reasoned. "You don't see them as I do. They are not the eyes those who know you will remember, love. They are darker. They are different in a way no one can dismiss."

He leaned back against the bed and seemed to relax, though inside he was enraged. "So, you're going to do the deed for me, is that it?"

"Yes."

"All for the sake of my soul," he teased.

"Yes."

He tried to appear accepting, though she could feel that he was not. "I will miss seeing Jahn die, but the result will be the same. Come tomorrow, I will be emperor."

"Will you forgive me?" she asked softly.

"I don't know."

It was the truth, but it could not change her mind.

She left Alix tied to the bed where they'd made love—and perhaps would again—and stepped into the hallway. She'd get lost on the hidden stairs, she imagined, and that would not do. She knew where the emperor resided, thanks to an earlier conversation with Alix.

The palace rose ten stories from the ground. Level One, which had once been the seat of power for the twins' father, was at the very top. It was rarely used these days. Level Ten was at ground level, and Alix had told her there were two levels beneath the ground—there had once been three levels there, but Level Thirteen had been filled in. He had not elaborated, but when he'd spoken the words "Level Thirteen," she had experienced a soul-deep chill.

Jahn now resided on Level Eight, which was three stories down from this floor where Alix made his home. All she had to do was get there and do what had to be done.

She walked slowly but with determination down the stairway, and when she reached her destination and stepped into the wide hallway, she was not surprised to see three sentinels standing guard at what had to be the entrance to the emperor's bedchamber. Instead of appearing alarmed, she gave them her best smile.

"Good evening. I'm here to see the emperor."

"At this hour?" one asked. Another poked him in the ribs.

It was no mistake that the dress she'd fashioned showed her figure to its best advantage, or that her shoulder was bare or that a hint of cleavage was revealed. No one would mistake the apparent reasons why she wished to see Emperor Jahn.

"The emperor will soon be taking a wife," one of the sentinels said with disapproval.

"But he has not taken one yet, has he?" Sanura asked with a seductive smile.

"No, but..."

"I am a gift from the King of Tryfyn," she said. "Would you send me away without even telling the emperor that I'm here? Would you rob him of the pleasure which is offered by a woman of the Agnese?"

"A woman of the... what?"

Sanura sighed. "Just tell him I've arrived, if you please."

"He might be sleeping," one of the guards said.

At that moment they heard a loudly delivered curse word which easily penetrated the large wooden door. Sanura smiled. "I think not. It sounds as if he's in great need of my ministrations."

Her heart pounded too hard and her mouth went dry.

She wasn't sure she could do this, but what choice did she have? It was her fault the shadows in Alix now ruled. Her fault! The least she could do was to save him from an act which would forever taint his soul.

She did not think of her own soul at the moment. Could not.

The youngest of the guards slipped into the emperor's room and was back a moment later with a nod to Sanura.

If they searched her for weapons and found the knife, they'd probably kill her. But the knife was small and there was not much in the way of hiding places on her person, especially since the sheet she wore parted and revealed her long legs as she walked toward the guards and the open door. She smiled at the men, men who at this moment wished to be Emperor of Columbyana simply because she was walking into his bedchamber.

The emperor awaited her, sitting on a large chair on the side of the room away from his massive bed. He was a handsome man, much prettier than Alix and more fair of hair, though there were darker streaks mixed with the blond. Even though the hour was late, he was still dressed in imperial crimson. His face was set in stone, but he was curious. Curious, confused, angry...and a good man, in spite of all his faults.

"King Bhaltair sent you?"

"Yes," she said as a sentinel closed the door behind her, leaving her and the emperor alone.

"I have heard a distressing rumor that Princess Edlyn was murdered."

"I'm afraid that is true."

"I also heard that my brother, Prince Alixandyr, did the killing."

"That is not true."

A wave of relief washed through the emperor's body. "Thank the gods. I knew he couldn't do such a thing, but I have received word from more than one quarter that he did this unspeakable deed. Where is he? Do you know?"

Sanura hesitated before shaking her head. Lying did not come easily to her, but what was she to say?

"You are Sanura, correct?" he asked.

She nodded. "I am. You have heard of me?"

"The sentinel who just yesterday delivered word of the princess's death told me that Alix escaped with a blue woman named Sanura. Though you are no longer blue, you do match the rest of his rather vivid description." His eyes raked her up and down. "There are also at least two Tryfynian soldiers in Arthes who insist upon taking Alix's head, as well as two very insistent wild men in residence who are adamant about killing Alix for touching you."

"Paki and Kontar are here?" she asked, her heart thumping.

"Yes. We've been doing our best to keep them occupied, but they remain quite insistent on killing my brother." His expression hardened. "I cannot allow that to happen."

"Don't hurt them," she said as she took a step toward the emperor. "They're only doing their duty."

"To protect you," he said, almost as if he did not quite believe what he said.

"Yes."

"Where is Alix?" he asked again.

"I told you, I do not know."

"I don't believe you."

Sanura stopped a few feet away from the emperor. The weight of the dagger which was tangled in her clothing grew heavier with each step she took. With three guards outside the door, it was unlikely she would survive once the emperor was dead, but if it meant Alix did not have to carry out this monstrous task . . .

She sensed something unexpected from the emperor, something which stopped her in her tracks and took her breath away. "You know," she said.

"I know what?" he snapped impatiently.

"You know about Alix's struggle. At least—you suspect that something is not right with him."

"Don't be ridiculous."

He was protecting his brother, he loved his brother.

"The shadows, the dark battle, the tight control..."

Emperor Jahn placed both hands on the arms of his chair and stood, moving slowly so that he coiled from his chair like a snake rising to strike. "You don't have any idea what you're talking about," he said tightly.

"I know too well, I'm sad to say," she said. "For years a darkness has lived within Alix, wishing to rise and take power, to take control. His determination has kept that darkness deep within until I unknowingly unleashed that which Alix has fought all these years." Was it safe to trust this man? Did she dare tell him everything? "What you do not know, what I have just come to understand, is that both parts, he who fought and he who tried to rise, are one and the same. Alix was fractured, but he is fractured no more."

"So you do know where he is."

"Yes." Sanura reached into her clothing and pulled out the dagger with which she had planned to kill the emperor. "I came here to murder you."

"Did he send you?" Sadness radiated from the emperor but there was very little surprise.

"No. He plans to do the assassination himself, but I cannot allow that to happen. He will never recover from such a dark deed."

"Neither will I, I imagine," the emperor said dryly. He pointed to her small dagger. "What made you think you could kill me with *that*?"

"My plan was simple. I would get close to you, promising all that I was meant to give, and when you were lost in desire, I would stab you through the heart."

"Ouch." He laid a hand over his chest. "Lucky for me I have enough womanly trouble at the moment and would not let you get so close."

She tossed the knife onto his large bed, knowing that she could not kill this man any more than she could kill Alix.

"I am responsible for the change in Alix, though it was unknowing. I would never hurt him, never." She looked the emperor in the eye. "I love him."

"Enough to commit murder in his name?"

She glanced at the dagger, which sat on the bed, out of reach. "Apparently not."

"So, what now?" the emperor asked testily. "Less than three months ago I set in motion a silly contest for the position of empress, and at this moment two of the candidates are dead, killed en route by accident or malicious intent; my brother is wanted dead by two burly, saber-wielding madmen and more than a handful of Tryfynian soldiers; Alix appears to have lost the battle he's fought for so long; and I . . ."

"You?" Sanura prodded.

The emperor shook his head and declined to continue. "My own problems matter little, at the moment. Where is Alix? Is there any way to save him from this?" He raked his hand tiredly through his loose hair. "As if you would know."

"But I do know," Sanura said. She stepped toward the emperor. "You love Alix, and so do I. Together we can save him. Will you help me, My Lord Emperor?"

Intelligent blue eyes looked into her own, searching for answers. The emperor had no reason to trust her, and yet he did. He had no reason to keep her alive, and yet he did not call for his guards and inform them that she'd come to his room with murderous intentions.

"What do you need?" he asked.

Sanura sighed in relief. "Time, m'lord. I need time."

His eyes went hard with determination. "There are ten days remaining until the first night of the Summer Festival, ten short days until I will be obligated to make my choice. Will that be enough time?"

"I hope so, m'lord. With all my heart, I hope so."

Chapter Eighteen

HE had managed to free one hand and was frantically working on freeing the other when the door opened and Sanura slipped inside. Alix's heart sank, and he hoped she would not see his instinctive reaction. How foolish of him. Sanura always saw.

"It's done?" he asked.

She shook her head and walked toward him, taking the dagger from the folds of her form-fitting sheet-gown and placing it on the table near the door. "The emperor is not in residence. According to the sentinels I spoke to, I missed him by no more than an hour."

"Not in residence," he said as she sat on the edge of the bed and began to work at one of the bonds on his ankles. "I don't believe you."

She shrugged her shoulders, unconcerned. "In the morning you can ask them yourself. I suppose I could lie, but it would be a lie easily undone when the sun rises and your brother appears."

"Where did he go?"

"The sentinels did not say."

No, they would not tell her. They would tell him, though, when he asked. "When will he be back?"

"By the first night of the Summer Festival, they said, when he must choose his bride." She looked him in the eye. "Are you horribly angry with me?"

"Yes," he said honestly.

"Will you forgive me?"

"Probably," he admitted grudgingly.

"I only wished to help you," she said. "I don't agree with your plan, I don't even want you to be emperor, but if it is what you want…"

"It is."

"Even so, you should not be forced to kill your own brother."

She often referred to Jahn as his brother, instead of as emperor. Did she think he needed to be reminded? That if he heard the word often enough he would change his mind? "I will do whatever is necessary."

"Too bad." Sanura placed her body next to his and reclined there quite easily and comfortably, even though she knew he was still angry with her.

"Why is it too bad?" he asked. "Don't you want to be the emperor's mistress and have everything any woman could possibly want laid at your feet?"

She tilted her head back and looked at him. "Should I tell you what I truly want?"

"If you wish to do so."

"You will not like it."

"I suppose I won't."

Sanura rested her chin on his chest and draped her arms across his body, making herself more at ease. By now she was quite comfortable using him as her bed, her place to rest at the end of the day. "I want to be your wife, not your mistress. If your brother marries and has children, you will no longer be directly in line for the throne, so the production of babies would be less crucial for us, and I would not have to share you with an empress who will give you children and hate me for loving you."

"You wish to be married to a man without power, without purpose? You would wish me to be nothing?"

"You will never be nothing, love. And you will always have power and purpose." She snuggled deeper. "Now, allow me to finish telling you what I want."

She had bound him to the bed and gone off to accomplish that which should be his, so he should be furious with her, he should deny her all that she wanted. He could not. He had done worse to her in weeks past and still she loved him. "All right," he said with a lack of enthusiasm. "Proceed."

Sanura wiggled and made herself cozy. Her wiggling made him decidedly uneasy. "We could build a house on the outskirts of the city, a big house for you and me and Mali and..."

"Mali? The demon child?"

"You said you would let me finish." She laughed easily.

This time he just grumbled.

"Mali and others like her," Sanura continued, "other children who need instruction and care and love." She rose slightly to look at him, and though he did not have her gift, he could see the heartache and the hope in her eyes. "Perhaps I cannot bear children, but that does not mean I can't know a mother's love, that I can't give that love to Mali and others who need us. Who need *you*."

"Why on earth would these demon children..."

"Half-demon," she corrected.

"Fine. Why on earth would these *half-demon* children need me?"

"Because you understand their struggle," she said. "Because you know what it's like to do battle in your soul every day, just as they do."

"Some of these children you speak of will be beyond saving."

"Some will not," she countered.

"This is a ridiculous conversation," he said gruffly. "What you wish for will never be."

"Perhaps that's true, but you asked me what I wanted,

and I told you," Sanura said confidently, unshaken by his response.

What she wanted and what he desired—what he needed—could not live in harmony. Once Jahn was dead and Alix's darkest dreams came true, it was likely that what he and Sanura had found together would wither and die. She would still love him, he knew that, but their love could not flourish as it did in this room.

"Jahn won't be back until the first night of the Summer Festival?"

"That is what I was told."

"I will ask in the morning," he said, still wondering if she was lying to him to buy Jahn more time in this life—to buy them more time in this room.

"Please do so," she said. "You will find that I told you only the truth. Like it or not, we have ten days before you can proceed with your plan. What shall we do while we wait?"

She knew full well how they would spend their time. "We will eat, and sleep, and shake the very walls of this room with sex, and I will dress you in proper gowns and show you off and..."

"Oh!" She jumped up. "I almost forgot. You'd best not show me off until you're emperor and have complete power. The sentinels also told me that Paki and Kontar are here, as well as two angry Tryfynian soldiers who wish to take your head. We'd best spend the next ten days right here."

"Paki and Kontar are in the palace?"

"That is what I was told."

Alix grinned and began to untie the red sash which held the sheet to Sanura's form. If they had ten days, he would not waste a moment. "Will your diligent guards have the blue?"

"I'M not going to change my mind."

Verity stared at the palace straight ahead. In nine days' time, the emperor would choose his bride. She'd been so confident that he'd choose her—and now she would never know.

Laris was being stubborn, a trait she had not known he possessed until he'd asked her, in his own way, to marry him. "You need to take a good look at what you might have if you make another choice."

"There is no other choice," Verity insisted. "I've told you that several times, but you refuse to listen."

"I just don't want you to be sorry you chose me—not now, not in ten years' time."

She smiled. Never. Since they'd been arguing and he'd been winning, she did not reveal the deep certainty of her love. Perhaps later, when he was being more agreeable.

They walked toward the palace, as his family's home was not all that far from Arthes, and she was in no hurry to rush to tell the emperor that she was withdrawing her name from contention. Really, a letter would be sufficient. But Laris had suggested—no, *demanded*—that she face the life she might've had, that she take a good, hard look at the palace that could be her home if she made another choice. The walk had taken most of the day, and even if they were able to take care of their business at the palace quite efficiently, it would be dark before they got home.

Laris did not know how stubborn *she* could be, that once she made up her mind, it was well and permanently made.

He held her hand, and frowned as she looked down at her dress. "You might've borrowed a better-fitting dress from one of the girls."

"I like this one," she said, plucking at the green skirt as if it were made of the finest fabric. "You bought it for me." And he liked the brightness of her eyes when she wore the drab color.

"I'll buy better, when I can," he promised.

Verity smiled. In the letter she'd written to her parents to inform them that she was not dead, she'd also asked them to send along her things. Dresses, jewels, shoes, hairclips...she would need them all in her life as a sentinel's wife. Perhaps she and Laris would be poor for a while, but that didn't mean she had to *look* poor. That certainly didn't mean she had to act poor. Social skills were very important, and her mother had taught her well. With her help, Laris would rise through the ranks in record time.

The palace was impressive, but it also looked cold and stern and devoid of the laughter she had experienced at Laris's family home. She had no doubts about her decision, not as she presented herself to the guard at the gate, a guard who allowed her to enter only because she was with a fellow sentinel; not as she prepared herself to meet with Minster Calvyno. She had quite a few things to tell him!

She and Laris waited in a small, finely furnished room which was intended for greeting visitors to the palace. There were a number of comfortable-looking chairs, not that either she or Laris wished to sit. They had walked for quite some time, but she was much too anxious to sit! On one wall there was a portrait of a man she supposed to be the emperor. He was handsome enough, but he was no Laris.

In short time Minister Calvyno arrived, appearing tired and more than a little put-upon. He had dark circles under his eyes and looked as if he could use some sleep, but that was not her problem.

"I am Lady Verity of Mirham," she said, presenting herself with all the dignity she could muster, ghastly green dress aside.

The old man sighed. "Your trickery is wasted on me, young woman." He took in her appearance with disdain, actually wrinkling his massive nose. "Lady Verity is dead."

Verity was not intimidated, as he'd obviously intended. "No, I am not dead, Minister Calvyno, but that is no thanks to the man you sent to collect me. Gregor Wallis himself tried to have me killed, with the assistance of a traitorous sentinel named Cavan. If not for the interference of this fine and brave sentinel"—she pointed an insistent finger toward Laris—"I would've perished in the river, been dragged down and bashed against the rocks."

"This is ridiculous," Calvyno muttered. "Lady Verity was killed in a horrible accident, and..."

Her patience disappeared. It felt as if what was left just flew out of the top of her head. Good heavens, someone had tried to murder her, and this man was being no help at all! "Was the body recovered? No, it was not. Because there *was no body*." She placed her hands on her hips in a pose of defiance. "I escaped death, thanks to Laris, and then we overheard those awful men talking about giving something irritating to my mare, Buttercup, to make her bolt, and we ran for our very lives." She nodded her head decisively. "And by the way, when Buttercup is recovered, I demand that she be delivered to me immediately. If what those horrid men gave Buttercup damaged her in any way, heads will roll."

Calvyno turned to Laris. His eyes looked more tired than they had just moments ago. "Is any of this true?"

"All of it, sir," Laris said, calling upon a very official and sentinel-like voice. "Deputy Wallis and Cavan conspired to murder Lady Verity. Wallis also mentioned that he had been hired by someone to see the murder done. Once I understood the situation, I thought it best to deliver Lady Verity myself. I did not know whom we could trust, so it seemed best to trust no one."

Verity felt a surge of pride. She had never heard Laris sound so commanding and fearsome.

Minister Calvyno, who had been dismissive of her, listened intently as Laris explained all that had happened. Well, he explained most, leaving out their most private matters. Some things were none of his business, after all. He conducted himself very well, not at all intimidated by the highly placed minister.

Though Verity had seen Laris in his official capacity during the early days of their travels, until someone had tried to kill her, he had not been called upon to act in any truly sentinel-like way. He was a very good sentinel, she imagined. Quiet and thoughtful, determined and smart, dedicated and more handsome than all the other sentinels.

A brilliant thought occurred to her as she watched and listened to the two men. She had not turned her back on her destiny to be the wife of a great man who came from humble beginnings. Not at all. Mavise and her mother, and even she, had been wrong about who that great man would be, but other than that, all was as it should be.

Yes, Laris would make a fine Minister of Defense one day.

Once Laris had convinced the annoying Minister Calvyno of the truth, the tired man moved to the nearest chair and sat. Hard. "I can't believe this. Deputy Wallis seemed so upset when he delivered the news of your . . . death."

Verity put her hands on her hips. "He's here? In the palace?"

"I'm afraid so."

Verity pointed a firm finger at the minister. "I want that horrible man tossed into in your deepest, darkest dungeon. You *do* have a dungeon, don't you?"

"Of sorts," Calvyno admitted.

"Put him there, and never let him out."

Calvyno regained his composure and stood with a tired sigh. "Done. Now, let me see you to your quarters. The emperor will be most pleased to hear that you are not deceased. He's not in residence at the moment, but . . ."

"I'm not staying here," Verity said. "And I'm not going to marry your emperor."

"But . . ."

She had planned a more gracious way of delivering the news, but was much too agitated to remember it all. "I'm sure he's a very nice man, but I have my own very nice man now, and I don't need another. Do you have a priest about?" She turned to look at Laris and smile. Now he would believe that she had no intention of changing her mind. The wedding, and the wedding night, could proceed. "We could get married here. Now." And if that could be arranged, perhaps they would take the minister up on his offer of a room for the night. It was the least he could do, considering the circumstances which had brought her here.

Laris smiled at her. "You're still willing to give all this up?" He looked about the lavishly furnished room.

"Yes. I don't change my mind, Laris. Not about *important* things."

"You changed your mind about being empress."

"That's not important," she said.

"One moment," Calvyno said. "You're declining the offer to possibly be empress so that you might marry this sentinel?"

Verity grinned widely. "Yes, I am. As soon as possible. I'm tired of sharing a bed with his sisters." She leaned in and whispered, "He has three of them, and they're all elbows and heels."

Laris took her wrist and attempted to lead her from the room, but she stopped him and turned once more to Minister Calvyno. "I should like to wait here until you inform me that Wallis and his lackey are in that dungeon, locked away for good. I won't have some hired murderer ruining my wedding day."

"It will be done, m'lady," Calvyno said. "As soon as possible."

Verity gave him her finest smile. "That would be *now*."

ACCORDING to the gossip from those few servants who knew Alix had returned and was hiding in his suite of rooms, the palace was in chaos. A potential bride who was believed to be dead had shown up alive and well, and now the deputy minister who had been sent to collect her was in the Level Twelve prison, along with the sentinel he had hired to assist him. Not only that, the woman in question had left the palace in the company of a lowly sentinel, choosing him over the chance to be empress. As they'd left the palace, the couple had been arguing about the date of their wedding. The bride wished to be married immediately; the groom wanted two or three days to plan a proper wedding ceremony.

The Tryfynian soldiers who were still searching for Alix remained resolute in their duty, even though it was now thought that whoever had tried to have Lady Verity killed might've also had a hand in the princess's death. One murder was a horrible tragedy. Two were a conspiracy.

Six messengers had left here months or weeks ago to collect potential brides. In just a few days Jahn was to make his choice, but thus far only one of the chosen women had arrived. From all Alix had heard, she was not at all suitable. If Princess Edlyn had been murdered and someone had attempted to do the same to Lady Verity, then was it possible the others had been killed as well?

To make matters worse, someone had stolen a valuable box from the visitors from Claennis, who spent their days and nights drinking, eating, and womanizing—all to excess. Alix had smiled widely as the servant who'd brought last night's meal had shared that gossip.

Taking the box while Paki and Kontar slept had been too easy. If they'd awakened, he might've killed them, but they'd snored on as he took what he wanted, and he'd left them to their dreams. He'd heard they'd raised hell the following morning.

No wonder Jahn had disappeared.

Alix swept a bit of blue on Sanura's back, stroking the bristles of the soft brush against her skin, watching as the remarkable powder colored her flesh, as the cosmetic became a part of her. Now no one but he would touch her. He would be the one who killed any man who dared to caress the forbidden blue. She was his.

"Many men in this part of the world don't like the blue," Sanura said as he continued his work. "I have felt revulsion and confusion and even intense dislike from the men who do not understand. I never felt anything like that from you." She turned her head and smiled at him. Her face was already blue. She'd applied the cosmetic to her face herself, but had allowed him the pleasure of taking care of the chore over most of the rest of her body. They'd started late in the morning, and it had taken most of the day. They might've hurried through the process, but he enjoyed taking his time...he enjoyed every step of the transformation...he enjoyed stopping often to love her. "I felt your surprise at first," she said, "but you never made me feel unwanted or disliked." Her eyes looked into him, in that way she had. "Why now, Alix? Why do I wear the blue now?"

"Because it is time," he said gently. "Jahn is back."

Her smile disappeared. "Not yet! He can't be. There are several days..."

"He was seen last night, love, by one of the servants who keeps the secret of our residence."

"You can't be sure that's true. It could be just another rumor."

"She delivered food to him, just as she has been delivering to us." He searched her eyes for the truth. Had Sanura lied to him? Had she conspired against him? "Jahn either returned early or else he's been playing the same game we have, hiding from those who would make his days...unpleasant."

"You wish me to be blue when I meet the emperor?"

"Of course, love. There is no use denying who and what we are. I fought that within myself for so many years, and it's a waste. You are a woman of the Agnese, a gifted treasure, a very special possession. And you're mine."

He knew what he had to do, and had already set the plans into motion. "We have an appointment, Sanura. We have an appointment with the emperor, with your keepers, and with the Tryfynian guards who think I killed their princess."

"One right after the other? All of them *tonight*? That's madness. You can't..."

"I will not confront them one after another. We will

meet them all at midnight, in the ballroom on Level Nine."

"Midnight is just a few hours away, Alix." He heard the fear in her voice, the fear that was more for him than for Jahn.

"Yes, I know."

With every day that passed, he was less and less sure about his plan. They'd been here for days, and every time Sanura said she loved him, every time they came together in his bed, every time she laughed or stroked his hair or looked into his soul, he grew less and less sure. Another day, and he might lose his determination. Another day, and he might give it all up for a woman.

Last night, as she'd slept, he'd been quite sure that the sound of her breathing and the murmurs of dreams and the crinkle of sheets as she moved made music. The music was for the man he had once been, not for the man he had become. It was for a man who did not have the heart or the nerve to take what was his, a man who had lived in shadows far too long.

Yes, midnight was an appropriate hour. It was time to leave the sanctuary of this room and this bed, time to build the life he so desperately wanted. No one was going to give him what he wanted; he would have to take it.

Either Jahn would die or Alix himself would. There could be no turning back.

Chapter Nineteen

THERE were no gowns in the palace which suited her, so once again Sanura wore a sheet which wound around her body and was held in place by ribbons which wrapped around her midsection. One shoulder was bare, and she was adorned with a few plain gold bracelets and a low-slung girdle constructed of tiny links of gold.

She'd tried so hard to change Alix's plans, but her efforts had not been enough. He was going to kill his own brother, take the throne, and he would never recover from what he'd done. Enough of the old Alix remained to make him miserably heartsick over the choices he was willing to make.

They walked down the winding secret stairs toward the ballroom where the emperor and at least four men who wished Alix dead awaited their arrival. Gently glowing rocks lined the steps, lighting their way. With every step her heart grew heavier. Her mouth was dry and her head spun. She patted the small knife which was hidden in the folds of her makeshift gown, wondering if she would need it—knowing she probably would.

"Don't do this," she said as the final flight of stairs came into view.

"I don't have any choice," Alix answered solemnly.

"You do!" she insisted. She stopped and planted her feet on the stairs, and since she was in front, Alix was forced to stop as well. "All the choices are yours!"

He placed his hands on her waist, where he could hold her without staining his hands with blue. "I am falling off a cliff and the ground's coming up fast. There is no avoiding the ground, Sanura. There is no stopping the fall." He gave her a gentle shove which propelled her onward.

"I can stop it," she said. "You can stop it. I know you feel how wrong this is! You can't convince me that you want to see your brother dead!"

"You're singing for me again," he said. "With every step, every word, you sing just for me. That song makes me question everything."

"Everything but my love," she said. "You don't doubt that at all."

"No, I don't."

"Let them wait," she whispered. "Let them all wait while we run. We can go anywhere, Alix, anywhere at all, and we can have a wonderful life together!"

"Can we?"

It was time for complete honesty. It was her only chance. "Unless you murder your brother, yes. If you kill him, we will never be happy again. You think taking all that he has will give you satisfaction, but it won't. It will destroy you."

"You can't know that."

"I can," she whispered.

They reached the narrow doorway that opened in the back corner of the ballroom. Two Tryfynian soldiers, as well as Paki and Kontar, watched the ballroom entrance. Only the emperor saw them enter by way of the hidden passage. He was not at all surprised.

"Interesting," Emperor Jahn said as he studied Sanura briefly before turning his eyes to Alix. "We are all here, just as you commanded. I understand you and I have some business to discuss, but why are these other men in attendance?"

If the emperor thought his brother would actually take his life, he did not show it in fear or anger. If he thought his life was in danger, he hid it well; inside and out.

Alix placed his hand at Sanura's back and led her toward the others. The Tryfynians placed their hands on their swords, but they did not dare move in the presence of the emperor. Paki and Kontar held their swords ready, but they, too, hesitated. They were in the presence of the leader of this country, and it was his brother they intended to harm. All were understandably hesitant.

"We'll take care of the easy tasks first," Alix said, walking toward the Tryfynians. "You morons, I did not kill Princess Edlyn. She was an annoying little twit and I won't miss her, but I did not kill her. It was Tari, who did the deed at Vyrn's insistence. I suspect the same person who attempted to have Lady Verity murdered also arranged the princess's murder, as well as arranging the scene to make it look as if Sanura and I were guilty." He glanced back at his brother. "Someone does not wish my brother to marry, or so it appears. Since only one potential bride has arrived, I would suggest that the others have had challenges and accidents, and perhaps even more deaths, along the way." He glared at the Tryfynians. "Besides, if I'd wanted the princess dead, I could have arranged some method of death which would not have pointed directly at me. I'm not an idiot."

The Tryfynians looked suitably humbled. The hands on the grips of their swords fell away as they recognized the truth of Alix's words.

Alix turned to Paki and Kontar, who were both bleary-eyed and very much on guard. "I understand and appreciate that when you tried to kill me, you were only doing your duty, but you must realize that you are no longer in Claennis, and you cannot murder a man for innocently touching a woman."

"Innocently?" Paki said angrily.

"In theory," Alix said, "it doesn't matter. Blue on a

man's skin means death, unless he is the one, the only one, who possesses Sanura."

"That is correct."

Alix reached out and raked his hand across Sanura's arm, and then he raked the blue stain from his hand to his chest, which was bare beneath a crimson vest. Sanura was stunned as once again Alix disarmed Paki and Kontar before the guards could react to his defiance. Instead of threatening them with their own weapons, he threw the swords of Claennis across the ballroom, where they skittered and screamed against the stone floor before coming to a stop.

Alix drew his own sword, which sang as it left its sheath. "If you cared at all about protecting Sanura, you would've used those weapons on the men who claimed to own her as if she were a pretty jewel or a strong horse. You would've used those blades to cut out the hearts of women who would rip her insides apart in the name of some damned man's convenience. If you cared for her at all, you would not allow any man to *own* her!"

Paki and Kontar backed away from Alix's dark stare.

"Go home," he said calmly. "Sanura is now mine to protect. Be assured that if any other man ever touches her, I will do what you could not."

The two men looked to Sanura, and she nodded. Kontar made a move as if he intended to retrieve his weapon, but Alix stopped him with a curt, "Leave the swords. You don't deserve them."

Without a word of argument, they backed toward the Tryfynian soldiers and the doorway. Alix shooed them all away with his sword, which caused some alarm among the four men. He dismissed the men and their threats, he ushered them to the door and tossed them out, and then he closed the ballroom door behind them and turned to face his brother.

"Now, on to our business," he said, stepping toward Emperor Jahn with long, purposeful strides.

* * *

GETTING rid of those who wished to kill him had been too easy. The Tryfynians were not beyond reason, and he'd barely broken a sweat disarming Paki and Kontar and staking his claim where Sanura was concerned. He looked Jahn in the eye and steeled himself for what was to come. An emperor should expect and be prepared for assassination, but Jahn was so trusting, so damned gullible. When *he* was emperor, he would be more cautious.

Alix's heart climbed into his throat. He should have no second thoughts, no doubts, no qualms about doing what had to be done.

He was so focused on Jahn he did not know what Sanura was intending until she planted herself in front of him, the dagger in her hand pointing to his heart, where he had marked himself with the blue from her skin.

"I can't let you do this," she said softly. "I'm sorry, but I can't."

Alix looked down at Sanura, disappointed and surprised. "You would kill me to save him?" He could disarm her easily, but she'd probably cut him in the process, and she would be hurt. Even now, he did not want that. Even now, he felt obligated to protect her.

"No," she said. "But I would kill you to save you."

"That makes no sense."

Jahn sighed, sounding tired and disgusted. "Cut my brother, and I will kill you," he said forcefully.

"I know," Sanura said in a voice loud enough to be heard by the emperor. "I understand completely."

"I don't," Alix said. "I don't understand this at all." He looked to his brother. "If she does manage to kill me, you will not harm her and you will not imprison her. Do you understand?"

"Not at all," Jahn muttered.

Alix looked down to Sanura, who had not moved. He could see no doubts in her eyes or in her stance.

"I broke you," she whispered. "I've tried to fix you. I've done everything I can think of, and it simply isn't working. I thought love would be enough, I thought *I* would be enough, but if I'm not... if I'm not enough, then I can't allow you to kill what is left of the man I love by committing this atrocity. You won't survive if you murder your own brother."

"Let him go," Jahn said. "Alix won't hurt me. We've been through too much together. He's my brother, for God's sake. He's my *twin*."

"You're a fool," Alix said, looking past Sanura to his brother, ignoring the knife she held to his heart. "I *will* kill you, if I get the chance. I will take the throne, this palace, everything you possess."

Jahn looked hurt, but was not as shocked as he should've been. Angry, yes, but not surprised. "Do you want the empress I'm supposed to pick?" he asked harshly. "Trust me, you can have her!"

"I don't..." He started to say he didn't need an empress. He had Sanura. But that wasn't entirely true. He would need an empress who could give him children. If they somehow survived this night, if both of them walked away from this, would Sanura stay? After he had done what he intended, would she still love him?

"Yes," she whispered, as once again she had reached inside him and touched his soul.

Tears flowed down her face. Those tears did not mar the perfect blue, they did not wash the cosmetic away, but they did leave tracks there. He knew it hurt her to hold that dagger to his heart; he felt her pain as if it were his own... and something inside him broke. Something inside him fractured and fell away. He moved quickly, grasping Sanura's wrist and pushing the dagger away. He pulled her to him and gasped for breath, holding her because only her touch kept the pain from sending him to his knees.

A sharp, wrenching ache shot through his body, and for the first time he felt physically broken, truly and honestly fractured in body as well as in soul. He could not breathe, and only Sanura kept him from screaming, from literally falling apart. There would be nothing left of him if he gave in to this pain, if he let himself be torn apart.

And then the pain was gone.

Sanura dropped the knife and launched herself upward, wrapping her legs around his waist and her arms around his neck. She laughed as he tried to catch his breath. She laughed and shed tears at the same time. She almost choked on the tears and the laughter, on happiness and relief and love.

She made music such as he had never heard before.

He dropped to his knees with Sanura still in his grasp. She continued to hold on tight.

Jahn walked toward them. "I'm so fucking confused," he said in a voice that was much more reminiscent of the man he had been before he'd become emperor. "Is this woman yours?"

"No," Alix said. "No one can possess something so bright and beautiful as Sanura. No one can own her. But I am hers, heart and soul. I belong to her in every way possible."

Sanura drew away and smiled at Alix. Her fingers touched his already marked face. "Your eyes, your beautiful eyes are more light than dark once again."

"The dark is not gone," he said. The shadows remained, not buried as they had once been but also not as strong as they had been in recent weeks.

"It never will be, love." She pushed back a strand of hair that had fallen across his cheek. "That darkness is a part of you, just as it is a part of all others, in some form or another. It doesn't matter whether or not the darkness exists. All that matters is the choices you make when that darkness speaks to you. Listen to your heart, and that darkness which tried to rule you will eventually be so small, no one will ever see it."

"No one but you, I imagine," he said. "You see everything."

"Especially where you are concerned, Alix, my love."

He wanted to ask her to be his wife, and he would. But not here and not now. That was a question which could wait until later, when they were alone. Instead he said, "I love you, Sanura. I can't survive without you. I don't want to survive without you. Will you have me? Will you sing for my soul forever and keep the darkness small?"

She smiled. "I will."

VERITY cuddled against Laris's fine, naked body. "I like being married," she said. "I like it very much."

"So do I."

Beyond the window of the bedroom they shared for tonight, the same bed she'd slept in for too many nights—but with his sisters for warmth and companionship instead of Laris—a bonfire blazed. His family and friends, her family and friends now, still celebrated the marriage, long after the newlyweds had retired. The fire was not terribly close, but Verity could see the light of it when she turned her head in just the right way. Somewhere out there were music and dancing, but she preferred the intimate dance she had just learned to anything that might exist beyond these walls.

Her wedding night was shaping up quite nicely.

She might've been an emperor's bride, but she could not imagine being any happier than she was at this moment, she could not imagine loving any man more than she loved Laris.

"I would've made a good empress, I'm sure," she said, "but I think I'll make an even better sentinel's wife."

"I have to agree," Laris said. Of course, he had been very agreeable all day, and why shouldn't he be?

She reached for the table by the bed and snagged the lucky talisman she had worn since leaving her old home to come to this new one. She hadn't taken it off until tonight, when she had not wanted anything, no matter how small, to come between her and her husband. "I have a gift for you," she said as she grabbed it.

"That's not fair," Laris said. "I didn't have time to get anything for you."

"There will be lots of time for presents later." Yes, she would have to teach him that she liked presents very much.

Her mother had told her that all husbands, even emperors, had to be trained, but Verity suspected Laris needed less training than most. She slipped the chain over his head. "This will bring you luck in all you do."

He lifted the amber stone which lay against his bare chest and studied it briefly. "I don't much believe in charms and such."

"You'd better believe in this one!" she insisted. "It brought me to you."

He let the stone fall against his chest and lie there. "Then it is already a lucky piece for me." He kissed her very well, as he had often on this night, and she settled her body against his.

Verity had not yet told Laris that he would one day be Minister of Defense, but that time would come soon enough. He was smart, he was loyal, he was dedicated...it was only right that he rise through the ranks.

"It's a lovely gift indeed," she said against his mouth. "You really should repay me in kind. A gift to mark the starting of our life together, an offering to remind me every day that you love me."

"I have nothing to give you," he said. "Not yet. Maybe..."

"Maybe a little girl," she said as she ended his protests with a long, wonderful kiss.

UNDER normal circumstances, the marriage of a prince would require months of planning. It would be a social and political event of great importance.

Sanura counted herself at least a little bit lucky that at the moment nothing was normal.

Knowing that there had been at least one murder and one attempted murder of the bridal candidates, Emperor Jahn had dispatched sentinels to join and assist the two parties that had not yet been heard from. General Merin had been sent east to collect the daughter of the leader of a powerful clan, and Deputy Minister Bragg had gone south.

Neither of them had returned. One potential empress had arrived at the palace weeks ago, unharmed and without tales of excitement, a fact which put her under immediate suspicion. If she was the one behind the violence, however, she was not a particularly smart strategist.

One of the chosen had actually refused the offer to be presented, so that accounted for all the women.

Because all was not well in the palace, and because Alix refused to wait, they were married in the Imperial Ballroom with a handful of guests in attendance. A distracted and decidedly grumpy emperor and a handful of shocked ministers observed the simple ceremony. The priest who said the words was beyond shocked. Sanura had never before seen a man quite that shade of red.

Alix did enjoy seeing her blue, and though she could not remain forever in that state, he wished her to be painted on their wedding day. He also wished to be able to touch her without worrying about marking himself. The solution was simple enough.

He was blue, too.

Sanura was surprised when Alix led her from the site of the marriage ceremony to the stables, where two horses had been prepared for a trip. The saddlebags were bulging with supplies, and he even carried a small roll-up tent on the back of his horse.

"Where are we going?" she asked as he checked the contents of one saddlebag.

"It's a surprise," he said, casting her a satisfied smile. His eyes were a lovely pale green marked with small slashes of a darker emerald.

"I do not care for surprises," she admitted.

"Every woman likes surprises," he protested.

"It appears you do not know as much about women as you think you do," she argued with a grin. "You have much to learn, husband."

"I expect you will teach me, wife." Alix assisted her into her saddle, then he hoisted himself into his own. He looked fearsome and content, happy and agitated, determined and loving. And very blue. She rather liked it, though she knew they would be anything but inconspicuous as they traveled to his surprise.

It was probably not fair to cheat, but she really did not like surprises, and if she looked intently, she could see anything of Alix that she wished to see.

Happiness, love, a hint of turmoil, plans to give Sanura everything she wanted, wondering if he would make a proper father...

Mali. They were going to fetch Mali and make her their own. She might be the first of many such children, but only time would tell.

They rode away from the palace at a leisurely pace. Alix did not look back, though Sanura did. Once.

"In just a few days your brother will choose an empress. Do you not wish to stay and see how events will unfold?"

"Not really."

"He might need your help," she argued. "And it isn't as if Mali won't be waiting for us if we are delayed by a few days."

Alix looked at her and sighed. "I will never be able to surprise you."

Sanura grinned. "I hope not. Now, about your brother..."

"Jahn will be fine, though I don't envy him his choice and the days to come." Alix's brow wrinkled. "I don't envy him at all. I want nothing he possesses. Nothing at all." He caught her eye and held it with is own. "I have you, and you are worth a thousand kingdoms."

He increased the pace of his horse and so did she, and after a few minutes Sanura was certain that the horses' hooves and the jangle of swords and bracelets and the rustle of leather and cloth created a heartsong that only they could hear.

Turn the page for a preview of the next romance
from Linda Winstead Jones

22 Nights

Coming December 2008
from Berkley Sensation!

AMONG the Turis, marriage was a simple thing. A man
and woman promised themselves to one another with their
actions more than with formal words. There was an exchange of gifts, a simple dance, a kiss, and then it was
done. The clan gathered to celebrate their union with food
and drink and general merriment.

Bela did not feel particularly merry at the moment. She
watched with sullen and openly acknowledged self-pity as
her friend Jocylen offered Rab Quentyn a bowl of stew she
had made with her own hands. He took it and drank some
of the broth, and then he placed a ring of brightly colored
spring flowers upon her head. They joined hands, and
while simple, slow music played on a single lute filled the
night air, they took a turn, skipped in unison, and spun
about. Jocylen laughed, and because he was so pleased
with her joyous response, Rab laughed, too. They kissed, a
joyous cry from families and friends filled the air, and it
was done.

Bela did not shout or laugh, but she did move forward to
offer Jocylen her congratulations. She wanted her friend to

be happy, she truly did, and she knew how very much Jocylen loved Rab. But no one else understood her, no one else knew all her secrets, and now Jocylen would spend her days cooking and making a home, and in short order there would be children to care for and the newlywed would begin to spend her time with other married women who were devoted to their husbands, women who spent their days talking about babies and sewing and how best to cook a tough piece of meat.

Bah! Bela had never cared for any of those things, much to her mother's dismay. She preferred hunting with her brothers to cooking, and she had no intention of taking care of any man. Not ever.

Jocylen smiled at Bela and took her hand. "You dressed well for my special occasion, I see."

Bela glanced down at the plain, drab green gown which draped simply and ended just short of her best sandals, sandals adorned with gemstones from the mountains which surrounded the village of the Turis. Unhappy as she was at the turn of events, she would not attend her beloved friend's marriage ceremony in her usual male-style clothing. Heaven above, she had even washed her hair! "Did you expect any less?" Bela asked, as if her efforts meant nothing.

"With you I never know what to expect," Jocylen responded.

The circlet of gold which adorned Bela's brow was heavier and less comfortable than her usual cloth or leather circlet. Yes, she had gone to great lengths to make herself presentable. Perhaps she was displeased to see her friend marry and join the ranks of the wives of the clan, but she also wanted to see Jocylen happy. Which she was. Blast.

"If he hurts you, I will gut him."

Jocylen's eyes widened. "Rab would never hurt me."

"Well, if he does . . ."

"He won't!" Jocylen rose up on her toes, as she was a good half-foot shorter than Bela, and kissed a reluctant cheek. "Don't worry so, Bela. We will still be friends. Forever, no matter what."

And then Jocylen was whisked away by new relations. Food and drink for all would follow, and then the newly-weds would retire to their home and do what newly wed couples did. Poor Jocylen. Bela had tried to warn her friend, but the warnings had been dismissed. Somehow the new bride expected bliss in her husband's bed.

She'd think differently in short order.

Alert as always, Bela was among the first to hear the quick hoofbeats approaching. She and a number of the men rushed to meet one of a pair of guards who had been posted at the western edge of the village, on this side of the river. Since so many riches had been discovered in the nearby mountains, mountains owned and protected by the Turis, they'd had to take measures to secure the safety of the people.

Some men would do anything for wealth.

Byrnard Pyrl leaped from his horse with a grace Bela admired. "A rider approaches. He wears an imperial uniform and his horse is clad in an imperial soldier's green as well, but of course that doesn't mean he's who he appears to be."

Bela's heart gave a nasty flip at the mention of soldier green. They did not see many soldiers out so far, not since the end of the war with Ciro, but still—her heart and her stomach reacted fiercely.

A handful of men gathered weapons and torches and collected their horses. The would-be intruder would be met and turned away from the village. None but Turis were welcome here. Strangers were not allowed simply to ride into their midst and be accepted.

Bela quickly collected her own sword and ran to her horse, intent on joining the men who would meet the rider. She was not surprised when her brother Tyman ordered her to remain behind with the other women. No one but she would see the glint of humor in his eyes. She looked to her older brother Clyn, who did not have Tyman's sense of humor. He, too, shook his head in denial.

Just because she was dressed like a woman tonight, that didn't mean she had to be treated like one!

A group of six men, her brothers among them, galloped toward the western edge of the village, their torches burning bright long after the men and the animals had vanished from sight. Bela watched those bits of light for a moment, and then she hiked up the skirt of her long gown and leaped into the saddle. Her sword remained close at hand, tucked into the leather sheath which hung from her saddle.

"Belavalari, don't!" a well-dressed and attractive older woman cried, rushing forward from the group of revelers. Bela knew that her mother would very much like to see her only daughter become a wife, as Jocylen had. She wanted to see her daughter among those women who cooked and cleaned and sewed and birthed babies.

"Sorry, Mama, I have to go."

"You do not..."

Bela set her horse into motion before her mother could finish her protest. Her loose hair whipped behind her as she raced from the village, her mare galloping into the darkness, away from the fires which lit the night celebration. For the first time this evening, Bela smiled. She was more warrior than woman, and when it came to protecting these people from intruders, it was as much her duty as it was her brothers'.

MERIN was not surprised to see the riders approaching with force and mistrust; this was a typical Turi greeting. It was for this reason that he had chosen to make the trip alone. He was sure that Valeron would send a chaperone, and perhaps a warrior or two, with his daughter when they left the village for Arthes, but on the initial leg of the journey other travelers would've only slowed him down.

And would've made this initial greeting more difficult. The Turis would not be suspicious of one traveler, especially when he was a soldier with whom many of them had once fought. If Merin had arrived with a contingent of soldiers, that would've been another story entirely.

Merin slowed his horse and held up both hands, so the

riders would see that he was unarmed. As they drew close, he was happy to see two familiar faces. Tyman and Clyn, sons of the Turi chieftain, had fought with him for a time, when the threat of Ciro's Own had come near their home. Even though they had not parted on the best of terms—he had wished for an army of Turis to fight with his sentinels well beyond the clan's lands, and they had refused—he trusted them. They were good, if somewhat primal, men.

The chieftain's sons were not happy to see him, but they wouldn't kill him—not right away, in any case. Not unless their sister had said too much after Merin had left their village.

"I bring a message from the emperor," Merin called out. His hands remained visible, even so three of the riders drew their swords. Tyman and Clyn did not draw arms.

"What do you want?" It was the fair-haired Clyn who moved closest to Merin. The elder Haythorne son was extraordinarily large. Clyn was probably Merin's age, or thereabouts. He was a full head taller and was wide in the shoulders. A long blond braid fell over one of those shoulders. His chest and arms were unusually muscled, but those muscles did not impede him in swordplay, as they might with some men. Clyn was an intense and gifted swordsman. In any fight, Merin definitely wanted Clyn on his side.

The big man did not look like an ally at the moment.

"As I said, I have a message..."

Tyman, the more hotheaded brother, rode forward and almost ran into Merin's horse. The animals danced on graceful hooves. Tyman's loose, long hair—reddish brown and wavy like Bela's—danced around his angry face and rigid shoulders. "Give me one reason why I shouldn't kill you here and now."

Judging by the expressions before him, Bela had talked. What had she told her brothers? The truth or her twisted version of the truth? Anything was possible. "One reason?" Merin looked Tyman in the eye. "Kill me, and an entire army will come down on your head. The Turi have many fierce warriors, I will give you that, but Emperor Jahn has you in numbers. Kill me, and they will crush you all."

It was true, and surely they knew that; yet Tyman still gripped the handle of his undrawn sword.

"And if you are killed by a woman?" an unexpectedly soft voice asked.

Merin's head snapped around. He had been so intent on Clyn and Tyman he had not seen or heard the seventh rider arrive. She moved into the light of their torches, the gold circlet across her brow glinting in the firelight, her wild chestnut hair shimmering. Her dress had been hiked up to allow her to ride astride, and so her long, strong legs were exposed to the night air. She simply did not have the reservations that others of her age and gender possessed.

"Lady Belavalari," he said.

She drew her sword, and something on the handle of her weapon caught the light in a strange way. He didn't have time to study the weapon's grip; he was more focused on the blade and the woman who wielded it. She could kill him, and at the moment she looked as if she had killing on her mind.

"General Merin," she responded, "I did not think ever to see you again. I did not think you would be so foolish as to come anywhere near the Turis."

Bela was older, leaner of face, more confident than he remembered. The shape of her body was a bit different: softer, a bit rounder, but maybe it was the unexpected dress. No matter what she wore, she was more strength than gentleness.

"I have a . . ."

"Message," she interrupted sharply. "I heard. Are you still a general, or have you been demoted to courier?"

"I am still a general," he said calmly.

"What foolish mission would lead you here, where your life is all but worthless? I would think a general would be smarter, though in my experience you're not known for your vast intelligence."

A couple of the men laughed, but not Bela's brothers.

"I need to speak to your father," Merin said, ignoring her gibes. Was she trying to provoke a fight so she'd have an excuse to cut him down? That was certainly possible.

"First you have to get past me," she said.

He had heard tales of female warriors who'd lived in the past, and he imagined they might've looked very much like this. Bela Haythorne was stubborn, strong, willful, skilled, and fearless. She was in many ways everything Merin had ever wanted in a soldier.

Unfortunately, she was also deceptive, manipulative, and determined to have her own way in every situation, no matter what the cost.

She was very close to him now, and she held her sword steady and thrust forward so that the tip of the blade came near his heart. Not threateningly close, not yet. Again the exposed portion of the grip caught the light from a torch and glinted brightly. Bela's arm did not seem to be strained, as she continued to hold the weapon steady.

"It is your decision, Bela," Tyman said in a low voice. "Kill him, and we will gladly fight the war that follows. You have every right to take his head, and any other part of him that strikes your fancy."

Only one man laughed that time, and the harsh sound was strained and short-lived.

Thanks to the darkness of night and the way she'd narrowed her calculating eyes, he could not see the warm, mossy green he remembered. After all this time he should not remember that particular detail, but he did. Narrowed or not, night or not, he *could* see the anger and the hurt in her eyes. "Is that what you want, Bela?" he asked. "Do you want my head?"

"Yes," she whispered.

"Then take it." Hands out, defenseless, he looked into her eyes without fear.

For a moment he thought she might take him up on the offer, but eventually the sword fell and she looked to Clyn. "Take General Merin to Papa, let him deliver his message, and when that is done, have him escorted to the other side of the River Hysey." Her gaze returned to him. "Consider my generosity a parting gift, General. If I see you again I *will* take your head."

BELA spun her horse about and urged the mare to a full run, not looking back, not acknowledging to anyone that her heart was pounding too hard and her mouth was dry.

Tearlach Merin, here after all this time. She'd never admitted to anyone, not even Jocylen, that she'd spent the better part of a year foolishly waiting for him to return. It would have been a ridiculous confession, considering the circumstances. She'd never admitted to anyone that she dreamed about General Merin now and then. Well, he'd had plenty of time to come back, and he hadn't. Now it was too late. Much too late!

Just when she had her life settled as she pleased, just when she was happy with her lot, he came waltzing back, looking just as pretty as ever with that dark curly hair that did not hang even to his shoulders, and those deep, dark brown eyes and that perfect nose and the lovely full mouth. She knew men did not like to be called pretty, but Tearlach Merin was.

Too bad looks were deceiving.

Bela held on tight and let the horse run free in the night. With every hoofbeat against the ground her worry eased. Merin wouldn't be here for very long. He'd deliver his message and then he'd be gone long before sunup. Maybe this time he'd know better than to come back. It wasn't as if he had returned for her.

And if he had . . .?

Many villagers were standing about, waiting to learn who had come calling at such a late hour. Bela dismounted, withdrew her sword from its sheath, and then, for her mother's benefit, she smoothed her wrinkled skirt and ran the fingers of one hand through her hair. "The man who entered our territory is a messenger from the emperor," she said simply. No reason to tell them all that it was General

Merin, come back to taunt her. They'd find out soon
enough. "He'll need to speak to Papa before he leaves." She
glanced around, but saw no sign of Jocylen. The poor girl
had probably already retired, not knowing what awaited
her in her marriage bed. Really, women should be told the
truth, instead of being fed pretty lies about love and pleasure.

Bela found her mother in the crowd. "I'm exhausted,"
she said. "It's been such a long day."

Gayene Haythorne narrowed her eyes suspiciously. Bela
was never the first to bed. She preferred staying up late and
sleeping long past sunrise, when possible. "Are you ill?"

Did heartsick count, Bela wondered. "No, I'm fine." She
looked toward the narrow lane that led to Jocylen's new
home. "I'm just a bit worried about Jocylen. Poor girl. You
know how I feel about marriage, Mama. It is a horrid and
unnatural state for women."

"It is not," her mother said genially. They'd had this argument many times, and had finally come to an understanding; they would never agree.

"In any case, I have worried about Jocylen all day, and
worrying is exhausting."

"As I well know," Gayene replied, not even attempting
to hide her true meaning.

Bela did not respond to that. She had given her mother
no reason to worry. Not today.

"I'm off to bed." Bela gave her mama, an attractive
woman who was almost as tall as she, a kiss on the cheek.

Bela's progress was stalled by a warm hand on her arm.
She did not pull away, but stopped to look directly at her
mother. "You look beautiful in a dress," Gayene said, "with
your hair down and your face clean." Her eyes flitted
briefly but with evident displeasure to the sword Bela carried. "You should pretend to be a lady more often."

Then they both smiled. Differences aside, there was an
abundance of love in the Haythorne family.

When Bela heard the approaching riders, who moved at
a much slower pace than she had, she said a quick good

night to her mother and hurried toward home. She did not look back. She would not give Tearlach Merin the pleasure. Oh, she felt like such a girl, with her heart pounding and her hands trembling, all on account of a *man*. The crystal grip of her sword vibrated, and she held on tight. "No need to worry about him, Kitty," Bela said softly. "He won't be here long."

Did Kitty vibrate because she wanted to take Merin's head? Did she long for battle in this time of peace?

The Turi village was laid out like a wheel, with the town square at the center, essential businesses around that square, and houses extending from that center like the spokes of a wheel. Beyond the houses were farms, small and large, and a couple of ranches. Even farther to the west ran the River Hysey, and to the east lay the gem-filled mountains where so many of the Turi males worked, where some even chose to live.

The Haythorne house was one of the finest in town, which was natural since Valeron Haythorne was chieftain. Still, the building, which was made of wood and stone, was simple. The long, single story house was clean, large, well built, and plain. There were sturdy furnishings and a few adornments, but for the most part it was a functional home. The Turis were not a frivolous people.

Bela's room was located at the rear of a short hallway. As the only daughter she had always had the luxury of her own bedchamber. Her father was Turi chieftain, and that meant she was all but a princess. Still, she did not fill her room with fripperies. There was no lace, no frills. The only concession to her femininity was a wooden rack built onto the wall where she stored her small selection of jewelry and headbands. Though she would not admit it aloud for fear of sounding frivolous, she liked the sparkle of the gems found in the mountains nearby, she liked the glitter of gold and the sheen of silver.

Bela placed Kitty upon another rack, one which had been built just for that purpose. Like the few feminine adornments Bela possessed, Kitty sparkled. The special crystal from the mountains nearby was alive in a way that was difficult to explain.

Sometimes Kitty spoke to her. Not in a voice that could be heard with the ears, but with a whisper in the soul. For weeks on end Kitty would be silent, and then she would begin to speak again, spreading wonder into Bela's life. Bela reached out and touched her fingertips to the crystal grip. Even though Kitty's existence had been known of for less than three years, she was already legend among the Turis. Every warrior wanted her, and some wondered aloud why Bela Haythorne, a mere woman, possessed such a gift. Many thought that her father had allowed her to keep it, a special gift for a spoiled daughter. What they didn't know, what very few understood, was that Bela had not chosen Kitty.

Kitty, a sword which was as alive as any person Bela knew, had chosen her. The village seer, a grumpy old man named Rafal Fiers, said that one day Kitty would choose another. But not today.

Bela heard the front door open and close several times. She heard raised voices that held a tenor of excitement. Kitty's grip shone bright, as if she were excited, too. Could a sword feel exhilaration? Could it crave and want and feel? Kitty could, Bela knew it.

Her bedchamber door opened swiftly, without the courtesy of a knock.

"The main room," her mother said briskly. "Hurry."

Bela left Kitty upon her rack and followed her mother from the chamber. She should've expected what she found in the main room of her family home, but she had not. The sight took her breath away.

General Merin, better lit here than he had been when she'd seen him on the road, was on his knees, head down, hands tied behind his back. She could not see his face for the fall of dark curls which were surely the envy of many a vain woman. Tyman stood behind the general, the tip of his sword at Merin's neck.

"Stop!" Bela cried.

Her brother lifted his head but not his sword. "We know what he did to you, Bela. He was foolish enough to come back here, and he will pay the price. As soon as he delivers his message to Papa, the general is going to die."

Merin tried to lift his head, but Tyman forced it back down with a tap of his blade.

"You don't understand," Bela began. There went her heart again, pounding too hard and too fast. Why was she alarmed? Maybe it would be best if Merin was dead. Hadn't she just threatened to take his head herself?

But not like this, and not for something that wasn't his fault.

"I do not need to understand!" Clyn bellowed. "He took a husband's rights, and then he rode away and did not look back."

"It was my fault," Bela said, the words hurting a little. She hated to admit that anything was her fault. "I insisted..."

"You were seventeen!" Tyman shouted. "He was a grown man who should've known better."

Even from this distance, Bela heard Kitty's urgent whisper as clearly as if the words were being shouted. *Tell all.*

Bela took a deep breath and exhaled slowly. Her mother tried to calm her boys. They would not kill Merin right away, not until her father arrived and the message which had brought him here was delivered. There had to be another way. How could she tell her family what had really happened that night? It was mortifying.

Tell all.

"Fine," Bela snapped. "Since it appears that you *must* know, I drugged the general until he was nonsensical, told him I was twenty years of age and a widow looking for physical comfort, and then I took off all my clothes and his and..."

"You didn't," Clyn said in a low voice which was much more frightening than his roar.

"I did," Bela said, lifting her chin in defiance.

"She did," Merin echoed.

"Why?" her mother wailed. "Belavalari, how incredibly imprudent!"

Bela sighed. Tyman still hadn't moved his sword into a less threatening position. "I couldn't do anything!" she said with evident annoyance. "Papa and you two said I was a maid who could not put myself in danger, that I could not fight or ride or wear the trousers you outgrew." She rolled her eyes. "You all wanted me to become something I was not, to wear dresses and be coy with suitable boys who might become husbands. I lied to General Merin so he would take my bothersome virginity and I would no longer be a maid."

"That is nonsense," Tyman said. His sword shifted slightly to the side.

Bela looked her brother in the eye. "Is it? I don't think it's nonsense at all. In fact, I believe my plan worked quite well. Merin left, so I was not saddled with a man I did not want, and once you knew what had happened, you two felt so guilty for not protecting me more diligently that you allowed me to do whatever I wanted. By the time your guilt faded, it was too late to turn back." Her trick had been childish, she could see that now, but it *had* worked.

Tyman's expression hardened. "You do share some blame, in that case, but the fact is, the general took your virginity and did not marry you. For that alone he deserves to die."

Bela pursed her lips. She had hoped it would not come to this, but she couldn't let them kill Merin under false pretenses. If anyone killed him, it would be her. "That's not entirely true."

"You said he took a husband's rights!"

Bela shuddered. That was a memory she could not forget no matter how she tried. "He did. He also married me, *before* the act was done, if you must know all the details."

Tyman's sword dropped away, and Merin lifted his head and looked at her. On his knees, bound, angrier than she had ever seen any man. He was still pretty, far prettier than her, but in this light she could see the years that had passed written on his face. A crease here, a toughness there.

"I did not marry you," he said tightly.

Idiot man. Such lies would lead to his death, if he were not careful.

Bela remembered that night much too clearly, and there was no denying it now. "According to Turi custom, we are very much married, General." It was the perfect marriage, in her mind, even though she had managed to keep her wedded state a secret until now. Merin was an absent spouse and she had her freedom. If her parents ever insisted that she needed to marry, if they ever tired of waiting for her to choose a mate and tried to force one upon her, she could inform them that she already had a husband. The marriage could be undone if there were no children, but not without both husband and wife present and participating in a ceremony not quite as simple as the marriage.

Her plan had been perfect. Until now.

There was stunned silence in the room, and her mother had gone so pale Bela was afraid the older woman might faint. Bela looked down at Merin, who seemed more angry than afraid. His eyes were so dark they looked more black than brown, so deep they seemed to be a bottomless pool of vitriol. She stared into them for a long moment before saying, "Welcome home, husband."